MY LADY OF CLEVES

Margaret Campbell Barnes

My Lady of Cleves is the powerful and moving story of Henry VIII's fourth wife. Born into a poor but noble Flemish family, she married the King of England to cement the alliance with the Protestant princelings of Germany. Resourceful and brave, she survived his passions and his fury, her divorce and finally his death.

"In Mrs. Barnes's skilful hands Anne herself becomes a real woman who will make many friends."—*Sunday Times*

"A real achievement."—*Saturday Review*

"Turns a brilliant light on one of the lustiest and one of the most dramatic periods of English history."—
Philadelphia Inquirer

"One of the best historical novels ... intimate, well drawn and entertaining."—*Daily Sketch*

MY LADY OF CLEVES

To the courage and endurance of all women who lost men they loved in the fight for freedom

My Lady of Cleves

MARGARET CAMPBELL BARNES

SPHERE BOOKS LIMITED
30/32 Gray's Inn Road, London, WC1X 8JL

First published in Great Britain in 1946 by Macdonald & Co.
(Publishers) Ltd.
First Sphere Books edition 1971
Reprinted June 1971

TRADE
MARK

Set in Linotype Baskerville

Printed in Great Britain by
Hazell Watson & Viney Ltd,
Aylesbury, Bucks

AUTHOR'S NOTE

Most of the remarks made about Anne of Cleves by characters in this book were in fact made by people who knew and saw her. Contemporary descriptions of her appearance are conflicting; but the three existing paintings of her are considerably more attractive than most of the portraits of Henry the Eighth's other wives. The popular idea that she was fat is completely belied by the neat, gold-belted waist shown in Hans Holbein's three-quarter-length portrait belonging to the Musée de Louvre, Paris. His exquisite miniature painted at the same time and now in the Victoria and Albert Museum, London, is less than two inches in diameter and still lies in the heart of the ivory rose in which it was sent to King Henry. There is a quaint charm about the painting of her by an unknown German artist which hangs in the Great Parlour of St. John's College, Oxford, in which she is shown wearing the same stomacher ornamented with Tudor roses. One likes to think it was a valued gift from her husband.

Several of Anne's letters—to the King, to Mary Tudor and to her brother William—are to be found among State Papers, while the Losely Manuscripts contain records of affairs connected with her estates and of domestic purchases made for her by Sir Thomas Carden, her tenant at Bletchingly, who appears to have acted frequently as her man of affairs during her enforced 'spinsterhood'. Her Will—surely one of the most human and endearing legal documents—makes delightful reading.

Although she outlived Henry by ten years she chose to remain in England, and perhaps the best proof of the affectionate terms on which she lived with the Tudor family is the place where she is buried. It is the exact spot which Mary, as a character in this book, considered most fitting for her.

My sincere thanks are due to the Acting and Assistant Librarians of the Epsom and Ewell Public Libraries for their unfailing helpfulness in producing reference books.

M.C.B.

Epsom, April 1945.

CHAPTER I

Henry Tudor straddled the hearth in the private audience chamber at Greenwich. Sunlight streaming through a richly-coloured oriel window emphasized the splendour of his huge body and red-gold beard against the wide arch of the stone fireplace behind him. He was in a vile temper and the huddle of statesmen yapping their importunities at him from a respectful distance, might have been a pack of half-cowed curs baiting an angry bull. They were trying to persuade him to take a fourth wife. And because for once he was being driven into matrimony by diplomacy and not desire, he scowled at all their suggestions. "Who *are* these two princesses of Cleves?" he wanted to know.

That didn't sound too hopeful for the latest project of the Protestant party. But Thomas Cromwell hadn't pushed his way from struggling lawyer to Chancellor of England without daring sometimes to pit his own obstinacy against the King's. "Their young brother rules over the independent Duchies of Cleves, Guelderland, Juliers and Hainault," he reported. "And we are assured that the Dowager Duchess has brought them up in strict Dutch fashion."

Henry thought they sounded deadly, and he was well aware that their late father's Lutheran fervour was of far more value in Cromwell's eyes than the domestic virtues of their mother. "Those Flemish girls are all alike—dowdy and humourless," he muttered, puffing out his lips. The audience chamber overlooked the gardens and the river, and from where he stood he could hear sudden gusts of laughter from the terrace below. He thought he recognized the voices of two of his late wife's flightiest maids-of-honour. Only yesterday he had heard his dour Chancellor rating them for playing shuttlecock so near the royal apartments. And because he was having his own knuckles rapped—although much more obsequiously—he snickered sympathetically. "And if

I *must* marry again," he added, "an English girl would be more amusing."

It was growing warm as the morning wore on, and a bumble bee beat its body persistently against the lattice. Obviously the graceless insect lacked all sense of the importance of the meeting; and—in self-defence—the King was doing his best to assume the same irritating attitude. But Cromwell was a born taskmaster. "Your Grace has already—er—tried two," he pointed out, looking down his pugnacious nose.

"Well?" demanded Henry, dangerously.

Naturally, no one present had the temerity to mention that Anne Bullen had not been a success, or to gall his recent bereavement by referring to the fact that Jane Seymour had died in childbirth. "It is felt that a foreign alliance—like your Majesty's first marriage with Catherine of Aragon——" began the Archbishop of Canterbury, who had obligingly helped to get rid of her.

Marillac, the French ambassador, backed him up quickly, seeing an opportunity to do some spade work for his own country. "Your Grace has always found our French women *piquantes*," he reminded the widower King, although everybody must have known that Archbishop Cranmer had not meant another *Catholic* queen.

Henry turned to him with relief, thinking irrelevantly that he looked like a brightly-plumaged popinjay strayed by mistake into a field full of sombrely-feathered crows. Like most bullies, he really preferred the people who stood up to him. He didn't mean to be impatient and irritable so that men jumped or cowered whenever he addressed them. He had always prided himself on being accessible. "Bluff King Hal," people had called him. And secretly he had loved it. Why, not so very long ago he used to sit in this very room—he and Catherine—with Mary, his young sister, and Charles Brandon, his friend—planning pageants and encouraging poets. . . .

"Your Majesty has but to choose any eligible lady in my country and King Francis will be honoured to negotiate with her parents on your behalf," the ambassador was urging, with a wealth of Latin gesture which made the rest of the argumentative assembly look dumb.

"I know, I know, my dear Marillac," said Henry, dragging himself from his reminiscent mood to their importunities. "And weeks ago I dictated a letter asking that three of the most promising of them might be sent to Calais for me to choose from. But nothing appears to have been done." He slewed his thickening body round towards his unfortunate secretary with a movement that had all the vindictiveness of a snook, and Wriothesley—conscious of his own diligence in the matter—made a protesting gesture with his ugly hands. "The letter was sent, your Grace. But, I beg you to consider, Sir—your proposal was impossible!"

"Impossible!" Henry Tudor rapped out the word with all the arrogance of an upstart dynasty that has made itself despotic.

"Monsieur Marillac has just received the French King's reply," murmured Cranmer.

"And what does he say?" asked Henry.

Seeing that the prelate had forced his hand and thereby spoiled his bid for another Catholic alliance, Marillac reluctantly drew the letter from his scented dispatch case. After all, he was not Henry's subject and his neck was safe. "He says that it would tax his chivalry too far to ask ladies of noble blood to allow themselves to be trotted out on approval like so many horses at a fair!" he reported verbatim. And many a man present had to hide a grin, envying him his immunity.

Henry gulped back a hot retort, reddening and blinking his sandy lashes in the way he did when he knew himself to be in the wrong. There had been a time—before that bitch, Nan Bullen, had blunted his susceptibilities about women's feelings—when he would have been the first to agree with Francis. Mary, his favourite sister, had been alive then, keeping him kind. Lord, how he missed her! He sighed, considering how good it was for a man to have a sister—some woman who gave the refining intimacy of her mind in a relationship that had nothing to do with sex. Someone who understood one's foibles and even bullied back sometimes affectionately.

Mary would have said in her gay, irrepressible way, "Don't be a mule, Henry! You know very well those stuffy old statesmen are right, so you might just as well do what they want without arguing." But even if they *were* right, and he *did*, it wasn't as simple as all that, he thought ruefully. For, after all, whatever foreign woman they might wish onto him, it was he who would have to live with her.

"How can I depend on anyone else's judgement?" he excused himself plaintively. "I'm not a raw youth to go wandering about Europe looking for a bride. I can't do more than offer to go across to my own town of Calais. Yet see them I must before I decide, whatever Francis says—see them, and hear them sing. I'm extraordinarily susceptible to people's voices, you know." The gay, light voices of the disobedient maids-of-honour still drifted up from the terrace, and in spite of Cromwell's disapproval they were pleasant enough. "That is why it would be so much simpler to marry an English girl," reiterated Henry obstinately. But this time he said it in the inconclusive grumble of a man who no longer feels very strongly about anything and only wants to be let alone.

"The young Duchess of Milan has just been widowed," suggested his cousin, Thomas Howard, Duke of Norfolk, dangling the last Catholic bait he could think of. And Henry, who had just called for a glass of wine, brightened considerably. "Coming from such a cultural centre, she should be accomplished," he remarked complacently, turning the well-mulled Malmsey on his tongue.

"But there is just one difficulty, your Grace," put in Cromwell.

"Yes?" prompted Henry, setting down his empty glass.

Cromwell cleared his throat uncomfortably. "The lady herself seems—er—somewhat unwilling."

The vainest monarch in Christendom stared at him incredulously. "Unwilling!" he repeated. He settled his new, becomingly-padded coat more snugly about his shoulders and shifted his weight testily from one foot to the other, to that he appeared to strut where he stood. "Why should she be unwilling? What did she say?"

But nobody dared tell him exactly what the lady had said; and the Italian Ambassador—less hardy than his French colleague—had found himself too indisposed to be present.

Henry glared at them like a bull that has been badly savaged. It was beginning to be born in upon him that he was no longer the splendid prize that had once fluttered the matrimonial dovecotes of Europe. So he blustered and blinked for a bit to hide his embarrassment, and everybody was glad when an ill-aimed shuttlecock created a diversion by smacking sharply against a window-pane.

The drowsy bumble bee was still banging its fat body against the inside of the glass, trying to get out. Henry wanted to get out too. The room was too full of contentious people, and the clever court tailor who had designed the widely-padded shoulders of his coat had considered only the slimming effect and not the heat. His shoes, with the rolled slashings to ease the gout in his toes, shuffled a little over the broad oak floor beams as he went to the window; but he still moved with the lightness of a champion wrestler. He pushed open a lattice and stood there in characteristic attitude, feet apart and hands folded behind his back beneath the loosely swinging, puff-sleeved coat. He had turned his back on the dull, musty world of diplomacy, and the world outside was alive and fresh. The wide Thames sparkled at high tide. He could smell the sweetness of the herb garden swooning in the hot sun and see the riot of colour in tall herbaceous borders. On the grass immediately below, four or five girls in different coloured gowns flitted like gay butterflies as they struck the shuttlecock back and forth. With the outward swinging of the window, their voices had come up to him, clear and strong, so that he could hear the careless things they said. There was one slender, auburn-haired child who laughed as she ran, and her laughter was like a delicious shivering of spring blossoms. Even his grave, embittered daughter, Mary—pausing on her way to chapel to watch the forbidden game—smiled at her indulgently and forbore to reprimand. Seventeen the girl might be—and, judging by her delight in the game, quite unsophisticated and unspoiled.

Henry wondered why he had been stuffing indoors all morning, when with a touch of his hand he could open a window onto this enchanting world of youth. And what would he not give to re-enter it? He, who had known what it was to enjoy youth with all the gifts that gods could shower! Music, poetry, languages, sport—he had excelled in them all. "*Mens sana in corpore sano*," he muttered, looking back over that splendid stretch of years and seeing, as men do in retrospect, all the high spots of success merged into one shining level of sunlight and strength. Alas, so easily had he excelled that gradually the strong impulses of the body had sapped the application of a fine and cultured mind! So that now, at forty-seven, while still hankering vainly after past physical exploits, he realized that had he developed that other side of himself, life might still mean growth, rather than gradual frustration.

Henry saw his daughter pass on, hands primly folded about her rosary; but he remained at the window, looking down benignly on the laughing, chattering players. They were girls of good family. And he had only to go down and lift up his finger. . . . "After all, why should I get married at all?" he suggested blandly. "There's plenty of fruit down there for the picking!" He threw the challenge over his shoulder to his disconcerted counsellors, and the answer he expected came back at him pat as a well-placed tennis ball. The careful placing, of course, was Cromwell's. "To secure the succession, Sir."

Henry swung round on him again in a flurry of purple and fine linen. "Haven't I already done that?" It was the vindication of the male who after twenty years of frustrated hopes, has produced a son at last. The only possible justification for his having divorced Catherine and defied the Pope. It had always seemed to him the supreme irony that weaklings could beget heirs whilst he, the fine athlete and lusty lover, had been able to sire only daughters and still-born sons. And now Jane's dying gift to him had both salved his vanity and satisfied parental yearning.

Archbishop Cranmer hated to prick the fragile bubble of

his pride, but felt constrained to point out that Prince Edward was far from strong.

Henry's anxiety for the child far outweighed theirs, but he never would look upon the things he did not wish to see. His light eyes flickered over the group of statesmen to the lean, imposing figure of the court physician, who began to understand why the others had pressed him to attend the meeting. "You don't think he looks any worse, do you, Chamberlain?" he asked.

Chamberlain caught Cromwell's compelling eye. As a doctor he was above coërcion, but in order to frighten the King into another marriage it was necessary only to tell the truth —a lamentable and half-understood truth beginning to be discussed in medical circles because it appeared to affect not only the King's heir but also a large proportion of the population. "There is a kind of wasting sickness," he admitted reluctantly, "which in its first stages frequently imparts a fallacious glow of health——" But seeing the stricken look on his patron's face and being essentially a healer, he tried hastily to allay the gravity of his own words. "With care, Sir, he may improve."

Henry had evidently been badly frightened, and when he was frightened he blustered. "Care!" he shouted. "Haven't we denied ourselves the joy of his presence so that he may be safe from all infection at Havering? Hasn't he every care that human thought can devise? A devoted foster-mother. Dr. Bull in constant attendance. His food—and even his tiny clothes—tested for poison. And haven't I recently given orders that no one—not even his own sisters—may go and dandle him and breathe on him without my signed permission?"

He cared so much that it almost swung his thoughts beyond the necessity of re-marriage. If anything should happen to his son—his little, lovable son—who already looked for his coming and talked to him with the marvel of first words. . . . What did all the women in the world matter compared with this precious replica of himself? And here were these wretched counsellors wasting his time when he might be on his way to Havering. He must get rid of them—promise them anything. He looked round and beckoned to Thomas Culpepper, a personable young man whose pleasant manners had already earmarked him for personal service. "Tell them to have the horses ready for Havering, Tom," he ordered. "I shall want you to come with me. And bring that toy puppet show we bought in Kingston and some of those big peaches from the south wall." It would be pleasant riding to-day. But how often had he set forth quite happily on such a morning only to worry himself into a frenzy on the way lest anything should have happened to the child before he got there! That was the worst, he supposed, of having only *one* son.

The Archbishop touched him on the arm. The austerity of his heavily-jowled face was softened by pity. Of them all, he alone guessed at the Tudor's inmost thoughts, understanding that mixture of sensitiveness and self-deception which men called the King's conscience.

"For England's sake, Sir, settle something definite before you go," he urged gently.

Henry relaxed from his defiant stance and smiled at him. Wolsey, the most powerful Archbishop of them all, had died lamenting that he had served his King much better than his God. But the King himself knew this to be much more true of Cranmer, who, however troubled in his conscience, invariably helped to get him what he wanted. So he listened to his appeal. Beyond the trivial pastime on the terrace, his eyes sought the Thames, bearing laden ships from half the world's ports to the wharves of his throbbing capital. The river that flowed past all his palaces—that was part of his daily life and the very life-stream of his land. A land weakened by the interminable Wars of the Roses and which he, born of a Lancastrian father and a Yorkist mother, had solidified and made strong. No weakling could have done that, he thought, expanding his mighty chest. The vigour of his manhood had both reflected and inspired the resilience that always lay coiled at the slow-beating heart of England waiting on necessity and some leader's call. In this he had not let England down. Strength and physical courage and heartiness he had shown his subjects—and these were the credentials they demanded of their rulers. His private life was his own. But he would do much to secure the succession —to keep England peaceful and prosperous as he knew and loved her now.

"I tell you what, milords," he suggested, turning towards the waiting group. "If I can't go myself and see these prospective brides, we'll send Holbein to paint 'em. For upon my soul, he catches people's expressions so marvellously and is so scrupulous of detail that this should help me to decide. Have them send him up," he ordered, almost genially. "I saw him down in the garden but a few minutes ago being besieged by ladies who hope to get their miniatures done."

While waiting for his court painter to come, Henry went and stood before his portrait of Queen Jane. He had ridden to Windsor the moment the breath was out of her body sooner than sleep in the same house as her corpse; but immediately on his return he had her painting hung where he could see it from his work table. And so truthfully had Holbein reproduced her fair gentleness that it seemed to all of them as if Jane Tudor herself looked gravely down at him. Only once—to Catherine of Aragon—could Henry give the clean, uncalculated love of youth, and his body had never burned for Jane beyond control of reason or religion as it had for Nan Bullen; but so happy had their short married life been that he felt no desire to replace her. In fact, after the first shock of her death he had rather enjoyed playing the new role of widower, and—giving himself up to an orgy of self-pity and sentiment—he had managed to wrap her memory in a shroud of perfections which would have startled diffident Jane. But all his life he would be sincerely grateful to her for the tranquillity she had brought him after the disappointing torments of his second marriage, and because she had died in giving him his son. Never, he knew, would she have defied him as proud, virtuous Catherine had done or deceived him like Anne. If he must marry a fourth time he could imagine himself marrying a Catherine or a Jane—but never, never another girl called Anne!

Hans Holbein brought into the room a breath of the wider life of art, unbounded by nationality and uncontaminated by scheming politics. The anxious statesmen breathed more freely and the King, always ready to turn from any unpleasantness, welcomed him with genuine pleasure. Here was a man whom he felt he had made and who—unlike Cromwell—had remained unchanged. His appreciation of the arts had been quick to recognize Holbein's genius, and it was his own generosity that kept him in the country. And because so many of the things he did made Henry feel shabby he found it comforting to warm himself at times in the glow of his own good deeds. So he laid an affectionate arm about the painter's shoulders and led him to the late Queen's portrait. "It's more than two years since you painted it, Hans," he said. "And I would sooner lose anything in the palace."

They stood side by side in front of the canvas, not wholly unalike in appearance. The fortuitous resemblance was accentuated by the light, spade-shaped beard Holbein had grown in deference to his patron; but the colour of it, like his eyes, was warmly brown and the width of his face was refined by half a lifetime of diligent seeking after perfection in his art. However unconventionally he lived, there was little of the gross or animal about him—it had all been whittled out of him by hard work. In his brown velvet of unassuming cut, beside the King's gorgeousness, he would have passed for any kindly, middle-class student. But he was master of his craft and that was the kind of equality the King recognized. With mutual appreciation they examined the texture of Jane's brocaded bodice and the fine network on her sleeves. "I remember that dress well and how happy we were when she wore it!" sighed Henry, his small, light eyes suffusing with easy emotion. "You know, Hans, I sometimes think if she were alive to-day my little son would be stronger. And there wouldn't be all this pother now about getting married again." He made a gesture as if to wash his hands of the whole wearisome business and turned Holbein over to his counsellors.

The Archbishop drew him into their midst and they discussed the commission at length.

Milan was a painter's paradise—particularly to one who had not been able to afford such opportunities in his youth.

But when they told him it was the young Duchess they wanted him to paint and Norfolk explained eagerly what a famous beauty she was, Holbein looked sceptical. He had usually found these famous beauties to be remarkably uninteresting sitters—smug and expressionless. "Are they expecting me?" he asked practically.

Some of the statesmen exchanged uneasy glances. Knowing the lady's objections, they had proceeded no further with the negotiations. Cranmer stole a glance at the King's uncompromising back. "We could send an envoy, could we not, milord Chamberlain?" he suggested uncertainly.

"Send Wotton," snapped the King, without turning round.

"But he is only a Lutheran doctor of divinity," objected the Duke, whose connection by marriage with the Tudors gave him considerable liberty of speech.

"He's the most discreet man I know for the business," said Henry. "And I don't want to be compromised until I've seen the portrait."

"And if there should be any hitch in Milan," demurred Thomas Cromwell obstinately. "Have they your Grace's leave to proceed to Cleves?"

"Hitch? Why should there be?" demanded the exasperated bridegroom-to-be.

Cromwell had learned his able statecraft as Wolsey's secretary but, being the son of a blacksmith, he had not been brought up to soften his blows. "Sir, we have combed Europe," he explained bluntly. "And, failing the Duchess of Milan, there seem to be no others available."

It was a humiliating thought and Henry swallowed it in silence. "I don't know anything about these two Cleves women. I don't even know their names!" he burst out presently, pacing back and forth beneath Jane's portrait.

Cromwell hastily consulted a document in his hand. To his legal mind, the ladies themselves had seemed relatively unimportant. "The Lady Anne and the Lady Amelia," he read.

Another Anne! And they would probably foist her onto him because she was the elder! "Oh, if you must!" agreed

Henry ungraciously. "But of what consequence is this Duchy of Cleves? Nothing ever happened there!"

Cromwell could have reminded him for the hundredth time that an alliance with Cleves would send up his stock with the Emperor and keep France guessing; but it was Holbein who unexpectedly relieved the tension. He looked up from a clever little cartoon of the King which he had been drawing surreptitiously on the back of a book. "Nothing —except that I was born near there!" he said laughingly. Not being concerned with the inner strategy of the projects they were pressing, he was far more at ease than the rest.

"Why, of course—one forgets you are really German!" exclaimed Henry, forgetting his annoyance. "You've lived here so long and you came to us from Basle——"

"My father had to go there to illuminate manuscripts. He used to paint people's portraits within the initial letters of their important documents. They were so small and exquisite, that their lovers used to cut them out and keep them in lockets. That's how I got the idea of making miniatures."

"But you remember Cleves?"

"As a small boy I lived in the lower Valley of the Rhine. I loved the vast skyscapes—the long, straight canals—and the windmills——" He broke off with a little deprecating laugh in a rather charming way he had when speaking of his own affairs.

Henry gave him a friendly punch. "Why, all this time we've been keeping a homesick man!" he laughed good-naturedly. "And avidly as the artist in you yearns for the art treasures of Milan, all the little boy in you wants the windmills! Well, go on there if you like, and paint all the Flemish princesses you want to. In all their stuffy petticoats! But mind you let me have young Christine of Milan's portrait first!"

Good humour was restored. Henry's great laugh rang through the room so that the maids-of-honour outside remembered their duties and scuttled from the terrace; and the solemn, middle-aged men within smiled as they were wont to do at home, without the closed and wary look that concealed their tortuous minds at Court. The King made a gesture of dismissal and they bowed themselves out, streaming thankfully into the ante-room and corridors. Only Cromwell and Cranmer and Holbein remained, arranging a meeting with Dr. Wotton; and young Culpepper who was to ride with his master to Havering.

"You can see how it is, Hans," said Henry. "The two parties on at me all the time. And the brides only cyphers for the men's separate ambitions. Religious faction wrapped up in romance!" He made a ribald grimace at the Chancellor's back. He felt he could talk to Holbein like that because a painter belonged to the world and not to any party.

"Like the carvings I'm designing for Hampton of the lion and the unicorn fighting for the crown," laughed Holbein.

Henry stretched himself luxuriously, looking down appreciatively at the great muscles that still swelled on either forearm. "Ah, well, now we can get out," he yawned, relaxing from a public character to a private individual. "Have they brought round the horses, Tom?"

"They're in the courtyard, Sir."

"Then we'll get going. I wonder now if Mary would like to come with us? If she's finished her everlasting devotions!" He was all brimming over with kindness now, and it pleased him to know how his proud elder daughter, now a grown woman, adored her half-brother. He stepped back to the window to see if there was any sign of her; but the terrace was deserted save for the slim, dark girl who had laughed so deliciously. Having nothing in particular to do, she was putting the shuttlecocks back in their box. "Who *is* that girl?" he asked idly, noting the untamed grace of her most ordinary movements.

Culpepper, helping him into his riding coat, craned over the royal shoulder to get a glimpse of her. "The Dowager Duchess of Norfolk has only just brought her to Court," he answered evasively.

"A poor relation of sorts, so probably her name is Howard," vouchsafed the departing Chancellor, gathering up his papers and his unbecoming little hat. "An undisciplined wench, anyhow," he added, remembering how she had distracted the King in the middle of a solemn Council meeting.

"I should like to paint her as Persephone," murmured Holbein.

The Archbishop joined them at the window. "Scarcely out of the schoolroom, I should imagine," he remarked indulgently. With an apprehensive side glance at the sensual Tudor whose whims he had cause to know so well, he did his best to defend the girl by placing her definitely in the category of the very young and unimportant. "Young Tom here should be able to tell us her Christian name. I saw them dancing together last night."

This time the good-looking gentleman-in-waiting could not very well withhold the information. "It is Katherine, milord—and she's a cousin of mine," he said, reddening. And he, too, glanced at the King.

But Henry had turned from the window, cheerfully humming one of his own songs. "Katherine Howard," he repeated absently, gathering up gloves and whip from a page. "A charming name!"

CHAPTER II

When Dr. Wotton and Hans Holbein arrived from Milan a flurry of wild conjecture stirred the quiet Duchy of Cleves. Within the walled town itself people gathered in excited groups about the Rathaus square or stood gazing up at the castle with as much curiosity as though they had never seen its famous Swan Tower and comfortable pepper-pot turrets before. Each house, with a pulley sticking out like a sharp beak from the granary in its high-peaked gable, was sure to hold *someone* who worked in the ducal household or stables and could bring home first-hand news of the bustle that was going on up there. There were important foreign guests, they said. And Cleves could scarcely credit her own importance when the Burgomaster himself was sent for and told to hang out all the civic banners because two envoys had come from Henry the Eighth of England.

As soon as the Dowager Duchess was sure that their interest in her impecunious family was really matrimonial she coached her son in diplomacy and told her two unmarried daughters to put on their best clothes. She realized, of course, that even their best clothes would probably seem dowdy to the messengers of a monarch who had outshone the French on the Field of the Cloth of Gold. But Amelia could be depended on to look sprightly in anything, and Anne was no raving beauty anyhow.

Mary of Cleves reviewed the situation hastily. Although her daughters were dowerless she had managed to marry Sybilla, the beauty of the family, to the Duke of Saxony. And what with her own recent widowhood and her son's ineptitude for affairs, Anne was too useful to be spared. She was so domesticated that she was capable of running the royal household, and had been so much in her father's company that she understood a good deal about estate management as well. It was she who had calmed the flustered servants and improvised a suitable banquet, leaving her mother free to

23

concentrate on saying the right thing. Mary had come to depend on Anne. So she sent for Amelia, who was always complaining that Cleves was dull and whose pleasure-loving mind worked with the tinkling briskness of a musical box. "The gentlemen from England whom you met at supper last night tell me that Henry Tudor is looking for another wife," she said, watchful for her youngest daughter's reactions.

Amelia's hard, bright eyes almost stuck out of her head with suppressed excitement. "I wondered if that was it— when Dr. Wotton asked us so many personal questions—and Anne was so dumb. But why—*here*, Madam?" she enquired, voicing what everyone else was secretly wondering.

The Duchess had not nurtured her family on false pride. In loyalty to her husband's religious principles she had even castigated her maternal satisfaction in their well-set-up young bodies by dressing them more unbecomingly than she need. She felt it wiser to let her daughters know that they were only a last hope. "They went to Milan first," she admitted. "But I suppose that after the way he divorced his Spanish wife and the—regrettable incident of Anne Bullen——" She left the sentence unfinished and began looking over a pile of mended bed hangings which a sewing maid had left for her inspection.

Amelia readily grasped both inference and warning. She had already given a good deal of superficial thought to the subject. Henry would be no romantic lover, and Anne Bullen's fate indicated clearly that it would be a risky business encouraging any others. But, as her mother had anticipated, she was prepared to sacrifice a good deal for the sake of a crown. Even as a child she had chafed against their uneventful family life, and here was promise of the biggest publicity that could happen to anyone. She hadn't sufficient depth of sympathy to imagine how Henry's first two wives must have suffered, and she had always been jealous of Sybilla's social triumphs. "Well, at any rate, his last queen died a natural death!" she recalled optimistically. One couldn't think seriously about blocks and executions in the peaceful security of her mother's room in the old Swan Tower. She stood watching the Duchess's busy hands until their familiar, methodical movements had soothed away her momentary trepidation. "Are the two gentlemen going to stay long?" she asked, helping to refold the hangings.

"Long enough for Master Holbein to paint you both." In spite of her campaign against vanity, Mary of Cleves couldn't prevent a certain amount of complacency from creeping into her voice as she surveyed Amelia's slender neck rising from the heavy metal embroidery of her collar and the neatness of her feet visible beneath a full round skirt. "Besides the full-length portraits he will do two of his famous miniatures to send immediately to King Henry," she said. "So naturally I want you to look your best."

It would mean sitting still for hours and Amelia wished it could be with Dr. Wotton. The suave doctor of divinity had plied her with questions which had made her feel important, whereas the self-effacing artist—apart from acting as interpreter—had said nothing at all. He had only watched her and Anne in an apprizing way which she found confusing.

"And I must arrange for you to have some English lessons," continued the preoccupied Duchess.

Amelia looked up quickly. "Anne as well?" she asked, in her birdlike staccato.

Mary met her glance with complete understanding. She was comfortably sure that Amelia was the right one to go. "Anne always seems to have so much to occupy her," she said, preparing to start on her daily inspection of the kitchens with a comfortable leisureliness that disguised the astuteness of her mind. "But, of course, she can learn English if she likes."

Later in the day, in the seclusion of their bedroom, Amelia passed on to her sister some of the information she had gleaned. Anne had come in from one of her frequent visits to the ducal tenantry. She stood just inside the door, a tall, serious girl with a pencilled list in one hand and a cheap earthenware bulb pot in the other. Anne was always making lists of things to be attended to and things the servants and farm workers needed. She knew that the various officials took advantage of her brother's occasional mental lapses if she didn't. And in return the tenantry were always presenting her with humble gifts. "Why must you accept the things?" her family would ask, between amusement and exasperation. But Anne was never embarrassed by them. She balanced the cheap bowl with its straggle of flowers some child had grown for her as carefully as if it were spikenard and looked across at her sister with beautiful, lazy-lidded brown eyes. "What on earth are you doing?" she asked resentfully, seeing Amelia's entire wardrobe spread out across both sides of the enormous bed.

"Looking out my most becoming dress to be painted in. Deciding that they are all old-fashioned. And giving Saskia a lot of things I shan't want any more," answered Amelia, categorically.

Anne glanced from her sister, preening herself before her mirror, to the plump, well-pleased lady-in-waiting holding an assortment of heavy-looking garments across her outstretched arms. "But you may be glad of them in the winter," she said stolidly. For Anne was what her upbringing had made her—a thrifty soul, given to hoarding. Besides, like most elder sisters, she had contracted the habit of looking after people. Because Sybilla had always been the show-piece of the family it had fallen to Anne, the second daughter, to shepherd an excitable younger sister and a small, neurotic brother through state functions, muttering firmly at intervals, "Don't dirty your dress, Amelia!" or "No, William, you can't possibly be sick in front of all these people!"

Glad that she would soon be finished with such admonitions, Amelia dismissed her laden lady with a smug little smile. "You must make William buy us some *new* clothes, Anne," she insisted. "You know as well as I do why that charming Dr. Wotton has come to Cleves. He says the King of England wants to get married again."

"Why?" asked Anne indifferently. "I should have thought three times was enough." She crossed the room and put down her latest gift by the window overlooking the moat. Like a fine etching in sepia, the whole façade of the palace was mirrored in the sluggish water. Anne often wondered why, with such rows of unused windows, convention demanded that unmarried daughters of a ducal household should share a bedroom. She wanted a room like William's, uncluttered with Amelia's fussy toilet accessories and Amelia's ceaseless conversation.

"Because they want an heir, stupid! I should hate that part, wouldn't you, Anne?"

"No. I should like lots of babies," said Anne. "But I thought his last Queen had a little boy?"

"People say he's delicate," snapped Amelia. "Which is more than anyone could say of you!"

Anne made no reply. People who liked her and wanted to speak well of her always said that she was not quarrelsome. But she was sufficiently honest with herself to know that part of that rather negative virtue was just laziness. At twenty-four she had come to realize that she saw most things from an angle so much simpler than most people's that even to begin arguing with them took more time and mental energy than she cared to expend. All this delicacy about babies, for instance. If one was expected to love them once they were born why should there be something shameful about either wanting them or getting them?

"You know, Anne, this visit is the most important thing that ever happened to us," Amelia was saying. "It appears that Henry Tudor wants one of us and doesn't mind much which."

"How revolting!" murmured Anne, picking up a comb to tidy her hair.

"I wanted to talk to you about it last night, but you were so disinterested and sleepy."

"It was one of William's bad days," Anne reminded her. "And what with Mother not wanting Dr. Wotton to guess—and the Margrave of Guelderland coming to see us specially about that dispute over his land—I had to go into all the details so that I can explain it to William when he's better. And then, of course, the stewards wanted extra money for entertaining our guests."

"I don't know how you can be interested in such dull things—specially when we so seldom have a really cultured and interesting visitor like Dr. Wotton!" Amelia came and seated herself on the broad window seat, prepared for a pleasant gossip. "You know Master Holbein is to make miniatures of us, don't you? I have asked him to show *us* a picture of Henry. It is only fair, don't you think? Dr. Wotton says that when Henry Tudor was eighteen and married Catherine of Aragon he was the handsomest and most sought-after young man in Europe."

"Whatever he was then, he must be quite old now," said Anne, making sure that every wave of luxuriant brown hair was well hidden beneath the severity of her round, winged cap. "Forty-five, at least, I should think."

"But he's very rich. And *much* more important than Sybilla's husband."

"William says he is fat and red-headed."

Amelia stared at her, finding it difficult to believe in such detachment. "D'you really mean you don't want to be Queen of England?"

Anne shook her head. "I believe I should hate it," she said. "I like our life here."

"Life!" scoffed Amelia, trying to make the high neckline of the blue velvet look less severe. "Stagnation, you mean."

Anne's only answer was a lift of her finely marked brows. She pulled an apple from her ample pocket and began munching it contentedly. Having a large frame that used up much energy, she was usually hungry. Her ruminative gaze strayed to the flat fields beyond the city walls, with industrious villages dotted comfortably here and there beneath a limitless canopy of sky. "And there again it's no use arguing," she thought helplessly. "It's all a question of what one means by life. Amelia's idea of it begins and ends with parties, while mine is made up of wide breathing spaces—and other people."

"But think, Anne, what it would mean being Queen of an important country like that!" Amelia leaned forward in her eagerness, hands tightly clasped and eyes acquisitively bright. "Dancing and masques and low-cut dresses—all the things our father thought wicked—amusements we've never been allowed here. Poets like Wyatt and the Earl of Surrey paying you compliments and other women envying you——"

"And hating you!" laughed Anne. Touched by her sister's naïve eagerness she stooped to drop a light kiss on her forehead. She hoped there would be some kind person at hand to guide her through the pitfalls of such a marriage.

But Amelia tossed her pretty head. "Who cares about the women?" she scoffed.

"I do," said Anne gravely. "And I should think they could make or mar one's life in a foreign country. Besides, I like other women to be fond of me and tell me things. When they're thrilled about something—or when they're in trouble. People do, you know." She paused to impress the fact on herself as well as her sister almost as if it were a new and pleasing discovery. "You do yourself—and William—and even Mother sometimes—and people like Dorothea——" Anne broke off with a little cry of consternation, and reached for the list of things she had to do. "Ach, dear God, I had forgotten——"

"Forgotten what?" asked Amelia.

"All about Dorothea's baby. The poor mite's terribly ill and none of the neighbours will help because he's come out in some sort of rash. You know how stupidly nervous they are about the plague!"

"You mean they won't help because she isn't married."

"But if they see me going into her father's house it may shame that prude of a doctor into making some attempt to save the poor little thing's life," sighed Anne, who didn't in the least want to go out again.

"Surely the shame is Dorothea's!" remarked Amelia primly.

Anne wanted to say, "So was the shining glory!" but remembered how shocked her father would have been. All the same, she couldn't help thinking of the Summer morning when her favourite waiting woman had asked leave to be excused from her duties. The roses had been in bloom and poor plain Dorothea had been transfigured by happiness and Anne knew that it hadn't seemed like sin then. "They were planning their wedding," she explained hurriedly. "And then the man was sent to Hungary or somewhere to fight the

Turks. He was a captain in the Emperor's army and he was killed."

"How awful for her!" agreed Amelia, with facile sympathy. "But you simply can't go now. You heard Mother's message. Either of us may be sent for at any moment to sit for those portraits."

"I promised," said Anne. And Amelia knew by long experience that Anne always kept her promises. "Well, if you must go, for Heaven's sake change your dress first. Then I can send Saskia for you if we're wanted. Look, I had her lay out your best brocade."

"Bless you, my sweet! But I should only crumple it," said Anne. "I'll have to change when I come back."

Amelia knew the dubious results of such a hasty toilet. She was too much accustomed to shining socially by comparison with her sister's gaucherie to look upon her as a rival. But there was something about Anne's smile when she wasn't worried or preoccupied. . . . And that famous painter had looked at her so persistently last night! It would be just as well perhaps if dear Anne *should* come in late, looking awkward and distressed, as she always did on the rare occasions when she caused her mother displeasure. "Oh, well, if you *must* go——" acquiesced Amelia, burying the mean little thought beneath the virtuous memory of putting out the brocaded dress. "But how you can do things in poky houses for people in pain I can't think! Particularly when our whole life may depend on looking nice this afternoon!"

Anne hastily gathered up some dill seeds and her recipe for a soothing syrup, and her purse and thrust them deep into the pocket where the apple had bulged. Still refastening the old, dull pink gown she had been about to change, she looked back from the doorway and laughed. "*Your* future, you mean, my dear!" she amended. "Who's likely to look at me?" She said it without bitterness or resentment. She was used to being the useful, untemperamental member of the family and she hadn't an idea how lovable she looked when she laughed like that. She only knew that Amelia had had several suitors, whereas she herself had been betrothed in childhood to the Duke of Lorraine's son who—as soon as he had grown up—had wanted to marry someone else. She had been too young to be consciously hurt by his repudiation; but her sisters' lively teasing on the subject had left her devoid of vanity. So it never occurred to Anne of Cleves that Henry Tudor might choose *her*.

CHAPTER III

Anne took longer over her errand than she had intended and—as usual—she didn't come away until she had persuaded people to do what she wanted. It was doubtful if Dorothea's baby would live; but at least the doctor had prescribed something to cool his feverish spots and because the Duke's sister had been seen to call at the head falconer's house, it would inevitably become fashionable for neighbours to help. But virtue had gone out of her. Torn with pity by the infant's pitiful crying, she herself had stayed to soothe him to sleep, and she began her walk back to the palace in weary pre-occupation. It was not until she had crossed the postern bridge and noticed an unusual smartness about the sentries that she remembered the important visitors from England. Dismissing her maid, she took a short cut through a walled fruit garden; and there, being screened from the observation of court dignitaries, she ran as fast as she could to the kitchen entrance beneath the private apartments.

Turning sharply out of the strong sunlight into the deep shadow of the backstairs cloister she collided with a man standing just inside the archway. He appeared to be sketching the Swan Tower and the waterlilies on the moat. Paint pots were scattered in all directions by the violence of the encounter and their annoyance was mutual. He cursed below his breath in some foreign language as he clutched at his impedimenta—then raged at her more explicitly in low German because she had broken his best brush.

"And you've ruined my dress!" cried Anne, surveying a splodge of yellow ochre dribbling down the front of it. "What a ridiculous place to stand, where people are bound to bump into you!"

Such practical considerations seldom bothered Hans Holbein. "It's the only place to get a view of the lilies *and* Tower," he retorted.

"No, it isn't," contradicted Anne, dabbing at her faded

skirt. "There's a much better one from the top of the dove-cote. All the views from the palace are stiff."

Holbein grunted. Rich man's sons who were privileged to work in his studio would as soon think of denying that the sun moved round the earth as of questioning his artistic judgement. "It wouldn't look across a typical Flemish garden or be framed in the perfect setting of a Gothic arch," he argued. "And in my case I don't know where your dovecote is." He was aware of her standing there, breathless and bare-headed, as he grovelled on the flag-stones to retrieve his gear; and in the gloom he took her to be one of the innumerable ladies-in-waiting he had seen about the place. They all looked alike to him, with their stupid good-natured faces and shapeless clothes. But because Anne's irritation seldom lasted long she was soon stooping with compunction to pick up the broken brush. The picturesque Flemish waterways drew many foreign artists to Bruges and Antwerp and the Valley of the Maas, and although her father had disapproved of their loose way of living he had always shown them hospitality because they were invariably hard-up. "You must let me buy you a new one," she said, more gently.

The great portrait painter laughed. He was in the habit of having squirrel hair brushes made specially for him by a man in Paternoster Row, and beautiful blondes had even offered him their golden locks. "I'm afraid you'd have to send to London for a brush like that," he told her.

"London?" Anne straightened up and regarded him more attentively. Her eyes were becoming accustomed to the cloistered gloom. "But how stupid of me! You are Master Holbein, of course..."

The pleasant twinkle came back into his eyes. He was used to people recognizing him as a celebrity. "And you, milady?" he enquired, getting up casually and dusting his knees with a paint-rag. She was almost as tall as he and his professional eye noted the excellent moulding of her profile and breast silhouetted sharply against the light.

"Don't you remember meeting me last evening? I am Anna," she said.

She pronounced the name as her family said it, and

33

Holbein had been introduced to so many people since he came. Her voice was husky with tiredness and—now that her annoyance was spent—there was a note of laughter in it which promised deliciously. "Well, Anna," he suggested, "perhaps one day when we are both off duty you will be charming enough to show me the marvellous view from your dovecote. And instead of your buying me a new brush we might go and choose some Utrecht velvet for a new gown."

Realizing his mistake, she moved into the little pool of sunlight provided by a small, barred window. "Anna of *Cleves*," she corrected quietly. He looked at her sharply enough then. Because her elaborate head-dress had been left clutched tightly in a sleeping baby's fist her brown hair was blown in a soft cloud about her face. Her cheeks, warm with hurrying, vied with the dusky pink of her gown. Yet there was a dignified composure about her which he had noticed during the previous evening's formalities. Holbein bowed sheepishly, cursing himself for an abstracted fool. How right his London friends had been when they said it was useless trying to make a courtier of him! "It's so dark here, Madam—and you look so different . . ." he stammered.

"I'm afraid I do," she agreed, thinking how vexed her mother would be that Holbein of all men should catch her at such a disadvantage. She smoothed her wind-blown hair without embarrassment, straining it back from a high, thoughtful forehead until all the artist in him wanted to cry out to her to stop. He would have flattened himself and his sketching materials against the wall that she might pass, but this homely Flemish princess—deeming it inhospitable to leave a guest ill at ease—paused for a few minutes to rest herself on the deep window-ledge. "Thank you, but I am not in such a disastrous hurry now," she explained. "It was only because I feared my mother might be wanting me to sit for you."

"Dr. Wotton is waiting for a further audience with His Grace the Duke who, we understand, was indisposed yesterday," said Holbein stiffly. "And it would be useless to begin work until the conclusion of the—the——" He made worried little circles with his hand, fumbling in an unbusiness-like mind for the correct word.

"Bargaining?" she suggested, mocking him—or possibly herself—with a forced smile.

He could have kicked himself for his clumsiness. It hadn't occurred to him how crudely hurtful those international matrimonial offers must appear to the woman concerned; and to relieve his obvious confusion she asked to see the sketch.

She was familiar with the meticulous detailed master-pieces of the Flemish school; but here was a vivid, modern impression created with a few lines. Yet the whole essence of her country was there—expressed in placid water and the long unbroken skyline that had bounded all her uneventful life. "I wish I could paint!" she sighed. "For so one can hold the places one loves for ever—even if one has to go away."

"I will make you a sketch, Madam—a better one," he found himself promising impulsively. "This is only a poor hurried thing I attempted as a souvenir."

She really smiled at him then—her wide, tender mouth curving with friendliness. "Then you like our unexciting kind of country? Even after having come from Italy?"

"I lived near here as a small boy, Madam."

"Then that settles it. I will show you my favourite view from the top of the dovecote," laughed Anne. "But you must get up early in the morning when the mists are rising over the Rhine and a pale primrose light shines through the lindens."

He saw immediately how right she was. It would break up the formality and recapture the legendary romance of the tower. He wanted her to stay and talk about it. He would have liked to tell her about the feast of pictures he had seen in Milan. But she got up and walked away down the long, dim cloister towards her own apartments. He watched her pass through a patch of sunlight by the kitchen courtyard, where some maid-servants were drawing water from the well. In spite of clothes scarcely less cumbersome than theirs, Anne walked with the untrammelled freedom of a Queen.

She was twenty-four and grave for her years. Her calm eyes surveyed all men with consideration. Holbein, who was almost twice her age, guessed that passion in her was as yet unawakened.

He bundled together his things and called to a passing servant to carry them back to his lodgings in the front of the palace. Creative fire began to kindle in him with a fresh conception. His gifted fingers twitched as he strode along, impatient to give it form. The half-planned construction of his subject teased his brain with that promise of perfection, superlative and ultimate, that drives the goaded servants of creative work. There was a baffling quality about Anne's face which reminded him of Leonardo da Vinci's 'Mona Lisa' which he had seen as he came through Paris.

On the main staircase he met Dr. Wotton coming from the Duke's audience chamber. With his wrinkled face and hurrying, black-clad legs, the English envoy looked like a worried monkey being prodded on from one difficult trick to another by the vast, pursuing whims of an invisible master. "How did you get on?" Holbein enquired, perceiving joyfully that he had escaped a diplomatic conference.

"It's a good thing the Duke's better as he's the only one of the whole crowd who speaks decent English," grumbled Wotton pointedly.

Conscience-stricken that he had not been there to help with his knowledge of both languages, Holbein drew his colleague into his own room and called for drinks. "At least they're straight-forward people to deal with—not half so Machiavellian as our amusing Marillac or those crafty statesmen in Milan," he observed consolingly.

Wotton sank into the nearest chair and frankly mopped his brow. "They're not as simple as they look," he said. "They want an undertaking that whichever daughter the King takes to wife will be crowned immediately."

"He certainly wasn't taking any chances with the last one!" chuckled Holbein. "'Time enough for that when she bears me a son!' I heard him say once to Cranmer when they were discussing how I should paint poor Queen Jane. Though I'm sure, had she lived——"

36

But Wotton was scarcely listening. He was too full of his own responsibilities. "I can't add anything to the marriage contract without consulting Cromwell," he said. "But I pointed out that as neither of these unfortunate young women has a dowry their Council can't expect much say in what the King spends on his new wife's establishment."

"He isn't mean," observed Holbein, who had benefited considerably from the royal exchequer.

"Everything depends on whether he likes her," muttered Wotton abstractedly.

Holbein poured him a beaker of the best Rhinish. He was beginning to appreciate what Anne had meant about the bargaining. "How did they take it?"

Nicholas Wotton took his wine at a gulp and felt more capable of reporting on the morning's haggling. " 'The Tudors don't need money,' the Duchess said, in that complacent way of hers. 'It's fresh blood they want.' You know, Holbein, although she looks like a well-to-do merchant's wife she says things our queens simply wouldn't dare to— and no one dreams of contradicting her."

"Well, most of what she says is common-sense," allowed Holbein. "And what did the Duke say?"

"He said he was uneasy about his sisters and he asked straight out if it was true that the Lady Elizabeth had inherited syphilis from her father."

"Good God!"

The little Lutheran lifted shocked hands to high Heaven. "If only milord Cranmer could have heard him!"

"They certainly don't mince their words," admitted Holbein, grinning at his discomfiture.

Wotton set down an empty tankard and closed his eyes. "Mercifully I was spared the pain of replying," he said. "The Duchess tried to slur over his tactlessness by pointing out with a wealth of embarrassing detail how well fitted her daughters were to bear healthy children—particularly the Lady Anne. Wide flanked, I think she called her. These people have no delicacy. If the daughters themselves talk like that——"

"It should cause quite a refreshing stir when one of them gets to Greenwich!" prophesied Holbein.

"Please God I shall have an opportunity to take them in hand first!" exclaimed the King's envoy piously.

Holbein made no doubt he would. "Well, I'm glad I've only got to paint 'em!" he laughed. "And talking of that, Wotton," he added, with the elaborate casualness of a man who has set his heart on something. "I suppose it doesn't matter which one I do first?"

"I should begin on the better looking of these two," advised Wotton, ever bent on pleasing Henry.

"And which would you call the better looking?" enquired Holbein, regarding his companion with quizzical amusement. Having contributed little to the diplomatic mission, he had had time to observe that Wotton was as wax in the toils of a designing little minx like Amelia.

The doctor of divinity looked up in innocent surprise.

"There is no comparison, is there?" He seemed about to expatiate on the younger lady's charms but, remembering his cloth, contented himself with a few disparaging remarks about the elder. "The Lady Anne is by all accounts an estimable woman. Docile, charitable and an excellent needle-woman," he declaimed in his best pulpit manner. "But as regards conversation and—er—polite accomplishments——" He smoothed down his white stock and ended on a more human and emphatic note. "I should imagine that a man like my master would find her about as entertaining as a meek cow."

Holbein dropped the quaint blue Delft wine-jug he had in his hand so that it smashed to pieces on the tiled floor. "There was nothing of the meek cow about her when I met her just now in the kitchen cloister!" he retorted, with unusual heat. "And if by having no conversation you mean she doesn't chatter like a magpie——"

Accustomed as Wotton was to his companion's deftness and tolerance, he was naturally taken aback. "I only meant that she has no animation," he explained hastily.

Holbein picked up the fragments of pottery and began piecing them together with remorseful care so that the stiff little barges fitted into the right bit of canal and the bundly Dutch women walked in their proper setting beside the blue windmills. "She *could* have, I suspect—were she awakened. Now, if *I* were the prospective bridegroom——" He was bending over his task, talking almost to himself when Wotton's scandalized remonstrance reminded him that even in Cleves such words had a treasonable sound. So he snapped out of a rather interesting reverie to assert aggressively, "Well, anyhow, when I saw her as she really is—with colour in her cheeks and her hair loosened from that dreadful cap arrangement they all wear, and flaring out at me because she's upset half my precious yellow ochre down her dress— I wanted to paint her. Really wanted to the way I used to enjoy decorating churches and books and rathauses before I became a royal lapdog paid to paint titled people!"

It was not in Wotton to understand the man's cause for self-contempt. To him freedom in one's work seemed relatively unimportant compared with money and the royal favour and an assured place in that pleasant hub of English life rotating between Greenwich, Westminster and Hampton Court. "I can't understand what you see in her," he said coldly.

"It isn't what I see. It's what I find myself looking for," said Holbein. "That younger one is pretty enough—if you like all your goods in the shop window. But there's something elusive about the Princess Anne—something to call a man back when he's tired of the obvious in other women." He paused to glance thoughtfully through the open window in passing. "It's like the lights and shadows chasing each other across those immense, flat Flemish landscapes. One minute they're dull, the next enchanting." He turned eagerly to the unresponsive cleric, his whole face alight with enthusiasm. "She doesn't often smile, have you noticed? But it's worth waiting for. Like the moment when a burst of clear sunshine lights up a mural painting on a dull day, revealing unsuspected beauty."

The unimaginative Englishman stared at him, open-mouthed. "What it is given to you artistic fellows to see!" he marvelled sarcastically.

exhausting thing to do," he said. "Won't you go and rest, Madam?"

She stood hesitant at the open window. Her normal decisiveness seemed to have deserted her. "I ought to join my sister for our English lesson," she sighed. "But it's so difficult and my head aches——"

Out of working hours Holbein was almost boyishly human. Acting on impulse, he picked up the English book which Amelia had wished to have painted in her hands. "The air on the lake would do you good," he suggested. "And if you will allow me to accompany you perhaps I can make the English seem easier."

"But I am not at all clever," she warned him, her gaze straying longingly to a tranquil stretch of sunlit water fed by the Roer.

"There are different kinds of cleverness," he observed, putting away his things.

She turned to watch him, leaning languidly against the casement. "I mean clever like Amelia. Look how easily she talked to you about art that first evening you came!"

Holbein laughed, taking a last look at his miniature. To-morrow he would mix a clear ultramarine for the background. "Milady Amelia read all that up in a book, but what you feel about colours comes out of your own heart," he said. "The Sunday before you were taken ill I saw you in church, standing like a wrapt visionary in front of Jan Van Eyck's 'Virgin and Donor'."

A twinge of conscience moved Anne to point out that her interest had not been even devout. "It's the homely little view in the background that I love—with the gay little ship and bridge, and the comfortable town," she admitted. "You wouldn't call that very discriminating, would you, when everyone thinks so much of the figures in the foreground?"

"I think I should. And you will be richer all your life because you have absorbed spontaneously some quality in a great master."

Anne thought that over. There were so many things that moved her to inarticulate delight—warm, colourful things like stained-glass windows and ceremonial processions and peasants dancing on saints' days. Her father had suppressed them and called them worldly temptations, and because she had grown up in his company, sheltered by his kindness, she had accepted them as such. But how much fuller and easier life would be if after all one found there was no need to stifle one's spontaneous reactions! She walked thoughtfully downstairs and across the terrace, followed by her reluctant lady, while Holbein hurried on ahead to unmoor a boat.

In the summer residence of that kindly, unostentatious Court it was not impossible for a celebrated painter to enjoy the company of a daughter of the ducal house. Particularly as it had suddenly become so fashionable to study English. And Nicholas Wotton, who frequently accompanied them, wrote home to Cromwell that although the Lady Anne 'had no languages, she was apt to learn'. Her methodical diligence succeeded better than Amelia's fitful brilliance; possibly because Holbein, having had to learn the language himself, knew all the pitfalls better than did their English tutor. "It's like learning several different languages at once—with so many words meaning the same thing!" Anne would complain sometimes, as they began to tackle more difficult books.

"It *is* several languages," Holbein reminded her. "British, Roman, Saxon, Norman. That is why it's so rich a heritage. And gradually—as you hear it spoken around you—you will get great joy of it."

"You talk as if I were going there!" laughed Anne, to whom health and strength were rapidly returning. Whenever possible during that golden autumn they studied out of doors, and looking from the dull book propped up between them in the boat to the golden sunburn on her cheeks, he knew how much he wanted her to come. He was old enough to be her tutor or her uncle and when they were alone he addressed her without formality. For the first time in her life Anne found herself being teased, just as if she were not a princess in a sober Lutheran land. At first she could never make out whether he were serious, but soon her own shy sense of humour waked to meet his. "Ze English gentlemens always make fon of ze ladies, yes?" she asked in her tentative, guttural English, not guessing that he himself did so expressly to bring the delectable dimples into her cheeks.

"Only if they like them," he assured her, rowing their little craft towards a bevy of fluffy cygnets she wanted to feed.

"Den if your King tease his wife—she know he really like her?" concluded Anne, trailing her lovely fingers among the flat green plates of water-lily leaves.

Holbein jibbed fastidiously from the thought of Henry's fat fingers pinching her cheek approvingly.

"Doesn't the Duke ever tease you?" he asked, remembering that solemn young man's dog-like devotion.

But Anne shook her head and made one of her queer, ungarnished statements. "No. He just needs me," she said.

Holbein would allow no one to see her miniature until it was finished. Realizing how much he wanted her to come to England he grew afraid that desire might corrupt his integrity. Scrupulously, even to the last jewel, he put in each detail exactly as he saw it. He would not even paint her with a flower in her hand, as a flattering German artist had done, lest it should give an impression of romanticism which Anne did not possess. Yet long before the tiny portrait was finished he knew that it had power to make her Queen of England. The knowledge kept him awake at night, sweating with anxiety. "But as God has given me insight I must have courage to depict what I see," he thought. And, being a dreamer, he saw Anne—Anne of the kind hands and homely heart—drawing the people of England to her with the common touch they loved. Anne with her quiet dignity and forthright gaze, walking among the gay, quick-witted women at Greenwich or Hampton Court, making their restless scheming and piquant gossip look tawdry. He knew that this vision had nothing to do with his own loneliness or desire. But thinking of her like that he did not see that, right as she might be for England, she might be all wrong for Henry.

At last there came an afternoon when he laid down his best squirrel-hair brush and called her to his side. "Come and look, Anna!" It was such a high moment for him that he didn't know he had used her name like that. They usually spoke in English now and Griselda Lowe went on dozing.

Anne got up, stretching herself luxuriously. Even now she was more interested in the man than in his limning of herself. She was watching the satisfied glow in his eyes and the way his hand cherished the precious piece of vellum. She smiled affectionately at his lapse. She knew by the lines round his eyes that he was tired, unguarded; and with her usual flair for getting inside other people's feelings she was wondering if artists, delivered of their creative riches, sagged in comfortable relief like a newly made mother whose body is her own again. "Look at your portrait, child, not at me!" he ordered, and his deep voice shook because for once the critic in him tasted satisfaction. He had done what he set out to do. He had shown a woman's whole nature in her face.

Anne obeyed him. And once she had looked, her whole world was changed.

She did not reward him with any extravagant expression of gratified pleasure. Had they not been of kindred texture he might have thought her unappreciative. She stood almost shoulder to shoulder with him, steadying his excited hand with her cool one—yet unaware that she touched him. Only the old Countess's rhythmic breathing disturbed the warm stillness of the room—the room in which their quiet friendship as well as his masterpiece had been born. She saw now why he had insisted on the dull pink gown. The richness it made against his favourite background of ultramarine was almost breath-taking in so small a circumference. The gold of her collar, the exquisite embroidery of her cap and the perfection of each jewelled ornament were all there; but nothing was allowed to detract from the interest of her face. Grave, pensive, and completely natural, she looked straight out on life from long, heavy-lidded eyes—a woman with fine brows and tender mouth. While faithfully recording each feature, genius had left unstressed her over-long nose and—being but head and shoulders—the portrait made her appear smaller than she was. Like all Holbein's work, it emphasized the refinement and spiritual attributes of the sitter. It was the most exquisite miniature Anne had ever seen—the most exquisite the world would ever see. She raised her head slowly to look incredulously at its creator. "Am I really like that?" she asked, in an awed sort of whisper.

He looked deeply into her wine-brown eyes. "As you look at me now," he vowed unsteadily, "you are exactly like that."

The troubled perplexity in her face gave place to a beautiful, shy pleasure. She felt herself recreated. "But I know I am often ordinary—and colourless—and clumsy——," she whispered humbly to this new friend to whom one could speak of even those ridiculous personal humiliations that blush wordlessly at the back of most people's minds.

"But this is the *real* you," he told her. "People don't see themselves when they are being spontaneous—or all gravely concerned with some kindness—or smiling—Do you know that all your soul pours itself into your too rare smile, Anna?"

She laughed outright. Already her staid gravity was beginning to be leavened with a becoming touch of coquetry. "Why didn't you paint me smiling then?" she asked.

He had wondered that himself. "I don't know. Perhaps because I never *have* painted anybody like that—or because I knew I was—gifted enough," he confessed.

Anne watched him place her portrait in the wonderful ivory case he had designed for it. It was carved in the shape of a Tudor rose, rising petal on petal to the lid; and sunk in that flawless setting the rich colours gleamed like the facets of a precious jewel. Anne bent over it, humbled by its perfection, and as she did so a new, overwhelming thought possessed her. "It seems possible now—that the King of England might—choose me," she faltered.

"If he has any sense he certainly will," agreed Holbein,

snapping the case shut. For the first time he was aware of a sense of personal animosity against his patron.

Anne's expressive hands, usually so still or so prosaically occupied, fluttered in a movement of distress. "But—suppose you have flattered me?"

"I've only painted what is there for all men to see."

"All men don't look for the same things in a woman."

Holbein, concerned only with driving the apprehension from her eyes, yet sought in his heart for the most sincere answer. "As long as you are fully yourself—as you have been with me—he must see in you the kind of woman who alone can assuage the devastating loneliness which is in each one of us." He took her hand gently in his and the still room wrapped them about with sad intimacy of a shared and finished interlude. "You have come alive, Anna. Don't ever shut yourself up again!" he implored.

She guessed then that he loved her and—woman-like—shied from the knowledge with an irrelevancy. "After all, you didn't put in the pock-marks," she reminded him.

"I never even thought about them," he laughed easily. "Besides, they will fade."

She smiled at him, touched by a demonstrative kindness so much more comforting than the matter-of-fact affection of her family. But when he would have laid the ivory casket away in its velvet-lined case she stretched out a hand to prevent him. There was something so irrevocable about his gesture. The portrait would go to England now. And Henry Tudor would bend over it as they had done—and make his choice.

She lifted her head to look round with new awareness at the pleasant room and a corner of the lake reflected in a rounded mirror on the wall—to let her senses drink in the familiar hotch-potch of small scents and sounds that meant home. Her face was drained of colour, and she seemed to crumple suddenly, so that Holbein caught her in his arms lest she should faint. And she—who so rarely cried—began to sob inconsequently against his heart. He supposed it to be the reaction from her illness. "Oh, Hans, I wish—I wish you had made me hideous!" she cried.

53

She didn't want to leave Cleves. She didn't particularly want to marry a king. Because Holbein had called her beautiful the slumbering passion in her was stirring. She was not as yet in love, but her body was vibrant with the knowledge that she could love lavishly.

CHAPTER V

A week or two later Henry stood with Anne's miniature in his hand. He was bending over it just as she had pictured him and already Amelia's portrait lay discarded among the books and sheets of music on his table. The five other men present watched his expression, motionless as mummers in a tableau; for the policy of a kingdom was hanging in the balance.

"I believe I'm going to be happy again!" he murmured; and a sigh for the fleeting freedom of his widower's estate lent weight to the words.

Men moved again. Relief was audible in the suave rustle of a primate's sleeve; frustration in the irritable clank of a ducal scabbard. All three Thomases made appropriate congratulatory sounds. Thomas Cromwell and Thomas Cranmer whole-heartedly because it was they who had baited the Lutheran trap; that fine old soldier, Thomas Howard of Norfolk, perfunctorily because he wanted a Catholic queen.

But Charles Brandon, Duke of Suffolk, said nothing. The religious issue scarcely affected his easy-going nature. He wanted Henry's happiness simply because he was his friend. He had known him intimately since they were both carefree youngsters, and he had seen him mature and suffer. Undoubtedly, most of Henry's suffering had been his own fault. But Suffolk was not censorious, and life at court was always much pleasanter when the King was happy.

Nicholas Wotton—the only man in the room who was a comparative nobody—stood near the door. Although it was he who had brought the momentous miniature, it was the first time he had been summoned to the King's private work-room and he knew his place among his betters.

Henry's beauty-loving fingers were caressing the ivory Tudor rose casket, appreciating both compliment and workmanship. Such subtlety always pleased him. "You do think she's beautiful, don't you, Charles?" he enquired urgently.

Suffolk came closer and examined it with him. They were much of a height, but the Duke looked the taller because he had kept his supple figure. The three Thomases couldn't resist smiling a little, covertly. They seemed to have watched their colleague being drawn into similar pre-nuptial discussions before. Only the King himself appeared to be untroubled by a hovering sense of the ridiculous.

"Holbein's a genius!" said Suffolk. And he said it with such honest conviction that Henry scarcely noticed that his question remained unanswered.

"It's quite the best thing he's done yet, isn't it?" he agreed. "By the way, Wotton," he added, looking round the pleasantly-littered room for his recently-returned envoy, "where *is* Holbein?"

The doctor detached himself from obscurity to join the finely-dressed group standing by a window overlooking the river. "He wished to remain abroad for while, your Grace," he explained with a formal bow. "I believe he has associations—er, early associations—with that part of Europe." Wotton was sufficiently astute to realise how eagerly the Catholic party would clutch at the least hint of frailty in Anne, and not for worlds would he have spoiled his spiritual superior's project by suggesting how dangerously recent was the association that kept Holbein from enjoying fresh laurels in London.

"He wrote for my permission," corroborated Cromwell. "And, seeing that he had worthily executed all three commissions, I trust I did not over-step my office in granting it?" Like most of them, he had a weak spot for the unconventional artist and—providing it cost his ambition nothing —could enjoy being indulgent to a friend.

Henry waved the matter aside benignly. "The man deserves a holiday," he agreed. Picking up poor Amelia's discarded portrait, he turned again to the envoy and said graciously, "We are much in your hands, Wotton, since you alone have been privileged to meet both ladies. Tell me, do you really consider these to be good portraits?"

"Most lively likenesses," Wotton assured him.

"Then it seems the Lady Anne of Cleves is even more

attractive than her sister, Sybilla of Saxony," postulated Henry pompously, passing the portraits round for inspection.

Cromwell remarked a little over-eagerly that Olsiliger, the Flemish chancellor, had been marvelling at some subtle change in her and considered that she had grown even more so during these last few weeks while her full-length portrait was being painted.

"Since learning of the possible good fortune that awaits her, no doubt," suggested Charles Brandon, with a smile.

"Attractive or not, I understand she has no civilized accomplishments and speaks nothing but guttural German," objected Norfolk. "I can hardly imagine that your Grace will find an evening spent without music or a bed shared without speech particularly entertaining!" To lend point to his carping remark he picked up a viol which was never far from the King's hand and began strumming a sophisticated little song which Marillac, the popular French ambassador, had introduced from Paris. Every maid-of-honour and page-boy about the palace was singing it, and it had helped to beguile many an evening for the King.

Henry looked a little crest-fallen. "That's true, Thomas. But, after all, we have plenty of paid musicians——"

"They might suffice till bedtime," laughed Norfolk, torturing the gut in a final tremulo which set Henry wincing. The Howards might be fine poets and fighters, but he wished the fellow would either leave other people's instruments alone or learn to play them more tunefully.

Cranmer was quick to smooth out his mounting irritation. "Beauty and accomplishments are what every man hopes for in marriage, Howard," he remonstrated sententiously. "But for the sake of the realm oughtn't we to attach at least as much importance to character?"

The prospective bridegroom stood irresolute, one sandy eyebrow cocked enquiringly in Wotton's direction, and that aspirant to diplomatic advancement made a movement towards Amelia's portrait as if to bring her back into the conversation. He felt that he should explain to them that she was really the more lively and suitable. He could picture the King with her—sitting contentedly beside her at meals, teasing her for her coquettish ways and feeling pleasantly masculine because of her stupidity. But Cromwell, ever clumsy in his movements, brushed against him in reaching for Olsiliger's latest letter; and as he did so his black, bull-like eyes snapped a warning. One Lutheran princess was as good as another to him; but since by good fortune the King seemed to have fallen for one, why confuse the issue? The Chancellor's ring flashed under Wotton's sharp nose— the ring that set seal to so many punishments and prefer-ments. And Wotton, who was no fool, abandoned the con-scientious impulse.

In any case, it was Holbein's responsibility. Any man, confronted with his two portraits, would inevitably choose Anne. So Wotton made a virtue of necessity. He had to admit that although Anne could keep accounts and write a good letter in her own language, she had none of the accomplishments in which the King delighted. So he harped enthusiastically upon her needlework, her kindness and her domesticity.

Henry gaped at him dubiously. "Good God, man!" he ejaculated. "I'm not engaging a cook!"

Cromwell pointed out blandly that the same simple up-bringing had produced Sybilla of Saxony, who gave her Duke counsel as well as sons. And Norfolk countered that with his trump card. "Naturally one doesn't know much about these minor royalties," he remarked languidly. "But wasn't this second daughter betrothed to one of Lorraine's sons?"

Wotton preened himself on having gone into all that. Both Duke William and Olsiliger had assured him that the match had been broken off years ago.

"By the bridegroom's wish?" insinuated Norfolk, finger-ing the pointed chin which, in defiance of royal fashion, he elected to keep clean shaven.

But Suffolk's common-sense robbed him of the trick. "My dear Howard, they were almost babes at the time! Besides, I doubt if he'd ever seen her." And Henry, looking from one to the other of them, smiled at him gratefully.

"I suppose there are no other—er—entanglements?" asked Cranmer, with a clever air of impartiality. He shrewdly suspected that it was a pretty safe question to put to anyone who had been forced to spend eight rather boring weeks at that innocuous court.

"She was never far from her mother's elbow, milord!" protested Wotton, just as he had been intended to. "Why, even her brother—who naturally has more opportunity— appears to enjoy no good cheer in his own country!"

The Duke of Suffolk was understood to mutter something about an insufferable prig and Henry, remembering their own hot youth, gave a rude guffaw. But the Archbishop of Canterbury reproved them.

"Apart from the question of morality, your Grace knows we can't afford to risk any more scandal," he said quietly.

And Henry, whose vanity still writhed at the lightest allusion to his second wife's lovers, was instantly sobered. "You're quite right," he said pressing the prelate's shoulder with a kindly hand. "And—added to this lady's unquestionable virtue—just think what a thorn a Flemish marriage will be in the flimsy friendship between Francis and the Emperor! Neither of them, without the Lowlands, will be strong enough to attack the other or to combine forces and invade *us*." He was so pleased with his own diplomatic acumen that he felt well disposed even to the man who had fostered it. "A nice piece of work, Cromwell!" he approved condescendingly. "Carry it to a swift conclusion for me and I shall certainly have to find you an earldom before I present you to my new queen!"

In high good humour he dismissed them all, remembering to soften the losing Duke's moroseness with a jest and to commend Wotton for his pains. But when all of them were gone except Suffolk he let fall the mask of omnipotence with which he faced his world. "It's all very well for them, with their everlasting party squabbles," he grumbled. "But I've got to live with the woman!" He carried Anne's minature to the light and seated himself on the wide stone window seat. "I would have preferred her a little younger—a shade more vivacious, perhaps," he muttered broodingly.

Suffolk, turning over a pile of new songs at the table, lowered his handsome head to hide a smile. It occurred to him that the lady might feel the same way about *him*. But, as always he was touched by the urgent need for reassurance in the King's 'off-duty voice'. "She looks comely—and amiable," he said. Long ago, even before he became the King's brother-in-law, he had determined never to lose his own integrity by saying what Henry wanted him to. All the same, he recognized Holbein's cleverness in attempting nothing grandiose—in painting Anne of Cleves as he saw her each day in her own home. The painting he had sent was essentially the portrait of a capable gentlewoman and as such was bound to appeal to the desire for sympathetic understanding and domestic comfort in a much married, middle-aged man with an over-sensitized ego.

"The pink and gold of her against that celestial blue!" sighed Henry, as much in love with the artistry as with the woman.

Suffolk stopped grinning and looked across at him with impatience. He had so often been called upon to witness the rising tide of the Tudors' tremendous enthusiasms and then left to clear up the ugly wreckage left by their inevitable ebbing. "But only two inches of vellum on which to stake all your happiness!" he pointed out. "With the other, you knew them—saw them almost daily—first."

"And could I have been more deceived—in the second?" demanded Henry, his voice sibilant with self-pity.

There was no answer to that.

"Besides, this is different," he went on. "With a diplomatic marriage one doesn't expect——"

"But that's just the trouble. You *do* expect—everything. . . . You know you do, you incurable old optimist!" Suffolk threw down the songs and came and sat beside him. "If you were content to consider it just as a thorn in the side of Francis and the Emperor it would be all right. You wouldn't be risking a domestic tragedy if she disappoints you. But already you're trying to turn it into a romance."

Henry laughed sheepishly and set down the exquisite little casket between them. "I suppose I am," he admitted, and sat there with his hands loosely clasped between his knees staring abstractedly at the square toes of his great slashed shoes. Sunshine and stained glass conspired to bring out the warm lights in his thinning reddish hair. When he looked up there was something at once gallant and pathetic about his forced smile. "I do so want it that way, Charles," he confessed. "Just once before the fires of my manhood go out."—It was the best part of Henry speaking. All that was left of the adventurous knight, the ardent lover. "You've been married three times, Charles—and always happily. There's peace and homeliness in your house. Something I envy every time I come. How do you manage it?"

Suffolk might have said that he didn't create dreams of ephemeral perfection and then expect his wives to live up to them. But he didn't answer immediately. It was his turn to sit and stare abstractedly. "Two marriages," he corrected softly. "And a brief taste of Heaven—with your sister."

Henry sighed and the gay little ghost of the first Mary Tudor who had joyfully laid down the crown of France to become Mary Brandon——flitted through the quiet room which she used to fill with laughter, garnishing its present stillness with a dozen well-remembered gestures for these two middle-aged men who had loved her.

In order to break the spell Henry left the window-seat and went back to his work table. Slumping into his wide chair, he pushed aside the score of a madrigal he had been composing and, with an air of conscious virtue, pulled towards him the inevitable pile of state papers Cromwell had left to be signed. "If only Katherine's sons had lived——," he muttered irrelevantly, taking up his quill. It was the weak man's typical kind of excuse for his own muddles. But he always felt things might have been so different. She wouldn't have grown ill and priest-ridden and old—so much older than the inextinguishable youth in him. And he might have been too occupied with the unbringing of his sons to get caught in the toils of that witch woman who had broken up his home. . . . He liked to picture himself the bluff, adored centre of family life, as Charles now was. After all, he was essentially a family man. Above everything, he

61

wanted legitimate sons. He hadn't wanted passionate inter-
ludes and all that underhand scheming—nor had he meant
to be a brute to poor dead Katherine and their only
daughter. He couldn't really afford to quarrel with Wolsey
either. . . . It was Anne—Nan Bullen of Hever—who had
involved him in cuckold ridicule and crazy defiance of the
Pope. And all for a few moons' madness—with nothing to
show for it but another daughter! Though Nan's sleek
head had rolled in the straw, he would never forgive her
for having fooled him.

And here he was deciding to take another Anne! The one
thing he had sworn never to do. And she not much more
than half his own age. He let the heavy parchments roll
back on themselves and beckoned Charles from the other
side of the room. "Tell me," he beseeched in panic. "*This*
Anne is no harlot? *She* wouldn't make a cuckold of me? I
couldn't go through all that again!"

Suffolk threw an affectionate arm about his shoulders.
"Of course not, Harry! Holbein's painted both of them,
hasn't he, and never were two women's faces more different.
All I'm worrying about is whether you'll be able to live
with her placid goodness?"

"I'm older now."

"But you know so little about her," reiterated Suffolk,
afraid for his friend's fastidiousness about physical details.
"Why, she might have flat feet or bad breath or something."

But Henry had already recovered from his hysterical
lapse. "I know more than you think, my friend!" he said,
his small light eyes twinkling with cunning. His podgy
hands fumbled at a silk neckcord and from somewhere between doublet and shirt he fished up a well-thumbed
document.

Suffolk took it with amused curiosity. All down one side
of the paper were questions, numbered and tabulated by
some clerk, presumably at the King's dictation. Opposite
each, in Wotton's scholarly hand, was the envoy's candid
answer. Its author had at least had the grace to make it 'Con-

fidential'. "Sit down and read it?" he invited, vacating his own chair and pushing Charles into it.

Charles sat down and read, and all the time the King fidgeted round him, pleased as a child who has outwitted his tutors. "They wouldn't arrange for me to see any of 'em but I fancy I've covered everything," he smirked complacently.

"I should think you have!" agreed the Duke ironically. He picked out one or two items at random and read them aloud. ' 'Q. To note her height. A. Tall, but by reason of her wearing slippers and the roundness of her clothing looks less.' She doesn't sound exactly modish, Harry, does she? 'Skin—fair and clear.' That's better. 'Hair—seems to be of a brown colour.' That must have been a bit of a teaser for Wotton with that chastely fitting cap!"

"There's a bit showing in the miniature."

"Thoughtful fellow, Holbein!"

"It's brown all right. I like 'em brown."

"I should have thought that after Nan. . ."

"That was *raven*——"

Suffolk slid a finger down the page. The smug audacity of the thing had begun to intrigue him. "Um—let's see. 'Teeth—clean and well set. Breasts—trussed somewhat high.' What's this? 'To endeavour to speak with her fasting, so that they may see whether her breath be sweet——' *Really*, Harry. . . ."

"So you *see*," chuckled Henry, "I *do* know a good deal about her!"

"Yes. But I shouldn't let the lady concerned see—ever. Nor any of Norfolk's crowd either." There were little commonesses about this flamboyant Tudor which, through long usage, Charles Brandon could stomach and even find amusing. But he hated the blue-blooded Howards to catch his friend doing things which not even the worst of the Plantagenets would have thought of. "Sounds like the catalogue of a horse fair!" he commented.

"Well, anyhow, all the answers seem satisfactory," said Henry, thrusting the inventory of Anne's points back in his bosom.

"Yes, quite satisfactory," agreed Suffolk, wondering how a man of such real culture could, at times, treat his women like cattle.

Henry consulted the dial of a great astronomical clock which had just arrived from France and was to be erected at Hampton Court. "If Cromwell doesn't bungle things she ought to be here by Christmas," he calculated. "We'll give her a real English Twelfth Night, like we used to have when Katherine and Mary were alive. I believe I'll write a masque for it myself."

"Well, by all accounts the poor girl should appreciate a bit of gaiety after Cleves! And if she's too straight-laced to enjoy it at least it'll do *you* good. You're looking years younger already, Harry."

"Wish I'd kept my figure!" grunted Henry, watching him enviously as he rose lithely from the royal chair.

Suffolk laughed good-naturedly and suggested a gentle game of tennis, but Henry's reddening neck warned him that he had said the wrong thing. "There usen't to be anything gentle about it, used there?" he hastened to add. "Remember when you made poor old Wolsey wager Hampton Court against a cardinal's hat on your winning, and how we were so evenly matched that we had to go on playing by torchlight?"

With a deep rumble of laughter Henry took up the tale. "And he felt it would be lése majestè to get up and go and the poor devil couldn't kneel at Mass next morning for rheumatics?" Henry loved to hark back to those far-off, colourful days. "You know, Charles, I miss Wolsey. Compared with this bull-necked Chancellor we've got now——"

"Still, you must admit he knows his job. Look how he's managed to—to straighten things out on the Continent——" Even Suffolk dared not say 'after you had made a mess of them.' Being a comparatively self-made man himself, he could sympathize with the blacksmith's ambitious son. And as a mere on-looker at the game of politics, he could see how disastrously Henry fancied himself as the arbiter of Europe and how both his Chancellors had played on that vanity to further their own reasonable policies. Why, even in this matter of Cleves the King was really Cromwell's pawn.

"Well, I've repaid him, haven't I?" snapped Henry. "From being Wolsey's secretary to a chancellorship, and now an earldom if he pulls off my marriage!" A week ago, yesterday even—he would have spoken of it impersonally as 'this cursed Lutheran alliance.' But now he was under the spell of Holbein's genius—obsessed with the idea of rejuvenating himself for a foreign bride. Already, pulling and puffing, he was half out of his doublet and shouting for Tom Culpepper to bring his tennis shoes.

"It's months since you played," warned Suffolk, with an anxious eye on the thickening veins at his brother-in-law's temples. But Henry laughed gallantly, drawing in his stomach and squaring powerful shoulders. "A few years ago you were the only man in the country who could give me a decent game," he boasted. "We must begin playing before breakfast again."

"I was going down to Westthorpe," Suffolk reminded him. "I promised Catalina. She's pregnant again, you know."

"Bring her up to Suffolk House then," said Henry. "It'll be far better for her than being buried in the country. She'll have all the best attention. My own doctors. And my daughters for company. She shan't want for anything, bless her!"

Suffolk knew that he meant it—that he would be generosity itself to this sweet, half-Spanish child-wife of his. But it wasn't the same thing. He wanted to get away from Court for a while. Back to that atmosphere of homeliness of which Henry had spoken so enviously. Somehow he didn't want to meet the new queen. To listen to all the pother and gossip of Henry trying out a new wife. To have to watch all over again the waxing and waning of a tempestuous royal love affair. He could hear Henry telling young Culpepper, in a voice charged with emotion, to have this elder Cleves woman's miniature placed on the tallboy beside his bed. But Henry had said, "I can't possibly spare you now, Charles"; so there was nothing for it but to stay.

They went out onto the terrace together, followed by a brace of pages with their gear. There was a pleasant nip of autumn in the air. An invigorating little breeze ruffled the grey surface of the Thames and rustled the great beech trees which were already laying russet carpets here and there on the sloping lawns. Henry linked an arm in Suffolk's as they turned briskly in the direction of the tennis court. He was effervescing with plans. "We'll have my new queen brought here, Charles."

"Not Hampton Court? You always say it's your favourite palace."

"For the honeymoon, yes. It's more intimate and rural. But consider the possibilities of Blackheath for a state entry!" Henry stopped to wave an histrionic arm towards the park gates. "The bride's procession arriving over there —heralds and City guilds and so forth forming an avenue all down Shooter's Hill—and me here in scarlet—no, gold damasked purple, I think . . ."

Suffolk considered it and allowed his friend the palm for showmanship. "I suppose you'll send Cranmer to meet her at the coast?"

"And some of the women, of course," agreed Henry, passing into the tennis court. "A pity Catalina won't be able to go. Her beautiful grave manners would give old Olsiliger such a good impression of England."

"Except that they're half-Spanish manners," laughed Charles, well pleased with the compliment.

"Are they? Very probably you're right because my daughter Mary has them too. As it is, I shall have to send Norfolk's old termagant of a second wife, and Heaven knows, the way she hates Lutherans, she's sure to make everything as difficult as possible for—for her." Suffolk could not help noticing that for all his exuberance Henry still jibbed at the use of Anne's too familiar name. "And listen, Charles," he was burbling on all the time Culpepper was scattering the eager pages as ball-boys, "When they've got as far as, say, Rochester, we'll get into some sober worsted clothes and ride down there looking like a party of merchants and take a look at her."

Suffolk glanced up across the bent head of the page who was fastening his shoe. "What on earth for—when you'll be receiving her here? In scarlet—or purple, was it?"

But Henry was terribly in earnest. "To foster love," he said. "Women love that sort of romantic gesture."

"You love dressing up, you mean!" thought Suffolk. Aloud he said, "My dear Harry, won't you ever grow up?"

Henry was too elated to take offence. "Delicious to hold a racquet again!" he murmured, selecting one from an armful Culpepper offered and swinging it to feel the balance. He limbered himself lightly on the balls of his toes and when Suffolk served a 'knock-up' ball he drove it well and truly back to the base line. "You don't seem to have lost your eye, Sir!" exclaimed one of the courtiers who had gathered to watch; and they all joined in the adulation although they must have known it wouldn't be long before he lost his breath. Henry loved a gallery and always played up to it. Soon he and Suffolk had settled to their game. It was like old times. The thud of hard, accurate hitting was a recaptured joy. The swift padding of their feet an echo of their splendid youth. Henry forgot that he was forty-eight and fat. Through a pleasant haze of applause and exhilaration he saw himself in a few weeks' time—fit and rejuvenated—riding down through the crisp Kentish lanes to meet his bride. He would get his tailor to devise some new clothes —becoming and slenderising—in which to play the gallant in a new drama of sex. He would enjoy strutting before another Anne. After all, he was rather glad she was unsophisticated. How much more fun it would be planning lavish entertainments to take her breath away than giving them for some bored French or Milanese beauty who had been everywhere and seen everything! He would take her about and show her how lovely and prosperous was his kingdom. She would think him the devil of a fine fellow and he would teach her—everything. It pleased him to picture her as a timid little woman. At any rate, she would be a foreigner —dependent upon him for everything. She would be like a frightened bird in his hand, and he would be very kind.

CHAPTER VI

Down through Antwerp and Bruges came Anne and, as Henry had predicted, she was on English soil before Christmas. But the sea still ran between them. She and her retinue had reached Calais. As she rode through the city gates she saw for the first time the proud lions and presumptuous lilies on his standard. "So like the English," she thought, "losing nearly all their French possessions and behaving as if they hadn't even noticed it!"

But in this important one they *had* kept, English voices sounded all about her as Henry's subjects thronged the streets, wanting to see what their new queen looked like, and liking what they saw. And Anne, on her side, gazed at their prosperous half-timbered houses and thought how squat and comfortable they looked after tall, angular Flemish gables. She loved the red and blue uniforms of the Governor's guard and the deafening salvoes of the harbour guns. There was a cosmopolitan flavour about the place—an 'aliveness'—something she couldn't put a name to. "This is quite different from the other towns we came through," she remarked to Olsiliger, who was riding at her elbow.

"It is a port, Madam," he explained briefly. He had no wish to admit that these self-satisfied English had the knack of infusing all their possessions with their own virility. And as Anne had never before visited a port, the explanation sufficed.

She was quick to appreciate the more personal quality of Calais' welcome. In the other towns there had been polite speeches and flower throwing and women watching from -their windows. But here Henry's sailors came pouring up from the quay to cheer her, making her arrival both a public holiday and a home-coming. And Henry's men-at-arms came out to meet her, dislodging her own astonished gentlemen with good-natured roughness, and riding side by side with them through the narrow streets to bring her to her lodging. Obviously, she was *their* responsibility now. It made her feel precious—and somehow very safe. She adored all this new experience of travelling and marvelled that her women could grumble at the cold, the strange food or the jolting of the cumbersome coaches. Like a child going to a fair, Anne would willingly have put up with any inconvenience for the sake of seeing a fresh town every day. Perhaps her enjoyment was enhanced because Holbein, who had proved himself invaluable as both friend and interpreter, had been invited to ride in her train.

Sitting straight and unflagging on a tallish horse, she looked about her with a friendly smile as her augmented party clattered across the cobbled market place. There was nothing but the sweating flanks of her mount to suggest that she had ridden from Gravelines since breakfast. Sharp frost and plenty of outdoor exercise had brought becoming colour to her cheeks and, like most large-boned women, she looked her best on a horse. She was interested in all she saw and not ashamed of it. And the crowd, accustomed to the comings and goings of bored, irritable or pre-occupied royal personages, appreciated her interest in themselves. A mutual satisfaction, which could be felt, pervaded the cheerful streets.

The Governor of Calais had ridden out to meet her. The gallant Captain of the Guard placed his garrison at her disposal and the King's Constable knelt before her with the castle keys. And at the entrance to the harbour she met the pompous old admiral who was to take her across the Channel.

They all began making speeches which Anne tried conscientiously to follow. When the townspeople had been speaking quickly to each other it had seemed to her only a disconcerting jumble of sounds in which she caught a familiar word here and there; but she was gratified to find that when more cultured men addressed her directly she understood well enough.

And above the confusing strangeness of their words, Anne was aware of a booming sound which no one else seemed to notice. At first she thought it must be more salvoes in her honour, but decided that it couldn't be because the smoke that had completely obscured the view was beginning to drift away. But it almost drowned the Admiral's bellowed apologies about some delay caused by currents, so that Anne, having a vague idea that they were some kind of fruit, supposed him to be talking about dinner and remarked, quite pleasantly, that it was a pity because she had got up early and was very hungry—a remark which sent his second-in-command into ill-concealed gusts of laughter.

"Milord of Southampton would have your Grace understand that it is very *rough*," explained the gallant Captain of the Guard and the kindly Constable in unison.

"Ruff?" repeated Anne uncertainly, fingering the new-fashioned frilling at the wrists of her gown. Lieb Gott, what a language!

Her eyes sought helplessly for Holbein. But he was separated from her by a surge of Calais dignitaries and the handsome second-in-command came to her rescue. "It's the *sea* which is rough, Madam," he said, pointing through the harbour gateway. "Listen."

Anne listened. The great, regular booming came from the direction of the cliffs; and now that everyone was silent she could discern, after each crescendo, a sibilant swish like the dragging of tons of stones. Her puzzled face lit up with eager interest. "The sea!" she exclaimed, and pricked her horse forward alone.

The screen of smoke had been torn by a freshening breeze and the sun had come out. Holbein, trying to escape from the fat Mayor's fulsome compliments, saw her recoil and set her horse motionless, framed in the rough stone archway with her back to them all.

She had always pictured the sea as something blue and placid—an unrevised concept of childhood compounded of the palace lake at Düren and the untroubled waters on which the Noah family cruised with their amazing cargo in her father's illuminated missals. Ridiculous, of course, because one knew that there were storms and wrecks . . . yet it came as a shock to her to look out at that expanse of angry, leaden water fringed with white breakers that lashed at harbour masonry and chalky cliffs, fell back in spouts of slopping spume, only to lash and lash again. The tearing wind took away her breath and the unaccustomed tang of salt was like a buffet on her cheeks. Overpowered by such majestic elements of nature, it was some time before she remembered her own importance or the waiting company. "Milords, it is ze first time I behol' ze sea," she told them simply.

Their faces expressed amazement and deep commiseration. With her uncanny insight into other people's minds, she understood how they must feel about it. As islanders, they regarded it as their own blessed and particular element —and pitied her accordingly. Proudly, they begged her to look again and observe the splendid ships their king had sent for her. This was Southampton's great moment. "The 'Lyon' and the 'Sweepstakes'—dressed with a hundred silk pennants apiece!" he shouted in her ear against the rage of the nor'-west gale, and with a sweep of the silver whistle which Henry had given him as insignia of his high calling, he indicated the harbour basin round which the whole of Calais huddled.

Anne looked and her stomach turned over beneath the smoke smutted purple velvet of her travelling gown. The masts of the two ships lurched drunkenly together, making the bare thought of dinner suddenly abhorrent. To her inexperienced gaze they looked like a bundle of sticks bobbing against the far end of a toy jetty, and the thought of trusting herself to such cockle-shells in so murderous an element, rendered her speechless. Lord Lisle, the consequential Governor, believed her to be overwhelmed by the honour paid to Cleves. And Southampton told her what hours of hunting his King had sacrificed in order to build up an efficient navy. And after that he really *did* say something about dinner.

But even Anne's hunger and healthy zest for sight-seeing were rather daunted by the grim Norman castle in which custom decreed that she must lodge. It sprawled, lion-like, along the cliffs, as if keeping a last aggressive foothold on the conquered shores of France. There was an ugly efficiency about the battlements and the still smoking cannon that made Henry's quartered fleurs-de-lis look less like a boastful jest. Passing under the iron teeth of the portcullis, Anne shivered involuntarily. She hated the hollow echoes struck by her horse's shoes from the flagstones in the chill shadow of the gatehouse arch. If this was the first taste of the queenly grandeur to which her journey must ultimately lead, then how much pleasanter, she thought, to sleep in one of those comfortable houses out there in the square in close contact with the friendly people! Already their voices were growing fainter as the thick, grey walls closed about her. Just for a moment she felt that she would give anything—even the hope of furthering her brother's interests—to turn back. But the press of men-at-arms behind her and her own strict training bore her forward into the palely comforting sunshine of the inner bailey. Irrevocably now she was in her future husband's stronghold. And, forebodingly, she had sensed his power.

She turned in her saddle and Holbein managed to press his horse through the throng. "That last gate seemed to shut out the fields," she complained, as if discussing the view.

It was the first time he had heard her speak carefully in metaphors. He didn't know that Olsiliger, her brother's Chancellor, had been grumbling at her for undoing his diplomatic work with her outspokenness; but he hoped this new subtlety she was learning would serve as armour in the arena of the sophisticated court towards which she was riding so defencelessly. "There are other fields in England," he reminded her gently.

Anne was beginning to feel overwhelmed by her reception. There was so much ceremony and every man presented to her seemed to have some strange title. It was beginning to be born in upon her that perhaps, over there, she wouldn't be allowed to see much of a mere court painter. Lowering her voice, she asked, "Does one walk in them with freedom —and friendship?"

"Not if one is wise," he warned her, with his usual uncompromising honesty. "But why not think of the gateway as the opening into a fine new city?"

She knew that he was right and rode resolutely forward.

At the foot of the castle steps people were waiting to help her dismount. They fussed kindly about her being cold and seemed anxious to hustle her upstairs to a fire. But she made a little deprecating gesture beseeching them to wait. She couldn't find the right words to explain to them how much she wanted a few farewell moments with her own people. Standing half-way up the short flight of steps, with her shivering women huddled about her, she watched her retinue come crowding into the bailey; and, seeing her there, they shuffled their horses into some sort of formation. Three hundred Flemish gentlemen who had ridden with her from Cleves. The cost of their upkeep and grants towards their new clothes had appalled her. "We *must* send you well turned-out," William had insisted, when she had suggested half the number to save him the expense. But, in spite of Francis's promise of safe conduct across the northern corner of his kingdom, she knew that her brother had feared treachery. "Union between us and England is the last thing the French want," he had kept saying anxiously the night before she left. So Anne smiled on her escort affectionately, suspecting that although many of them were past middle-age they had not come with her merely for show. Now that she had seen more of the world and could compare their comfortable, befurred figures with the lean and hardy English they didn't look quite so martial a body as she had supposed when they first set out. There was a suggestion of play-acting about their antique culverins which made her wonder whether, after all, they would have been of much use in a scrap. But they were dears to have come. Many of them she had known all her life—some of them had taught her to ride when she was a child, and told her the fairy legend of the Swan Knight who had come long ago to woo a princess of Cleves, and some of them she had cured of various ailmets with her famous herbal remedies. And as if to keep them with her a little longer she beckoned to the white-haired count who led them. "Will you thank them for me all over again, Waldeck Harderwijk?" she said. "And give my tender love to my brother and assure him how kind everybody has been." And because she had caught some of the well-equipped English men-at-arms looking superciliously at the culverins, she leaned down and kissed the old man on both cheeks; whereat the three hundred gentlemen from Cleves raised feathered velvet caps which Anne reckoned must have cost enough to keep the Düren servants in liveries for a year. To-morrow, as soon as they were rested, they would be going back. Back through the gay, evil-smelling French towns; through Antwerp, where the English wool merchants had made her a lovely torch-light procession; and through Guelderland, where a regiment of little whirring windmills manned the frozen dykes and grey wild geese flew into the wintry sunset. Back up the Rhine valley, where fields grew flatter and peaked gables higher, until the unpretentious palace of Düren and the famous Swan Tower of Cleves became dear realities. . . . The tiled stoves would be lit there and the embroidery frames brought out—her mother and Amelia would be talking about her, perhaps, as they stitched at their Christmas gifts or the new spring bed-hangings—and William, pacing back and forth along the snow-covered City walls, would be worrying about how the English were treating her and how he would manage without her when the trouble in his head next took him. . . . Poor, nerve-racked William. . . . Anne shut her eyes hard and quickly until the hot, home-sick tears were pressed back into her heart and she could turn and face these foreigners without shame. Up till then it had all been a holiday, a splendid adventure—and she was such an unimaginative fool that only when it came to saying 'Good-bye' had she begun to realise that this was the end of her familiar world. She clutched the decent defences of courage about her, grasping desperately at the things which were left. At least there would be her women. Even if they went on grumbling and snivelling, they would still be part of home. Particularly Dorothea, whose baby had died after all, and who had begged to come with her— poor, sad, shamed Dorothea who *never* grumbled but tried to show her gratitude in a comforting gift of unobtrusive service. And stiff, grumpy old Olsiliger—until he went back after the wedding.

After the wedding. Her wedding—to a complete stranger. Now that it had come so close, Ann wondered how she could have gone on placidly from day to day, concerned with the small things of life, not bothering to find out what this bridegroom of hers was like. Everyone knew that Henry Tudor was massive and ruddy. But what was he like to *live* with? Suddenly, as she stood there on the threshold of this castle which was the southern bulwark of his kingdom, it mattered tremendously. Why hadn't she been more curious, like Amelia? After dinner she must get away from all these people. Somehow she must get Hans Holbein alone. . . .

Anxious to get the ceremonials over, she motioned to her party to follow the Constable inside. Two high-born matrons—friends of the dowager Duchess—supported her with their stolid propriety. But in the darkness of the winding staircase she managed to hang back a pace or two until her searching fingers caught at Dorothea's. Regardless of the fact that she was only the least of the waiting women, Dorothea squeezed them hard. And Holbein, who had never before touched Anne deliberately, bungled one of the steps so that she might feel the warm strength of his shoulder against hers. It is in one's worst moments, Anne decided, that one knows one's best friends.

And just as she reached the royal apartments on the first floor a door opened near the serving screens of the hall, emitting a delicious smell of roasting meat which brought things into good, everyday prospective again and cheered her considerably. It reminded her of warm kitchens and the pleasant bustle that always, in any country, precedes royal arrivals; so that she sniffed knowledgeably, trying to decide whether they were to have boar or venison. Then she hurried on, with an amused smile, remembering that she would no longer have to concern herself about culinary preparations. From now onwards she would be the royalty.

The Constable's wife carried her off to wash and to take

off her heavy riding cloak. She told her that the rooms had belonged to the English royal family for nearly two hundred years; adding impressively that the bedroom in which they stood had not been used since Henry himself came across the Channel for the Field of the Cloth of Gold. Anne glanced apprehensively at the resplendent four-poster on which those savage, snarling leopards were blazoned instead of the gentle swan to which she was accustomed. "I 'ope you have air ze bed," she said prosaically.

In the hall they had placed a chair of state for her in front of a huge central fire which roasted her wind-nipped face until it reflected the blaze. Anne bore it as best she could. She had yet to learn that the crazy English either freeze or fug. And anyhow she was ravenous and bed and board and fire were as nothing compared with the fact that all those people seemed prepared to like her. But while they all talked and ate she did some hard thinking about those lurching ships and before the company retired she caught at the finely-slashed sleeve of the handsome, swaggering second-in-command. He had kept the table lively with laughter and seemed to her more easy and human than the rest. "Tell me," she whispered urgently, "do your ships always—gambol—like that?"

He looked like a swash-buckling pirate with his trim beard and fine golden chain, and he smiled down at her kindly from his great height. "Don't worry, Madam, we shan't put to sea until the wind changes," he assured her.

"Then I hope it won't change for a very long time!" she said involuntarily; and so great was her earnestness that only Olsiliger's dry cough and her ladies' shocked faces made her realise that she had made another unfortunate remark. But the tall, blond Englishman only laughed. He had done full justice to the French wines and liked a woman without affectation who didn't finick with her food. "I, too, Madam, begin to feel less eager to weigh anchor," he confided, scanning her with bold blue eyes.

Anne withdrew her urgent fingers from his sleeve but pursued the matter with true Teuton persistence. "Haf you no flat bots?" she asked.

The poor man looked mystified.

"Like I saw on the canals as we came through Bruges."

"Oh, *barges——*"

"Yaa! They would be more safe."

He threw back his head and laughed, showing enviable white teeth. "But they wouldn't carry your Grace to England!" Impulsively, he lifted her hand to his lips. Anne had very lovely hands and he felt that they were beginning to get on well together. Evidently he stood in no particular awe of potential queens. Yet there was something about this one that made people want to serve her. "We've had the best cabin on the flagship prepared for you, and we shall do everything for your comfort," he promised more gravely.

"And you will persuade the Admiral to wait until it is quite calm?"

He looked quite surprised. "Dear lady, it doesn't rest with him—or with any of us. The king's orders are that we sail as soon as we can make it."

But the idea of a King who presumed to rule even the sea was new to Anne. "With or without safety?" she demanded, with a little spurt of anger.

He shrugged tolerant shoulders. "What man among us, Madam, can condemn his impatience?" he asked, with his most engaging smile.

Anne herself couldn't help smiling at his roistering impudence. "Then I shall be sick. In the best cabin of your flagship," she prophesied. "And, God in Heaven, when I am sick I look horrible!" she added in her own tongue as soon as he was out of earshot.

When he had bowed himself out with the other Englishmen she drew Holbein aside and sat down in a window recess. "Who was that man I was talking to?" she asked.

"Sir Thomas Seymour."

"Seymour. I seem to remember the name. But they introduced so many——"

"He's Queen Jane's brother. Didn't you know? I thought perhaps that was why you favoured him."

Anne leaned forward eagerly, interested in anything to do

with her predecessor. "Then it was generous of him to be so nice to me. Is he like her?"

"About as boisterous as she was gentle."

"All the same, he is very attractive."

"Most of the women in London seem to think so."

"Oh, so that's why he preened himself so when I asked him to sup with us! And why Olsiliger disapproved. 'Can you not hide your likes and dislikes, Madam? It will only land you in trouble over there,'" mimicked Anne. "Mercy me, I only wish I could! But if this Seymour is the King's brother-in-law he certainly must sup with us and tell me all about him."

Holbein thrust out his full lower lip like a lovable but disagreeable boy. "I can show you the King—in a few strokes," he declared, remembering the cartoon he had made of him on a book at Greenwich and rummaging through coat and doublet for the bit of paper and stump of charcoal without which he never seemed to move.

But Anne wanted more than that. "To live with—in his own home, I mean," she said.

Besides being altogether too good-looking, Seymour had the advantage of him there. Holbein slapped the paper onto the lid of an oak muniment chest and began scratching a few strong, square lines. "*Will* you speak English, Madam?" he growled.

Anne laughed affectionately. "Oh, Hans, you old bear, I've had such a morning of it!" she protested, deliciously conscious that he was jealous. "Tell me honestly—how did I get on?"

"You were a credit to my inspired tutoring," he allowed.

"Oh, I'm so thankful. They will hardly believe it at home."

He went on drawing in silence for a few minutes, then glanced cautiously down the length of the hall. Her stolid ladies-in-waiting were gathered round the fire, discussing the English food. The Flemish Chancellor had gone to talk business with the Governor and Mother Lowe had gone to bed. "Anne," he said, lowering his voice to a monotone unlikely to attract the attention of the passing servants, "why

78

do you always speak as if you were less clever than your sisters? You were so—capable—this morning. Managing them all, and yet not seeming to."

"Yes. Because you were there—encouraging me—thinking my English better than you had hoped. And because they all seemed to like me. That makes all the difference, doesn't it?"

"It wouldn't to everybody."

"Well, it does to me. But, of course, it works both ways. Directly I feel people dislike me or I think they're laughing at me—I'm hopeless. My mind just goes all dull and stupid and I do clumsy things—although I'm not really clumsy." She wandered to the window, fancied she could discern a faint smudge of land in the direction of Dover, shuddered and came back. She was wondering for the hundredth time if Henry himself would like her. "Hans," she asked suddenly, "would *you* put your impatience before your wife's comfort—and safety?"

He looked up sharply. "That's near treason," he warned with a non-committal smile. But Anne laid a hand on his shoulder. In the light of approaching separation he was very dear to her. "You know you wouldn't. You'd be kind. You'd put your wife first."

He appeared to have lost all interest in his sketch and sat with crayon poised staring at her—trying to decide . . . . For weeks past there had been something he felt impelled to tell her. Several times he had tried but the words had seemed to bear too much significance. They could only be said casually. And here was the perfect opening. "No. You're all wrong," he said. "I left my wife. She's still living in Basle."

The charcoal snapped between his tense fingers and—because she felt that he was watching for her reactions—Anne stopped to grope for it among the dried rushes which covered the floor. "I didn't know you were married," she said quietly, dropping the pieces into his open palm.

He crammed them somewhere in the swinging folds of his coat, not noticing that she waited on him—not even thanking her. "I gave her all the money I had and walked out," he reiterated.

79

After a moment's pause, Anne's voice floated down to him, cool and compassionate, against a background of guttural jabbering from the hearth. "My poor Hans! Were you —so unhappy?"

He pushed his tool aside and got up, moodily leaning a shoulder against the tapestried wall. "It wasn't her fault. She was what is called a virtuous woman. It was just that she nagged—and that as I learned to paint my world grew bigger," he tried to explain.

"Had you any children?" she asked presently.

"Yes."

"And you left them too?"

"That would have been unthinkable to you, wouldn't it? However wretched you were." Even then, in spite of her rigid upbringing, he could wring no word of condemnation from her. Unconsciously, during her quiet, useful life, she had acquired the supreme Christian charity of condoning in others' sins which she could not pardon in herself. She had seated herself on the muniment chest and Holbein came and rested a knee on the other end of it. It was as if they two, talking in low flat voices, were alone in the lofty hall. Yet the very fact that they were not alone made it possible for him to assume that she cared—to dare to assume it. "You see —and perhaps it is better that you should see—that I am just a swine like your . . . like the rest."

Anne didn't answer, but her dark lashes dropped beneath the searching intensity of his gaze. Absently, she ran a finger round the edge of an elaborate iron hinge. "How long ago was it?" she asked.

Common sense told him that it would be better that she shouldn't care, but hot joy leaped within him because she did. "Oh, years ago," he told her, as casually as possible. "I was barely nineteen when I married—and just physically in love."

For the first time in her life, Anne felt awareness of a man's demanding body near her own. Because she had grown to maturity devoid of sex experience her heart raced to the new delight. "And isn't it a good thing," she asked breathlessly, "to be physically in love?"

"A marvellous thing. But for perfection one must love the mind behind the flesh even more, and I knew nothing about that—until now." In his sincerity, Holbein found himself floundering for words like any callow youth.

"You mean that happier marriages can be made when one is older? That Henry and I, for instance——" He had not meant that at all, and she knew it. Blindly, she picked up the crumpled sketch that lay between them. It was, as he had promised, a picture of the Tudor—limned in a dozen or so clever lines. Or were they merely cruel? Anne stared down at the arched brows, the square face, the little pursed mouth. . . . What did it matter, after all, what he was like to live with? What was the good of willing herself to make a success of their married life? She was sure that she could never love him. All she would be able to do now would be to compare. She screwed the paper into a stiff little ball and stuffed it into her pocket. All the lovely, long-denied excitement of life beckoned and clamoured at the prohibitions of her soul. "Perhaps the wind won't change before Christmas," she suggested softly.

His hands closed over hers. There was an adorable directness about the woman, almost dispelling the last fragments of his caution. Yet he knew that they were both walking in a dangerous dream, and he meant to wake her in time. "I hope that too, Anna," he said. "It seems all that is left to us. A week—ten days perhaps——"

Darting a defiant glance at the women grouped round the fire, she leaned closer to him. The dimple he was always waiting for dented her cheek, hiding the pockmark he had forgotten to paint. "Hans, am I growing very wicked? I want to crowd all the enjoyment of a lifetime into these few days. And I don't even mind about your being married," she whispered.

He stood up abruptly, shielding her from the curious glances of two of her younger girls. No one must surprise that lovely awakened look on her face. "What does it matter, anyway," he laughed harshly, "when you've got to marry the King?"

CHAPTER VII

Anne stood in the middle of a room in the Bishop's Palace at Rochester, trying to be polite to Agnes Tilney, the Duke of Norfolk's second wife. She was still feeling the effects of a bad Channel crossing and it had rained ever since she landed. The journey from Deal had been a nightmare. Christmas frost had given place to an unseasonable January thaw so that the Kentish roads were just winding quagmires and the whole of the countryside was blotted out. Everything was so wet that she had been obliged to travel in a stuffy coach with the curtains drawn. Three times the cumbersome vehicle had stuck in the mud, and—when at last the imperturbable English peasants had dug it out—the jolting had been intolerable.

And now this gaunt Catholic duchess and a Lady Rochfort had been sent by the King to welcome and advise her. Or—it seemed to Anne—expressly to criticise her clothes. To her all her new possessions seemed like part of a fairy tale—fantastic as the good fortune of that ancestress of hers for love of whom a stately knight had come down the Rhine guided by two white swans. William had made considerable sacrifices to pay for them and poor, envious Amelia had been sullen over them for days. But according to English standards nothing apparently was right—not even the gorgeous purple velvet.

"So unbecoming, don't you think, with the short round-cut skirt?" sniffed Jane Rochfort, smoothing her own modisly cut yellow satin. "Particularly if one happens to be on the heavy side." Anne had offered the elderly duchess the best episcopal chair and she seemed to have taken root in it. Under the guise of 'being a mother to her' she was making Dorothea bring out all the bridal finery for their inspection and doing her best to destroy Anne's new self-confidence.

"Isn't it a matter of taste?" suggested Anne, scowling uncertainly at her reflection in the Bishop of Rochester's unflattering mirror yet loath to have her new dresses cut about. After all, the gentlemen at Calais hadn't seemed unfavourably impressed!

But the crabbed Duchess preferred to make it a matter of morals. "In this country no woman of breeding wears skirts that balloon out and show her ankles. I only mention it, Madam, because the King is so fastidious." She tapped the floor impatiently with her silver-headed stick to summon a young girl whom she had brought with her from court. "Come here, Katherine, and show her Grace of Cleves how modestly a gown in the Paris fashion should hang to the toes." And Katherine Howard, who had been standing behind the tall backed chair lost in admiration of Anne's open jewel box, came and pirouetted obediently before them. Anne thought her grey gown a poor affair, with its plain square-cut bodice and insignificant underskirt; and considered that only the girl's youthful grace saved it from a suggestion of genteel shabbiness—though not for worlds would she have hurt anyone's feelings by saying so. "But then your—your——" She hesitated, not sure—since the Duchess had not bothered to present her—whether this young woman were relative or maid.

"Granddaughter," supplied Katherine, with a shy smile.

"Your granddaughter is much younger than I—and not going to be a queen," protested Anne. "So naturally the same kind of clothes wouldn't be suitable."

But the Duchess's thin lips folded themselves into what Henry called her 'obstinate bitch' expression. "If that delicate boy of Jane Seymour's should die," she said, voicing a hope which even her husband would not have dared to utter, save behind the drawn curtains of their conjugal bed, "his half-sister, Mary Tudor, will be queen in her own right. And *she* wears the *plainest* of gowns."

Something in Anne could afford to leap and laugh with warm, secret joy. Had the old fool forgotten the fine sons she was going to rear? "I see. Thank you for telling me," she said, more meekly. "And you think the King won't like me in such bright colours? Though my mother chose them because we've always heard he dresses so sumptuously."

Cunning Jane Rochfort was ready with an answer. "It's not so much the colour of your dresses as the colour of your *hair*," she told Anne confidentially.

Anne swung round from the depressing mirror in surprise and as she did so her multitudinous petticoats displayed a pair of ankles far too well-turned to please either woman of the Norfolk faction. "My hair!" she echoed, well aware that it was long and dark and lustrous. "What on earth is the matter with it?"

"Nothing, Madam, as far as I know. But the late Queen was a *blonde*."

"But what about Anne Bullen—the one he was so crazy for?"

That was a subject Lady Rochfort preferred not to talk about. She had married a Bullen and only saved her own skin by denouncing him, and even the Duchess looked profoundly shocked at such forthright mention of her unfortunate niece's name. "Well," she drawled, putting a hand as if by accident to the pearls at her wizened throat, "I suppose they have told you what happened to *her*?"

Words and action were so sinister that Anne's eyes widened in terror, and young Katherine Howard made an impulsive movement as if to shield her from their cruel significance. But Anne could have sworn that her grandmother pinched her arm. "As that third marriage turned out so well, naturally the King has a penchant for blondes," the scheming old woman went on. "And it is so much *safer* to please him."

Poor Anne felt herself engulfed in waves of intrigue beyond her understanding. She felt that they were trying to frighten her. Her helpless glance passed beyond them to the comforting sight of Dorothea patiently putting back into the dower chests all the dresses this terrible old woman had made her take out. She watched her swoop with a pair of scissors to scrape at a mud-bespattered hem; but what she saw with her mind's eye was the shining axe falling inhumanly on that other Anne's slender neck. The disparagement of her own appearance at which she had been seething seemed negligible now. For the first time she was realising fully that in a few days' time she would be married to a murderer. Well, not quite a murderer perhaps .... If Anne had really committed adultery while she was queen, it was the law; and they held life cheaply over here. But to a man who could let such brutal violence happen to a woman he had slept with—to someone who was the mother of his child. . . . "I don't see that I can do anything about it. I can't change the colour of my hair," she said drearily.

The Duchess's desiccated chuckle showed her that she must have said something stupid again. "If your women haven't any more *nous* than that it's a good thing I *did* drag my rheumatic old bones half-way across Kent to help you!" she said. "But don't worry, Madam. We'll soon put a small thing like that right." She jabbed with her stick in the direction of a box her servants had left on the table. "Katherine, child, pass that to the Princess of Cleves. Its just a little wedding gift, Madam—from one woman to another."

Anne lifted the lid reluctantly. She had no wish to accept anything from her persistent mentor. And when she saw the flaxen wig it contained, all the tradition of her up-bringing was outraged. "It's very kind of you, Madam," she stammered. "But I couldn't—possibly——"

"No one need ever know and it may be the key to your husband's heart!" urged the Duchess.

Anne tried to push the box away but Agnes Tilney's bony fingers were already diving into it, drawing out a mane of curls, fair and flowing as the locks beloved of minstrels—and as utterly irrelevant to homely, practical Anne as a halo. Even in the midst of her annoyance she wanted to laugh, imagining the candid comments of her family at the bare idea of her wearing such a thing. It was absurd of Henry to expect her to be blonde. "But Master Holbein specially painted a piece of hair on my forehead," she pointed out.

"A pity he didn't paint a bit more then," sniggered Lady Rochfort. "Only a week ago I heard milord of Suffolk and the French Ambassador laying a wager about the colour of it."

Anne didn't know that Suffolk was the King's brother-in-law and Marillac the most kindly, incorrigible gossip in

Europe. Distastefully, she pictured even the pages and backstairs lackeys betting about her. "Well, at least my caps are modest if my skirts aren't. And if so little of my hair shows what does the colour matter?" she demanded with asperity.

"You forget, Madam, that it is customary for brides to wear their hair loose. If you don't, the people will think you are no maiden," the Duchess reminded her. "And the King will be riding close beside you in the procession."

"Besides, you'll have to sleep with him, won't you?" added the Rochfort woman, with vindictive relish.

That was one of the aspects of this marriage which Anne preferred not to picture at all. "I'm certainly not going to bed in a wig—like a prostitute!" she muttered obstinately.

"Surely you're not so unsophisticated as to suppose that most of us don't," soothed the Duchess. "My step grand-daughter here is lucky enough to have inherited a tinge of copper from her Plantagenet ancestors, but you'll find half the girls who come to take up posts in your household turn auburn out of compliment to the royal family. Here, let me put it on for you." In her eagerness, Agnes Tilney got up without the aid of her stick, removed Anne's elaborate cap and fitted the wig to her sleek, dark head. "There, it's beautifully made—by my husband's *coiffeur* at Framling-ham. No one would know it from natural, would they, Jane? You'll see—it'll make all the difference——"

It certainly did. Anne raised shamed eyes to the mirror. A stranger—hard, bright and fashionable—confronted her. The sort of woman she would instinctively have hated at sight. "Thank you," she murmured, her only immediate desire being to get rid of these two persistent Englishwomen and rest.

"Then you will wear it?" urged Lady Rochfort.

"I will try it for a little while, Madam—to get used to it," temporized Anne.

The Duchess drew a sigh of relief. She wasn't so young as she had been when baiting the last Protestant queen to her downfall. "And now if I can just advise your Grace about lengthening those skirts——"

But Anne had reached the end of her endurance. "I'm afraid my maid is much too tired," she said.

The première duchess of England turned and stared haughtily at Dorothea as if she had not previously been aware of such a person's presence in the room. How bourgeois of this Flemish woman to pamper her servants like that! Probably she sat and gossiped with them, and even poked about in the palace kitchen at Cleves like any hausfrau. But then, poor thing, she had no genteel accomplishments. "If that is all, my granddaughter will help. It will be good for her to have something to do," she suggested, remembering how susceptible the King was to a pretty pair of ankles.

But Anne, who had allowed herself to be browbeaten because she was sick and in a foreign land, was not quite as meek as all that. "Madam," she said quietly, "I regret that I too am tired." And—over-wrought as she was—her voice somehow managed to combine politeness with finality. She nodded to Dorothea who rose with alacrity from her labours to hold open the door. And the Duchess, who had supposed that she could intimidate this simple foreigner into the same state of submission as any of her husband's penniless relatives, took Jane Rochfort's arm and went out. For once she didn't even look back to call her granddaughter to heel. And halfway across the room Katherine Howard hesitated and turned back. There had not been too many likeable women in her short life. The tall, foreign princess was still standing in the middle of the disordered room with her hands folded before her. She looked terribly tired but—in spite of her inadequate English—she had routed Grandam Norfolk. Katherine's slippers slithered across the polished boards and slid into the familiar motions of a hurried curtsey. "It is true, Madam, that the King's daughters *do* wear plain dresses," she whispered breathlessly. "But Princess Mary is very religious. And if the lady Elizabeth doesn't wear trimmings and jewels it is because—like me—she hasn't any." Her voice sank to an awed whisper. "And since she was declared a bastard, Mrs. Ashley, her governess, can't even get enough *nightgowns* for her——"

The intimate disclosure came tumbling out impulsively and the girl was already poised for flight, when a cool, detaining hand was slipped under her chin. She dodged involuntarily, so that it was easy for Anne to guess that she was more accustomed to cuffs than to caresses. And when Katherine looked up, half-frightened at what she had said, most of the tired lines seemed to have been wiped from the Flemish woman's face. In spite of the unbecoming wig, she looked smiling and warm and beautiful. "You ought to have rubies, bless you, to vie with the warmth of your heart!" she was saying, in that deep, husky voice of hers. And Katherine wondered if she had noticed how greedily she had been looking at them.

With ears still strained for the Duchess's returning footsteps, she was confusedly aware of the wonderful jewel case being brought and two pairs of generous hands scuffling hurriedly through the contents. Of the Princess of Cleves saying —in a tone so different from any ever addressed to the Framlingham servants—"Let's find her the deep red ones the Duke of Saxony gave me, Dorothea!" And next minute the necklace was lying in her own outstretched, cherishing palm. The real ruby necklace she had always longed for even when young men had bought her gaudy imitations at the fairs—as payment for cheap love. "Oh, Madam! How lovely—and how kind!" she stammered.

Katherine's blue eyes were grateful as a recently beaten hound's. She threw a quick, apprehensive glance over her shoulder and with furtive stealth let the valuable jewels slide down inside the out-grown bodice already strained across the burgeoning roundness of her breasts.

"Are you so frightened of her?" Anne asked compassionately.

"So *dependent* on her," explained the girl, with a gamin pout which, in spite of her obvious breeding, savoured somehow of the backstairs. "My father was only a younger son and my mother died." Unimportant as she was, she knew quite well why her family wanted this new queen out of the way; but they were wrong about her being a boorish, strait-laced Lutheran. Katherine heard the Duchess's strident voice calling to her from the end of the gallery; but there was something she had to say. "Madam, don't let them make you any different. Please—stay just as you are!" The words were spoken with such intensity that she might have been pleading for something affecting her own life. And in saying them, she gave Anne back some of her lost assurance —just as her broken warnings gave her food for conjecture.

As soon as Anne was alone with Dorothea she told her to leave all the dresses. "Time enough to alter them when I get to Court and see what other women are wearing," she decided sensibly.

"And the wig, Madam?"

Anne had forgotten she was wearing it. It fitted so well that it was difficult to take off and a promise was a promise to her. Wasn't her family motto *"Candida nostra fides"*? "I said I would try to get used to it—and, after all, there may be something in what she said. . . ." She sank exhausted into the chair her disturbing visitor had vacated. "How I wish I had just one woman friend in England!" she sighed.

"Is your head very bad, Madam?" asked Dorothea, giving each of the Bishop's austere, leather-covered cushions an experimental punch, and slipping the softest of them beneath the throbbing nerve centre at the back of her mistress's head.

"Terrible," admitted Anne, wondering how delicate people like William could bear such pain frequently. It was all so different from the peaceful days at Cleves and Düren where one could be alone sometimes instead of being part of a page of history.

"You weren't fit to travel when you came ashore but they must needs hustle you on from place to place," complained Dorothea indignantly.

"And I did so want to stay and enjoy Canterbury!"

"And to-morrow, I suppose, all these important people who have come to meet us will insist on our rising at the crack of dawn again to push on to Greenwich." A grey vista of wet roofs and dripping trees didn't make the prospect any the more alluring. Dorothea's devoted fingers itched to take off the unbecoming wig; but all she could do was to unfasten Anne's stiffly-trussed dress and iron-busked stays and put her, unresisting, into a favourite old wrapper that reminded them both of home. "Couldn't you ask this Archbishop Cranmer to let you rest here another day?" she ventured.

"And disappoint all those poor people waiting so patiently along the route? Why, Dorothea, you know we were never allowed to do that sort of thing!" Anne scolded gently. "Besides, it doesn't rest with milord of Canterbury any more than it did with the Admiral. It's always the King who's so——" She stopped short and bit her lip. 'Impatient' was scarcely the word Olsiliger would approve of her using of her future husband.

Dorothea covered the lapse with cheerful tact. "Well, at least it looks like clearing," she said, declaring that she could see a break in the clouds across the shipping in the Medway. She pushed a stool beneath her mistress's feet and begged her to try to get an hour's sleep before dinner.

Anne smiled her gratitude. "That sounds heavenly! But are you sure there is nothing we ought to be doing?"

"Master Holbein dared the other woman to disturb you," smiled Dorothea, pulling a curtain across the window. "And even that dreadful lady in the yellow gown said, as I held the door for them, that it would be a good thing if you took your stays off and relaxed!"

"Perhaps she isn't really as bad as she seems," smiled Anne, with her usual readiness to believe the best of people. Thankfully she closed her eyes and drifted off into a somnolent reverie. Even after two days on dry land she could still feel the roll of the ship and see in imagination the dreadful swaying of the masts. The bluff old Admiral had said she was very brave but it was only that she hated making fusses and was determined not to let her country down. During the worst moments in mid-Channel when he and Sir Thomas Seymour had merely joked more casually and behaved more kindly, she had tried to play up to them. Ghastly as she had felt, she had managed to allay her women's tendency to hysteria by acting normally. She had even persuaded Seymour to teach her some of the King's favourite card games; and afterwards he had confided to her that the crew who hadn't relished taking 'a hold full of squeamish women' aboard in such foul weather, had appreciated her good spirits.

Mercifully, the weather had improved so that they had been able to make the little port of Deal. The King had sent his brother-in-law, Charles Brandon, and the Archbishop of Canterbury to meet her at Dover; and when they congratulated the Admiral on bringing her safely to *any* port in England he had told them bluntly that in his opinion it was the people of England who were to be congratulated. And Anne, longing only for a bed that didn't rock, had liked that better than either Suffolk's courtly manners or Cranmer's long Latin speech. Such appreciation did something to one's personality. It was like sunshine, making the seeds of all sorts of unexpected talents grow.

Sleepily, Anne reviewed her life. For years everything had gone one just the same until that drowsy summer afternoon in Düren when she had held Holbein's miniature in her hand and realized quite suddenly that she might become Queen of England. Since then every day had brought some fresh experience, some widening influence—changing her, making her dormant emotions thrive and glow. Then had come her momentous journey, bringing her first sense of importance. At first, out of her long habit of self-effacement, she had involuntarily looked round for her brother or Sybilla or some other important member of her family, incredulous that the flags and the cheering were for her alone. There had been processions and pageantry, partly spoiled at first by early inhibitions. Movement, colour, excitement—all the forbidden things she had felt the capacity for enjoying—were pressed into her inexperienced hands. She had tried to take these things soberly, as they were taken in her own land. But the torchlight procession at Antwerp, where a handful of East Anglian wool staplers and their apprentices and made the frosty night a thing of warm beauty for her, had broken down her reserve. In the flame-starred darkness she had found herself stretching our eager hands for these new subjects of hers to kiss—felt the tears of mass-emotion on her cheeks. Anne's wide mouth curved into a satisfied smile, remembering how easily she had made contact with these people. This liking of the English had given her confidence. She could almost feel herself changing from a gauche personality into a gracious one. "I *will* make a success of my marriage—like Sybilla," she determined. "Hans was right. I must make it the main thing in my life—put all my endeavour into my high destiny—and not let even let my love for him mar it."

How near she had come to this at Calais was at once her glory and her shame. It was the only love episode in her life. It had unfurled all the warm petals of her womanhood. Yet she thanked God now that Holbein, for her sake, had kept his head. Apart from prodigious danger, she was no more the sort of woman for illicit love than for a golden wig.

Thinking of him, she fell asleep. She had drifted into a jumbled and improbable dream in which she found herself addressing the Parliament at Westminster in perfect English. The subject of her discourse was flat-bottomed boats for their Navy; and when she had finished Henry Tudor, sombrely clad in the Archbishop's black gown, laid aside a hunting horn he was carrying and declared that he would do anything to oblige a blonde.

CHAPTER VIII

Anne's slumbers were rudely disturbed by shouting and laughter and the barking of dogs. She awakened with a start, the Bishop's cushion slipping to the floor as she sprang to her feet. The baying hounds that had surrounded Henry in her dream had turned into real dogs in Rochester. Pandemonium seemed to have broken out beneath her window and a justly incensed Dorothea was tugging back the heavy curtain. "It's just *too* bad—when you were in such a lovely sleep!" she cried. But the crowd only cheered expectantly when she pushed open a casement. The rain appeared to have stopped and a gleam of watery sunshine filled the sombre room.

"What is it now?" asked Anne wearily.

"They're calling for you to come to the window, Madam. Half the people in the town seem to be down there between the palace and the river. They've brought a bull—and dogs leashed two or three together."

"It must be one of the English sports Sir Thomas Seymour told me about—baiting I think he called it."

Gazing down at the shifting crowd, Dorothea could judge of its popularity by the eagerness with which men and women alike placed bets on the dogs. Some rough Kentish farmers had roped off a ring into which the poor, terrified bull was being driven. "How horrible!" she exclaimed as half a dozen large terriers were unleashed to the attack. One was gored instantly, another tossed like a ball above the men's heads, while a third succeeded in hanging by the jaws from the beast's bleeding throat.

"I don't enjoy seeing animals suffer. But if English ladies can stomach it, I must," said Anne, rising reluctantly.

Dorothea would have brought one of her grand new dresses but—as Anne pointed out—only part of her would be visible through the casement and the sooner she showed herself the sooner the good townsfolk would be finished with their crude entertainment and go away. "And I needn't really look," she added, as a vociferous cheer greeted her appearance.

"I can just stand here and watch the crowd."

Anne loved watching crowds. There was a jolly little puppet show down on the strand and most of the river craft had dusky red-brown sails. Rochester really wasn't so bad now the sun was shining and one could see some colour.

"I should think it must be market day by all the people streaming in over the bridge," said Dorothea, looking over her mistress's shoulder.

"And look at those children climbing on the coping to get a better view of the puppet show! I'm sure they're not safe. And of course they must do it just as a bunch of horsemen are coming along, crowding everybody to either side."

"What lovely mounts they have!" murmured the daughter of the Cleves head falconer, who knew a good horse when she saw one. "They're smaller, but much finer bred than ours."

"Much too fine for a pack of merchants or whatever they are!" snapped Anne, still concerned for the safety of the children. "See how that jolly, fat man in front swaggers along as if he owned the place. He must be pretty confident of picking up a good bargain in Rochester to-day." But he was too good a horseman to jeopardize the youngsters and his good humour was so infectious that she couldn't help wishing him well of his deal.

"Oh, look, Madam, he's thrown them some money, and all the party are roaring with laughter and staring this way——"

But Anne had lost interest. "I suppose that type of person finds bull-baiting amusing," she said—adding, with customary fairness, "or, of course, they may be enjoying some joke of their own." As the soberly clad little company clattered up the main street and were lost to view round an angle of the palace wall, she turned from the window to smother a yawn. She was still heavy with frustrated sleepiness—still slippered and capless. Her ladies, roused from their afternoon nap by the tumult, came bundling into the room in much the same state. Anne almost giggled at the sight of them as they stood around gaping at her yellow wig. They were absolutely horrified. "Dear old Madame Willicke's cap is on crooked and poor Guida Hagalas has got on odd shoes," she noted. "As soon as this revolting spectacle is over we must really go and make ourselves presentable."

She was not sure whether it would be considered discourteous if she left the window, and wished Olsiliger or somebody would come and advise her. In any case, the people seemed to have forgotten her for their sport; and her attention was distracted by a commotion nearer at hand. Dogs seemed to be barking now *within* the palace. Doors banged and servants began scurrying along the gallery outside her room. Anne thought she could distinguish a great raking of fire in the kitchens and a woman's spiteful laughter on the stairs.

"Milady Rochfort," muttered Dorothea. She ran to the door, opened it a crack and peered out; while her slower-witted companions pivoted on shapeless heels to stare after her in cow-like bewilderment. "It's those men we saw on the bridge. They're in a huddle with milord of Suffolk and the Archbishop, and the skinny duchess is hovering round them like an anxious moth!" she reported irreverently. Further revelations were forestalled by someone hurrying along the gallery from the opposite direction and pushing past her into the room.

It was Hans Holbein, looking angry and dishevelled in a paint-stained doublet and shirt. He went straight to Anne with a lack of ceremony which would have betrayed their friendly intimacy to a more observant audience.

"It's the King!" he warned breathlessly. "He's just ridden in with four or five of his gentlemen, done up like honest, middle-class men."

Anne's hands flew to her blonde, disordered head. "Are you *sure*?" she gasped, incredulously.

"Quite. I was in my room, working. But I knew those

damned hounds wouldn't bay like that for anyone else. And I've just passed poor Cranmer all in a flutter."

"But why—why—must he come *to-day* when he arranged to meet me at Greenwich *tomorrow*?" demanded Anne, trying to straighten a dozen different deficiencies in her toilette.

The painter's critical gaze swept over her, eloquent of dismay. "Oh, one of his boyish pranks, I suppose!" he burst out with bitter irony. "Entertainment for the consuming moment—*his* moment—and never mind any woman's convenience!" It was rank treason, of course, but he spoke in English and no one but Anne understood a word of it. "I see now what that Norfolk woman was sniggering about," he added, more soberly.

"You mean—she knew he was coming here?"

"Oh, she knew all right. Her husband must have told her."

"And that Rochfort woman made me take off my stays!" murmured Anne.

"Ssh! They're coming!" warned Dorothea, from her vantage point.

Anne could hear their approaching voices, tittering and whispering about their silly escapade like a lot of grammar-school boys. Only Cranmer's voice sounded formal, and faintly disapproving. He was speaking a little louder than usual, trying to give her time.

With a resourcefulness belied by her bovine appearance, old Mother Lowe waddled to a door communicating with the Bishop of Rochester's bedroom, which had been appropriated for Anne's use. "In here, Madam," she urged, her own leather stays creaking with suppressed emotion. "We can say you're resting—while some of us change your clothes."

But it was not Anne's habit of mind to think only of herself. "What do my clothes matter compared with Master Holbein's predicament?" she remonstrated. "Don't you understand? He came to warn me, and if the King finds him here——" Realizing how those two awful women might distort the significance of his presence, she turned imploringly to her guiltless lover. "Hans, it is you who must go in there. I beseech you—it's your career—maybe your life!"

In her distress she would have pushed him towards the small, arched doorway; but he detached her hands gently from his breast. "Your clothes *do* matter—more than you realize. I want him to see you beautiful," he insisted "Quick, Dorothea, come and take off this damnable wig!"

But the girl was too petrified to move. The whispering had ceased and firm footsteps were at the door. "It's a gentleman bringing some furs," she announced, helplessly.

"The King!" muttered Anne, closing her eyes. "If he suspects that you stayed behind because of me—Hans, it may be my life, too. I don't want to die—like Anne Bullen——"

She looked so distraught that he thought she would faint —and in any case there was no time for her to dress. He appeared to have no option. He passed into the Bishop's bedroom, so incongruously strewn with feminine finery, and allowed the old Countess to close the door softly after him. He had no thought of hiding. He just stood on the other side of it, his ear pressed to the oak. He cared for Anne so much that he had to know what was happening. And he knew Henry Tudor well enough to be sure that the Duchess's diabolical plot would prosper. Man and artist, he hung upon the fate of the woman he loved and the vindication of the portrait he had painted of her.

And Anne, all retreat cut off, turned back to the window. The terriers had got the bull down and were snapping with bloody fangs at its entrails. She stood there with pounding heart, staring blindly at the brutal scene, trying with all her will power to regain her composure. Acutely aware of every sound and movement behind her, she recognized the sweep of velvet as her ladies made obeisance, and Cranmer's premonitory cough. Then his suave voice, speaking very clearly, to help her. "Will your Grace permit me to present Sir Anthony Browne, Master of the King's Horse?"

A reprieve. At least it wasn't the King himself! Anne turned—awkwardly, ungraciously, conscious that she looked her worst. Her reluctance gave the impression that she was more interested in bull-baiting than in the kindly Master of Horse. And the belated sunshine, that could not shine until that hour, made things worse. It outlined her uncorseted figure in the bundly Flemish bed-wrap and lent a tawdry brilliance to her borrowed hair. Never was a woman taken at greater disadvantage.

In her confusion, Anne had no idea what Sir Anthony looked like. She was only vaguely aware of the richness of the gift he offered, though even then she didn't realize that the sable collar and moufflet were a far finer gift than anything Henry had ever given to his other wives. "A New Year's gift from my master," announced the bearer proudly, making an impressive bow.

But as he straightened himself Anne surprised the abashed disappointment on his face. Seymour and the Admiral had sent glowing accounts of her, no doubt. And then there was Holbein's miniature. . . . This was what she had feared, that he had flattered her. "*Danke—danke schön,*" she muttered, awkwardly as any chambermaid. The simplest English words had been scattered from her mind. And when she raised her eyes she saw another man standing in the wide span of the doorway. The fat man who had laughed on the bridge—laughed because he was so confident of making a good bargain. But he wasn't laughing now. And when he doffed a plumeless cap from his closely-cropped, red-gold head, Anne knew him to be Henry Tudor and herself to be the bargain.

Their eyes met across the disordered room—met and held. She knew that she must look like a startled rabbit. She saw the same disappointment repeated in his eyes—but far more poignantly. She watched his cheerful, rubicund face work painfully like that of a child deprived at the last minute of some promised treat. He looked half ludicrous, half pitiful, so that even in her humiliation, some mothering instinct in her wanted to comfort him. But she was far more sorry for herself.

Henry recovered himself almost immediately. He strode into the room, brushing Sir Anthony and the staring women

98

aside, and bade her welcome with a fine gesture. Although his presence seemed to fill the room, he no longer looked fat or ludicrous. One was aware of him rather as a mighty personality. One knew that whether he were clothed in cloth of gold or worsted, he would always—inevitably— take the centre of the stage. Mentally, he was master of the situation and his ruddy vitality was such that other men, crowding respectfully into the room on his heels, looked nondescript as the figures on some faded tapestry. In her distressed state of mind, Anne felt him towering over her. His voice was warm and cultured and kind; but she had read her doom in both men's eyes and all she could think of was Hans Holbein in her bedroom and Nan Bullen on the scaffold. And because—after all the strain she had been through—her legs felt as if they would collapse under her at any moment, she very sensibly went down on her knees before her future husband.

Henry was magnificent. Nothing he had rehearsed in his rejuvenated lover act could possibly have been more gallant than the way in which he lifted her up and embraced her and forbade a daughter of Cleves ever to kneel to him again. He made her sit down while he presented his friends. Probably he saw how ill she felt and Anne only hated herself the more for behaving like a weakling. "Even if I'm plain as a pikestaff, at least I'm healthy enough to rear him a dozen children!" she thought savagely, remembering all her mother's reassurances to Wotton on this important point.

Because he hated gaucherie, Henry made an effort to set her at ease. Much as he might have gentled a horse, he sat and talked with her. When he enquired after her comfort and whether everything possible had been done for her, poor Anne could have screamed, remembering how very much the Duchess of Norfolk and Lady Rochfort had managed to do for her in one short hour in this very room. And all the time she could feel the man controlling some inner fury and trying to avert his eyes from her unbound hair and the feminine disorder of the room, as if by not looking at them he could make them cease to exist. She could almost hear the punctilious Duke of Suffolk enquiring afterwards if it were

99

customary in Cleves for well-bred women to strew their living-rooms with clothes chests; and could have died with shame on observing that her discarded stays were obtruding from beneath the cushion beneath which the careless Hagalas girl had so hurriedly thrust them.

When the King called for wine, she tried to tell him that she never drank anything stronger than hippocras; but, wiser than she, he insisted on her swallowing a beaker of Malmsey and she was thankful to feel the blood coursing warmly through her veins again and to find that she could begin to answer his questions with some degree of intelligence. Actually, his clear, concise English was extraordinarily easy to understand and she even achieved a smile when he would have had the wine circulated among her women. "Better not, I think," she warned. "Your wine is so strong—and they are so——"

"Quite so," agreed Henry hurriedly, after one glance at their dazed, innocuous faces. "Most of 'em have their headgear on crooked now," he added, in an aside to Suffolk, who was standing near as if to support him. "God knows what they'd look like after a nip of the Bishop's best vintage!"

Anne was amazed to hear him ask by name after most of the people she had met on her journey, and touched to find that he himself had planned even the smallest details of her reception at Calais and Dover. "But that was before he saw me!" she thought, longing—yet dreading—to be alone with the knowledge of his disappointment, to absorb it and to adjust herself to the new outlook on life it would necessitate.

She guessed that the cooks were preparing an elaborate meal; but she was spared the tedium of this, for when at last the Bishop's steward came in to announce dinner, the King said something to Cranmer in Latin about what we have already received and got up to go. Being on his best behaviour, he turned to chat for a few minutes with her ladies on his way out; but—after raking the lot of them with a selective eye—he seemed to think better of it. Anne could scarcely blame him. Now that he was really going, several quite amusing remarks occurred to her, most of which she found herself capable of saying in impeccable English. But he turned abruptly on his heel. He appeared to have forgotten all about his betrothal gift, and Sir Anthony, at a loss what to do, followed him out with the furs still hanging over his arm.

So there was nothing more to be done but stand and watch the little scene of the King's departure. Agnes Tilney hovered by the door fussing about what she had done for his bride, and he thanked her perfunctorily. Just outside the room, her granddaughter, Katherine, stood flirting with one of the younger men who had been sent to Calais. Although it was still broad daylight, the servants had set torches to light the dim monastic gallery; and the light from one of them shone down on her exquisite little head, warming the mischievous curve of her cheek and her moist, red mouth. Evidently the young man adored her, but Anne saw her make a little secret gesture to check his ardent talk. She lowered her eyes respectfully, and flattened her childish body against the wall to let the King pass. But he stopped squarely in front of her. Clearly his mind was utterly, desperately on his own affairs. Yet in the midst of his absorption he seemed to find something in this girl's childlike torchlit loveliness to comfort him. "It's her freshness and vivacity. Or maybe just revulsion from our Flemish stolidness," thought Anne, with one of her swift flashes of intuition.

Whatever it was, he cupped Katherine's little chin in his great hand and gazed at her disconcertingly, although half his mind was still elsewhere. "You look like a rose with the dew still on it," he said, and sighed prodigiously. Presently he let her go and turned to the young man beside her. "*What* did you tell us her name was, Tom, that morning she annoyed milord Cromwell by playing shuttlecock at Greenwich?"

"Katherine Howard, your Grace," said Tom Culpepper, blood hotter than any torchlight flushing his own ingenuous face.

"Ah, yes. I remember thinking what a charming name it was." Henry turned back to the delighted Duchess. "And when you bring the new Queen to Court, Madam, be sure you bring this child as well," he ordered affably.

And the Duchess, perceiving that her family had every prospect of taking Cromwell's queen with a Howard pawn, ceased to plague Anne about her clothes.

CHAPTER IX

The curtains of the great four-poster were drawn. All except the two at the foot which had been left sufficiently apart to form a narrow frame for two tall candlesticks standing on the tallboy. Anne lay and stared at them until their silver sconces and the golden heart of each pointed flame ran into one beautiful nimbus of light seen through unshed tears. "I can bear it," she thought, "if only he gives me children!"

The nuptial procession, headed by the Lord Chamberlain, had seen her bedded and had at last departed. Her embarrassed women had undressed her and gone. At the last moment Dorothea—still yearning after her own lost baby—had managed to slip a sprig of fennel beneath the pillow. And now the softness of the down bed and the blessed quietness of the room were like a benediction after all the ceremonies and fanfares of the day. Faintly through the closed casements Anne could hear the strains of viols and hautboys from the Great Hall. People were still dancing at her wedding. But she—the bride—was alone. Alone in the great four-poster, waiting for her bridegroom.

Her hands lay clasped on the coverlet before her. They looked pale as ivory against the rich crimson damask. Pale, above the straight mound of her body, as carved hands upon a tomb. . . . The thought gave rise to others, equally unwonted. What of the other three women who had lain here, snug in the royal bed at Greenwich? Where were their cold bodies now? Had poor Nan's severed head been buried with her? Anne felt she must ask someone. But there wasn't anyone she knew well enough. And what did it really matter? She jerked her mind violently from such morbid humours. She wasn't concerned with death. She was too healthy—too prosaic—to speculate about dead bodies on her wedding night. Too much in love with life. And yet here she was—waiting for Henry—when it might have been Hans.

Desperately she strove to kill all realization of what ecstasy that might have been—drive from her all thought of him, of where he was or what torments he must endure this night. All she knew was that when they had parted hurriedly at Rochester she had been almost too wretched to care. Her hands were clenched now, nails biting into palms as if to mortify the flesh. She lifted the left one curiously, conscious of the unaccustomed weight of a wedding ring. The heavy golden hoop glistened against the light. She knew what was written on the inner surface. Milord of Suffolk, in his courteous way, had shown her before handing it to the Archbishop to be blesed, "God send me well to keep." Henry had had the comfortable words engraved before he met her. And now, she thought bitterly, he finds it's too late to alter them!

"But God knows he has tried!" she muttered, turning her head on the great embroidered pillow so that even the lovely candles could not light her shame. The hot blood of humiliation burned face and neck to the miniver edging of her nightgown. He had given her formal welcome—turned his kingdom into a pageant ground for her reception—failed in nothing which might honour Cleves. He had sent her sables and ridden in splendid state by her side; but never once had he lingered to speak with her alone. And ever since he had first seen her at Rochester he had wanted to be rid of her. Anne knew it. Everybody about the Court must know it. She read it in the Duchess of Norfolk's complacency, in Cranmer's kindness and in the way Cromwell avoided her.

And lying there in the great bed, Anne went over all that had happened since she landed—trying to determine, in her conscientious way, how much of it had been *her* fault. She could laugh now—or scream—recalling the good resolutions she had made. She would take no joy with her lover but devote herself to high destiny—make a success of marriage. As if it had ever rested with her! How puffed-up with conceit she must have been! She, who all her life had been just an unromantic, useful sort of person. Just because a famous painter had found her beautiful and a handful of boisterous English seamen had liked her pluck.

And then Henry had arrived unexpectedly at Rochester and caught her in that shapeless wrapper and abominable wig. Pretending to be absorbed in a brutal sport of the common people. Afraid for her neck because, like any slut of a serving wench, she'd a man hidden in her bedroom.

He had come brimming over with kindness and good humour, prepared to stay and dine with her. But he had ridden away within the hour, disgusted. In her writhing self-abasement Anne didn't blame him for that. If only she could have behaved naturally—making the best of a bad situation—explaining how they'd been trying to dress her *à l'anglaise*! Perhaps she could have made him laugh as he had laughed on the bridge. But it was over and done with now, the tragic comedy of their first meeting. And nothing could mend the pitiful mischance of it though they both lived to be a hundred.

Afterwards, of course, she had thought of plenty of things she might have said—things that would have amused him and shown that she wasn't quite dumb and stupid. But he had gone so quickly. "If he hadn't noticed that Howard child I might, even then, have put things right," she thought. "I'd have run after him and pressed him to stay. Maybe for all his power he's vain and lonely, and he'd have liked that." But she knew that he had forgotten even her shortcomings whilst he stood out there in the gallery holding Katherine's chin in his hand. "And what chance had I—against the budding youth of her?" Anne asked herself. "Why, even in that shabby frock she'd young Culpepper crazy about her. And what would it have mattered if *her* hair had been tumbled and her body untrussed? She would but have drawn men's eyes the more."

Anne raised herself to a more dignified posture against the pillows, and arranged the miniver more modestly across her rounded breasts. "It's women who're a few years older—large-boned women like me—who must dress carefully all our days," she thought. "We don't look so bad then. That's why poor Hans always minded so much about my wearing things that suited me. And why the people always liked me when I rode, dressed in my best, through the streets. I can make people like me—if I'm given time. Dear God," she prayed in sudden panic, "let me go on believing they *did* like me, and it wasn't just my imagination!"

Having a horror of succumbing to the hysteria that tormented her brother, she tried hard to relax. In order to take her mind off Henry's coming and the approaching hour, she went on trying to fix each day's incidents chronologically in her mind as she had not been able to during the emotional whirl of living them. She preferred to have things unequivocally clear—even the sequence of events leading to her own shattered pride. And this was such a personal, intimate grief that it couldn't be spoken about like people's illnesses or bereavements. It was something to be born secretly and pretended about even to one's own family until gradually the bruised roots of one's self-esteem began to grow again. And even that, she foresaw, could only come about if one stopped being broken-hearted and brought one's self to accept it.

So Anne, waiting in the bridal bed, spared herself nothing.

She recalled how carefully she had dressed the next morning for the journey from Rochester to Greenwich. In spite of all the previous day's worry, she had slept well. The last trace of sea-sickness had left her and there was colour in her cheeks, which always made the unfortunate pockmark at the corner of her mouth less noticeable. It wasn't fair, she had felt indignantly, that a man one didn't love could hurt a woman so! She had sent for a more flattering mirror than the Bishop's and decided that, whatever Henry thought of her, he couldn't deny that she was bravely turned out and held herself erect. She wasn't fat or middle-aged like him. Neither had she been allowed to grow up spoiled and childish. She'd enough common sense to recognize that the failure of their first encounter had been as much her own fault as his; and sufficient courage to be willing to start all over again and try to please him better. And now that the moment of departure for this final stage of her journey drew near she had been eager to seize the first opportunity of putting things right between them at Greenwich.

And then—just as the horses were being brought round to the door—word had come from Henry that she and her people were to ride to Deptford.

No apology. No explanation. Just peremptory orders to remove herself there without any of the expected ceremony and to await the King's pleasure like a lackey. A last-minute change of plan as utterly devoid of consideration for herself as his inopportune arrival at Rochester.

She had gone quietly, deeming it to be more dignified than ineffectual protest. For days she had endured the slight of waiting to be sent for. The embarrassment of having to face her perplexed people and answer their distraught questioning. The misery of trying to answer her own. She had paced up and down her room, making all kinds of wild conjectures. Had she, in her half knowledge of the language, committed some unforgivable solecism? Had Henry found out that Hans loved her? In her bewilderment she even began to cherish a wild hope that William—faced with the prospect of facing his mental lapses alone—had sent after her to stop the marriage. Deptford became a prison indelibly connected with her tormented thoughts. All her life she would hate the place.

And in the end it was Olsiliger, not she, who was sent for.

Anne recalled the day of his return. She had sent for him privately and he had at least been able to kill conjecture. "They are probing into your Grace's former betrothal to Lorraine's son," he had told her, with choking indignation.

"But that was broken off years ago!" she had exclaimed, not at first seeing the drift of their machinations.

"I know. I told them so. But they wanted proof." She had waved him to a chair and he had sunk into it gratefully. But she herself could not sit. "I don't understand," she had said. "The papers about it are in the muniment room at Cleves. I remember seeing them when I was helping my father to catalogue some estate rentals for Sybilla's dowry."

"But it would take me at least three months to get them," the Chancellor had pointed out. "And they want them *now*—before the wedding day. That's what all the delay is about. They're questioning the validity of your Grace's present marriage." The poor man seemed to be ageing visibly with the worry of it all just when she had needed someone strong to turn to. "Who's they?" she had asked. She remembered now, with compunction, how she had snapped at him.

He had waved an impatient hand. "Cromwell, Cranmer, those sumptuous dukes of Norfolk and Suffolk—the whole pack of them. I don't know who raised the scent, but obviously it's the King himself who's hounding them on."

Anne remembered how the walls of that horrible, impersonal room had seemed to drop away from her, leaving her shame exposed to all the world. "You mean—he's trying to —get out of marrying me?" She could still hear the way her voice had rasped like a rusty door latch.

Even then the old diplomat had winced at her unvarnished speech. She supposed that in his own anxiety, he scarcely saw how she suffered. "It's the first time my word has been doubted!" he complained. And, noticing, how his hands were shaking, she had sent a servant for some Malmsey, because it was the only English wine she could remember. "My poor Olsiliger! It must have been horrid for you," she had sympathized, momentarily forgetting how much more horrid it had been for herself. And when he would have pushed the heady foreign abomination aside, she had taken it from the servant and coaxed him herself. "The King insisted on my drinking some at Rochester, and it made me feel better," she had reminded him; and he had patted her ministering hand with the nearest approach to demonstrative affection of which he was capable, and obediently swallowed the stuff.

Obviously the wine had merit for after the servant had gone he had begun chuckling almost humanly. "It's funny to see that man Cromwell!" he said, glad perhaps that the English chancellor must feel as big a fool as himself. "He was so cock-a-hoop arranging it all and now he's biting his nails as if his life depended on finding a way out."

"Perhaps it does," she had murmured, without any particular pity. She was far more anxious about the repercussions on Holbein and her own family.

"Your mother will be furious, and I am afraid it may—er—unbalance the Duke again," Olsiliger had prophesied, voicing her thoughts.

She remembered how she had moved to the great, open fireplace to avoid one of the perpetual draughts in which English families appeared to live, her own slow anger beginning to mount like the heavy wood smoke. "And does it mean, do you suppose, that we we must stop in this dungeon of a house until someone from home brings those wretched papers cancelling the Lorraine contract?" she had demanded.

But however Henry might juggle with women who were his subjects, he couldn't afford to treat a Flemish princess like that—yet. Cleves, Guelders, Barre and Hainault together formed a tempting make-weight in the European balance of power and—as Olsiliger was at pains to point out—to repudiate her now would be to push William into an alliance of retaliation with the Emperor. And what is more important, thought Anne, it would make Henry Tudor look a fool! So the King had sent for her at last. And she had to admit that there had been nothing mean about the sending.

She had ridden in a gilded chariot with the two sumptuous dukes, as the austere Olsiliger always called them, attending her. And when they reached the last hill overlooking Greenwich it had seemed as if all the inhabitants of London must be waiting to welcome her on the open plain below. The place was called Blackheath, Charles Brandon had told her; though she couldn't imagine why when it was as full of colour as Holbein's palette. The crimson of velvet coats, the glitter of halberds, blazing heraldry, multi-coloured tents and white discs of expectant faces stretching away to a splendid palace flanked by a blue river. And all about the wharf the craft of all the City companies, decked with cloth of gold pennants. She had exclaimed aloud at sight of it and could have shed tears of vexation because her family weren't there to enjoy the honour paid her. At a word from Norfolk her coach had begun to rumble down the hill, and with a feeling of complete unreality she had passed between ranks of knights and merchants and aldermen lined up in a respectful silence that was far more impressive than any of the informal cheering to which she had become accustomed. It was the final touch of some inspired pageant master and had made her realize suddenly how near she was to being a queen. Henry had remembered, too, to give a place of honour in all that splendid throng to the merchants from her own country. And when one of them had stepped forward to present her with a jewelled purse she had declined Thomas Howard's offer to take charge of it and insisted upon carrying it herself, just as she used to do when people made her gifts at home.

When her new English chamberlain had met her at the bottom of the hill and presented to her the officers and servants of her household, she had felt that for the first time in this strange country she had found something that was really her own. And then the King's two nieces—spirited Margaret Douglas of Scotland and Charles Brandon's gentle daughter, Frances—had taken possession of her, and led her into one of the tents to wash and warm herself by a scented log fire. She couldn't help noticing how dainty they were compared with her younger Flemish girls and how quickly their nimble wits dealt with her halting conversation. She had kissed them heartily and would have given much to stay and talk to them. But a fanfare of trumpets had warned them of the King's approach and the grooms had brought her horse. And so she had ridden to meet her bridegroom.

He had dismounted, bared his ruddy head and embraced her. And so excellent were his manners or his miming that it had seemed incredible that his courteous greeting and protestations of affection were merely a conventional gesture to please the hood-winked, show-loving populace. I have never seen so many peoples!" she had exclaimed. looking for the end of his retinue which reached like a glittering serpent half-way across the heath to the park gates.

"Nearly six thousand horsemen, Madam," he had told her, taking her hand and presenting to her some of the foreign notables in his immediate entourage.

"It is grand like the Field of the Cloth of Gold, yes?" she had asked, abashed that so much money should have been expended on her account. And the elegant French ambassador, who had been quizzing the foreign cut of her gorgeous clothes, had assured her gallantly that at least she could not be outshone as his poor countrymen had been. And so she had ridden on at Henry's side, almost enjoying herself in her golden dress and glad that her mother had insisted upon having the black lions of Hainault embroidered on her horse's trapping. White swans were well enough embroidered on her underwear, but the fierce lions looked better able to vie with the Tudor's leopards in public.

Henry himself had taken her to her apartments and left her there. And the great palace of Greenwich had engulfed and overwhelmed her. All the week-end it had seethed with guests and guards and servants—so different from the drowsy ducal palaces to which she was accustomed. One was always changing one's clothes for some banquet or other, and there wasn't an hour of privacy. Only feverish comings and goings and whispering, even in the Queen's apartments. People didn't seem certain whether they were preparing for her wedding or for something they called Twelfth Night. Until Sunday supper time, when Henry announced suddenly that he had fixed their marriage for the following morning. He had omitted to consult the startled bride and then sulked because her poor women hadn't finished dressing her by the stroke of eight. And after all that hurry and pother the ceremony had not taken place—as they had all anticipated—in some splendid cathedral, but privately in the palace.

And during her wedding day, between a confusion of meals and masques, she had attended Mass and Evensong. Both William and Olsiliger had warned her that she would be expected to do so, and she had intended allaying her Lutheran scruples by conforming with blank or abstracted mind. Once she had become sufficiently familiar with the office to follow it automatically, she would use this as a quiet time for following her own thoughts. But the beauty of Henry' private chapel had held her spellbound. All the candles on the altar had been lighted for the feast of the Epiphany and the silver star of the Magi shone softly through a haze of incense. Never had she seen anything so wonderful as the embroidered chasubles of the officiating priests or heard singing like the pure, sweet voices of the King's choristers. She had stood in a daze beside her new husband, following his movements and listening uncomprehendingly to the Latin responses that fell so tunefully from his lips. She had offered her lighted taper with the rest, and even raised her eyes with a sense of guilt to the pictured face of the Madonna. And she had come away oddly comforted.

The remembrance steadied her now. After all, other women had endured this suspense of waiting for Henry. Anne fell to thinking of them. Catherine of Aragon couldn't have been afraid. She was a daughter of mighty Spain, armed with learning and accomplishments and she had known Henry from childhood. Besides he was young then— young and handsome and kind. And Nan Bullen, eighteen years later, had no need to wait, for already she must have carried the seed of his child within her. Their first ecstasy must have spent itself in some more secret bed. Else how could Elizabeth be a tall girl of seven?

Elizabeth. Elizabeth Tudor. Out of the gorgeous kaleidoscope of the day's doings—the sea of strange faces—there swam up into Anne's consciousness the pleasing memory of a bright-haired child. A dutiful curtsey and an unresentful kiss, followed by shrewd inspection from eyes absurdly like Henry's. The child had been presented to her by a grave elder sister. That must have been Mary. And they were both her step-daughters. The very nature of the relationship was a challenge; but it was the kind of relationship with which Anne felt qualified to cope. She was homesick and avid for affection. Perhaps, after all, life with the Tudors wouldn't be so bad. If only Henry's ready-made family accepted her. . . .

But the only Englishwoman she had made any real contact with so far was Katherine Howard. And although the King had arranged for her to become one of the new maids-of-honour there had been no further opportunity to talk to her. She wasn't important enough. Anne had caught sight of her in the Hall after supper and had been glad to see that someone had given her a new dress and that her grandmother was being quite affable. Perhaps that was why Katherine had dared to flaunt the Saxony necklace. She looked like a newly-opened rosebud and her voice had rippled with low, excited laughter as she danced past the dais in Tom Culpepper's arms. But Anne, watching them, had wished that she had given her pearls. Rubies, as Dorothea had pointed out at the time, were just the thing to brighten up a dull grey gown. But they contrasted so sharply with white damascene that one could almost imagine they were drops of blood encircling the girl's white throat. Anne had had plenty of time to notice things like that because when Henry had invited her to tread a pavanne she had to confess that she couldn't dance. He must have known this from Nicholas Wotton, but he had raised his eyebrows a little and turned away to talk to Cranmer. And presently he had left the dais and he, too, had danced a turn or two with the radiant little maid-of-honour. And she—the bride, had sat there all the evening, feeling prim and mature and unwanted, while other girls enjoyed themselves.

And now at last all the Twelfth Night revelling and the distant dance music had stopped; and Anne became aware of men's voices and convivial laughter outside her door. She could picture them standing there in an unsteady group, their fine clothes a bit dishevelled, capping each other's threadbare jokes—the kind of jokes men make in their cups about brides. She caught only a sentence here and there and most of them she didn't understand. But her face burned and her heart seemed to go hammering up into her throat. And then she heard her husband's voice, deadly sober and enunciating each syllable too perfectly for her to miss a word. "If it were not to satisfy the world and my realm I wouldn't have put my head into this yoke for anything," he was saying to somebody. And then more clearly still, with his hand on the latch—brute careless whether she heard or not—"That fool of an admiral knows I like 'em small. He ought to have stopped her at Calais—instead of bringing me a great Flanders mare !"

What woman could look her best after that? It was so like the Tudor. Pitying himself because the fairy-tale princess he had conjured up had turned out to be an everyday flesh and blood woman. But calling upon none of his riotous imagination to pity *her!*

Poor Anne lay rigid as a corpse beneath the crimson damask, gripping the sheet defensively beneath her chin. She knew just how that baited bull must have felt at Rochester. Her gaze turned entreatingly to the comforting candles, as if they were God. In her extremity she even crossed herself, an act she had been taught to regard as idolatrous.

Then Henry stood at the foot of the bed, holding one of the drawn curtains in either hand. His bulk blotted out the candlelight. Blotted out everything that was dear and familiar in life. It was the first time they had been alone; and although his eyes were only wells of shadow, Anne could feel them stripping her straight body—assizing it point by point like a farmer buying a heifer.

She stared back, hating him. Outlined by a yellow rim of light like that, he was ridiculously like the crayon sketch Hans had made of him in Calais. She had thought it cruel then. But now she saw how exquisitely clever it was and guessed how sensitive its victim must be about his obesity. All the baffled fury of sex antagonism was rising in her, swamping inherent meekness. So that now—at the most momentous hour of her life—she must needs hit back. "You look exactly like——" she began. But some residue of caution in her brain held back the words for Holbein's sake.

"Like what?" asked Henry coldly.

"You look so *square*," she amended lamely. Even in her own ears the words sounded perfectly inane.

He turned away, contemptuous of her gaucherie; and began to snuff the candles. Even had he come to her in co-operative mood there was nothing she could have said more calculated to mar their marriage from the outset. But she was glad she had hurt him.

Henry in a bad temper was incapable of assessing the smouldering disgust of those who suffered him. He had been told his bride had no languages, and he had not bothered to find out how much she had improved her English for his sake. And—as his cousin of Norfolk had prognosticated—he didn't find a bed shared in silence particularly amusing.

Yet presently in the shameful darkness Anne had to endure the resentful fumbling of exploring hands.

CHAPTER X

Anne spent her honeymoon at Hampton Court; and from the moment she stepped ashore from the royal barge she felt she had recaptured something of home. This was no pretentious palace of comfortless mediaeval castle; but a pleasant manor, modern and convenient, sprawling along the river meadows in a mellow warmth of red brick. Even the moat and drawbridge on the landgate side were a mere sop to architectural convention, making no pretence to fortification but providing a formal setting for the casual beauty of the courtyards. The rooms were gracious with wide fireplaces and the latest linenfold panelling, jolly little gilded weathervanes gleamed on the pinnacles of the great hall, and the kitchens hummed with good cheer and well-ordered service.

"I love this place," she told the Archbishop of Canterbury when he came to visit her.

Because he had something difficult to say to her, Cranmer had chosen a day when the King was at Westminster. It would have been less difficult, he felt, had she received him formally in her private apartments. But he found her strolling in the privy garden. Some of her younger women, more shapeless than ever in their winter wrappings, followed her in a chattering bunch. Apparently she felt that everybody should take the opportunity of enjoying a burst of early February sunshine. And although Cranmer hunched the collar of his gown almost to the lappets of his tight-fitting cap by way of protest, he soon found that the beautiful walled garden was soothing away some of the fret and anxiety of the awful weeks since her arrival. "Everybody loves Hampton," he agreed. "And the King himself prefers it above all his other palaces."

Anne—the bride of a month—had just discovered a bunch of snowdrops, half hidden, like harbingers of better things to come, among the brittle wintry stalks of an herbaceous border. She straightened herself in surprise, a few pale buds dangling from her hand. "Does he?" she said, her naïve joy in the spring flowers instantly masked by an expression of hard indifference. "I should have thought something more ostentatious—like Greenwich——"

Cranmer deplored her scarcely veiled hostility. It bore out the King's complaint that she was 'waxing wilful and stubborn,' which wasn't going to make matters easier for either Cromwell or himself. But, realizing how much she must have suffered at Greenwich, he spoke more gently than he might have done. "He liked this place so much, Madam, that he took it from my predecessor, Cardinal Wolsey," he told her.

Anne had never heard of the man. But she glanced back consideringly at the comfortable huddle of roofs and turrets and twisted chimneys. "There's a cardinal's hat still carved over the Clock Court gateway," she observed. "And every time I go upstairs I see the Bullen falcon decorating the vaulting of the roof." She sighed, and resumed her walk towards the river. "I suppose it's easier to get rid of people than to pull down bits of buildings."

Cranmer paced beside her, deliberating how best to rebuke this new, unseemly bitterness. He glanced back at her attendants to assure himself that they were following at a discreet distance, and wondered why women giggled so inanely. He was unaware, of course, that he looked like a black and white magpie against the honeymoon gorgeousness of their mistress. "I would suggest that your Grace has scarcely time to know—or to judge—him," he said.

But she only quickened her pace, her back uncompromisingly rigid and the fur-lined folds of her mantle bunched aggressively on her stomach in typical Flemish fashion. "I have slept with him," she made so bold as to remind him.

He had to concede her the point. Primate of England as he was, it was a distinction to which he couldn't lay claim. "But I have worked with him for years," he pointed out. "And just as a finely-cut jewel has more than one facet so I assure you there is another side to him. Perhaps one day, Madam, you may be privileged to find it." They had reached the terrace that separated the garden from the Thames.

Below them lay the Barge Walk. The water-gate steps were busy with the constant arrival and departure of people who had business with the royal household, and the noonday peace was broken by the rough badinage of boatmen waiting for passengers or mooring their craft against the landing-stairs. It was scarcely the place Cranmer would have chosen for conducting so delicate a remonstrance. "In the meantime, is it possible that you are not showing your best side to him?" he probed. "When you first arrived you were so meek and reasonable, whereas now even I am aware of the 'high-stomached humour' of which he complains."

"Would you have me fondle myself into favour like a prostitute with a man who insults me?" demanded Anne, her generous mouth drawing itself into a hard, resentful line.

Cranmer was too shaken by her out-spokenness to offer the usual platitudes about wifely duty. "I would have you try to render yourself more agreeable to your husband, Madam," he countered, with equal bluntness.

"You met me before ever I saw him and no one knows better than your lordship how hard I have tried," she reminded him. And something in the directness of her gaze must have shamed him, for he added almost defensively, "It was Thomas Cromwell who asked me to entreat you to consider the expediency of continuing to do so in spite of —everything, Madam."

"Then why doesn't milord Chancellor come and talk to me himself?" she asked. "I have besought him to often enough."

"Being under the King's displeasure, he was afraid to meddle further in the matter," admitted his friend. "And now he can't come because he is in the Tower."

Anne didn't ask which tower. She felt sure that he meant that grim, four-square building further down the river. Passing it once on her way from Greenwich, she had remarked on its strong portcullised water-gate, and an awkward silence had fallen on the company. Only Lady Rochfort had taken pleasure in whispering to her that Henry's second wife had gone there to her death. And now Cromwell, who had manoeuvred her own marriage, was helpless behind those dreadful gates. Realizing the implication, she stood there with her hands folded over her bunched-up skirts staring at the animated river scene from which all cheer and sunlight seemed suddenly to have been wiped out. "Does Henry hate me as much as that?" she asked, in a stricken sort of way. In a spasm of fear and homesickness her thoughts flew distractedly to Cleves. If only she could tell William! If only her mother or Sybilla would advise her what to do! Dared she send for Holbein?

She was scarcely aware of the Archbishop telling her how Norfolk had arrested his rival in the King's name just as he was about to take his place in council. But there must have been some humanizing effect about the busy waterfront or maybe the first hint of spring had moved the prelate to compassion; for presently—out of her stony abstraction— Anne heard him say quite kindly, "Does it make it any easier to know that I would willingly serve your Grace if it were in my power?"

Separated from the love of her family, she was compelled to live on small kindnesses. She turned at once to thank him and he could scarcely credit the sudden beauty of her expression. Standing there in her bunched-up blue velvet, she reminded him of his favourite Albrecht Dürer Madonna. "Have you made no friends in England?" he asked. Her disproportionate gratitude had jolted his sensitive mind into realizing the painful isolation of her position, and if the tone of his enquiry were sharp it was due to an uncomfortable feeling of participated guilt.

Anne shook her head and sat down comfortably on the low garden wall. She had ceased to be either a tragic queen of a famous Madonna, and had become just a lonely woman arranging a few spring buds in her lap. "But since I have your lordship's goodwill——"

He waved aside the tactful formality as if warning her not to expect too much from any overtures of his. "Among the women, I mean," he hastened to explain.

Anne considered the matter gravely. "There was a young niece of the Duke of Norfolk's who showed me some kindness," she recalled, with a reminiscent smile for the spontaneity of the girl's hurried confidences about the Princesses' clothes. "The King has since appointed her to be one of my maids-of-honour; but so far I have had little chance to talk to her. Katherine Howard, her name is."

Thomas Cranmer started. Could even this placid unsophisticated foreigner be so simple? So ignorant of all the stale gambits of court intrigue? Churchman as he was, he could almost have shaken her for her complacent goodness. "I would not advise your Grace to make a confidante of *her*," he warned drily.

"No?" Supposing that he spoke out of antagonism towards the girl's religion, she surveyed him from beneath drooped eyelids with covert amusement. "Strangely enough, the only other English woman who has gone out of her way to befriend me is a Catholic too," she said to plague him. "No less my enemy than Mary Tudor herself."

"Naturally, as a member of the family, she would wish to show you hospitality. In spite of all this increasing divergence in religious opinion you mustn't think we're all savages, entrenched in two separate camps." The learned archbishop permitted himself the informality of sitting beside her, and his personal charm melted the last of Anne's reserve. "But it wasn't merely hospitality," she assured him; and in her eagerness to show him what sort of things she had to put up with, and to do justice to Mary's unexpected kindness, most of her newly acquired mastery of English verbs deserted her. "In the procession at Blackheath I do something foolish. I am over-joyed to see among so many strangers a group of merchants from the Hanseatic ports——"

"Given place there by the King's forethought—to welcome you," murmured Cranmer, with a smile.

"Hans Holbein often spoke to me of them. They were good friends to him when he first came to England. They commissioned him to paint their portraits and to decorate their buildings in some place called the Steelyard, yes?"

"Their wharf extends like a walled city all along Thames Street from Barking Creek to Dowgate," explained Cranmer. "All the nobles go there to buy their falcons and all manner of rich stuff, and it's quite the fashion to invite one's friend to caviare washed down with Rhinish at the Steelyard Inn."

"So?" Nodding her head appreciatively, Ann savoured the welcome fact that her countrymen were held in such high esteem. "Well, these rich merchants offer me a purse and I keep it. It appears I should have passed it to one of your fine dukes to distribute to the poor. But at home my brother's people were always hurt if one so gave away a present. So I carry it to my apartments in the palace. And afterwards that old——" out of respect for his cloth Anne bit back the low-German epithet which best expressed her feelings—"that old Norfolk woman told everybody I have the manners of a chambermaid. That I am greedy and hold out my hands for—how do you say——"

"Gratuities?" suggested Cranmer, interpreting the rubbing gesture of her finger and thumb.

"They are all laughing about it in the long gallery after supper," went on Anne. "I think sometimes my husband encourage those pretty girls to amuse him by making fun of me. But when my step-daughter pass I see her bite her lip. Two spots of colour come high up on her cheek bones as if she is angry. And she take the trouble to turn back and remind them that perhaps I do not know your English customs." Gradually her resentment gave way to a sort of pleased pride. "It was a beautiful thing for her to do, don't you think, milord Archbishop?"

"Katherine of Aragon's daughter is always scrupulously fair," admitted Cranmer, a little absently. "But as regards power to help you she is—negligible. Whereas only a few short weeks ago Thomas Cromwell ruled England." His voice dropped so that he seemed almost to be communing with himself. "And now the Norfolk star is in the ascendant. It is like the swing of a pendulum. And what has happened once can happen again."

Anne made an exasperated little movement as if to brush all these vast, perplexing contentions from her. In Cleves things were so much simpler. Conscientious councillors didn't walk in fear of their lives, hanging on her brother's moods or his fancy for some woman. "Can I help it if the King is indifferent to me?" she asked wearily.

"Indifferent? Would that he were!" thought Cranmer, rousing himself. But he tried to speak patiently. "Don't you see, Madam, that nothing remains static—least of all the King's affections. You tell me that you love this place. You seem prepared to settle down sensibly and make the best of your new life, enjoying the sports, the jaunts to London and the people's liking for you. To put up with your husband, in fact."

"Well, isn't that what you all want?" she asked, wondering if she would ever do anything right in this mad country.

"It's not enough. Particularly if he should come to realize it. You must make every effort to please him—to keep him."

"To—keep him?" repeated Anne. Nothing would have pleased her better than to lose him; yet the thought of doing so raised a cloud of frightening possibilities.

Cranmer had no wish to emphasize them. "It's not for a mere man to suggest the means to your Grace," he hurried on, with nervous urgency. "But I beseech you to forget your pride and use your wit. For your brother's sake—for all our sakes. Most of all, perhaps," he added, more quietly, "for the sake of England!"

Such fervour coming from so self-possessed a dignitary could not fail to impress Anne, and the thought of William had power to shake her out of her own personal sense of grievance. Besides, as the Archbishop must have observed, people seldom appealed to her good nature in vain. "I will take the first opportunity that offers," she promised.

Cranmer's thin body seemed to settle a little more comfortably into the voluminous folds of his gown. "It may save Thomas Cromwell's life," he said, with a sigh of relief.

Anne laid down her snowdrops on the sun-warmed bricks between them and glanced at him anxiously. Although he was about the same age as her husband, he seemed much older. Much of the fine energy of his youth had been consumed by study and—like most people whose original purpose in life has been frustrated—he lived largely on his nerves. "I am afraid I have been stubborn and tired you," she apologized in her best English. "It is difficult to think of others when one has been so badly hurt oneself."

But having accomplished his errand, the Archbishop allowed himself to relapse into the kindly theologian; and, in the rôle nature had intended for him, he was at his best. "Life is so full of various kinds of hurt," he said, thinking perhaps of the cruelties he had unwillingly helped the King to perpetrate in the name of conscience. "That is why a wise man builds for himself some sort of retreat to which he can occasionally retire. And because the young are very vulnerable it is as well to begin building early."

He looked up to find Anne's eyes fixed on him—no longer sleepy or gently mocking; but wide, surprised and full of intelligence. "What does one build with?" she asked.

He was pleased. He hadn't supposed that she would appreciate a spiritual lead—which was the only kind of help he had to offer. "Oh, with very ordinary things. One's talents and hobbies and interests."

"I haven't any talents. That's just the trouble," she told him.

He left it to born courtiers like Marillac to offer her the momentary balm of flattery; but he found himself sincerely desirous of giving her some chance of lasting consolation. "No," he agreed, recalling several painful occasions during the last few weeks when she had only averted fiasco by confessing candidly that she couldn't sing or dance or play upon the virginals or whatever people expected her to do. "But there must be *some* things you are good at. What can you do best?"

Anne considered the question. "I suppose—just sew and cook and see that things are properly run—like any hausfrau."

Cranmer regarded her with fresh interest. He liked her candour and her common sense. She seemed devoid of petty vanity; and it was always easier to put things right when dealing with people who had been brought up to see themselves without blinkers. "Then why not specialize in that?" he suggested. "Take pride in running your household efficiently. Study the King's comfort and keep your servants from quarrelling. And try to do it all a little better than—than his other wives."

Anne indulged in a small complacent sniff. All these things were as child's play to her; but she was surprised that he should set any store by them—and a little sceptical. "It would be interesting to know what the Duchess of Norfolk would have said had I insisted upon inspecting the kitchens at Greenwich!" she remarked grimly. "I should have the mind of a cook as well as the manners of a chambermaid, no doubt! Besides, surely all the fine new officers of my household would resent it?"

"Perhaps, just at first. But here at Hampton things are more homely. You'd be surprised how much interest the King himself takes in the vacheries and wine cellars and so forth. Underneath all his regal trappings, he is really a very domesticated man."

Anne had already found that out, although whether he wanted a domesticated wife was another matter. But it was certainly a relief to be asked to shine at things which she had been taught to do at home instead of being expected to compete with the English court ladies in their more fanciful sphere of accomplishments. "I could plan a proper herb garden with plants that really cure people,' she admitted. "And the way you heat your houses is hopeless."

They sat in companionable silence for a while. Anne was a restful woman to be with and he had evidently given her an idea to turn over in that deliberate mind of hers. Her maids had moved away to a lily pond where they were feeding the rising carp. Before him stretched a lawn of smooth, verdant grass; while from behind came the dip of oars and creak of rowlocks in pleasant, familiar rhythm. It was all vaguely reminiscent of the college backs at Cambridge from which he had been dragged unwillingly to fame. "I've a lawn almost as fine as this at my palace at Lambeth," he mused aloud. "But I never wanted to live in palaces."

Anne studied his thoughtful profile. Although he looked

so austere, there was a lovable courtesy about him. "Is that how you came to understand—about the need for making some kind of retreat?" she asked.

She spoke so quietly—hands idly folded, inviting confidence—that he found himself telling her how it had all come about. "The happiest part of my life was spent at Cambridge," he said. "Men sought for truth there—not how to confound it for their own ends. Men like Erasmus of Rotterdam. And I found vast contentment in teaching theology. You see, when I myself was at school my master was so severe that he daunted even the finest wits among us. His harshness dulled our memories. So that when I grew up and found the beauty of words for myself, I wanted more than anything to present literature to the young people of this generation in such a way that they must needs enjoy it."

Anne's brown eyes were soft with pity for his hurt youth. "How I wish I could have been one of your pupils!" she laughed ruefully. "I might have learned to talk to you in Latin as all the Tudors do. But how did you come to be connected with them?"

"It was pure chance really. I'd taken two of my pupils to their father's country place in Essex, because of the plague. It must have been in fifteen twenty-nine, the year it was so bad in Cambridge. We were reading Tyndale's *Obedience of a Christian Man*, I remember, when Fox and Gardiner, the King's almoner and secretary, happened to be quartered in the same house during a royal progress. We were old college friends, so you can imagine I was glad to see them." He chuckled reminiscently, in a way that made her feel what the stimulus of such intellectual friendship must have meant to him. "We used to sit up till all hours talking and—coming from Court—they were full of the proposed Spanish divorce."

"What had Qeen Catherine *done*?" interrupted Anne. People had talked a lot about it in Cleves; but it had meant nothing to her at the time. Now she wished she had taken the trouble to find out what it was all about, and here was the very man to ask.

"It was rather what she hadn't done," explained Cranmer. "She hadn't given England an heir."

"But she couldn't help that, poor woman!"

"No. But there it was. And she was getting old——"

"And I suppose Henry had met someone he liked better?" The words slipped out before Anne could stop them and Cranmer pursed his lips and didn't reply. But surely the man must realize that she of all people wanted to know what happened? That anything of which the Tudor was capable concerned her intimately? Perhaps, if she put the question differently, he could tell her. "On what grounds could he divorce her?" she asked, more respectfully.

"He couldn't—for a long time," admitted Cranmer. "They'd been married for eighteen years and there was never a breath of scandal against her. But there *was* the question whether their marriage were regular or not."

"How like Henry to think of it—after eighteen years!" thought Anne, who was learning unwonted cynicism.

"She'd been married to his elder brother, Arthur, who died before he was sixteen," explained Cranmer. "So it all turned on whether that first marriage had been consummated."

"I see," said Anne.

He was too preoccupied with this well-worn thesis of the past to notice that she seemed to be gravely assimilating some new idea which might affect her own future. "All the—er—evidence about it seemed to disagree," he told her solemnly, "and, as you probably know, half the eminent lawyers in Europe argued over it for months."

"And what did Catherine herself say about it?" asked Anne, wondering how clever men could behave so much like a lot of pompous asses.

"She swore it had not. Obviously it was to her advantage to do so."

"You don't suggest that she——" began Anne, hot in her defence. But the Archbishop silenced her protest with a deprecating gesture. "It was the King's word against her's, you understand."

Anne understood only too well.

"And it appears Prince Arthur had said things which gave the people of their household reason to think otherwise. . . . But, be that as it may," he went on, shying hurriedly from the vexed subject, "the Catholics held that as dispensation had been granted at the time of the second marriage, there could be no divorce. And the Protestants took the view that if the second marriage were proved irregular, there was no *need* of a divorce. And as the Pope himself happened to be in custody at the time, many enlightened people felt that it was rather an anomaly for England to accept religious jurisdiction from one in secular bondage."

All Anne could see about it was that it must have made a bitter split throughout the country, and that it was monstrous after eighteen years to get rid of a faithful wife.

"Having no particular interest in the matter—apart from one's natural sympathy with the Queen, and a scholar's impatience with legal delay—I, for my sins, happened to suggest to my two old friends that the matter might be laid before the divines of the Universities," went on Cranmer. "I suggested it because they seemed to me the most enlightened and disinterested people to decide. Professional prejudice, no doubt. But Fox and Gardiner must have repeated my words to the King."

"And what did *he* say?" prompted Anne, the perfect listener.

A wry humour curved Cranmer's clever mouth. "He said, 'Mother of God, that man has the right sow by the ear!' and sent for me immediately to Greenwich. And—as I have already complained to your Grace—I've been living in a palace instead of a college ever since."

"And you feel uprooted—as I do?" asked Anne gently.

"I did at first." In the rare easement of telling someone about it, he forgot the formality due to her rank and began to speak as if they were old friends. "And since then it has been nothing but religious controversy and straightening out the King's matrimonial affairs. I did think that when Jane Seymour——" He pulled himself up with comical dismay;

but Anne only smiled and finished the train of thought for him. "But she died when her baby was born. And now you've got me on your hands."

He sighed, taking up the burden of the present again. "And Cromwell's life and my own may be gravely influenced by the way you behave."

Impulsively, Anne stretched out a hand and touched his knee. "You're not afraid—for yourself?" she asked, with real concern.

For a moment his fine, scholarly hand closed over hers. So many people listened attentively to what he thought—so few cared about what he felt. They always brought *their* troubles to *him*. "No, Madam. For the present God has spared me that," he said. "For although I have been forced to meddle with statecraft, I have managed to keep the King's affection. Though only, I fear, by allowing myself at times to become his tool." Only Anne's own unaffected candour and humility could have drawn such a confession from him.

"It wasn't being anybody's tool to fight as you did to give the English people the Bible in their own tongue—to have one put in every church so that they could read it for themselves," she argued. "My father was telling us about it not long before he died and he said it was one of the most significant reforms in Europe."

"Yes, I had to fight for that." The memory of how he had fought warmed him, mending his self-esteem as she had intended. "And one day I want to give them a book of prayer simple enough to comfort them and yet fine enough to voice their approach to God. Each man's personal approach, not some set of half-understood Latin words mumbled through a priest. But to do this would be to tilt so hard at the long established power of the Catholic Church that then indeed I might be put to the fear of death. And I doubt if I am of the stuff from which martyrs are made."

Anne looked around her at the greening hawthorn and the cheerful little gold and silver plumes of young willow fringing the river. She spread the folds of her new blue velvet caressingly, preening herself in the warmth of the sun. Such intensity of religious conviction had never moved her. She knew only that she was young and strong and that, in spite of her uprooting and humiliation, life was still full of lovely things she wanted to enjoy. "I've always felt it would be easier to die for someone one loved—or for pity's sake . . ." she murmured diffidently.

But he was too deep in introspection to hear her. "I often think that accursed pedagogue of my youth mutilated all my audacity," he was saying wretchedly, "for this fear of being afraid is an ever-present torment."

Anne kept silence. She had the sense to realise that through some chance blending of mood and encouragement she was being vouchsafed a glimpse of an integral flaw that was eating the heart out of the man. Something beyond her full comprehension, but not beyond her compassion. She had been in this country barely six weeks and here was the awesome prelate who had met her with such pomp at Rochester and worn that wondrous cope at the feast of the Epiphany, talking to her as if he were any tired and rather timid middle-aged man. Apparently the same thought struck him, for he straightened himself up and laughed shamefacedly. "I came out here to rebuke you, and then I wanted to comfort you," he admitted, almost irritably. "And now—I don't know why I should be telling you all this!"

Anne didn't know either, but she dismissed her incomprehension with a shrug and a smile. "People do tell me things, you know," she said simply, as if that were all there was to it.

They had both become aware of some sort of commotion further down the river towards Kingston. People were standing up in their boats or running to the water's edge; and her *jauntlewomen*, as she called them, had forsaken the greedy, rising fish to see what was going on. They were hurrying to the wall with little cries of excitement, their round, beaded caps bobbing together like large sunflower heads in the wind. Cranmer, who knew by the cheering that it must be the King coming back from Westminster, stood up and smiled at her. "That, too, is a gift. A very rare and precious one," he said. "Cultivate it, my child, along with those domestic virtues. For if it seems to heal only the teller, in time it may come to be the means of healing your own hurt."

CHAPTER XI

Anne waited dutifully at the top of the water-gate steps,
with the archbishop beside her and her women hovering
behind. She stood without fuss or fidget, as she had been
trained to do, hands folded placidly before her. Because she
made none of the commotion that used to herald the spectacular movements of Nan Bullen, and could move without
the formal entourage imposed by the rigid etiquette of Aragon, it was some time before the people noticed her. But
when they did, the cheering was no longer all for Henry.
Right from the first they had approved her quiet dignity and
because her household reported that she had no exotic, tem-
peramental ways they scarcely thought of her as a foreigner.

"Next to a public hanging, there's nothing they enjoy
staring at so much as a royal bride," Cranmer was explaining
with a quiet smile.

Anne supposed it must be just that mixture of toughness
and sentiment that made them so difficult to understand.
She smiled at them benignly but was far too tactful to seem
to appropriate any of her husband's ovation to herself. Instead, she turned towards the Kingston reach to share in
their orgy of sightseeing.

With a new little thrill of pride she realised that the King's
home-coming was a sight to be proud of. Like so many of
the everyday bits of English pageantry to which she was
becoming accustomed, it had an air of unrehearsed spontaneity. It was as if the observance of it were so deeply
embedded in the national life that each man, according to his
degree, fitted naturally into the colourful picture and played
his part just as his forebears must have done during some
earlier reign. They wore their clothes, too, as if they were unaware of them—the humblest fiddler and the most resplendent courtier looking equally at ease—so that in all the
sparkling scene there was none of that solemn, ordered

pomposity that often made Flemish ceremonies such dull affairs.

The great crimson upholstered barge came smoothly over the water with a full tide slapping at her golden prow. The rippling muscles of the royal watermen and the dipping of their blades were part of one satisfying rhythm, while decoratively—with great gold roses embossed on their green uniforms—they helped to weave the background for this casual Tudor tapestry. Henry himself was hidden by the silk-fringed awning; but every now and then, between the flutterings of his proudly quartered standard, Anne could see his knee and part of the fur-wrapped lap of a lady sitting beside him. Scraps of light-hearted conversation from his attendant gentlemen were sufficient indication to the initiated that he was in a good humour.

Sharp as the snapping of a twig, the barge master gave an order. The long oars rested motionless and, with that consummate skill that makes precision look so easy, his craft fetched up through the shallows until her side bobbed gently at the stonework of the palace landing-stage. A rope whistled through the clear morning air and was effortlessly caught. In the well of the moored barge there was a graceful uprising, a doffing of velvet caps and the flurry of laughter that rounds off a well-savoured joke. Henry stood up, balanced himself a moment and stepped ashore. Tom Culpepper, his favourite gentleman of the bedchamber, whom he had sent to meet Anne and transferred to her household, stooped solicitously to the lady beneath the awning, threw the fur wraps to one of the boatmen and passed her safely along the barge. The others made way for her—rather too much as if she were royalty, the watchful archbishop thought. Even the King himself turned back to stretch her a helping hand.

It was little Katherine Howard, in a new rose pink cloak and hood.

Henry came almost running up the steps, followed by the French ambassador and the rest of the party, and a grinning page or two incongruously laden with an assortment of gaily-painted toys. All eyes were focused upon the *rencontre*. Seeing the Queen standing there, Katherine changed colour and—in her inexperience—hung back with noticeable confusion until Tom Culpepper nudged her to go forward. The chatter of his companions had died down suddenly and his gay young face was set like a decorous mask to hide the sullen welter of his feelings. Cranmer, who had often been called upon to calm the jealous paroxysms of Nan Bullen, glanced anxiously at the new queen; but only by a tightening of her clasped hands did she betray how thoroughly the episode had clarified his recent warning.

Of all the people present only the King seemed completely at ease. "But then he must have had more experience than most of us in carrying off such moments!" thought Anne contemptuously. Swaggering forward in his short, swirling coat he bade her a pleasant, unabashed 'Good morning,' and grinned defiantly at his friend. "Look, Thomas, what we've bought!" he cried, beckoning breezily to a small page whose merry eyes scarcely topped the assortment of wooden animals steadied by his chubby chin. "Katherine's bright eyes spotted them on a stall in Eastcheap and I made Culpepper buy up the lot. The stall-holder will probably retire on the proceeds! They're for Edward, of course," he explained, taking a fierce-looking hobby horse with improbable orange spots from the top of the pile and handing it to Anne. "Don't you think the young rascal will love them?"

Poor Anne was busy telling herself that her husband had a perfect right to go shopping in Eastcheap and junketing up the river with any court lady he liked; but any delight she would normally have taken in the quaint quadruped could be only perfunctory with such a storm of enlightenment raiding her mind. "They are very cleverly carved," she said, trying to speak politely.

He turned from the stilted flatness of her voice to toss a toy to Katherine, who was still standing dumb and hesitant half-way up the steps. "Here, Kat, you said you wanted to keep the lamb for yourself," he invited, with his great infectious laugh.

The little maid-of-honour caught it deftly with one of those wild fawn movements that made Anne feel mature and clumsy. She nestled her soft cheek against it; but clearly her action was but the joyless reflection of some former playful mood, for she looked up miserably at her new mistress's grave, still dignity, and her husband's casual neglect. Her hand went to her throat where the coveted rubies had gleamed so becomingly of late; but the King's pearls lay there now. Anne noted the instinctive gesture while she was greeting the French ambassador, and guessed at the shamed pity in the girl's warm, undisciplined heart.

"Lady Katherine is still half a child herself!" laughed Marillac with tactful suavity.

Henry smiled blandly, made a gesture of dismissal to his barge master and bade the pages take the toys up to the palace. "Mary will take them to Havering to-morrow," he told the company in general. "She asked leave to go again this week."

"Judging by her care for her brother, her Grace must be a born mother," remarked Marillac, and—lowering his voice—went on to discuss with Anne the rumour of Mary's betrothal to Philip of Bavaria, who had come over ostensibly for the King's wedding. Was it right that the princess was not—over-enthusiastic? Some prior attachment perhaps? Anne was not in a position to satisfy his curiosity but felt it was kind of him to try to draw her into the family circle like that; particularly as, in his efforts towards a French alliance, he must have worked hard to keep both Philip and herself out of the country. She was rather afraid of his polish and perspicacity, but couldn't help wishing that some of the English would emulate the philosophical good grace with which he had accepted political defeat.

Cranmer and the King were standing a little apart, watching the skilful turning of the royal barge against the turn of the tide. One could imagine it was the sort of thing each of them would have enjoyed doing in his youth. Through the Frenchman's whispered gossip, the half-understood wit of which only confused her, Anne could hear the archbishop prompting Henry to a simple kindness. "Perhaps little Elizabeth would like to go to Havering too and participate in her brother's pleasure?" he was suggesting.

Having served Henry for ten years, he was expert in

choosing his moment. Even Anne could see that her husband was in just that expansive humour in which he had ridden into Rochester the day she first set eyes on him. Ripe for some rejuvenating romance, no doubt—though not with *her* this time! "Oh, Elizabeth can go along if she likes," he agreed, in the careless way in which he usually spoke of his younger daughter. "It's time she went back there anyway now the wedding's over." He never referred to her unless he was obliged, and then only to call her his 'red-headed little bastard.' But there was something in Nan Bullen's daughter —some spark of his very self—that drew his grudging approval; whereas most things about Mary seemed to irritate him, except her manners and her devotion to Edward. But it was his elder daughter he was looking round for at the moment and, because she didn't immediately materialize, he automatically began to bully his wife. "Why isn't Mary out in the sunshine with the rest of you?" he demanded. "She sits indoors too much for her health."

Just so, thought Anne, he must often have spoken to Nan Bullen when her sleek arrogance had ceased to entrance him.

It was Katherine Howard who spared her the indignity of replying. "If your Grace will excuse me I will go and find her," she offered, curtseying herself gracefully out of an awkward situation and leaving most of the others relieved that she had gone.

Henry looked after her desirously as she flitted like a nodding pink rose up the lime-sheltered path. That was the nimble kind of wit he liked his women to have. Everybody about him ought to have learned enough subterfuge to hide up unpleasant things and so deliver him from embarrassment. It made life so much easier. He sighed and glanced uneasily at his latest wife, standing like an unwanted stranger in their midst, unhelpful save for her silence. She had been so damned uncompromising over that pre-contract business, which might have saved them both from this travesty of marriage. . . . Probably if he tried to get rid of her now she'd raise hell, and gloss over nothing to that righteous brother of hers in Cleves! He shrugged the prospect aside with the long-suffering patience of an ill-used man, and turned to the diplomat who had had the sense to urge him to marry a Frenchwoman. "Well, Marillac, you'll want to be getting along!" he said jovially. "That looks like the Northumberland barge coming up-stream for you. One can always tell her—she's so much grander than Suffolk's or mine!" Annoyance showed through the frayed edges of his sporting show of laughter, as he registered a mental note to speak to Cromwell's successor about limiting the pennons of ducal barges as well as regulating the clothing of the common people according to their trade or craft. But he explained to Anne courteously enough that the ambassador was going on to one of Sir John Dudley's famous parties at Northumberland House.

"The one on the other side between here and Richmond Palace," recalled Anne, who was beginning to know most of the great family mansions built all along the banks of the Thames. She couldn't help noticing with a twinge of envy how his voice changed as he rested a hand on Cranmer's shoulder and urged him to stay and dine. It was such a beautifully modulated voice when he spoke of music or poetry or to somebody for whom he really cared.

But Cranmer was in no mood for company. He may have been feeling self-conscious still at having told his troubles to a comparatively unknown lady; or perhaps he needed time to forget what his master looked like through the eyes of an unwanted wife. "If your Grace will excuse me, I have a conference at Lambeth," he demurred. "I only came to pay my respects to the Queen."

"Well, next time be sure to come when I am at leisure," said Henry. "I want to play over to you my new setting for 'The Song of Songs'."

Cranmer's face lit up with so much pleasure that Anne decided that this love of music must be one of the facets of her husband's personality to which he had alluded. "Will it be ready for the Children of the Garter to sing at Windsor for Easter?" he was enquiring eagerly.

"Not if half the congregation drown it with the scraping

of their spurs, as they did last time I allowed something of mine to be sung," complained the royal composer.

"Does that mean that because some of your Garter knights behaved like vandals the rest of us must be denied the delight of hearing one of your Grace's anthems?" pleaded Marillac.

"Even the choristers themselves were indignant about it, your Excellency," Culpepper told him. "My young brother, who is solo boy on the descant side, told me they had put in extra practices before school hours for weeks so as to do justice to the honour paid them."

"I suppose they could be brought to Westminster and sing it there," cogitated the archbishop, "for there are no such pure trebles in the country."

Henry stood with arms akimbo in the middle of them, his mouth pursed consideringly. Clearly, he enjoyed being pressed. "Wouldn't it be simpler to forbid the Knights of Windsor to come to church in spurs?" suggested Anne, who wasn't at all clear what this cherished Order of the Garter really was.

"That's not a bad idea," agreed Henry, surveying her abstractedly. "Except that it might give offence to some of our foreign visitors." And presently his frown gave place to a fat chuckle. "I know what we'll do, Culpepper," he said. "We'll levy a fine of five pounds on anyone who enters Windsor chapel in spurs, and I'll let the boys collect the money and keep it themselves. That won't start a European war, and I think their keenness deserves it."

"And I warrant, Sir, they won't let a single culprit escape!" laughed Culpepper.

"So now we may all pass our time in rest and quietness until Easter," smiled the archbishop. And seeing that—thanks to the Queen—the matter was amicably settled, the archbishop made his adieux, remembering to send his loving duty to his little Grace at Havering. "Though I make no doubt he will prefer the toys!" he added, with charming diffidence.

"Of course he will!" laughed Henry. "But I'll charge Mary with your message." He turned away as if to make a tour of inspection of his vines and newly-planted mulberry trees; and suddenly Anne had a sense of being excluded from everything. They were all going about their various occupations while she—whose life had been so full of every-day concerns and of people depending upon her—seemed no longer to matter to anyone. She had hoped to be able to show some kindness to her neglected step-daughters; but almost before she had got to know them they would be gone. Gone to live under the care of this Mistress Ashley she had heard so much about, with the delicate, motherless boy who was in a sense her own son. The only son, perhaps, that she would ever be given. This new thought was fraught with such dismay that she caught in panic at her husband's finely-slashed sleeve as he passed. "Please, Henry——" she entreated, to detain him.

He swung round in surprise. It was the first time she had asked for anything—the first time since their wedding night that she had called him informally by his name. And never before had he—or any of them—seen her look like that, with her eyes wide and shining and her eager mouth. "What is it, my dear?" he asked involuntarily.

Her skin was flushed softly with embarrassment, her voice so low and hesitant that the harshness he hated in her accent was blurred. "Do you think—I could go and see Edward too?"

"But of course!" Henry's face became a florid disc of pleased surprise, and Cranmer, noting how much better that touch of flattering hesitancy pleased him than her usual forthright calm, wished she would always speak to him like that.

"You don't think Mary will mind?" she asked.

Henry soon disposed of such a scruple. A daughter's whims were of about as much consequence to him as thistle-down floating across the grassy rides of Windsor when he was hunting. "Mind? Why ever should she?" he scoffed. "It'll be company for her. The girl's too much alone, or closeted with that infernal confessor of hers." He looked at Anne quite attentively and added "I forgot you hadn't seen Edward." He loved showing off his son. And because— like most parvenus—he prided himself on doing the right thing socially, he was relieved that she hadn't resented his lapse. "Come to think about it, I'll take you myself," he offered magnanimously.

"Thank you," said Anne simply. She couldn't explain that besides wanting to go for her own sake she wanted to hold the boy in her arms for poor Jane, who had had to leave him so soon. Sleeping as she did in the late queen's bedroom, she often thought of the joy and anguish that must so fleetingly have filled its comfortable, sunny-latticed loveliness.

"If this weather holds it should be a pleasant ride," predicted Henry. "We'll get to bed early and Culpepper can order the horses to be ferried across soon after daybreak." He glanced at a sundial on the wall and saw that it was past noon. "Let's go in now," he added, grape vines and mulberries forgotten. "I'm famished."

"So am I," agreed Anne.

They went bustling up the garden path together, two gorgeous figures in cloth of gold and blue velvet, followed by the foreign maids-of-honour and a whispering coterie of courtiers. And as they went they appeared to be discussing the best position for a new herb garden.

Archbishop and ambassador stared after them.

"Such heavy, tasteless clothes are enough to make those girls look frightful even if they were *belles comme des anges*," summed up Marillac, before mincing elegantly down the steps to the Duchess of Northumberland's waiting barge. "But your new Queen's no fool!"

"No," agreed Cranmer, sending a servant to hail his own.

Anne had certainly seized her opportunity of pleasing the King; but he was not so sure that expediency had had anything to do with it. She was such an unusual woman—so incalculably uncomplicated. Perhaps after all she had begged to see Edward quite simply because she wanted to—because she, too, was what that gossiping Frenchman had called a born mother. And if so, well——She was healthy and kind and comfortingly sane . . . while that poor, pampered child at Havering was by all accounts disturbingly delicate. . . . He was still thinking of her when the familiar roofs of Lambeth began to show between the bare trees on the

Surrey bank. And of Henry, who had done nothing but complain about her since she came, and who was already flattering the Howard girl into becoming his mistress. And, stepping ashore at his fine episcopal palace, Cranmer—confirmed Erastian as he was—caught himself thinking what a fool Henry was!

CHAPTER XII

At Havering-atte-Bower Anne was able to take stock of the other four Tudors. "At last there are just the five of us together," she thought, looking round her little step-son's over-heated nursery. And in spite of her original reluctance to become one of them and all that she had suffered in the process, the feeling gave her an odd sense of satisfaction. But then she was essentially a family sort of person.

The ride from Greenwich had been a pleasant, informal jaunt with only a handful of followers. The sunny weather had held, the roads were in good condition and young Elizabeth's excitement had been a joy to behold. Realizing how seldom Nan Bullen's child could have been invited to accompany her father on such an expedition, Anne remembered with gratitude the archibishop's kindly thought for her loneliness. "How well she rides!" she had exclaimed involuntarily, watching the tall, straight-backed seven-year-old race across a stretch of common land with the wind in her crisp, red-gold hair. And Henry had looked pleased and had said complacently, "Yes, she has my hands."

Though less spectacular, Anne herself was no indifferent horsewoman; and it had increased her pleasure to find there was at least one thing she could do as well as these talented new relations of hers. She had been particularly interested, too, in the flat country north of the Thames because it reminded her of home. And, finding that she could talk intelligently about beasts and crops and buildings, Henry had enjoyed assuming the rôle of guide. Anne couldn't have had a better; for there was a likeable pride in him, and a robust grasp of the common man's conditions, when he talked about his villages and towns. And—best of all—almost throughout the journey he had been affable with his daughters.

Elizabeth, sunning herself in this rare intimacy of family life, was all high spirits and self-importance. It was good to see her discard for once the unnatural assumption of grown-up discretion with which she had learned to parry the dangers of her pitiful youth, and to give rein to an unspoiled interest in the exciting-looking parcels of toys piled on a pack-horse for her brother. "Which do you think he will like best—the spotted hobby horse or the dragon that belches fire or the lovely red unicorn?" she had kept asking of all and sundry. Tom Culpepper had teased her by pretending that the bundles were full of the household stuffs her nurse, Mrs. Ashley, was always writing for; and the King had laughed and reminded her that they were bringing Edward a new stepmother as well as toys. Whereat the child, all unconscious of the travesty of their marriage, had paid poor humble Anne an unwitting compliment. "He won't be able to help liking her best of all, will he, Sir?" she had said, in the fearless way she had of talking to her neglectful father.

But Mary's conscience was always making her fight down envy of people who drew to themselves quick liking. "He doesn't take to strangers as a rule," she had warned them, with a prim puckering of her mouth. And Anne had hoped that she wasn't going to spoil everything by being jealous.

But only as they had neared Havering had the shared pleasantness of the morning been spoiled, and that by reason of Henry's growing uneasiness. He had hurried them all on, getting himself and his horse into a sweat lest his son should have caught another of his frequent chills. When Mary had lagged behind, complaining that the jolting made her head ache, he had barked at her impatiently. And Anne—torn between a conscientious instinct to keep her company and the natural desire to prove her horsemanship—had felt relieved when Culpepper, seizing an opportunity to prick his horse close to hers, had explained in a hurried undertone that his master always behaved so and that there was usually no cause for anxiety.

Anne had heard a lot about Havering-atte-Bower, the sequestered Essex mansion where the royal children were brought up. She had made it her business to talk with Lady Margaret Bryan, who had charge of them, because she felt—

both as queen and woman—that it was one of the places of which she should take an active interest. She had carefully verified Katherine Howard's words about Elizabeth's shameful need of clothing. She knew also all about the care with which the little prince's food, and even his clothes, were tested for poison; and how none but members of the household could come near him without a signed permit from the King. As she dismounted in the courtyard her practical glance took in the double guard at the gatehouse and the gloom of encroaching woods which would, it was hoped, ward off any tainted breath of town-bred pestilence. Following Henry into the house, she noted the splendid proportions of the room in which the heir of England played —the expensive toys, the carefully-closed windows, the tapestries thick enough to exclude every possibility of draught. And how everything—from the vigilance of picked servants to the ridiculous way her companions began to tip-toe anxiously from room to room—gave the impression of a gilded cage. The great Tudor had lavished everything on his only son. But the place appalled Anne. Should she bear him children, she would want them brought up in the fresh air and sunshine. She had imbibed enough austerity from her own parents to believe in untrammelled growth, and she had enough common sense to realize that half the perils that beset childhood come from *within* the home. Spoiling, for instance, and half-formulated fears. And this house was full of both. It was clear to see that Henry's fear of infection had communicated itself to everyone who was forced by his orders to take dozens of petty precautions on the prince's account and to carry out, day after day, all that mediaeval ritual about testing dishes and counting how many times the child sneezed.

But this time it seemed that his fond forebodings were not without foundation, for the spacious playroom was deserted and the royal visitors were greeted by the thin, protesting wail of a child in pain; and when a flustered major-domo conducted them to the boy's bedroom they found Edward muffled to the eyes in his heavily carved, hooded cradle before a blazing fire. To Anne, coming in glowing from her ride, the room seemed unbearably stuffy; to add to which a bevy of women were bending over him stifling him with well-meant attention. One shook a toy set of jester's bells before his face, so jangling his nerves that his peevish crying turned into hysterical screams. Another rocked the cradle with a ceaseless, maddening motion of her foot; while two elegant young girls sat on the floor offering him sweet-meats from an assortment of expensive comfit dishes. As the King strode into the room they sprang up and scattered, leaving a tall, anxious-faced woman to face his inauspicious arrival. By the way Elizabeth ran to her, Anne guessed her to be the Mrs. Ashley of whom the child so often spoke.

"How long has he been crying like this?" Mary demanded, going straight to the cradle with that air of bridling importance which even the most self-effacing of women can assume in a sick room.

"Since the dial stood at noon, Madame," replied Kate Ashley, who—although on the defensive—was clearly relieved to see her. "Nothing seems to sooth him. We have given him the tansy syrup milady Bryan recommended and the cooks have been making his favourite almond paste all morning."

"Which rather explains things!" thought Anne, glancing with horror at the rich contents of the abandoned comfit dishes.

"Where is Margaret Bryan? And that ass, Bull? Why isn't he in attendance?" bellowed Henry, above the yelling of his son. But this only caused the four younger women to sink deeper and more helplessly into their skirts, for had not Lady Margaret applied for permission to visit a sick relative? And was not Dr. Bull himself abed with a quinsy? And wasn't poor Mother Ashley, stumbling through these explanations, already in a frenzy lest he should have given the infection of it to her precious poppet?

"Then have a man ride hell for leather for another doctor out of Barking and send all these useless women away!" shouted Henry, keeping as far from the cradle as possible because—hero of the tilt-yard as he had been in his youth—

the bare mention of infection could make an arrant coward of him. "A fine thing," he went on blustering to his new wife, "to keep a resident physician and a room full of women who are supposed to understand their job, and when I come to see my son he roars too lustily to notice me and no one can sooth him!"

His complaint was not without reason, for Mrs. Ashley seemed to have come to the end of her resources and the royal nursemaids had been thankful to scuttle out before his wrath, like rudderless ships careering in a gale.

And now, except for the middle-aged nurse and young Culpepper, the five Tudors were alone.

Standing unobserved in the shadow of Kate Ashley's discreetly-curtained bed, Anne of Cleves had time to look at each of her new English relatives in turn. Now was a good time to observe them—while they were completely unself-conscious and the attention of three of them was centred on the youngest. Henry—who hated illness—straddling the hearth, utterly useless. Mary, suddenly come into her own, lifting her little brother tenderly from his embroidered coverlets. The child Elizabeth, forgetful for once of the need to dramatize her own burgeoning ego, watching in an agony of genuine concern. And Edward himself, an adorable three-year-old, pleasantly curved but too transparent of skin, beating at poor Mary's prim spinster bosom with tight-clenched fists and screaming until his face was like a round, red moon. Instinctively, Anne noticed that he was too big to be coddled in a cradle and that he was sweating profusely from the stuffiness of the room. But—although she had ridden many miles specially to see him—she was scarcely thinking about him. She was looking at Mary. Seeing Mary for the first time—with understanding. Learning the story of her frustration, just as she had learned about Thomas Cranmer's the day before.

Mary Tudor's slight body looked over-burdened, holding the heavy boy in her arms. All her longing for her own adored, persecuted mother and for children of her own, found escape in the way she strained him to her poor, love-starved heart. Her thin, tightly-buttoned mouth was relaxed in tenderness; her short-sighted, Spanish-brown eyes were beautiful with devotion, the way they looked before the candle-lit altar in church. Seen like that, all her cold reserve was belied, all her waspish irritability excused. One remembered only what a mother she would make.

But such fervour was scarcely soothing to a welling, perspiring boy of three. And Anne, accustomed to dealing with children in humbler walks of life, foresaw exactly what would happen when his closely-cuddled cheek came into painful contact with the jewelled cross which was the sole ornament on his sister's dark velvet bodice. As she had expected, he stopped in mid-yell, outraged by the sudden scratching of his tender flesh, took one indignant gasp and held his breath. His limbs stiffened alarmingly and his face assumed the purple hue of the velvet against which he found himself squeezed. Poor Mary herself, already sallow from her hurried ride, went white as death.

"Oh, quick, Mrs. Ashley! What's the matter with him?" shrieked Elizabeth, instinctively turning to the only fount of succour she knew.

"It must be some sort of fit," declared that much harassed woman, reaching unceremoniously behind the King's broad back for a shovelful of wood ash to heat the warming-pan which was her very present help in time of trouble.

"Fetch that fool Bull out of his bed if he's dying!" shouted the King to Tom Culpepper.

In face of such concerted family panic, Anne decided that she had been a spectator long enough. Reluctantly withdrawing her leisurely mind from further fascinating discoveries about her elder step-daughter, she stopped her departing gentleman with a decided gesture. Heedless of the King's command, she told him to open a window instead; and so astonished was Tom that, after one hesitant glance in his master's direction, he obeyed. There was a tussle with a long-disused latch and suddenly the room was freshened by an unwonted inrush of sun-warmed air. Meanwhile Anne, noting Mrs. Ashley's formidable approach with the warming-pan, had forestalled her at Mary's side. "I am afraid he's too heavy for you," she said tactfully, holding out her arms for the breathless boy. In her panic, Mary yielded him up without resentment. And—to the horror of his watching family—Anne proceeded to turn the future King of England ignominiously onto his stomach and slap him smartly on the back. "Please, will someone pull back those heavy curtains?" she asked pleasantly, and carried him to the open window.

Not least surprised was Edward Tudor. Shocked by such unaccustomed treatment, he allowed himself to relax, gulped and lay limp but breathing. She cuddled him up then and after one final sob of self-pity he settled himself comfortably, staring up into her face with comical confusion. "New pwetty lady," he lisped gravely.

Because Mary had said that he didn't take to strangers, Anne forbore to kiss him. "Silly boy, what a fright you gave us all!" she scolded unsteadily. "Now stop crying and try to tell us what's the matter."

Her voice was low and bantering, as if they two understood each other, and Edward found her strong young arms reassuring. She didn't hold him as if he were made of glass or seem in the least afraid of dropping him. Neither did she fuss like the rest of them. She just sat down on a chair, made a wide, comfortable lap and took off his elaborate night-cap. For a long time Edward had been wanting to get that cap off, and the way her cool hands stroked the damp hair from his forehead was lovely. One didn't *want* to be cross any more. He leaned back wearily against her breast and continued to stare at her with blue, tear-drenched eyes. Evidently he approved of her; for after another whimper or two and a gusty hiccough he indicated without undue delicacy that the pain was in his belly.

"Stuffed with sweetmeats!" thought Anne, rubbing it gently. But she had more sense than to say so. Instead she tried her most persuasive smile on his nurse and begged for a bowl of warm water and a napkin to bathe his face.

"But, Madam, he'll catch his death of cold under that open window—and without his cap too!" protested Kate Ashley.

In a score of emergencies Anne had learned to rely on her

own judgement in such matters. "I don't think so. It's so mild to-day," she said; and although she was well aware that the woman was shocked at the idea of a queen knowing how to do such things, she began placidly freshening him up herself. Elizabeth brought his jewelled comb and Anne let her tidy his straight, fair hair. It was so much better for him than having half a dozen anxious underlings hovering over him. "Now you look fit to kiss your father," she declared, plumping the little fellow round on her knee to face his family.

Edward held out his arms and smiled enchantingly. And his great, red-headed sire came and kissed him so tenderly that Anne, looking down on the back of his closely-cropped head, felt a stab of pity for him.

"May he see his toys now?" begged Elizabeth, whose love for this one being smaller than herself was probably the only completely spontaneous, uncalculating emotion in a nature already beginning to be warped by her precarious bastard state.

Henry was as anxious to see him play with them as she; but he had been badly shaken. "Ask your step-mother," he said, hiding behind the usual domestic formula of a domineering man who finds himself at a disadvantage in a sick-room.

"Just one, Elizabeth," decreed Anne. "The nicest you can find—for him to cuddle while he goes to sleep. You see," she added at sight of their disappointed faces, "he's quite worn out with all that—that——" Not being certain of the exact significance of the English verb 'to yell' she substituted the euphemism 'weeping.'

Elizabeth, who adored bright colours, danced away to select the lovely red unicorn. But she stopped short with the creature in her hands and—with a politic sense unsuited to her years—offered it soberly to her father.

Henry glanced uneasily at Anne. He was beginning to have a glimmering idea that she wasn't as slow-witted as he had supposed, and that behind that meek mask of hers she was often criticizing him. "Give it him yourself," he told the child, with the rough awkwardness of a man unaccustomed to making even small sacrifices; and went back with pompous virtuousness to his favourite stance before the hearth.

The unicorn was a vast success and Edward beamed impartially on them all. But soon his sandy lashes were drooping and a healthy flush was warming his cheeks. Anne wished she could come often and play with the two children, banishing that shrewd look from Elizabeth's pointed face and the sickly petulance from Edward's and bringing a more careless happiness into their lives. She began to sing softly and tunelessly under her breath. Some nonsensical nursery rhyme in her native tongue. She had forgotten the grown-ups. She might have been back in Cleves, soothing Dorothea's sick baby. And presently her little step-son fell asleep on her lap, his round head tucked into the soft hollow of her neck and his father's gift clutched in his arms.

She looked up to find Henry watching her. He was thinking how much her placid ways resembled his gentle Jane's —except, of course, that Anne was a hundred times more capable. He could almost imagine that it was the boy's own mother who held him and—had Anne but known it—her neck was safe on her shoulders from that moment. But the soft, sentimental expression on his face embarrassed her. So she beckoned him to her side as if he were any ordinary husband and had to laugh at the docile way he came, stepping with exaggerated caution from rug to rug for fear of waking the boy and undoing all her labours. Quite unwittingly, to cover her lapse, she said the thing that never failed to please him. "He's ridiculously like you, isn't he?"

For the first time in a month of marriage, they were talking in intimate domestic whispers. "He has the Tudor colouring," he agreed, "but less pronounced than Elizabeth's. You see, my wife had honey-coloured hair like yours." The woman who had given him an heir would always be 'my wife' to Henry. He had never been violently in love with her, but she had earned her status and it satisfied his sense of fitness to put her on a different plane from the rest.

But Anne was suddenly too conscience stricken to notice

—much less to feel slighted. "My hair isn't really honey-coloured. It's dark, like my eyes," she confessed. She had always wanted to tell him the truth; and now, with his son warm in her arms, somehow she was no longer afraid to.

Mary looked up sharply and Elizabeth's eyes were wide with astonishment.

"Show me," he ordered curtly.

With her free hand Anne fumbled at her head-dress until the hated yellow wig was on the floor and her own warm, brown tresses about her shoulders. Her cheeks burned with shame. Why had she allowed herself to be persuaded into wearing the thing when such deception was so utterly alien to both her upbringing and her nature? How vulgar they must think her! "It wasn't just silly vanity," she stammered; and was touched to the heart when Mary, who would have shrunk from doing such a thing, came and stood by her defensively and said, "How could it have been when your own hair is so much more beautiful? I only wish mine were half as thick!"

Henry himself stood blinking at the becoming revelation. "As Mary says, I don't see why . . ."

"I didn't want to deceive your Grace," explained Anne desperately. "But you took me unawares at Rochester—when one of the English ladies you sent, had brought me a wig. She said you would be disappointed—because you usually liked—because the late queen was fair."

Henry's arched brows came down in a prodigious frown. "Oh, she did, did she?" he said; and waited for the usual tale-bearing. But Anne sat mute. And finding, much to his surprise, that he was not going to be furnished with the lady's name, he couldn't resist making a guess at it. "Sounds to me like that poisonous Rochfort woman!" he said, with a malicious grin for her ingenuity.

Anne neither confirmed nor denied his guess. She tried never to think of that unfortunate meeting—the one meeting when they might have started differently—before he had looked into Katherine Howard's face and been caught in the sweet spell of her youth, "I'm afraid it never suited me," she murmured ruefully.

"Neither do those stiff, elaborate dresses of yours," he told her. "You would have done better to take her advice about that."

Anne recognized in his criticism the same personal resentment which had tinged his laughter when he had poked fun at the grandeur of the Dudley's barge. Evidently she had been doing the wrong thing again in trying to dress up to him. Involuntarily, she recalled a splendid peacock she used to watch at Greenwich as he strutted with gorgeous spread tail before his trim, neat hen. Probably that was the way all male creatures really thought things ought to be.

"I will ask Mary to help me," she said meekly, bending to retrieve her pearl-studded cap from the dangerous proximity of his heel and to hide a smile which brought that elusive dimple to her cheek. Was she, perhaps, beginning to understand this difficult husband of hers? And, in getting amusement from his foibles, to find that he wasn't quite so formidable as he seemed? At any rate, it had been stupid of her not to appreciate sooner the similarity between Henry and the peacock and to choose her clothes accordingly. By the time he began to fidget about his dinner she had regained sufficient confidence to try her hand at humouring him. "Why not go and eat now," she suggested, "and let the child have his sleep out?"

"His little Grace can go back in his cot, Madam—away from the draught," suggested his nurse pointedly.

Anne was hungry too; but there was Kate Ashley to humour as well, and she realized that if any good was to come of this visit, she must establish friendly relations with the woman. "I think I will have a dish of well-seasoned capon and a draught of Malmsey sent to me here if I may, Henry, so as not to disturb him," she said. And—surprisingly enough—he backed her up tacitly about the open window. Already halfway to the door, he collected up his daughters and Culpepper with a nod. Obviously, he was glad enough to quit the hushed room and get his knees under a laden table.

As soon as they were alone, Anne turned to Mrs. Ashley with that comfortable, receptive movement which invites confidences between women. "To tell you the truth, I wanted a chat with you," she admitted. Human nature was much the same, she found, whether in Cleves or Havering; and however ignorant she might be of book learning she was well versed in conciliating people. "I've been wondering all the time how you've managed to bring up a delicate, motherless baby to look so plump. What did you feed him on? And what sort of foster mother did you get for him at first?"

The flattered nurse was only too willing to tell her; and in the telling all sourness went from her thin, kindly face. Anne insisted upon her sitting down and drinking some of the wine brought for her own meal, and so free from haughtiness was she that—as Kate boasted afterwards—it was 'as good as a gossip with a friend.' She had never had so good a listener; and all the time Edward slept peacefully, breathing in the good fresh air. While Anne—by means of judicious prompting—was able to form a pretty clear picture of her step-children's lives. She appreciated the wisdom that kept them away from court; but perceived the flaw. While receiving the best possible mental instruction and—in the case of Edward—almost fanatical physical care, their characters were being moulded mainly by dependants. A flaw which Henry was probably aware of and which, in marrying her, he had done his best to remedy. What they needed was a woman of their own class to love without fear. She must do her best to help him. . . .

"I hope I've not talked too much, Madam," apologized Kate at last, seeing that the Queen was absorbed in some considerations of her own. "It's so wonderful having someone who understands all the difficulties—begging your Grace's pardon. Specially when one is stuck right away in the country away from all one's friends. . . ."

"That must be trying for you, Kate. But it's worth it, don't you think, to be so trusted?" said Anne, smiling down at the rosy boy asleep in her lap.

"Of course, Madam!" agreed the refreshed nurse fervently.

"I hear you have been very kind to the lady Elizabeth

too. She speaks of you so often that it is clear she loves you."

Kate's face suffused with pleasure. "Small wonder, poor lamb! I've let her have her will more than is good for her because she suffers so with her teeth all these years." The woman stopped abruptly, glancing nervously over her shoulder. Making a martyr of Elizabeth was dangerous; but it was clear where the woman's heart lay. "Perhaps," she ventured with a cautious glance at this latest step-mother, "things will be better for her—now?"

Anne put aside her plate. "Does she know—about her mother?" she asked, in a low voice.

"It is difficult to tell, Madam. I *think* she sometimes wonders why she doesn't have a lot of pretty things like her cousin, Lady Jane Grey, who sometimes comes to play with them."

Here was a problem most new step-mothers are spared. "Wouldn't it be kinder to—to tell her?" suggested Anne.

"The child resents it if her mother is mentioned."

"Surely that is very bad for her."

"She is still a child in some ways, Madam, but growing so secretive in others."

"Don't be hurt by it, Kate," advised Anne kindly. "I'm sure it's only her armour against life." Edward began to stir as the servants came to clear, and she put him into his nurse's arms. "You were worried, I believe, because the Lady Elizabeth has need of clothes?" she said, in a more business-like manner.

Kate looked abashed that she should know. "Chancellor Cromwell always scolded me so for bothering them. But believe me, Madam, I never wrote before I had need——"

Evidently the news of his downfall hadn't filtered through to Havering yet. "I don't think he will scold you any more," said Anne. "It was nightgowns, I heard someone say, that she is shortest of. I will see that she has some."

"Oh, Madam!" The gratitude in the woman's eyes was greater than could have been inspired by any gift to herself; but it was swiftly chased away by fear. "But—if I might make so bold as to warn your Grace—you won't bother the King about it? He hates to be reminded of—*her*."

Anne rose, thankful to ease her stiffened limbs. "No, I won't speak of it to the King," she promised. Did these people never realize, she wondered, what it felt like to be constantly reminded that one was successor to a beheaded wife? To know oneself undesired—to be far from the protection of one's own people—to lie awake wondering and fearing—to keep pushing away that picture of the wide arched, portcullised water-gate that led to Tower Green.— She sighed, gathered up her gloves and riding whip, and went with a sort of forlorn dignity to join her step-daughters.

Later on in the hall, while Henry and Elizabeth romped with Edward and his new toys, and the boy's midget jester and half a dozen dogs added to the din, Anne found herself standing beside Mary to watch the fun. The shyness of two reserved women who are beginning to like each other was upon them. Mary had that 'buttoned-up look,' as her younger sister called it, which made it so difficult for peeople to approach her; but Anne remembered how she had looked when she held her brother in her arms. "It was good of you to remind all those people at Greenwich that I was not acquainted with your customs when I kept the Steelyard merchants' purse," she said.

Mary smiled stiffly. "My mother must have gone through much the same annoyance with their boorishness when she first came," she replied. And the disdainful way she spoke seemed to include her vociferous relatives and their horseplay, and to make Anne realize for the first time that Mary herself was half a foreigner.

"As a matter of fact I didn't keep it," she explained. "I sent it the next morning to a lazar house. It must be so dreadful to be diseased and cut off from all the enjoyment of life !"

Mary looked at her admiringly, wondering perhaps what enjoyment she could find in her present unenviable position. "I knew you couldn't be mean with a mouth like that," she said, trying not to envy her such health and zest for living. Presently she went and sat in a chair and passed a hand over her eyes so that Anne enquired anxiously if she were ill.

"It's only one of her headaches," vouchsafed Elizabeth,

with youthful hardness. Prettily flushed and tired of play, she had come to join them. Her manner implied that Mary's headaches occurred too frequently to be anything but a bore. But Anne was all concern at once.

Mary begged her rather irritably not to fuss because it only annoyed her father. "It was riding so fast, I think—and the worry of Edward holding his breath like that." She raised her head and peered anxiously across the hall. "Look, he's made poor Dr. Bull get up from his bed and is telling him all the symptoms. I do hope Edward hasn't caught the quinsy!"

They all three watched in silence for a minute or two while the King and the pallid looking doctor and Kate Ashley went into grave consultation over the boy. Through a hustle of servants beginning to clear up the chaos of toys they could see Dr. Bull tapping Edward's chest and making him stick out his tongue.

"They seem to think now that his Grace may have been suffering from excess of bile this morning," whispered a passing nursemaid, hurrying towards the serving screens to fetch something the doctor had called for.

Anne felt Elizabeth pulling at her arm. "What do you suppose was *really* the matter with him, Madam?" she asked, in that terribly penetrating young voice of hers.

Anne looked down into the shrewd green eyes that saw through everything. She couldn't help laughing. After a swift glance to make sure her husband's back was still turned, she laid a finger to her lips and—catching Mary's eye to include her in the confidence—whispered "Mostly temper!"

CHAPTER XIII

After her honeymoon was over Anne often longed to go back
to the informal life at Hampton Court. But affairs of state
made it necessary for Henry to stay at Greenwich. Since
their visit to Havering she had seen less of him than ever.
He seldom slept with her now; but, on the other hand, he
was never rude. And at times, she thought, he seemed
almost afraid of her.

After supper, he would sit awhile watching her covertly,
as if he were planning something and wondering what her
reactions would be. Once or twice she even felt he was on
the verge of discussing some important matter with her quite
amicably. But for the most part he was away at Westminster,
meeting his Parliament she supposed, or shut up in his
private work room with Cranmer. Wriothesley, his secretary, came and went with an air of importance. Worried-
looking counsellors hung about the ante-rooms. And by the
way they all stopped talking whenever she appeared, Anne
felt sure that whatever was going on concerned herself. She
was filled with unhappy foreboding, but had no means of
finding out anything definite because Olsiliger had gone
back to Cleves. And whereas she had begun to feel one of the
family, she now found herself very much alone because Elizabeth had remained at Havering and much of Mary's time
was taken up by the attentions of her unwelcome suitor,
Philip of Bavaria. And whenever Henry *did* break away from
these seemingly endless and mysterious discussions, he was
always hunting with the Duke of Norfolk or supping with
his pretty niece.

In spite of her smouldering resentment Anne found life
much easier without him; but she hated it when the English
ladies of her household made a point of coming early to her
room and staring at her husband's undented pillow and asking impertinent questions. She knew that they gossiped

about her. Once Lady Rochfort, who was related by marriage to the Howards, asked with an exaggerated air of sympathy whether she had 'acquainted old Mother Lowe of the King's neglect.' They were at one of the Dudley's popular river fêtes at the time, and Jane Rochfort took care that her spiteful words should carry across the water to their hosts in the Northumberland barge. Anne had seen the smiles begin to spread on their faces and had answered a little louder still, so that their final sniggers should be for Henry. "If it eases your ladyship's curiosity, I have not," she had said, in her carefully enunciated English, "since, truth to tell, I receive quite as much of his Majesty's attention as I wish."

She had been so angry with the woman that she had to say it, straight out of her wounded pride. And it was not until Dorothea spoke anxiously of the matter that she began to wonder what the consequences would be should any of them repeat her words to Henry. She tried to recollect how many of her enemies had been in the other barge. It was a dreadful thing to Anne to realize that she *had* enemies. And so beset and bewildered was she by all this mysterious intrigue that she began to suspect Jane Rochfort of having angered her in public on purpose to make her say something indiscreet.

But however true her scornful words, Henry's neglect left Anne with long, empty days. And she, of all people, was ill-equipped to endure inactivity. When her loneliness and anxiety became more than she could bear she asked Dr. Kaye, her almoner, to take her to the Steelyard—ostensibly to encourage the crafts of her countrymen—but in reality to see Holbein. She had heard that he was painting Hans of Antwerp, the goldsmith, while he made a christening cup the King had ordered for Catalina Brandon's baby; and it seemed natural enough to everyone that the Queen should linger to watch two such famous men at work. So there— amongst exquisitely wrought sword handles and crucifixes and goblets—Anne managed to tell him hurriedly about her predicament. "You know the world, and you're the only person whose advice I can trust now Olsiliger's gone," she pleaded, lest he should imagine that she was trying to blow upon the smouldering embers of their relinquished love. "If only I could see you and talk to you sometimes!"

But he couldn't even promise that. "As you know, I am out of favour these days," he reminded her gently.

Anne picked up a massive shoulder chain and seemed to examine the workmanship. It was fashioned from a series of interlocking 'esses' in a design which was all the rage at Court. But it might just as well have been made of peascods. "Because you made me beautiful," she whispered back, with compunction.

"Because a man who has routed for shoddy charms can no longer perceive your kind of beauty, Anna."

"You used not to talk about him like that."

"I had come in contact with only one side of him. The widely informed amateur—the generous patron. His sex life didn't concern me—then."

His words—half regretful and half contemptuous—corroborated what Cranmer had said about the different faces of the King's character. "Since everybody seems to agree that he can be generous, I will ask him to have you back at Court," offered Anne, who hated asking him for anything. But Holbein began mixing some pigments with concentrated fury. "Do you suppose I should enjoy seeing the way he treats you?" he muttered.

His caring like that was oil to her wounded self-esteem. Her glance passed like a caress over the worn velvet of his favourite painting coat, and the practical part of her that was good at adding up accounts began to wonder if he had enough money. She handed the chain to a hovering apprentice and in order to get rid of him asked him to take it outside and show it to her ladies. "Without all the commissions at Court——" she began anxiously.

But the great painter only laughed. "Ever since I did my first portrait in this country for Sir Thomas More—God rest his lovely soul!—I've had more work than I want," he assured her. "And surely you know by now that however much I earned I should never have a groat?" Under cover of bending to select a finer brush from one of the little ledges at the side of his easel, he turned to smile at her. "So don't worry about me, liebchen, even if you hear that Horenbout or even that woman painter, Livina Teerlinc, has been commissoned to paint this new Howard hussy."

Anne hadn't even heard that Henry wanted a portrait of her. "So everybody in the City knows about her too?" she exclaimed, through stiff lips. She looked sharply from the goldsmith's absorbed face to the long window that lighted him at his work, and her soft brown eyes held a hunted expression reminiscent of one of the King's stags before the kill. A sharp squall of rain had whipped the grey Thames into angry little wavelets and made the cobbles on the quay glisten beneath an unnatural, stormy light. From where she stood she could see sweating labourers bearing crates of merchandise from the dark cavern of an open hold to the tall warehouses that shut out the busy streets and were only dominated by the spire of St. Paul's. A Flemish ship with furled sails was being unladen in the Pool and some of her crew were lounging against her bulwarks. The arrival of the Queen's party must have been a Godsend to their tedium. But one man spat expertly in the direction of the royal barge moored alongside with its impressive standards; and Anne imagined that he spat at the failure of the alliance they portrayed. She heard their outbursts of coarse laughter and wondered if they were laughing about her. About the unwanted bride. The bride, who, two or three months ago, was supposed to be making such a brilliant match. Some of these men might even have seen her set forth from Cleves with so many grand new clothes and so much pother. Suppose they too had heard rumours of a rival—already? They would carry back the story of her degradation to all the lowland ports and a dozen busybodies would ride hot-spurred with it to Cleves. How anxious and disappointed her brother would be! Half-formed fears for her future were blotted out by present shame. Staring out across that rain-swept London wharf, Anne suffered all the unmerited humiliation of a woman scorned. But Guligh, her devoted man-servant from Düren, was having a closed litter brought to the goldsmith's door so that she might not wet her feet on the way to the landing steps. She must pull herself together and go. And, going, she must look serene.

As a parting gift Holbein presented her with one of the new ostrich feather fans with ivory panels of his own design; and as he did so she felt his fingers, warm and strong, close momentarily about her own. She heard his comforting voice saying, "This infatuation of his can't last, Anna. What has this girl with her baby face to pit against *you*? *Au fond*, he's a man who wants more than that. . . . Beat these alluring English women at their own game, my Anna. Let yourself laugh and dance. Get rid of that accent that irritates him . . . learn all you can. . . ." He turned back to his easel as Mother Lowe appeared like an anxious hen in the doorway. "God knows it's the last advice I *want* to give you!" he complained, grinding a stump of crayon to powder beneath his heel. "But you've got to be happy somehow. I can't bear to see you look like this. . . ."

In her anguish at parting from him Anne's heart was deaf even to the Flemish seamen's cheers, and the fact that she had been mistaken about their feelings scarcely comforted her. Out of habitual graciousness she managed to smile at them and to thank her hosts. And then—somehow—she was on the water, being rowed home to Greenwich. Home to her magnificent husband—when all the homeliness she knew in this perplexing country was with that kind, unconventional man in the worn velvet coat. The rain drops spattered down so smartly that they drilled little white holes all over the grey expanse of water, and Anne thought, "My life is like the river. A little while ago it was smooth and sunny. And now it is all overcast and pricked with annoyances and pain."

Her women were chattering excitedly about their visit to the Steelyard. Most of them were either too stupid or too lazy to have picked up more than a word or two of English in all the weeks they had been in the country, and loosening their tongues for an hour among men who spoke their own language had been almost as good as going home. But during all the trivial conversation of the journey Anne held Holbein's advice in mind. "Learn all you can," he had said.

Hard words—to a queen. Particularly to one who had already tried so hard—and failed. But by the way they were torn from him, she knew he must feel them necessary to her safety. "And how can any stumbling drudgery of mine," she asked herself, "compare with the way he must have worked?"

She sat apart under the awning and let her thoughts close tenderly round him. The boy Hans, full of the exploits of Christopher Columbus or crime stories about the Borgias, wearing his woollen hose shiny on the benches of some Augsburg school; and, later on when it was time to leave, painting a signboard for his master so that he might go on learning the Latin in which he now answered letters from famous people all over Europe. Holbein the apprentice, helping his father to illuminate manuscripts and patiently acquiring the incredibly fine art of limning for woodcuts. Holbein the travelled man, still learning to illustrate books and embellish altars and paint people until he could cover walls with such splendid perspective that his figures seemed to come alive. And then picking up a playing card and making a miniature so small that a man might wear it on his heart! "Surely," thought Anne, "no other man has ever worked so hard or made himself so versatile! And if he, a world-famous painter, is not too proud to go on acquiring knowledge in his early forties, why can't I, a dullard, begin to educate myself at twenty-five?"

Back in the palace, she waylaid Cranmer coming from the King's work closet and asked him to help her about books. He was, she felt, uncommonly eager to do so. Feeling that French and Latin, begun at her age, would probably prove beyond her powers, her persuaded her to confine herself to striving after fluency in the one language she already spoke quite passably. He read aloud to her to improve her accent, and for the first time Anne began to perceive the beauty of the thing she laboured at. He lent her Tyndale's translation of one of the simpler books of Erasmus and the beginnings of his own liturgy; and, very astutely, insisted upon her reading her husband's treatise on the Seven Sacraments. Anne thought it all very dull and stodgy; but Mary pointed out that it was her lack of theological training that was at fault and helped her through the harder parts, trying to hide from her the humiliating fact that Elizabeth could already read it in French and Latin.

Patiently, doggedly, Anne worked, setting so many hours a day aside for study. Hours when most people believed her to be playing cards with her ladies or trying on new dresses. Sometimes, when her head ached with tasks at which she was naturally lazy, she would ask herself why she was doing all this. She knew now that Henry wanted his freedom, and it wasn't as if she wanted to live with him. But there were other things driving her. Fear, perhaps. And duty to her brother. And more than either, dislike of failing to perform anything she had undertaken.

She knew that had she had good tutors as a child she would have been as well informed as the next woman. Not brilliant, of course, like the Tudors. But she was both intelligent and observant. All that she had lacked was opportunity, stuck away all her life in one monotonous country where book learning for woman was counted temptation, and accomplishments to pass the idle hours in sin.

In the matter of the arts Anne relied upon her own judgement. She had real feeling for line and colour, coupled with some acquaintance with the Flemish school; and these advantages had been fostered recently by friendship with a master. One of her chief pleasures was studying the good collections of pictures in the royal palaces and in the great houses where she visited. But knowing herself to be hopelessly unmusical and having observed how her husband winced at a wrong note, she declined the offer of Master Paston, the princesses' music master, to teach her to play upon the virginals. No matter how frequently the Duchess of Norfolk or Lady Rochfort remarked that *in this country* such accomplishments were considered indispensable to a woman of breeding, she remained adamant. After hearing her younger step-daughter practising at Havering, she felt sure that a smattering of them would only make her look ridiculous against a background of family proficiency.

Her dancing gradually improved. Neither she nor her

instructors had any illusions about her ever being able to romp like thistledown through a gavotte or hold the company breathless in a stately pavane; but before long the rhythm falling sweetly from voils and hautboys in the minstrels' gallery began to guide her unaccustomed feet through the maze of steps, and the steps themselves to form a gracious pattern. The very fact that she had been brought up to consider dancing an abandoned pleasure would always flavour it with the spice of excitement for Anne. Where other women danced with boredom, she brought to each new measure a smiling zest which her partners found flattering. And there were plenty of men at Court who, whichever party they belonged to, secretly admired her spirit. Suffolk and Marillac were particularly punctilious about asking her to dance—the one because he was her husband's brother-in-law and the other because he liked her. And to spare her embarrassment Culpepper practised over all the new French dances with her in her own apartments.

Anne often wondered whether Henry had appointed this likeable young man to her household because he wanted him to see less of Katherine or whether Tom himself had asked for the appointment because he couldn't bear to see them together. "Why are you so kind to me, Tom?" she asked, after trying his patience even more than usual in an intricate measure. "Particularly when you ought really to be on the other side."

They were in a room overlooking her new herb garden. The candles had not yet been lit and he stood before her with the gold of an April sunset touching his fair hair and lacing his white doublet with the diamond pattern of the leaded casements. "What side, Madam?" he asked cautiously. In the throes of a fourth domestic Tudor crisis when even skilled diplomats skimmed over realities it was the only way to meet her embarrassing refusal to beat about the bush.

Anne sank rather breathlessly onto a brocaded pallet and looked him up and down apprisingly. She was thinking how dangerously attractive he was in the first strength of his manhood, and what an ideal couple he and Katherine would make, and what a shameful pity it was that Henry should want her too. There was an uneasy elation about the girl these days that ill became her and and—remembering how she had seen the cousins standing together in the gallery at Rochester —Anne guessed how grievously Culpepper must feel her growing response to the King's blandishments. "Well, you are related to the Howards, aren't you?" she pointed out lightly.

"Only by marriage, Madam." He placed a refreshing drink and the fan Holbein had given her within reach and, preparing to depart, looked round to see if there was anything else he could do for her comfort. "May I send someone to light the candles for you? And shall I call Mistress Dorothea?"

In all walks of life, Henry chose his servants well. Tom Culpepper was the perfect squire, combining a charming deference with unobtrusive efficiency. But he had been far too glumly efficient these last few days. He didn't go round chaffing people and challenging other exuberant young gallants to exhausting games. Anne sensed that he was at breaking point; and that only talking to somebody about it could ease that strained expression which was beginning to harden his good looks. She was only a year or two older than he; but now that he was of her household she felt responsible for his well-being and happiness. And she, too, endured strain and needed some outlet. . . . "And this girl Katherine——" she prompted.

"Her mother was Jocunda Culpepper——"

"What a pretty name!" murmured Anne politely.

"So she is my kinswoman," he explained carefully.

"And nothing more, Tom?" To her practical mind it seemed so absurd that they shouldn't speak of this thing— they two who, each in a different way, must suffer for this fresh love outburst of Henry's.

But Culpepper's proud young reserve was still unbroken. And after all, was she not the last person to whom he could speak of the King's infidelities? He bowed himself from her presence and it was not until he was at the door that some sort of response was wrung from him. And because he cared

164

so much it came haltingly. "She is also your Grace's maid-of-honour——"

"Only by title," sighed Anne. "She seldom sups or sleeps here—now."

He winced, but went on as if he hadn't heard her. "And if she isn't always—very circumspect—I pray your Grace to remember that her mother died when she was a child."

Anne had to check herself from harsh laughter. The word 'circumspect' seemed so inadequate when they both knew her to be supping at Durham House with Henry. But she sat there with her new fan in her lap, looking gravely across the room at him. She saw that his eyes were dark pits of anxiety above the modish white velvet and guessed that he hadn't been sleeping. "I am glad you told me. And whatever happens—I will try to remember," she promised.

Culpepper went out and shut the door quietly—almost reverently. He felt oddly comforted. By the window of the deserted ante-room he stood for a minute looking down on the orderly pattern of her small, healing herbs. It reminded him of a less formal garden where Katherine had sometimes come to play with him when they were children. Of late, his world had been largely made up of the flatteries handed to one near the person of a king, of royal kindnesses that could be withdrawn at a whim, and the worthless promises of self-seekers. But there were still people who meant what they said. Dependable people like those he had loved at home. In that simpler world where his father had taught him old-fashioned virtues and his mother had put up preserves with her own pretty hands. Where every April the fruit trees were a froth of pink and white. At Holingbourne Manor, in Kent.

CHAPTER XIV

Anne knew by now that Henry would give anything to get rid of her. Time-servers avoided her. Even her well-wishers walked warily. Everyone at court who had watched the break-up of the King's first two marriages knew that she touched tragedy. But she warded it off by good temper and good sense. There was a comfortable sanity about her which rendered her immune from drama and made even the statesmen who were planning her downfall look faintly ridiculous.

Perhaps it was because she never paraded her suffering, and was intensely interested in the lives of other people. Not being in the habit of exaggerating the importance of her own feelings, she managed to keep a sense of balance. Friendly contacts and the everyday pleasures of life would always be warmly lighted feasts for Anne. There were letters from home, and good horses to ride and masques with lovely music and costumes to attend. She never tired of watching London street scenes or the ever-changing life and colour of the river, and every now and then her world was ruffled by small excitements such as the Duchess of Northumberland's latest extravagance or a boat over-turning in the dangerous maelstrom between the wide piers of London Bridge. And always, of course, there was the drudgery of her books. And so the days slipped by, devisedly too full to wait upon tragedy. And at evensong in the King's private chapel, listening to sonorous Latin chants she couldn't understand, she would thank God simply that the first winter of her exile was over and that the pangs of homesickness were growing more bearable.

And now it was nearly May and the springtime beauty of her adopted country was beginning to catch at her heart. The skies were no longer grey nor the roads quagmires. It was as if everything, from the great English oaks to the wayside flowers, had been washed in dew and painted afresh. Little hawthorn bushes hung red and white veils about the park and the delirious scent of them drifted in all the palace windows. And she was no longer alone, for Henry had allowed her to invite Elizabeth to Greenwich for the May celebrations and Mary's Bavarian suitor had gone back unbetrothed.

"What do you English people *do* on May day?" Anne asked, wondering why all her servants were too excited to work.

She and her two step-daughters were sitting in the sunny south gallery desultorily looking through her dower chests which she had had brought out for their entertainment. Dorothea was spreading out all the ugliest garments for Mary Tudor's inspection, and a little group of sewing maids by a far window were altering some of them in accordance with her suggestions. Elizabeth, enchanted at being allowed to finger so much finery, was gathering notions for the still more elaborate wardrobe she meant to have when she was grown up. "We have revels, Madam," she vouchsafed, hugging the nightgowns Anne had just finished embroidering for her.

But that was a word seldom to be found in dull theological books. "Revels—what are they?" Anne enquired, selecting a strand of gay embroidery silk. "I don't think we ever had any in Cleves."

"Well, for one thing, there is a sort of set dance," Elizabeth explained a trifle absently, her envious gaze lingering on a length of green damask stitched with seed pearls. "With everybody dressed up as Robin Hood and Maid Marion and the Devil——"

"Not *another* dance?" protested Anne, who had scarcely mastered her latest lesson from Culpepper.

Mary looked up from a distressingly bundley Flemish kirtle. "*We* don't have to do them," she assured her stepmother. "The Morris dancers come round."

"With bells on their ankles," supplemented her sister, weaned from the silks and jewels to something she loved still more. "I wish we *did* do them, Mary! I am sure I could take the Maid's part. And imagine Uncle Seymour as the Devil!" Curbing her rippling laughter at sight of Mary's reproving frown, she hurried on before her pertness could be scolded. "And then there's 'Jack in the Green,' Madam. A man walking about in a little house of flowers. And garlands hung on all the people's doors."

"Where do they get the flowers from?" asked Anne idly.

"The girls go a-maying on Blackheath and in Moor fields."

Seeing the eagerness on the child's face, Anne looked out of her window at all the inviting loveliness of lilac and gilly flowers and golden broom. "Suppose we go maying in the park this afternoon?" she suggested. And Elizabeth clapped her hands because nobody had ever bothered to plan a treat like that for her before.

"You must see some of the May poles, Madam," Mary said. "They are hung with multi-coloured ribbons and the children plait them as they dance round, and all the people flock to watch."

"What lovely ideas! And yet the same people will flock to see a hanging, or even a woman who is to be beheaded!" marvelled Anne, perplexed by a race that seemed half poets amd half brutes. Mary understood how upset she had been a few days earlier by a chance encounter with the aged Duchess of Salisbury being taken to the Tower, for no better reason than that she had more Plantagenet blood in her veins than the King. But Anne, happening to look up and see the hot colour dying Elizabeth's fair skin, could have bitten her tongue. She was certain now that the child knew about her mother, and she wanted to take her in protecting arms and pour over her the shielding love of which the cruel block had denied her. But by the age of seven Nan Bullen's daughter had already learned to hide under an uppish manner anything which added to her feeling of inferiority. She handed her nightgowns to Dorothea and told her to fold them, and began talking about something else with a composure which Anne found very pitiful.

"I had a train of this sort of stuff for Edward's christening," she said, pulling at the green damask. "It was four yards long and afterwards Mrs. Ashley made me a dress from it.

Uncle Seymour carried me in his arms and I carried the crimson. And Queen Jane was all in crimson and ermine."

Anne glanced questioningly towards her elder step-daughter. "Surely she can't remember——"

"I do! I do!" insisted Elizabeth. "She was lying on a pallet sort of thing with halberdiers and tall candles all round her." But Mary, who knew that most of it was what the child had been told, shook her head smilingly. "You're thinking of the wax effigy the chandler made of her for her lying-in-state," she said kindly. "That wasn't *really* Queen Jane."

"Well, anyhow, she looked lovely and I envied her."

"But she wasn't queen for very long," pointed out Anne, laying down her embroidery to draw her into the circle of her arm. "And, why should you suppose it to be such an enviable state, sweet?"

The child's green eyes looked levelly into Anne's kind brown ones, reading perspicaciously all the bitterness she hadn't meant to express. "It could be—for a queen *regnant*," she argued, with pitiless logic.

Mary hastened to interpose. She felt responsible for her younger sister's manners. "There hasn't been such a thing in this country since Matilda!" she said. "And if you listened to what Master Cooke teaches you instead of indulging in such worldly fantasies you would remember that it was Stephen who really ruled. It would be such a terrible responsibility for a woman."

"But what fun to make all the men obey!" persisted Elizabeth. "If I were Queen I'd dress in gorgeous clothes like our new mother's, so that they'd write verses about me and go sailing the seven seas to bring me back galleons of gold."

Dorothea laughed indulgently and Anne felt somehow that it wasn't the verses or the gold the child wanted so much as a chance to strike back at a regime which had humiliated her. But then neither of them remembered Nan Bullen. Whereas Mary, seeing young Bess standing there talking exactly like her mother, was goaded to a depth of feeling far deeper than the occasion warranted. "Don't be a little fool!" she said, her voice low-pitched with contempt. "Ruling a country isn't dressing up and ogling men and grasping all you can get. It's working—meeting your Council—writing far into the night. Trying never to punish for personal spite nor yet reprieve for pity. And lying awake, no doubt, wondering if you have done right. Feeling the souls of your people pressing upon you . . ."

Her white hands were clasping her suffering temples in a familiar gesture; her beautiful, short-sighted eyes staring abstractedly into space. And her words were laden with such prescient earnestness that the others stopped whatever they were doing to look at her. Anne sat with needle suspended and Elizabeth's hand still warm at her neck. Of course, she thought, if little Edward were to die . . . But even so, what about her own children, waiting to be born? They, at least, would grow up strong and capable, shielding poor conscientious Mary from such a fate.

"I believe I could rule that way too—without losing any sleep," Elizabeth was boasting inexcusably.

Mary sighed, and relaxed with a shrug of exasperation. Her fingers strayed to the cross on her breast as if in search of strength or patience. "It is not likely to be required of you," she remarked coldly. And, having snubbed the self-assertive little bastard, turned back to the business in hand. "Suppose we settle which dress you will wear for the Bachelors' Pageant at Durham House, Madam?"

By a process of careful elimination she had selected the two most becoming, which Dorothea now spread before them. Anne's chastened gaze lingered on the more colourful. "I do *prefer* the flowered crimson," she admitted. "But I suppose the King would think it too elaborate."

Mary of the severe and impeccable taste looked consideringly from the fantastic garment to its owner. "I think he's wrong there," she decided, with surprising firmness. "On some people, yes. I should hate it. But bright colours and jewels become you, Madam." She rose to plump up the stuffing of a slashed sleeve, and smiled at Anne affectionately. "They make you look—well, just your generous, cheerful self—when other people would look merely over-dressed."

"And after all, Madam," urged Dorothea, "these gallants are arranging a real old-fashioned tournament in your Grace's honour."

Mention of the tournament reminded Mary of an awkward contingency. "Suppose, Dorothea, the Queen's dress should clash outrageously with their colour scheme for the competitors and stands?" she said, rather surprised to find herself so anxious for her new Lutheran step-mother to make a good impression.

"Your Grace may keep an easy mind," proferred Elizabeth politely. "They're all going to wear white velvet."

Mary turned and surveyed her, suspecting her of sulking by the way she addressed herself exclusively to the Queen. "How do you know?" she asked sharply.

But Elizabeth had seated herself virtuously before one of Anne's newly-acquired books, and if there were malice in her eyes it was concealed by diligently downcast lashes. "Uncle Seymour told me when he came to say 'Good-night,'" she said, studiously turning a page. "He and Sir John Dudley and Tom Culpepper are all going to compete." She knew it annoyed Mary that people didn't tell her things. But why should they want to when she cultivated that prim, Spanish reserve instead of the open Tudor touch?

Deprecating their inherent antagonism, Anne turned to give Dorothea instructions about the exact cap and shoes and ornaments to go with the dress. Tall, devil-may-care Seymour wasn't really Elizabeth's uncle. He was Edward's. But the child preferred him to all her own grown-up relatives—either Tudor or Howard—a penchant which Anne was human enough to share. She remembered that the gallant Sir Thomas hadn't found her unattractive even in her winter travelling clothes at Calais and—whether her husband approved or not—she wanted to look her best.

So the new Flemish queen rode through London on May Day in her brave crimson velvet with flowers embossed in oriental pearls. Blackbirds sang in rich merchants' gardens and the garlands she had been told about decorated all the doors. A pleasant breeze from the river scattered the last of the blossom from cherry trees along the Strand, and on the blue line of the Highgate hills away to the north a dozen busy windmills turned, reminding her of home. And she certainly looked her best. "Though not so placid as when I painted her," thought Holbein, standing on his friend's balcony in Goldsmiths Row to watch her pass. "She has lost that grave, 'going out into the unknown' look."

And Holbein was right. Anne was no longer the same naïve person who had left Cleves six months ago. She had learned more than a language out of her books, and from the massive tyrant who rode by her side. She had learned to be patient and to mix humour with renunciation and to take gracefully such pleasures as were left her. And at the sight of the smile that beautified her face, children pressed forward for the pleasure of strewing posies in her path. And the people who leaned from windows and lined the streets—remembering her many unobtrusive kindnesses—called to each other that surely she was the sweetest and gentlest queen they had ever had.

Henry overheard them and frowned, fidgeting at Dappled Duke's glossy flanks with golden spurs. He knew his Londoners. Were they not the pulse of his kingdom? They might manifest an almost childish passion for holidays and processions; but underneath they were inflexible. They gave loyalty, but they stood on their rights; and neither he nor any of his forebears had ever been able to bend them to subservience or make them accept what they did not want.

Once he had tried. He had pitted his will against theirs. He had had his sweetheart Nan brought through their streets to her coronation. And, though the bells rang and the conduits ran wine, they would none of her.

She was the one thing he had ever wanted enough to cross them for. God, how he had wanted her! For three years the clever little bitch had made him sweat with fear lest he shouldn't get her in the end. Made his heart murderous to the dying woman who had been his wife for eighteen years and loved him still. So that he had defied them, and ordered their Lord Mayor to see to it that the City was en fête, the proper speeches made and the flattering masques performed. It had been a day such as this, with the hot sun and the crowds. He could see her now, carried in a litter—carried carefully between two white palfreys because she had the shameful seeds of their love child within her. His little Nan, with her pointed piquant face . . . and her bewitching cloud of night black hair . . . It all came back to him now in the mingled smell of perfumed gloves, Fleet ditch and Eastcheap dust, so that a resurgent gust of the old hot passion swept his ageing body. And yet these Londoners had looked on her beauty unmoved, except to hate her as a usurping harlot. They had paid him back with silence, so that when at last he and she were alone instead of sliding into his arms in weary surrender she had wept and upbraided him, beating at his breast with her fists in her shrill, spit-cat way. And although he was King, there had been nothing he could do about it. He would have given anything to make them shout as they were shouting now—for this ordinary Flemish woman with her firm bones and her painstaking English. It was their damnable sense of fair play, he supposed. . . .

Besides the carefree pleasure-lovers in that May Day procession there were others who thought along the same lines. Cranmer, noting with a more spiritual eye how this new Queen was riding straight into the people's hearts, thought in his wisdom, "Here is a new and unforeseen complication—more powerful than we know." And Wriothesley, the King's Secretary, going in fear of Cromwell's fate, was heard to whisper later beside the lists, "We must see to it that there are no more public demonstrations until this Howard wench is Queen."

Yet in spite of their separate, secret thoughts Anne managed to enjoy the Bachelors' splendid pageant. For three whole days she was able to watch shifting crowds of people, to take note of other women's fashions and to make new friends. Under the lofty marble pillars of Durham House the Governor of Calais's charming daughter, Katherine Basset, begged humbly for a place in her household, and out in the sunny lists Sir Thomas Seymour begged—far less humbly—for her favour to wear in the fray. The two 'gorgeous dukes' with their retinues seemed to fill the grounds with stir and heraldry—Norfolk, as hereditary Marshal of England, directing the jousts, and Suffolk with his charming wife, Catalina, explaining all the complicated pageantry. And, best of all, there was Culpepper's tilting prowess to watch. A devil of recklessness appeared to possess him. Again and again Sir John Dudley and other more seasoned knights went down before him to sprawl in the dust with splintered lance, so that each time his charger thundered along the barrier the women waved and cheered. But he had eyes for none of them. It was enough for him that he wore his cousin Katherine's favour and that it was stained already with his heart's blood. "And if she isn't crazy about him she must be ambition blind!" thought Anne, glancing down covertly from the Kentish squire's hard, young limbs to her husband's massive knees. Henry was too heavy now to enter the lists himself and it never occurred to Anne that he was longing to. She didn't realize how a man can suffer, watching others enjoy a sport at which he once excelled. Or that there had been a time when the King could easily have unhorsed Culpepper or any of the other young competitors with a pikestaff. She only thought how complacent he looked, sitting there applauding the bouts, talking sport with his friends, leaning forward from time to time to catch her maid-of-honour's eye.

After the tournament came feasting in Whitehall, lights and music on the river, and Morris dances on the village green at Westminster. And after the dancing, prayer. In the dim old Abbey where her parents-in-law were buried in a lovely new chapel that looked like stone lacework. And— Lutheran as she was—Anne no longer went to vespers as in duty bound. She was beginning to find comfort in the lighted candles and more colourful ritual of which her father's churches had been shorn—the sort of groping comfort that the perplexed and homesick find. Outraged inhibitions tormented her at times, and she thought unhappily of her own dead father and of how he would grieve for her soul. But it was *her* soul. It was she who had to live here, plotted against and alone. With Mary, a Catholic, for her only real friend.

As she and her ladies stood in the dim interior waiting for the King she noted how Mother Lowe sniffed disapprovingly at the rich carvings and incense-laden air. "It's wonderful to be prayed for in all the solemn Cathedrals and little village churches up and down the country," she said, trying to placate the old lady for her own apparent lack of reforming zeal. "I ought never to be unhappy or afraid, ought I, having the prayers of so many people?"

Mother Lowe's hawklike countenance relaxed into grudging gentleness. Perhaps she was comparing Anne's humility with the self-assurance of her sisters. "And after to-day, Madam, you may rest assured they mean them!"

Anne turned to Culpepper who had escorted them. He was still in his pageant finery and she gave one of the silver tassels of his shirt a little, friendly tweak. "Do *you* mean it, Tom, when you say 'we beseech Thee to bless our gracious Queen Anne'?" In spite of all his triumphs and popularity he looked drawn and glum and she spoke with rallying affection. But he moved sharply so that her hand fell foolishly from his breast. "Rest assured I do!" he answered, almost roughly. "And God knows no one in England has greater cause to pray for your safe keeping than I, Madam."

For one crazy moment she thought that he must be drunk or fancying himself in love with her. Wine had been flowing freely and there had been other men that evening who had whispered things that would have been dangerous—had her husband cared. But Tom Culpepper was neither.

Anne wanted to get him alone—to ask him what he meant. But by his sudden rigidity and the quenched fire in his eyes she knew that the King must have entered the Abbey. She shook herself mentally for a fool and moved to meet him, pacing regally up the aisle at his side. And, kneeling before the High Altar, she let all her fears and frustrations float up on a swell of music to a pitiful God somewhere beyond the dim vastness of the roof—beyond the frontiers of countries and the bitter arguments of ambitious men.

CHAPTER XV

The letter lay on a table beside the Queen's bed. No one had dared to give it to her. Immediately the pageant was over Wriothesley had handed it to the Earl of Rutland, her chamberlain. And he, good man—guessing what it contained—had felt that it would be kinder to let her read it when she was alone.

She had just returned from Westminster. Her ladies were half asleep after three days of unaccustomed gaiety and, with her usual consideration, Anne had dismissed them and gone straight to bed. She was unusually tired herself. Much as she had enjoyed it all, it was good to be alone at last.

As the servant who had lighted her upstairs closed the heavy oak door behind her, shutting out all sounds from other parts of the palace, she looked round her room with the satisfaction of a holiday maker come home. It seemed to have taken on a new simplicity since Henry no longer came to fill it with his over-riding presence. It might almost have been the 'room to herself' which she had always wanted at Cleves. Only Dorothea was there, kneeling to warm her mistress's nightgown by a new-fangled coal fire which Guligh had had lighted against her return and which looked ridiculously small in the widely-arched hearth built for mighty logs. After the warmth of the day the May evening was turning chilly and they had drawn thick curtains against a light-fingered frost which would silver the lawns in the privy garden before dawn. Firelight and shadow danced cosily over the half-drawn curtains of the fourposter. As the weeks passed Anne had come to think of it as her bed—a blessed square of privacy—and no longer as a monstrous piece of furniture significant of the bonds of matrimony. Her glance rested appreciatively on inviting pillows and turned down sheet. And then she noticed the letter lying on her bedside table with her husband's royal seal dangling like a splash of blood from the ribbon that tied it.

"Strange," she thought, "when I've just spent the best part of three days in his company and parted from him only an hour since!"

She crossed the room briskly and picked up the small rolled parchment; then hesitated, her cloak still about her shoulders, weighing it on her open palm. If Henry had anything pleasant to say, surely he would have said it. She recalled Culpepper's disturbing words in the dimness of the Abbey, and shivered. All the warm comfort of her room seemed to fade away, leaving her bleakly at bay. "Do make up the fire," she called over her shoulder with such unwonted irritation that her kneeling woman looked up in surprise.

When Anne had gathered courage to break the seal she stood reading her letter by the light of a single tall candle. The stillness of the room was broken only by the spatter of fresh coals in the iron cresset and the whisper of the silk-lined cloak slipping from her shoulders. Dorothea rose from her knees and came and picked it up. She had been watching her mistress's face, sharp edged against the candle flame. "What is it—now, Madam," she asked anxiously.

The Queen stood still as a carved statue. "You are all to go back—to Cleves," she said tonelessly.

Dorothea gave a cry of dismay. "All!" she exclaimed, with the jewelled garment bundled heedlessly in her arms. "But surely—not I?"

Anne turned and tried to reassure her. "Not you—God help me!" she promised unsteadily. "Not if we can find any means under Heaven to keep you."

"We must. I will do anything. I would rather turn a spit in the kitchens than go back. Say I am your laundress—that none of these English girls can see to your beaded caps."

"But everyone knows you are one of my *jauntlewomen*."

Freckled, flaxen Dorothea blushed furiously. "I could marry Guligh. He was here just now—more dumb and devoted than ever. He doesn't dare to ask me; but I think he has always wanted me."

"Anyone can see that, my dear. But—invaluable as Guligh is—he is only a servant."

"That's why they wouldn't bother about sending him back. And are we not all your Grace's devoted servants?"

Anne smiled very tenderly at her touching humility. She had always hoped that someone kind would take the place of Dorothea's dashing soldier and give her other children to assuage the longing for her dead baby. "He is certainly big enough to look after you," she said, conscious that being attached to William's court the girl's straight-laced parents probably didn't *want* her back.

Dorothea seized her hand and kissed it as if everything were settled. "Oh, Madam, you know I couldn't leave you!" she cried, as if that were of far more importance than whether or not she were in love with poor Guligh. The gorgeous cloak was cast across the bed, and despite the difference in their rank, the two women clung to each other in relief.

Tears stood in Anne's eyes as they drew apart. "It isn't that I mind their going so much," she said. "Poor old Mother Lowe often irritates me with her narrow, domineering ways and one doesn't need to be told that half the girls are counting the days to get home. Besides, of late I have felt that it only makes me look ridiculous going about with a bunch of dowdy women." In spite of the hurtful letter, a smile began to curve the corners of her mouth. "I can see now why even the chivalrous French ambassador thinks they're not exactly 'belles'; and why the King always called their favourite terrace at Hampton Court the 'vrou walk' and avoided it like the plague." She began to pace up and down, tugging at the fastening of the metal belt circling her trim waist. "But why couldn't he have told me himself? Consulted me as if I were a reasonable human being. Haven't I shown them all—dozens of times—that I try to be reasonable?" Coming back to the foot of the bed she gripped a fold of the hangings with their everlasting pattern of Tudor roses, and lent her forehead against her clenched knuckles. "And why—why—can't I bear him a son?" she demanded, in a voice muffled by brocade and anger. "He wouldn't do these cruel things to me then."

Dorothea knew that was the one thing that would bring

security and happiness to her ill-used mistress. Scarcely less than Anne she wished for it as a weapon with which to make a mere plaything of the blue-blooded maid-of-honour who basked in the King's smiles and shared none of the work. "There is plenty of time, Madam," she soothed, coaxing the Queen into a chair and drawing off her shoes.

But Anne wasn't so sure about that. The way Culpepper had spoken in the Abbey had taken away her sense of security, made her feel on the verge of some calamitous happening. In spite of all the people's prayers! And it was characteristic of her that in the midst of her own disappointment she considered theirs. "The whole nation will be so frightfully disappointed too if I don't have children!" she thought. And for a moment the armour of self-restraint deserted her. She leaned forward, her eyes shining like stars, the cruel parchment crumpled in her lap. "Once he gives me a child everything will come right!" she reiterated. It was the old proviso that she had tried to comfort herself with on her wedding night. In the astounding importance of it everything else appeared puny—the machinations of her enemies, Henry's infidelity, the burgeoning affection of her step-children—even her abiding love for Hans.

Sinking back at last against the inviting pillows, she tried to picture herself living the safe, pampered existence Queen Jane would have enjoyed. It might still be possible. All those horrid, half-understood things that Lady Rochfort had hinted at need not be true. People whispered about the sore on the King's leg but it didn't necessarily prove that he was sterile. Anyway, it wasn't so very long ago that Edward was borne. And apparently if one produced sons Henry wasn't such an ogre. Anne had brought herself to accept the obligations of her birth. She had dutifully renounced the authentic flame of love almost before it had flowered. And she might even yet find that other facet of her husband's character which people spoke of, and sun herself in the ordinary contentment of living with a man for whom she had some liking. Like any other healthily tired young woman she indulged in optimistic day-dreams while she lay lazily blinking at the dying fire; then fell asleep, still smiling at the thought of Elizabeth getting four yards of pearled green velvet out of another christening train.

In the morning she collected all her women together and told them the King's wishes. Most of them tried to hide their joy beneath perfunctory expressions of regret; but she cut them short. "There is nothing to be ashamed of in wanting to go home," she said, with a wistful smile. "I would give almost anything to be going there myself." Whereat some of the younger ones wept in genuine pity.

But Anne was determined to be business-like. She would show these high and mighty Englishmen. "I want no commotion—no fuss," she told Mother Lowe. "Please see that everyone's things are neatly packed and you must all be ready to go at an hour's notice."

On one point she was adamant. She wouldn't answer the letter, either to Henry or to his secretary. She would see them, face to face. But Henry had cautiously withdrawn to Oatlands. So she had perforce to send for that reptile, Wriothesley. And she made sure that before he was shown into her presence he must pass along a gallery stacked with chests of women's gear, already marked with the cipher of her brother's court. Such promptitude unnerved him. He was a man who enjoyed bullying and he had come expecting tears and exhortations. Instead he found the Queen calmly arranging a bowl of late tulips. Because her interests were not intellectual he had, in common with many others, made the mistake of supposing her to be stupid. But like most people who say little she was mistress of the situation; and she further upset his calculations by receiving him with an inclination of the head more regal than anything he had seen since Catherine of Aragon left court. "I have sent for you, Master Secretary," she said, "to assure you that the ladies of my retinue will be ready to return to Cleves as soon as arrangements can be made for them to do so."

He muttered something about the Council not wishing to hurry her, but she silenced him with a gesture. "Only in the case of a woman married to my body servant, John Guligh, I would crave his Grace to make exception. My English maids do not understand our Flemish way of stiffening beaded caps and it will spare me embarrassment if she may stay."

Rather red and flustered himself, Wriothesley hastened to reassure her on so minor a point. "With so many foreigners gone it will be easier to remove your Grace's household to Richmond," he observed, being balked of all the other unpleasant things he had come prepared to say.

"Richmond?" The Queen's lazy-lidded eyes snapped wide open, and he was gratified to detect in them consternation. That, at least, had shaken her.

"It is the King's wish that you should go there as soon as possible," he told her smugly.

"Why?"

"Fearing for your Grace's health——"

"My health is excellent," said Anne.

"That is obvious to us all, Madam," he smirked, knowing how much she must wish at such a moment that it gave interesting cause for concern. "But the plague attacks the weak and the strong impartially."

"The plague?" Mistrustfully, Anne stared at him across the stiff tawny tulips in her hands. That England suffered periodic scourges of the bubonic disease, she knew; but only a week or two back, on May Day, the Londoners had been laughing and dancing in the streets. "We've so recently been in all those town crowds," she said. "And surely if there had been any fear of infection the King himself would have been the last person——" She stopped short, aware that she was on the verge of saying something tactless again and Wriothesley allowed himself to smile in his beard. Perhaps, after all, she wasn't so undiscerning. "He has gone to Oatlands, Madam. But he bade me tell you he will join you at Richmond—later."

There seemed no more to be said. Anne knew that the man was watching her—enjoying her discomfiture. And all the time her mind was groping for Henry's motive. Often in her barge she had passed the splendid palace at Richmond, with its fantastic pinnacles and great oriel windows built almost to the water's edge. But she had never been inside and nobody appeared to live there now. It was neither grim like the Tower nor homely like Hampton. What was the special significance of Richmond? She must ask Mary—or the archbishop. But in the meantime she must get rid of this dreadful little man. She beckoned a page to show him out. It never occurred to her to protest or to fly into tantrums as the other Anne would have done. "That of course is for his Grace to decide," she acquiesced with quiet dignity.

Wriothesley bowed himself out obediently. From first to last he had said no more than half-a-dozen sentences. Outside in the gallery he sat down on one of the 'vrou's' clothes chests and wiped the sweat from his forehead with a gesture suggestive of the gutter from which he had sprung. The wretched Lutheran woman had accepted his master's orders meekly enough; but somehow the interview had fallen flat. He would have enjoyed boasting to his colleagues in anterooms of how he had baited the Flemish Mare. Henry's brutal conjugal epithet had gone the rounds. Quite a good joke, of course, though wearing a bit threadbare with rough usage. But for the King's secretary it had lost some of its savour. He had had no idea that one defenceless woman could make a man feel so uncomfortable.

It would, perhaps, have mollified him to know that the defenceless woman was at that moment hurrying through a maze of royal passages to her step-daughter's apartments.

"Mary," she said without preamble, the moment they were alone, "the King is not only sending away my people. He is moving my household to Richmond."

Mary Tudor had risen from her book-strewn desk, her pale heart-shaped face serious from the task of translating a Latin treatise; her soft, kind eyes blinking blindly for a moment or two as they focused on her unexpected visitor. "They held a long council meeting this morning," she vouchsafed.

"Then you've heard?"

"Only rumours, Madame."

Anne tapped an impatient foot. "Rumours of *what*? If only they'd come out into the open and tell me!"

But Mary shrugged her slim shoulders noncommittally.

She was humiliated by the prospect of yet another step-mother. Why must her father make such a laughing-stock of himself? "Aren't there always rumours—if a King looks at someone else?"

Realizing what Mary must have gone through as a girl, Anne plucked up courage to ask her what she had been too proud to ask of anyone else. "Is it true that he is trying to divorce me like—like your mother?"

She spoke with averted head because it wasn't easy, and presently she was aware of Mary's small firm hands pressing hers, of Mary's voice, deep with pity, giving her the truth. "Yes," she admitted with her usual directness. "But I don't think you need fear—anything worse—since he is sending you home to Richmond."

Anne sank down on the nearest chair. Both women were aware of the stark tragedies which could strike so suddenly at their kind. "On what grounds *could* he do it?" she demanded. "Osiliger disproved all that nonsense about a pre-contract."

"On what grounds could he divorce my mother—after eighteen years?" echoed Mary, with concentrated bitterness.

"At least it wasn't because he'd always thought her undesirable. Am I so very plain?"

Mary regarded her gravely. "I wish I were as tall as your Grace," she said formally. But Anne laid a swift, entreating hand on her arm. "Please—please—my dear. I am only a few months older than you, and I too know what it is to be parted from my mother. I am well-nigh sick for friendship —and my name is Anne."

Mary turned and smiled at her—the slow, shy smile of one whose bruised affections are being reborn. "To those of us who love you, you will always look beautiful—Anne," she said.

Anne kissed her with gratitude. "A little while ago it wouldn't have hurt so much—being repudiated like this," she explained. "You see, my elder sister was supposed to be the beauty of our family, and my younger sister the conversationalist. One tried to be sensible about it. To make oneself capable or to foster a reputation for being kind. But afterwards when I had been chosen, and told I was beautiful—and been fool enough to believe it. . . ." She broke off and laughed at herself confusedly. "Well, it makes something inside a woman grow. I don't mean just self-confidence. But all the graces and desires she has as a birthright if she is born beautiful. . . ."

"I know. But with me it has been the other way round. I started with everything. Health, good looks, accomplishments. My parents adored me—all the more because their other sons and daughters didn't live. I'd the happiest possible childhood. And then I lost it all." Mary picked up the quill she had dropped at the Queen's entrance, and began bending it between tensed fingers until it snapped. "I fell ill with grief when my mother was sent away to Kimbolton. And such was her tenderness towards me that she wrote to the King begging to be allowed to nurse me in her own bed. But I never saw her again—not even when they knew she was dying. And when I rebelled she wrote me the loveliest words of advice any daughter ever received." From a small gold reticule hanging from her girdle, Mary extracted a letter so worn with frequent folding as to be almost illegible. She paid her step-mother the rare honour of showing it to her so that Anne was able to see for herself the love there must have been between them. And when Anne had handed it back she said proudly, "I wouldn't shame her by acknowledging myself a bastard or changing my faith. But the King hounded my mother to death and tried to make me wait on the love child of that Bullen strumpet!"

"She paid for it with her life," Anne reminded her gently.

"And even then she had to be different from anyone else. She made the King send for a swordsman out of France. 'I've such a little neck!' she said." Mary mimicked her mercilessly, implacable resentment patent in every line of her straight back and neatly coiffed head, as she stood in the deep embrasure of a window, staring out unseeingly at the Park. "And even when she'd mounted the scaffold on Tower Green she looked with warm eyes at the executioner so that he remembered it was a May morning and pitied her and hid the thing in the straw until the moment he struck."

Anne shivered, picturing the uplifted faces, the hushed silence and the grim Tower walls. And the tragedy of having to die on a May morning. "It's a good thing someone pitied her," she said.

"Why?" asked Mary. "She never had any pity for anybody else—not even for my father. She was as selfish as she was seductive. Even after he tired of her temper and suspected her cuckoldry, she tempted him back. And she'd have saved her precious little neck if only the boy he gave her had lived!"

"I never knew she had any other children," said Anne, for whom every day seemed to unravel some unsuspected thread from which the lives of these tempestuous Tudors were woven.

"It was born dead—and her chances with it. But it was a boy all right."

Mary turned back to her books. Her hands were shaking and it is doubtful if she saw a word; and Anne sat there wondering if Henry would dare to do to death a wife who hadn't been born his subject. She thanked God fervently that Hans, in his worldly wisdom, had saved her from the fear of detected guilt. And presently, in a low voice, she asked Mary the silly, morbid thing she had always wanted to know. "Where did they bury her?"

"They didn't. They just left her there. Uncle Charles, the Duke of Richmond, Cromwell and all of them. With her long black hair dabbled in blood and her women weeping and swooning over her." Even the scorn of Catherine of Aragon's daughter was muted in the description of so agonizing a scene. Anne herself felt sick. "But they must have—have put her somewhere," she faltered.

"Mary Wyatt, her favourite woman, implored a passing fletcher to help them and he brought a disused arrow chest from the armoury. They put her body and her severed head into it—just as she was except that Mary washed the blood from her face—and got him to dig a shallow grave under one of the flagstones in St. Peter-ad-Vincula, the chapel in the Tower bailey."

"What an ending to so much pageantry and passion!"

murmured Anne. But was it the end? She couldn't very well tell Mary that it was Nan's name the King still murmured in his sleep.

"There's a rumour that the Wyatts smuggled the arrow chest out of the Tower and took it to their place at Dereham, in Norfolk," admitted Mary, dispassionately. "But, even if they did, they would never dare to have her name inscribed on it."

The Queen rose and kissed her. "Yet in spite of all your bitterness you love Elizabeth, don't you?" she asked, almost pleadingly.

Poor Mary was always at the mercy of her conscience. "As a sister, yes. But as a—a public character—I hate and even fear her," she confessed, with painful honesty; so that Anne began to understand why sometimes she lavished gifts on the child and sometimes snubbed her, hurting herself in the process and building a barrier of wariness between them. She lifted a hand to her forehead now in the familiar gesture that betokened a headache and Anne, blaming herself for being the cause of it, remembered how Henry had complained that his elder daughter stayed too much indoors. "Let's go out into the sunshine and play bowls," she suggested lightly. Fresh air had always seemed to her a panacea for most ills.

Mary clasped and locked a newly-printed book and came reluctantly; and as they strolled across the smoothly-clipped lawn, a view of the sparkling Thames reminded Anne of something that had puzzled her. "Does this Duke of Richmond you mentioned own Richmond Palace?" she asked.

"Oh, no!" laughed Mary. "He was my illegitimate brother. The only one I ever had, as far as I know. When my own baby brother the Prince of Wales died, my parents were so terribly disappointed that I believe my father would have tried to make Harry Richmond, King. He even married him to Norfolk's daughter. But they both died childless when they were eighteen, poor things! So you can see what it meant to him to have Edward."

The hopes of the whole house were pinned on Edward, it seemed to Anne. "And why did you say just now 'Go *home* to Richmond?'" She persisted, determined to find out something about her new residence.

"Well, it *is* home to all us Tudors," explained Mary, entering the bowling alley. "Particularly to my father. He was brought up there and his parents died there. He was devoted to them. Afterwards I lived there myself for a little while—when the Council didn't quite know what to do with me." A couple of pages had brought a box of woods and she was occupied with selecting her favourite set or she would scarcely have spoken so carelessly. "It's used as a kind of dower house now."

A dower house sounded rather pleasant and peaceful. The sort of place where one could live one's own life without being ordered about at the whim of some man. Anne threw up the jack as Henry had shown her. Carefully she set the heavy wood on her palm so that the bias turned inwards. "But what should a married woman want with a dower house?" she asked herself, watching it roll away and lie wide. She was beginning to understand the peculiar significance of Richmond.

CHAPTER XVI

Dry-eyed, Anne had watched her women go. By them she had sent loving letters to her family. She had written of the affection shown her by her step-daughters, of the amusing pageant given in her honour, of the spaciousness of Richmond Palace; but she made no mention of her husband's neglect. She didn't want them to worry about her and she had her pride. Yet she had barely settled into her new apartments, and the May garlands were scarcely withered in the City streets before the final blow fell which would make her private humiliation succulent meat for gossip all over Europe.

The King's ministers came to her early one July morning. Not as visitors, but with grave faces and disturbing formality. Cranmer and Suffolk, surfeited with experience in clearing up the Augean stables of their royal master's matrimonial muddles—and Wriothesley, full of new self-importance. And such was Henry's impatience to be rid of her and free to pluck his fresh English rose that they came early enough to catch Anne still abed. Her flurried new English ladies had to confess that the Queen, who so seldom slept late, had not yet breakfasted. But when shy little Katherine Basset, diligent in the duties she had begged for, waked her royal mistress with the news that they insisted upon seeing her, Anne obligingly called for a wrap and received them in her bedroom. This queer custom of talking to people of importance in one's bedroom had at first shocked her sense of propriety, but she was growing accustomed to it.

When they were shown in, Charles Brandon's cheerful 'Good-morning, Sister' was a shade too jaunty to be convincing and the archbishop's eyes were shifty with compassion. Clearly they hated their errand. And the fact that they liked Anne made them both so nervous that even the suave prelate bungled it.

"We are come from the King," he began portentously.

Dorothea had set a chair for her mistress; but Anne, sensing the ominous importance of their coming, preferred to stand defensively with one hand grasping the back of it. "I had thought to have the pleasure of His Grace's company by now," she observed politely.

They all knew that he had promised to join her in a day or two and Charles murmured something about urgent affairs of state. But Anne's reactions were always so disconcertingly practical. "What a pity, then, that we didn't lodge at Westminster!" she observed blandly. "It would have been so convenient with Parliament lying——"

Her brother-in-law hastily suppressed an explosion of nervous laughter. "'Sitting' is the word," he corrected. "But no matter, my priceless Anne. They were probably doing both. And then, of course, there is the plague——"

"Don't you think your presence there might have kept up the spirits of the people?" she asked imperturbably. If there was any truth at all in this ever-recurring excuse there was nothing she would have liked better than to stay and help the poor Londoners who had welcomed her so warmly.

Charles was reduced to shamed silence. He had been no unwilling instrument in bringing about the Bullen's downfall. It was true he had even taken young Richmond to see her die. But it was one thing to be callous about an ambitious fellow countrywoman who had finessed for the throne and another to bring humiliating messages to a generous-hearted foreigner who had never tried to triumph over anyone. He himself had married wives who had kept him kind. He fell to wondering if Mary Tudor, his first love, would have softened her brother's heart towards women and how far the loss of her had made him hard. He remembered their shared grief as they laid her to rest in the great Abbey of St. Edmund in his own duchy of Suffolk, and how Henry —when he turned out the monks—had had her little coffin transferred to the church of St. Mary the Virgin and spared it to be her shrine. Because she still lived in both their hearts his mind wandered from the urgent matter in hand.

Thomas Cranmer, standing beside him, was for the hundredth time cursing the chance words that had been the means of drawing him into public life. For him there was no escape. Only a life-long adjustment between his God, his conscience and his King. He liked this Lutheran queen and knew her to be wholly worthy of the high state from which the Tudor was about to spurn her. He hated having to sanction her divorce. But he believed it his duty to obey the King in all things—even when the King disobeyed God. And because Cranmer was no self-seeking opportunist the flail of God's disapproval fell heaviest upon him. That same fine sensitiveness which enabled him to write exquisite prose rendered him oversensitive to pain, whether in himself or for others. Because he needed more courage than most men to meet it, he knew the added dread of acquitting himself unmanfully. And in this valley of apprehension he wrestled daily with his own private hell. "It has been my painful duty to call a convocation of clergy," he told the Queen. And while he was still seeking words to soften the blow he must deal, Wriothesley said the brutal thing for him.

He said it bluntly, without any fancy wrappings. And while he said it he stared unmoved at her defenceless face. "It is useless to expect the King to come to you at Richmond or elsewhere, Madam, because the convocation pronounced your marriage to be null and void."

She went from white to red as if he had struck her. "Why wasn't I told—that I might have been there?" she stammered. And Cranmer explained gently that the King had thought to spare her on account of her being a foreigner and unacquainted with their language.

"*Spare* me!" she gibed, and turned to her brother-in-law with gesture of exasperation. He could only shrug and smile back at her sympathetically. They were both aware that Henry chose to remember only her sorry efforts at English on the day he first met her and that, prejudiced as he was against her, he would continue to ignore the progress she had made until such time as he gained his freedom. It made

191

his case against her sound more plausible. And there was nothing they could do about it. "A bill to invalidate your marriage has already been read before the Commons," Charles told her, "and it was passed unanimously on the thirteenth day of this month."

"Unanimously?" murmured Anne, thinking of the loving welcome of the people.

Because he said the thirteenth day Basset crossed herself. Although she had been but a few weeks in her new employment, Anne's life had already become precious to her. And Dorothea, although now officially only Guligh's wife, defied etiquette to move closer to her mistress.

"You mean—he has divorced me?" said Anne. Her voice was low and husky as it always was in moments of deep emotion, and she looked from one to another of them for an answer. No man gave her one. But she could read it for herself in their respectfully bowed heads.

"Divorced!!" She repeated the word in her own tongue as if she had forgotten their presence. There was something infinitely forlorn yet dignified in the way she stood there, trying to take in the full significance of her situation and schooling herself to get used to it. True, it was half expected; yet the finality of it came as a cruel shock.

Out of the ensuing silence winged things seemed to rush at her, striking her down. Vague hopes and fears reshaped as definite facts. Failure, frustration, insecurity, humiliation. . . . Blackest of all—humiliation. Shame in the eyes of her family—shame in the eyes of the world. An indignant voice protesting that in spite of all she was desirable, a desolate voice crying that she was made for mothering children. A furious voice shrieking that it was Henry—Henry—who was old and fat and sexually diseased. Stabs of hot hatred, searing all the essential decencies of her nature. Confused displacement of familiar thought in her own mind to make room for so many new and irrevocable facts. And then—suddenly—a small, insistent voice blotting out everything else. The voice of fear. Fear born of broken bits of sentences hurrying through the echoing halls of memory, beating more and more sharply on her brain, hustling her to the edge of a dark abyss over which neither hatred nor humiliation would matter any more. . . .

"She made them send for a swordsman out of France. . . . She thought it would be quicker. . . ." And then the hush and the upturned faces. "They just left her there—her fine dark hair all dabbled with blood. . . ."

"Why did they have to tell *me* about it?" thought Anne piteously. "I, who am one of his wives!" But, of course she had asked. And Mary had even said that Cromwell and her exquisite Uncle Charles . . .

Through the shadows closing about her Anne's wide, distended eyes sought Charles Brandon accusingly. She saw him only as a blurred, resplendent outline against the haze of light from a window. She threw out a hand as if to ward him off. She wanted no spectators. . . . "You were there—you saw it——" she said thickly. To the rest of them it must have sounded crazy. They hadn't the least idea what she meant.

The shadows were resolving themselves swiftly and horribly into a picture that Anne had been staving off for months with a more determined effort than she knew. The picture of a low archway between dank walls, with slimy mud at low tide and the river sucking people in beneath a grim, iron-shod portcullis. All sorts of innocent, inconvenient people. Priests who were faithful to their creed, innocuous old gentlewomen like the Countess of Salisbury, anyone who had a drop of Plantagenet blood and—all the King's unwanted wives. . . .

Without warning the room went black and the waters rose and engulfed her. Married or divorced, she loved life. She clutched at a bed-hanging—at the warmth of a human hand. She was aware of an angry wind which might have been the swish of skirts—of loving arms trying to hold her up—of a humble waiting-woman's voice denouncing the Great Ones of England. "Between you you have killed her, milords!" Of an hysterical desire to laugh because Dorothea's voice, with its execrable accent, sounded like a snarling tiger's. And then darkness. . . .

The strong swirl of Thames drawing Anne of Cleves—the most innocent and inconvenient of them all—through the dread gateway into the stillness of the Tower moat. . . .

CHAPTER XVII

When at last Anne regained consciousness she was lying on a pallet by an open window. Consternation reigned round her. Dr. Chamberlain, the King's own physician, was beside her replacing the stopper of a phial. Basset was offering her something from a cup and Dorothea was putting a hot brick to her feet. Anne drank the potion obediently and lay readjusting herself to life.

As she collected her fumbling thoughts she observed that her three visitors were still in the room but had withdrawn themselves into an anxious huddle by the door. The concern on their faces gave the lie to her own ears. Evidently the King wouldn't have been at all pleased if their news had killed her. She frowned consideringly at the phial and the doctor's fine fingers which loomed larger than anything else at the moment because they came within her direct line of vision. After all, she decided, if Henry had intended to send her to the Tower an overdose from so expert a hand would have been much cheaper than an execution, and would have saved everybody a lot of bother. Always supposing, of course, that Dr. Chamberlain were as accommodating as the Commons. In an idle, detached sort of way Anne studied his face. It was an interesting face and she believed that Holbein had once painted it. He would have enjoyed that, she thought, for in the stern lines and decisive chin one could read the map of a great physician's life. And he certainly didn't look the kind of man who would betray his high calling. Experimenting with a limp hand, she managed to stretch it palm upwards across the coverlet in his direction. "Forgive my people for troubling you for so small a matter," she apologized. And when his long, clever features relaxed into the smile he reserved for patients who made light of their ailments, she added almost aggressively, "I have never fainted before."

Hearing her stir and speak, Cranmer hurried to her side.

He smiled down at her as he had done that day at Hampton Court when he had told her of his own problems, and Anne felt as if being divorced had lifted some ban on their nascent friendship. She loved the protective way he stood there, purposely trying to block out the Secretary's oppressive girth with his own spare, sombrely-gowned frame.

And Charles, presuming on his position as one of the family, came and sat on the end of her pallet. "It is we who should do all the apologizing," he said courteously.

It seemed such a friendly little party with people daring to like her again, and her two favourite women hovering to do the least thing for her comfort, that Anne wondered how so short a time ago she could have succumbed to the grip of tragedy. It had been terribly real at the time. But now a thrush warbled comfortably from a leaden gutter spout across the chapel courtyard, and when she turned her head towards the open window the world seemed full of sunshine. "It was foolish of me," she murmured, "but I thought. . . ."

The Tudors' family physician, whose mind must have been a sealed storehouse of royal indiscretions, tactfully withdrew to write a prescription; and Charles, in his suave way, gave her no opportunity to put into words what they all guessed she *had* thought. "We have bungled this badly, I am afraid," he hastened to admit, including his spiritual colleague with a friendly gesture. "We should have told you at once that although the King's conscience won't permit him to prolong this pretended marriage, he has the highest regard for you and wishes you to be his entirely beloved sister."

His sister, Henry the Eighth's sister. This certainly was a new way out.

Anne lay with closed eyes letting the fantastic idea sink in. Even as his sister one would still be more important than most men's wives. And it might not be an entirely distasteful relationship. At least she would no longer have to share her bed with him. Resolutely discounting the personal slight, she began checking over the possible advantages, for surely in such a crisis in one's life one needed to be sensible rather than proud. When she opened her eyes again there was more colour in her cheeks. "Does that mean that I may go home?" she asked eagerly.

But they shook their heads and said they thought not.

"Or marry again?"

They looked profoundly shocked. It was a suggestion they would scarcely dare repeat to the King. Although he had treated this fourth wife of his abominably, she should by rights have been broken-hearted like Catherine of Aragon. But then Anne hadn't known Henry when he was a personable young man. And now that the blow really *had* fallen and it was so much less heavy than she had feared, her natural cheerful resilience was beginning to assert itself. "Then if I am neither to go home nor to marry again what am I to live on?" she asked.

It sounded dreadfully mercenary; but then she was essentially a realist. And after all that was what they had come for—to make terms. But Suffolk and Cranmer preferred to leave financial matters to Wriothesley, the man of affairs. "His Majesty is graciously pleased for you to make this palace and manor of Richmond your home, Madam," he advised her unctuously.

Since she was no longer to be Queen, Anne would rather have lived in something less pretentious. "It will cost a great deal to keep up," she pointed out dubiously.

"To which end I am to arrange for you to be endowed with estates amounting to three thousand pounds."

Anne tried not to look too pleased. It was more money than she had ever had in her life. However niggardly Henry had been about necessities of life for Elizabeth, at least he showed every sign of being generous to *her*. As a matter of fact he always had been—in everything but affection. Wasn't everyone agreed that he had given her a much grander reception than any of his other wives? And then there had been the sables and any number of new dresses. Probably that was the way it worked. If you really loved a person you didn't need to provide the shams. After a few moments reflection she asked—almost wearily—on what grounds she was being divorced and what Charles had meant when he alluded to her 'pretended' marriage? Most women would have asked this immediately, she supposed.

Apparently, this was the question the deputation had been dreading most and by common consent it fell to Cranmer, as a churchman, to answer it. That he did so without hesitation was perhaps a demonstration of that sorely-tried courage of his. "His Grace has made a public statement, Madam," he told her, "in which he affirms on oath that it has never been consummated."

Anne sat up slowly, resting on her open palms and blinking a little as if she had not heard aright. "Not—not *consummated*?" she repeated. She looked from one to the other of them. Perhaps she was mistaken about the exact meaning of the English word. It was, of course, one of those delicate subjects about which people weren't too precise. . . . But, no, by the confusion on their faces she knew that it meant exactly what she had supposed. And Henry had dared to say that—the scab! Her bewildered glance slipped past them to Dorothea, her only confidante, halted in mid-career across the room with a bowl of water in her hands. Their indignant glances met and held, their brows went up. Anne turned back to Cranmer for enlightenment, but Cranmer stared fixedly at a coat-of-arms emblazoned on the leaded casement above her head. Charles had strolled to the fireplace and was examining a carved Tudor rose with as lively an interest as if he had never before come across one of the ubiquitous things.

Evidently she must figure this thing out alone. She was accustomed to being a stranger in a very strange land and she, too, was capable of calculating—of working out the move that would suit her best. Flooding into her mind came remembrance of how Henry had rid himself of his first wife by raising this very question about her marriage with his brother, Arthur. It was becoming quite a stock gambit in his game for freedom. It had worked then. So what was to prevent it from working again? It was something almost impossible to fight, as Catherine had found to her cost. But then Catherine had everything to lose, and Henry nothing. The poor woman was past child-bearing. Whereas now it was Henry who was almost impotent and she herself who had youth and vitality. This time the clever gambit might cost him dear. Anne knew that for all his lust there was something he wanted even more than freedom. She believed he would give up all his fancy loves to found a family of sons. There was a little contemptuous smile on her mouth; but she neither confirmed nor denied her husband's statement. "It is only his word against mine," she had the temerity to point out. "There can't possibly be—witnesses."

Cranmer withdrew his gaze from the emblazoned Richmond arms. He could scarcely believe that the expected storm of indignation had not burst. "No," he conceded. "But there is Thomas Cromwell. It was he who advocated your marriage, and from the Tower he has been forced to bear witness to the King's unwillingness to proceed with it."

But this was more than Anne could stomach. It was as if she, the unwilling bride, had thrown herself at Henry. "But the King chose me!" she protested indignantly. "After seeing Holbein's picture he begged my brother to send me—although I was dowerless. And if I hadn't been compelled to marry him——"

Cranmer lifted a rebuking hand. "Being already condemmed to death," he said sadly, "Cromwell would hardly damn his soul with lies."

So Cromwell was to die? It was he—not she—who must face that expectant hush and those up-turned faces and pay the price of Henry's disappointment. She tried to feel compassion, and could not. After all, it was just—if any justice were to be found in this mad subservience to tyranny—for wasn't Cromwell the schemer and she the helpless victim? And after bringing her to this sorry pass had he not, each time she sought his aid, avoided her to save his skin? And now, of course—because he was about to die—everybody would believe him when he bolstered up even Henry's wildest statement.

Anne allowed herself to relax against the cushions Basset had been piling behind her. Her sharp spurt of anger had been damped down by the shock of Cromwell's sharper fate. It was true, as she had been about to point out, that she might have married someone of her own age—someone stolidly good like Sybilla's husband. But in no circumstances would she have been permitted to marry a painter, however famous. So what did it all matter? Parrying the listlessness that was creeping over her, she became aware that Wriothesley was daring to bait her. "His Majesty's unwillingness appears to date from the day he met you at Rochester, Madam," he took pleasure in informing her.

Anne glanced in his direction as if she had only just noticed he was there. "Or from the day at Rochester when he met one of my maids?" she suggested coldly.

Not being prepared to counter such forthrightness, the wretched man sought to cover her words by shuffling the ominous-looking documents in his hands. And Anne felt it was only fair she should know what was in them. "If those papers you are fidgeting with contain a report of milord Chancellor's testimony, I pray you read it," she snapped.

Sheepishly, Wriothesley unrolled them. He began with the evidence of the King's anger because he had found his bride less fair than Holbein and Wotton had represented her. " 'If it were not that she is come so far into my realm,' " he read in a thin travesty of Henry's mellow voice, "and the great preparations that my States and people have made for her and for fear of making a ruffle in the world, and of driving her brother into the hands of the Emperor and the French King, who are now together, I would not now marry her.' "

"Go on!" ordered Anne.

And Wriothesley went on with the condemned Chancellor's testimony—how when he had asked hopefully the following morning if the King liked her any better, Henry had replied coarsely that he couldn't overcome her aversion enough to beget sons on her.

"Thank you," she said, after an uncomfortable silence. "Such clarity of expression makes his Grace's meaning clear even to *my* limited knowledge of English, and should leave no doubt in any woman's mind as to his unwillingness. But I should like to know what particular blemish in me gave rise to it." From where she lay she could see a reflection of herself in the metal mirror on her toilet table, and she took stock proudly of her well-poised head, her rounded breasts no longer trussed high in the Flemish manner, and the long well-shaped limbs outlined beneath her summer bed wrap. "I pray you," she asked, "what did he say of my appearance?"

"Madam——" entreated Cranmer, and made a sign to Wriothesley to put away his intolerable papers. It seemed cruel to kill all hope of reconciliation between these two in their new relationship, and he couldn't bear to see Anne unnecessarily hurt. But it was truth she wanted, not clemency. She had lived too long in an atmosphere of humbug and uncertainty to tolerate any half-tones now. She stopped making a hard round ball of her kerchief with angry fingers and lifted her chin defiantly. Her eyes were unnaturally bright. "I know that he called me a great Flanders mare," she said. "Do you suppose that anything else can hurt very much after that?"

All three men reddened with discomforture. They had no idea that she knew that. Even Wriothesley flinched before her withering honesty. "He must have said that in the heat of anger," he hastened to protest, "because milord Chancellor remarked on your queenly manner that day you arrived at Greenwich and the King agreed with him. 'Her person is well and seemly,' he said." And even he had the grace not to tell her that Henry, in a desperate bid for escape, had impugned her honour. That in a burst of post-nuptial confidence he had said to Cromwell, "I have felt her breasts and her belly, and to my way of thinking she is no maid."

Suffolk and Cranmer breathed a sigh of relief. They began to feel that the worst of this painful interview was over. To their surprise this strange woman had made no protest about the injustice shown her—had laid no claim to speak passionately in her own defence as the other two discarded queens had done. Could it be possible that she was going to agree meekly to everything they had come to say—to relinquish her crown without a struggle? Would there be no appeals to this or that power, no indignant complaints to Cleves involving England in war, no undignified personal struggle? The kind of struggle which would wring beholders' hearts because it could end only in still further persecution of the defendant. Could it even be possible, they wondered, that this particular wife didn't really *mind* being divorced?

Charles eyed her covertly. He was beginning to suspect that this was the truth and to derive considerable enjoyment from the situation. He would have liked to clap Anne on the shoulder and say, "Good for you, my girl!" But instead he cleared his throat rather pompously and delivered the rest of Henry's message. "If you will be reasonable about this and renounce your title of Queen, Anne, the Council is agreed that you should take precedence over all other ladies at court."

"Except, of course, the King's daughters," put in Wriothesley.

Charles had not liked to say that a child of seven—and a bastard at that—was to be put before her. Being more or less a parvenu himself, he was touchy about precedence; and it seemed to him a big thing to expect a woman who was a princess in her own right to accept. But surprisingly —and to his intense relief—she made no protest even about that. "What are the children to call me now I am no longer their step-mother?" she enquired, almost idly.

"You are to be styled the Lady Anne of Cleves," said Cranmer.

Anne received the information almost indifferently. It was their affection, not titles, she wanted. She knew well enough that if she was to be the King's sister they would all call her 'Aunt Anne' in private. She even smiled a little, picturing them doing so. Elizabeth and little lisping Edward and solemn little Jane Grey, their second cousin, who was Charles's and Mary's grandchild. 'Aunt Anne' was a good name to hear being shouted joyfully about a house. And now that she had a home of her own and would have no children to fill it with she would like to invite them often. "May I sometimes see Elizabeth?" she asked tentatively.

"As often as you wish," they assured her. They were

only too pleased to offer her anything—now that she had passively agreed to give up her husband and her crown. They almost beamed upon her, basking themselves in the certain approbation of their master. Life at court hadn't been easy since she came, with the King like a raging bull kept from the cow of his choice and the last Chancellor's fate hanging over them like a dreadful warning. But now with Anne's amazing acquiescence the worst of the tension would be over. There would be another wedding and another spell of royal smiles and expansive moods. And instead of all Europe being set by the ears or England being bled by war, only one person would suffer. And by that one woman's loneliness and humiliation everybody but Thomas Cromwell would benefit. Was it any wonder then that they viewed the unresisting sacrificial victim with new appreciation?

The business part of their meeting was over. Sir Thomas Wriothesley had withdrawn with his papers—probably to gather commendation by being the first to set the King's mind at rest—and the mid-summer morning seemed sweeter without him. Out in the Queen's gallery Basset was taking instructions from the doctor and Dorothea was fussing with some food a servant had brought on a tray. The homely smell of freshly-baked bread and new-brewed ale pervaded the room and the rest of the deputation suddenly remembered that milady of Cleves hadn't yet breakfasted. No wonder she had fainted. How inconsiderate of them!

Before leaving, Charles Brandon lingered for a moment or two by the open window, watching a wain laden with fresh hay from the Richmond meadows lurch through the gatehouse arch and turn in the direction of the stables. "Mary, my first wife—who, as you know, was Henry's sister —was very dear to him," he told Anne. "She made him— kinder—I think. She was his confidante in youth and even now he misses her more than most people guess." Not being an expert liar he floundered a little and turned to Cranmer for co-operation. "Do you not think milord Archbishop, that in suggesting that Anne should be his sister and wishing her to remain in England he may be prompted by a desire to regain something of the happy relationship he lost?"

Cranmer was grateful to him for the inspiration, which sounded plausible enough. But Anne was nothing if not logical. "If he can divorce me behind my back is it likely he would ever tell me anything he really felt?" she thought. And, not wishing to hurt Charles's feelings, she only smiled that Mona Lisa smile of hers.

They were all trying to be kind, but she rather wished they would go. Her long nose wrinkled a little, sniffing appreciatively at the crisp manchets and golden honey. Her brother-in-law and Dr. Chamberlain were preparing to depart together; but apparently milord archbishop had something more to say. "There is one other thing, my child——"

He spoke too low for anyone else to hear and Anne waited apprehensively, her dark eyes raised to his kind ones. "*Can* there be anything else?" she murmured with an almost comical grimace. Her face had lost much of its unlined serenity during the six months of her disastrous marriage, and he realized that she had minded all that had passed that morning much more than she had shown.

"I shall no longer be able to have public prayers said for you in all the cathedrals and churches," he was obliged to tell her.

The beautiful dark eyes filled with tears. "That too?" she whispered back. One or two tears brimmed over and she made no effort to hide them. "I am sorry. I loved having the people's prayers," she said. "And sometimes I need them so much." It was the only admission she had ever made about her private suffering—and there could be none bitterer, he deemed, than that of a woman publicly spurned, and denied the children she desired. Her simplicity touched him, and he was torn with envy for her courage. "Wherever I am—in Canterbury, Lambeth or Croydon—you will always have my personal prayers," he promised.

She bent her head beneath the hand he lifted in blessing. For the moment he was her confessor, not the King's servant. He would render only unto God what was God's; so it didn't matter what she said. "I don't mind so much about

Henry—or even the shame of it all," she stammered hurriedly. "But I did love being Queen of England."

Nan Bullen, too, he recalled, had loved being Queen of England. But how different their conception of the honour! To one it meant adulation—to the other service. And as once before, being rowed home to Lambeth, Thomas Cranmer's thoughts were with this unwanted Flemish woman. But this time he pondered, too, on the loss that was England's.

CHAPTER XVIII

All day Anne had wandered alone in the privy garden, trying to decide what her attitude should be to this strange new life in which she would be neither wife nor widow. To her methodical mind it seemed that—if she would preserve any semblance of dignity—she must approach all its eventualities, both large and small, according to some consistent plan. "Because I am stuck away in a dower house I needn't be useless," she thought. "I must turn myself into a sort of universal Tudor aunt."

During the afternoon Mary, who dared not come to her, had sent her confessor instead. A strange thing to do, perhaps, since Anne was still supposed to be a Lutheran. But besides being beset with pity for someone she loved Mary was full of zeal for her faith. At such a moment Anne's soul, which she longed to save, would be very vulnerable. The kind old priest was well versed in consoling the hapless women of Henry's first family, and since his counsel confirmed her own instinctive desire not to make a fuss, Anne felt even more than ever that the Church of Rome was a haven of refuge. "Acceptance takes the sting out of adverse fortune; and smiling acceptance may even turn it into moral victory," he told her, with an endearing mixture of spiritual and worldly wisdom. So Anne strove to relinquish her grandeurs with good grace and to gather up gratefully the good things which were left. For her there would be more than for most women. She had good health, good sense and good temper, and there would be everyday loves and pleasures which she must cherish and lay as comfort to her cheated heart.

When at last she returned to her apartments she found Wriothesley waiting for her. He had brought a large sum of money from the King. An advance on her pension to cover current expenses, he called it. Anne called it conscience money. A hardy little sprig of cynicism was growing up in her mind, providing a certain amount of protection from the vagaries of men. And she accepted without a qualm the manors of Lewes and Bletchingly and the rent roll of Denham Hall and another new dress, to say nothing of a pearl-dropped pendant which she remembered seeing in Holbein's portrait of Jane Seymour. Everything had its price, she supposed, trying on her predecessor's jewellery – even the crown of England. And loading her with gifts probably made Henry feel less uncomfortable. But in return he wanted her renunciation in writing. Otherwise, he had explained to Wriothesley, he had but a woman's word and she might change her mind. Which was funny, coming from Henry.

But only by keeping her temper could Anne hope to keep the remnants of her pride.

So after they had supped—quietly in her own part of the palace because the great hammerbeam roof of the disused hall had long been shrouded in cobwebs—she wrote to Henry agreeing to 'repose herself in his goodness' and dutifully subscribing herself his sister and servant. Laboriously her pen scratched over the paper. Such fulsome compositions didn't come easily to her and when she had finished—not knowing how to sign herself now she was no longer his wife—she indulged in a defiant flourish and an unnecessarily flamboyant 'Anna, daughter of Cleves.'

And finally, seeing that the insatiable Secretary was still waiting, she drew the wedding ring from her finger. The words carved on the inner surface mocked her in the shifting gleam of a taper as a page came to light the candles on her desk. 'God Send Me Well To Keep.' Ah, well, she had worn it for only a short six months—but she had managed to keep her head. She would wake to-morrow and the next day and the next, please God, to the homely smell of brewing and baking and the warmth of sunshine. How long, she wondered, would Katherine Howard wear it? Anne laid the magnificent, misleading thing on her folded letter and pushed them towards the King's Secretary with a gesture indicating that they were his for the taking. "That finishes the whole business, I think," she said as unemotionally as if she were concluding a deal with her wine merchant or her chandler; and bade him an unresentful 'Goodnight.'

When she was alone she sat gazing for a minute or two at her ringless hand. There was something naked and unprotected-looking about it. Like an abandoned child, she thought longingly of home; and pulling a fresh sheet of paper towards her, she began another letter—to William. "My dear and well beloved brother——." This time the words flowed swiftly, straight from her heart. As she wrote the very walls of the Swan Palace seemed to spring up round her so that she felt herself to be surrounded by the family to whom she addressed her thoughts. There was one point on which she could still fight. If William insisted, perhaps Henry would let her go home. It would be wonderful to be there again. To take up her old uneventful life—to help her mother with the household accounts and ride with her brother along the banks of the mighty Rhine. To forget all that had happened to her in England so that it faded like an ugly dream. And yet—and yet—it hadn't all been ugly. There were things she didn't want to forget. Elizabeth gathering armfuls of may in Greenwich park, the warm hearts of the people in the narrow London streets, sports and pageants and dancing such as they never had in Flanders. And some elusive spiritual value that these things represented—something fair and laughing as the hilly Surrey fields, robust and reliable as the oxen that ploughed them. Something in the English which her receptive senses had touched, but scarcely got to know.

Her hand began to lag a little across the page, only half conscious of the new tie that dragged it. The real argument against going home, of course, was failure. She remembered how her father had championed the new, reformed religion; how hard her brother had worked for a Lutheran alliance with England. Both as a woman and as an instrument of policy she had failed them. And if she went home now against Henry's will it would mean the breaking-off of friendly relations—the weakening of her country—perhaps war. Eager young men slaughtered, as Dorothea's lover had been, with the cup of life still full and sparkling in their hands. The eager, spontaneous sentences slowed down. A blot fell from the end of her pen.

Another, and more personal, consideration set her biting at the feather of her quill. Could she face the people at home as an unwanted bride, sent back like a bale of stinking fish to the vendor? Wouldn't her name always be associated with ridicule—the cruellest weapon of all? It was bad enough here, where no one knew about the exultation and preparation there had been when the English envoys came. But at least no one here had seen her setting forth in her hideous best clothes with her three hundred sober gentlemen —in a pomp which seemed so paltry now. Nor would they ever guess that the poor Düren servants had had to go without new liveries to pay for all that finery. No, no, she couldn't go back now. And—refusing to hide behind the last shreds of self-deception—she had to admit that as long as England held Hans Holbein she didn't really want to.

Anne tore the untidy, blotted sheets across and across. In the morning she would write to William and assure him that everything had been done with her consent and that she was being generously treated. But now she would go to bed. She seemed to have crammed a life-time of emotion into a day. . . . How merciful of God to set a gulf of sleep between one limit of endurance and the next!

But when the moonlight etched a pattern of the casements across the floor, and the maddening scent of jasmine invaded the stillness of the room, and a nightingale poured its love song on the summer night, Anne rose from her great double bed. Tearing the elaborate nightgown from her body, she stared searchingly at her reflection glimmering faintly in the mirror. Her moon-bathed limbs looked tall and pale as a silver birch; the cleft between her breasts, half shrouded by masses of dark disordered hair, an exciting secret place, the softened outline of her finely drawn brows and pointed chin was enchanting. Surely, only a madman blinded by his own unlawful lusts could say that as a wife she was undesirable! She was twenty-five—a woman whose sex instincts had matured late—and now all her frustrated body was afire with a vitality which could know release only in the natural begetting of children. Counsellors, lawyers, thin-blooded churchmen—all that they saw in her predicament was death to ambition and slight to pride. But what right had any libertine to take her, experiment, awaken her sleeping senses and then betray her with the foulest lie a man could tell and leave her unfulfilled and mateless? The long years stretched ahead, full of such nights as this. . . .

Glancing back at the tumbled bed, a cavern of mounded coverlets in the ebony darkness of the curtains, Anne wondered in what house Henry lay to-night. Knowing with whom, and knowing that all men knew. Not caring for that, but for all her wasted, passing, passionate youth. He had babbled to other men about his aversion, she remembered, smoothing her well-turned flanks with hands that had once been prudish in their austerity. But no aversion that he could prate about could ever have equalled hers that first night when she heard him outside her door likening her to a Flemish mare. Yet because he was her husband, who had never frittered away her forces on light loves, would willingly have given him sons. And now, to suit his worn-out desires, she must go childless all her days.

As if to shut out the sight of herself, Anne threw up a bare arm across eyes hot with anger. Why hadn't she sinned when she might have done? Why, why hadn't she given herself to the man she loved, that night in Calais, when all the new sweetness of awakened desire and the holiday atmosphere of a foreign port conspired to urge her to his arms? Why hadn't she lived once—fully and wonderfully—as other women did, risking even the shameful price Bullen had paid for lovers? For what could be worse than the neglected shame and the half-death of sterility meted out to her own virtuous self-denial? Self-denial spawned from a lot of inhibitions which all the rest of the world appeared to flout. "Why, why did I deny my body for the sake of some silly scruple about my soul!" she moaned.

But in the morning she was sane. She was the 'straightly' brought up daughter of a Lutheran duke. Nightgowns were garments to be primly fastened and scruples the dividing line between adulterers and people who lived decent lives. She thanked God that Holbein was older and wiser and—though she hated to admit it—more platonic in his affection than she. It was enough to face the world clear-eyed and to know that he lived in London with the same river running by. That he lived in safety, enriching the world with his work, and not easing Henry's divorce proceedings by a dangerous dalliance and risking his own handsome head to the gruesome publicity of a pole on Tower Bridge. It was so like Anne. Not sinning herself, but through her temptations learning sympathy with sinners. And as she grew older it was largely for this incapability of being censorious that people loved her. And now that she knew where she stood in this mad Tudor pattern, there were a hundred and one things to do. Ordinary, kindly duties which she could take pleasure in doing.

There was that letter to write to William. And a parting present to choose for Tom Culpepper, for now she was no longer Queen no doubt he would have to return to the King's household. She must set young Bess to cajole him into telling her something he really wanted, for lovelorn and forgetful as poor Tom had been of late she would miss him sadly. And now that she had a permanent abiding place there would be the orphans and poor on her estate to look after. She must consult Mary about that. And then she must make another visit to the Steelyard to buy that pet monkey Edward had set his heart on. Anne made a note of these things on the tablets jangling from her waist. And then, of course, there were her books. . . .

She went to the little closet where she worked and looked at them with loathing. An imposing array of ponderous, leather-bound, brass-clasped tomes spread out just as she had left them. And suddenly she realized that she needn't pore over them any more. No longer need she try to live up to Henry. Every day for the past six months it had been dinned into her that she must please him—and now she could stop. She could spend her time doing the things that she liked. She heaved a prodigious sigh of relief and walked back to her pleasant sitting-room where Culpepper was trying out on Basset a song which everybody knew he had written for his cousin Katherine. The high heels of her new French shoes tapped cheerfully along the oak floor-boards as she went. "I want all those books taken away, Tom," she announced, bustling into the room on a pleasant swirl of Tuscan silk.

Katherine's hands were stilled on the clavichord and Culpepper, inspired script still in hand, asked in surprise what he should do with them. "Oh, give them to a church or some library," said Anne airily. And when he had gone she bade Basset play a pavan while she picked up her scarlet skirts and danced down the sunny length of the room. And Dorothea, coming in at the opposite door with a pile of freshly laundered caps, stood with her mouth open, shocked to her correct Flemish soul. Considering that the news of Anne's divorce had been made public only that morning, it was as bad as seeing someone dance at their own funeral.

Catching sight of her face, Anne burst out laughing and kissed them both. "Don't you see, my dears, that I am free?" she explained, with all the joyful amazement of one who is only just beginning to realize it herself. "Free to run my own home as I like and spend my leisure with people I love. Free to do anything I like——"

But Dorothea looked dubious. Nothing would ever persuade her that any good thing could come out of a country that had insulted her mistress. "Except to marry or go home," she reminded them.

Anne's face clouded momentarily. "Well, at least I don't suppose the King will ever come here," she prophesied, having been taught to count her blessings.

She had forgotten that Henry delighted in surprise visits. That the consternation on the faces of unprepared hosts appealed to his prankish sense of humour and the stir caused by his arrival fed his vanity.

CHAPTER XIX

From that day Anne took the reins of her new household between her own capable fingers. She bade farewell to the exalted personages who had clamoured for office about her when she became Queen, and found to her surprise that many of them had in six short months so far forgotten their ambitions as to weep at parting. It had, apparently, been their first taste of a royal household unruffled by jealousies and malicious back-chat. After their departure she took the trouble to welcome personally each member of the humbler entourage that would now be hers and to see to it that they understood their duties and performed them to her liking. She sent for the account books, checked stock with the cellarer and inspected the kitchens. And because she and cobwebs could not live together she spent part of the advance on her annuity on refurbishing the great hall and showed her ladies how to repair the costly, old-fashioned tapestries.

And one hot August afternoon in the middle of all this pother, the King arrived.

Anne, who had been making sure there was adequate bedding in the maids' dormitory, heard the clatter of hoofs and looked down to see him riding into the outer courtyard. The round, brown-centred sunflowers topping the red brick of the garden wall were not more joyful than his face; and his splendid, bejewelled bulk seemed to emerge like the midday sun from the cool shadow of the gatehouse archway. "He had had his way with Katherine," she thought, noting how Royal Benignity shone upon her running grooms. And even as she hurried along the wardrobe corridor to change her dress, Hawe, her comptroller, was at her heels and the head cook wringing his hands before her. Both the Imperial and the French ambassadors were come with His Grace, it appeared. And the High Admiral of England. And a dozen other gentlemen—and their servants. And there was nothing—positively nothing—fit to set before them.

Anne raised sceptical brows at such unseemly confusion, for this was precisely the kind of crisis with which she had been trained to cope. Even if one couldn't converse in Latin or strum a lute one did derive *something* from being 'brought up straightly' at a domesticated mother's elbow; it seemed. "Nothing to eat in my palace?" she scoffed gently. "What about the plump pigeons I saw in the lofts and the fat carp in the stew pond? And the dozens of hogsheads of good Gascoigny laid down in Henry the Seventh's time? And it is extremely unlikely," she added, with a twinkle in her eye which belied the displeasure in her voice, "that the King will be staying the night."

"How shall I have the tables set, Madam?" panted the comptroller.

Anne regarded him calmly. "Use the pewter dinner service, of course. There's no need to panic, Hawe, even if all the gold and silver ware *has* been removed to Greenwich."

"But the matter of precedence," he persisted. "Now that your ladyship is no longer——"

Of course, the good man was right. It was a nice point, and one mustn't offend against the complicated etiquette of this English Court. As the King's sister she mustn't give place even to an imperial ambassador, but as his subject she couldn't very well sit at Henry's right hand without being invited to do so. Anne's sensible mind easily solved the problem—all the more easily because she had no touchy personal pride. "Lay my cover at a separate table—just below the dais," she ordered. It would be terribly inconvenient for conversation and she hoped maliciously that it would make Henry feel uncomfortable.

The putty-faced cook still hovered. "And how am I to serve the carp, milady?"

Anne raised exasperated hands to Heaven. As if there were any question of how to cook carp fit for a king! "Fry it in butter, imbecile, and garnish it with bay leaves!" she hissed, brushing past him to her own apartments and the comfort of Dorothea's ministrations. For even if it meant keeping Henry waiting she didn't intend to be caught a

second time looking anything like she had looked at Rochester.

But she needn't have worried. She had learned a good
deal about clothes since then. Mary had seen to that. Judi-
ciously, she had imposed the restraint of her own good taste
upon her friend's tendency to flamboyancy. And now the
constraint of her unhappy marriage had fallen from Anne,
and the fear of death. For the first time she moved with the
cool assurance of individual freedom, so that a new vivacity
lightened her manner and a sly humour crept into her
speech. One couldn't live in Tudor England and retain the
straight-laced solemnity of Cleves. Anne went to welcome
her unexpected guests in a gown of warm brown velvet,
with kirtle and sleeves of dull pink which matched the
flustered colour in her cheeks : but her emancipation suited
her so well that she would have made a comely hostess in
any dress.

She showed no sign of resentment, and the King's relief
was patent. All eyes were covertly upon their meeting. No
longer fettered, they greeted each other pleasantly as ordinary individuals, and because she no longer stood between
him and his desires nothing about her annoyed him any
more. In fact, the deep harmony of her speaking voice
pleased him so much that he wondered how he could ever
have likened her to a mare. Although he would never admit
it he knew he had wronged her deeply, and he was only too
anxious to show her every courtesy consistent with her
present state. It was interesting, too, to find himself back in
his boyhood home and when Anne tactfully suggested that
he should show them round her own garden, he was only
too pleased to do so. He didn't guess, of course, that she was
giving her people time to deal with the carp and the pastry
for the pigeon pie, and he thoroughly enjoyed pointing out
to the assembled company the great mulberry tree beneath
which his beloved mother used to sit, the lawn where
his sisters Margaret and Mary once played and the butts
where he had often beaten his elder brother Arthur at
archery.

Apparently he wasn't worrying about his supper and after a while he drew Anne apart into the neglected rose garden. She guessed what he wanted to say, but judging by the way he hummed and hawed he didn't find it easy. But it wasn't her place to speak until she was addressed, and in any case she had no intention of helping him out. It was such a pleasant change to feel perfectly cool and collected while a Tudor sweated with embarrassment. "I feel you should be one of the first to know," he blustered out at last, "that I intend to marry the Lady Katherine Howard immediately."

He had stopped short by a little splashing fountain at the end of a grass alley and Anne cast a sidelong glance at his pompous stance. She knew that he really felt as nervous as a braggart schoolboy. "He wants to know if I'll make a fuss," she thought. "And he's not quite sure how the nation will react." And a she had heard nothing of any wedding preparations at Westminster, she guessed that he was already married to the wench. Secretly, no doubt, in one of his private chapels. Remembering her manners, she dropped a formal curtsey in acknowledgment of his graciousness. "I hope your Grace will be very happy," she said politely.

Possibly her voice was a shade too cheerful. Henry began to frown, kicking at a loose stone with his great, square-toed shoe. "You don't seem to mind much," he complained sulkily. It was one thing to be let out easily, quite another to be indecently expedited on one's way. Poor Catherine had been suitably heart-broken.

Anne realized that she must choose her words more carefully. Stopping to detach her flowing sleeve from an untrimmed briar, she tried hastily to compose something noncommittal. "It has always been my wish to please your Grace in all things," she submitted meekly. She had often heard glib young Bess say that when taken in a fault.

Henry ignored the familiar platitude. "Yet you fainted when they came to tell you about the divorce," he observed. Of course, that *would* please him, the smug sheik! Anne was wild that he should suppose she had done so for love of

216

him. She even dared to open her lips on a pert retort. But disaster was averted because, jerking her head up angrily, she became aware that he was looking her over as if she really were a brood mare of sorts. In her new high-heeled French shoes she stood almost as tall as he and she read anxiety in the small, light eyes so near her own. Suddenly the cause of his unceremonious visit and their tête-à-tête in the rose-garden dawned on her. Of course he had wanted to find out her reactions to this swift fifth marriage—to assure himself that she would make no trouble. But there was more to it than that. He had sworn publicly that their marriage had never been consummated—and now the blundering old fool wasn't sure that he could get away with it. Someone— probably some inventive member of the Protestant Party— must have started a wild, wishful rumour in a last-minute essay to prevent his marrying Katherine. One of those un-founded, intimate rumours that are always flying round royal households. After all, during most of their marriage— willingly or unwillingly—he had slept with her almost every other night of his life. It was common knowledge among the ladies and gentlemen of the bedchamber, and every little backstairs page must know it. And now he half believed she might be pregnant. Delicious, secret laughter bubbled up in Anne as she perceived his dilemma. He must be feeling rather like the dog in the old wives' tale of the bone and the shadow. It was possible that Katherine mightn't give him any children, while she herself still *might*. Here indeed was a weapon with which to pay off old scores. A delectable weapon with which she could play off Henry's passion for her maid-of-honour against his very real concern for his realm.

"Would you like me to send Chambers to see you?" he suggested awkwardly.

Anne assumed an expression of bland density. "I thank God I have always enjoyed very good health," she assured him piously. "This was the first time that ever I fainted in my life."

That, of course, only seemed to confirm the rumour. Henry stared at her yet more uneasily. "You don't think

——," he began, with the familiarity of any anxious husband.

But Anne was occupied with a rose-bud she was sticking in her belt. "What should I think," she murmured humbly, "being but your Grace's sister? Except that your Grace must be hungry and the supper will be burned."

Anne heard him swear savagely under his breath. She knew that he could have shaken her. But he wouldn't dare to lay a finger on her. Neither would he dare to make a laughing-stock of himself by insisting upon his physicians examining her. She had him in a cleft stick and she meant to keep him there as long as she could.

And as he allowed himself to be coerced back to supper the sight of his perplexity was so refreshing that some of her loathing for him melted into something akin to pity. She understood him so well that she felt towards him as a mother towards her spoiled boy. Her desire to revenge his insults resolved itself into a queer vow that she would fool him wherever and whenever opportunity presented itself until she had him eating out of her hand. A revenge tinged with laughter which might buy back her self-respect without corroding her soul.

Henry had expected a make-shift meal in her private apartments and was gratified to find the tables laid in the hall just as they used to be in his father's time. There was no pomp of gold dishes nor any music from the gallery, but the tall oriel windows had been polished until they winked with sunlight reflected from the sparkling Thames and there appeared to be enough food for the unexpected suite with which he had so inconsiderately burdened his hostess. The dish of well-seasoned carp presented to him smelled appetizing and completely restored his good humour. "You've done something to the place," he remarked, looking round at the familiar walls.

"My ladies and I have been trying to mend the tapestries," admitted Anne modestly, from her lowly table.

"But you don't have to do that," Henry shouted down to her from the high table. "It's an expert's job—and endless.

I'll send Frances Lilgrave. Her family have kept our hangings in repair for years. They work for the Howards too."

Anne thanked him pleasantly. She didn't want a woman who worked for the Howards and felt she could probably make quite as good a job of it herself; but naturally she didn't like to say so.

"I hope you find yourself comfortable here?" her ex-husband added kindly.

Anne could feel both ambassadors hanging on her reply. It could, of course be weighted with international significance. Something they could report to their royal masters. But she had no ambition to start a European war. "I am overwhelmed by your Majesty's generosity," she replied placidly. "The only trouble is that the place is almost too large for me. And I could wish perhaps that the meat jacks and sinks were a thought more modern." The ambassadors sagged back in their seats. Here was a woman deprived of a crown, and she complained only about meat jacks and sinks. But Anne was, of all things, an opportunist. After all, she argued, if Henry were in a sufficiently expansive mood to send an expert about the tapestries he might perhaps do something about the old-fashioned kitchens. Her genius for getting things done lay in the fact that she had never been troubled by a sense of the incongruous.

Henry grinned. He knew all about the sinks. He knew, too, why he had been glad to make her so lavish a gift. "My first wife found it too large," he admitted. "But my mother was an extraordinarily capable woman. No one seems to have been able to manage the place since her day."

His complacency was a challenge to any daugher-in-law. Anne pounced upon it as upon a glove cast in the domestic lists. "Couldn't they?" she murmured politely. For a moment or two she bent over her plate recalling some advice Cranmer had once given her—something about doing whatever she *could* do better than Henry's other women. She had almost to shout in order to make him hear her across the shaven head of an intervening bishop, and presently she shocked the entire company by saying quite loudly, "Perhaps your Grace would honour me by bringing your bride to Richmond in a few months' time?"

An instant hush fell upon the tables. Visitors and household alike looked up with portions of pigeon pie suspended between plate and mouth. Even the servants stopped their soft-footed ritual with the dishes. It was simply unheard of. The King's wives—past and prospective—didn't visit each other. If they were still alive, they hated each other. They always had done. And so had the Catholic and Protestant parties who had proposed them. But if it came to anything so indecent as this. . . . The Imperial representative almost choked, seeing his job sliding from him. For if discarded queens started living in amity with their rivals where would the need for religious parties – or ambassadors – or, come to that, for all the evil, hatred and uncharitableness mentioned in Cranmer's new liturgy?

But somehow the audacious thing sounded natural enough as Anne said it. And after one suspicious glance at her, Henry gave a great burst of genial laughter. It rang healthily to the rafter, relieving the tension so that his parasites—however badly shaken—could at least get on with their food. "Why not?" he agreed, secretly applauding her common sense. And—being in all senses a big man—he capped her unconventional invitation by suggesting courteously that after he and Katherine returned from their honeymoon she must visit them at Hampton Court. He was quick to perceive how much easier her attitude of natural acceptance rendered his position, and although most people might attribute it to some lack of sensibility in her, he couldn't but be grateful. Had his other wives behaved like that, how many unpleasant crimes his tender conscience might have been saved. It was as if Anne were deliberately making it easy for him to get his pretty Katherine without bloodshed, and generosity in others invariably stirred something reciprocal in him. So now, having got his own way in everything and finding Anne so amenable and entertaining, he insisted upon her coming to sit beside him though it meant moving the bishop and disarranging the whole table.

And after supper, while people sat in groups about the hall, he waxed so merry and affectionate with her that the irrepressible Marillac went round trying to find out from her women if it were indeed true that she was pregnant and some of the Howard faction were terrified lest the King meant to take her back.

When at last he took his departure a midsummer moon was silvering the Twickenham meadows and his sleepy servants reckoned that it would be past midnight before he drew rein at Hampton, where his new young bride must be wondering what had become of him. Anne had followed dutifully into the courtyard to see him mount and even then he had tarried to ask if she felt lonely away from court. And Anne, just as if she were really his sister, had asked if Elizabeth might come and keep her company. Because he had been telling her how worried he was about a cold young Edward couldn't shake off; she had even suggested that Mrs Ashley might bring the boy too for a change of air. "You know he will be safe with me," she had pleaded ingenuously.

And Henry—who wanted to be free to take a long holiday after all the strain of the divorce proceedings—knew that his precious son *would* be safe at Richmond. Like most successful kings, he had learned to be a remarkably good judge of his own subjects. Blind as he was to his own failings, he kept a clear eye on the characters of others and seldom laid a charge on the wrong kind of man—or woman. He had watched this Flemish woman handling Edward at Havering; and he knew that she wanted to have him not because he was heir to the throne or the Protestants' hope, but simply because he was an ailing and lovable child. So he gave his consent, knowing that the gesture would help to appease the Londoners, who had taken Anne to their hearts.

But for himself, he intended to enjoy the Howard girl quietly in the country. And this time there would be no attempt at processions. He remembered only too well the humiliating silence with which they had greeted her cousin.

So he rode away from Richmond, taking Tom Culpepper with him. And Culpepper bade Anne an affectionate and rather incoherent farewell, going sullenly as a man must who resumes his duties as gentleman-of-the-bedchamber to a master who sleeps with the girl he loves.

They were followed by the rest of the distinguished party; and the Imperial ambassador, being a disappointed man, climbed heavily to his saddle. Sorely puzzled, he watched milady of Cleves re-enter the palace. "If there be any truth in this rumour that she is with child," he grumbled in under-tones to his French colleague, "she must be marvellously stupid not to harp on the only string which could hold him!"

But Marillac, whose mind was infinitely subtler, paused with one elegant foot in the stirrup noting how a lighting of tapers at upper windows preceded Anne's leisurely pro-gress up the grand staircase, along endless corridors to her own apartments. "Marvellously prudent, you mean, mon ami," he chuckled appreciatively, swinging himself into the saddle. "She has kept her head in both senses of the word, and now everybody can be happy and she can get anything she likes out of him as long as she keeps him guessing."

They were joined by the bluff High Admiral. As they clattered slowly across the courtyard all three of them looked back uneasily as though their thoughts were still with the woman who had come in such a whirl of ceremonial gor-geousness and was going out so quietly, so unprotestingly. Although the susceptible Frenchman was on the winning side, he couldn't suppress a sigh as some unseen hand drew the curtains across the bedroom windows, so symbolically blotting her brief blaze of light into obscuring privacy. But the diminishing sound of hoof-beats warned them that the King and Culpepper were already half-way across Richmond Green and heading for the honeymoon palace at Hampton; and whether they wished or not they must follow in the flower-strewn pathway of the new girl Queen.

The portly High Admiral of England rode with the two ambassadors under the gatehouse and out into the warm silvery night. It was no concern of his, of course. But he had watched Anne, homesick and sea-sick, with scarcely a coherent phrase of English, trying to learn card-games to please her future husband. "Well, it pleased milord the King to get rid of her," he summed up with a gusty sigh, "but for myself she always appeared to be a very brave lady."

CHAPTER XX

Henry Tudor lingered long over his fifth honeymoon, as if hating to set down the last loving-cup that life would offer him. Quite humbly he reduced his girth by exercise and simple living, and tried to live worthily during this Indian summer of his days. There must indeed have been a sweetness about this rose of his that so drew the hearts of men. Court life about London faded as a forgotten dream, time killed the worrying rumours about Anne's pregnancy and by the beginning of November Marillac was writing in his chatty despatches that no more was heard of the repudiated Queen than if she were dead.

But Anne was very much alive. For the first time in her life she was free to arrange her days as she chose. She bought some more dresses and having finished with her books she went out a good deal visiting her neighbours, riding in the home park and going to parties. And before long people who hadn't set foot in Richmond for years were coming to visit her. A little furtively at first, perhaps; but it was difficult to be furtive about Anne and hadn't the King himself set the fashion by supping with her?

Her riverside home with its garden-wall built so close to the strand that trees and turrets, flowering bushes and blazoned oriels were all reflected like some fairy palace on the surface of the water, lay conveniently between Hampton Court and London. Jaded statesmen, mooring their barges for an hour or two at her landing steps, could always be sure of a well-cooked meal, a good listener and an atmosphere where nobody was interested in politics. Mary came often, of course—and Charles. Cranmer felt it his spiritual duty to call occasionally. And Seymour, the adored uncle, came while the children were staying and made it seem like a real home with his boisterous laughter and lavish presents. Sometimes Anne's visitors happened to arrive on the same day and, seeing that she had friends in both parties, there was frequently a little stiffness between them. But Anne couldn't be bothered to sort them out and she felt it was probably very good for them. The more often they met in such an unceremonious atmosphere the more chance they would have of ironing out their differences of opinion, or at least of coming to respect each other's intentions.

"The King is still away," they told her each time they came.

"They say he has taken up archery again and plays tennis for half an hour before breakfast," boasted Charles, as they gathered round her fire after a conveniently cadged dinner. Rain was lashing the river outside most depressingly and each of them must have been struck with the same idea—that it would be pleasant to visit the divorced Queen.

Mary stiffened in her straight-backed chair. She was always at her harshest when Cranmer was present, although she tried hard not to be for Anne's sake. "There is very disturbing news from Scotland and he has never neglected affairs of state for any woman before," she remarked. With all the humourless dignity that was in her she resented the ridicule her father's amours piled upon their name, and because her own mother had been set aside for a maid-of-honour she was all the more sore for Anne.

Charles stretched a still shapely leg towards the blaze. "She makes him feel young and irresponsible, no doubt," he said, suppressing a yawn. It was always so comfortable in milady of Cleves' rooms that one was apt to forget one wasn't at home—except that at home his affectionate young wife often plagued him to pet and cosset her when he was tired. Whereas Anne never teased or nagged or intruded. She just went cheerfully about her own affairs and was there—always ready to listen intelligently—when one wanted her. He couldn't imagine why Henry. . . . But then, of course, Anne had changed so much of late. Charles Brandon looked across at her, trying to remember why they had all laughed at her when she first came. She had turned from him to remonstrate with Elizabeth who was coaxing Seymour to come and see Edward's new monkey, but there was a cheerful lilt to her voice as she bade them both make less noise and a detached sort of smile on her lips as she watched him lift the child to his shoulder and carry her, squealing delightedly, on their quest. And Charles began to wonder whether this woman for whom they had all been so sorry might not be well out of this marriage business and hoodwinking them all. Somehow it had simply never occurred to any of them that she might have a lover, for instance.

As if aware of his scrutiny, she had picked up a fan of flame-coloured ostrich feathers—ostensibly to shield her face from the fire. "Is Tom Culpepper with them?" she asked, in leisurely pursuance of the conversation.

"Yes," replied Cranmer, with his gentle smile. "And I imagine he has to slow up his tennis considerably, poor fellow—for there is no one else except the servants."

"Poor Tom!" sighed Anne. But she was not thinking of the tennis. And Mary, supposing the sigh to be for her own self-esteem, explained kindly that her father always had preferred small women.

Anne moved irritably, tumbling her beautiful fan to the floor. Like most tall women, she secretly yearned to be called by diminutive endearments that would make her feel frail and cared for. "Then why did he have to choose me?" she demanded.

"The miniature Holbein first sent, showed only your head and shoulders," pointed out the archbishop reasonably.

Anne stood there in the middle of the group with the firelight dancing over her. Six months of crowded experiences had added interest to her face and smoothed out that faint suggestion of raw-boned gawkiness. Since life had become more peaceful she had put on more flesh, which suited her. "And you all think he flattered me?" she challenged, looking from one to the other in good-natured defiance. They all knew that Holbein was too great an artist to flatter anyone; but before they could answer she added, with a kind of naïve exultation, "You see, Hans said he was painting my soul."

Only Mary noticed her use of the painter's Christian name. Charles smiled in his trim, brown beard, knowing how little

226

any woman's soul would count against Katherine Howard's smallest finger until his brother-in-law's desire had burned itself out. "Perhaps if Henry could have seen your soul——," he ventured teasingly.

To his surprise he detected laughter beneath Anne's provokingly long lashes. "Perhaps he will now he doesn't have to look at my body," she came back at him as wittily as any French-bred court beauty. But almost immediately she was grave again. She always was when she spoke of Holbein. Presumably she had a great veneration for his art. "Where is that miniature now?" she asked.

They had to admit they didn't know. "It used to stand on the tallboy beside his bed," Charles remembered vaguely.

But he needn't have felt uncomfortable. Anne was so free from sentimentality. "Well, if he doesn't want it I wish he'd give it to me," she said. "I've a feeling that one day it may be worth a lot."

They had to laugh at her prosaic business acumen. But Mary wondered if there were another reason. Stooping to retrieve the fan from the floor beside her, she decided that only one master hand could have designed the exquisite scroll of swans carved across the ivory struts. And Anne had carried it everywhere with her these last few days. "Perhaps you could get another done," she suggested casually, "now that Holbein is in your house."

Everyone present looked up in surprise. But Mary spoke advisedly, not to betray her friend's confidence but to protect her good name. There were always plenty of malicious tongues ready to wag about a woman left in Anne's peculiar position; and it wouldn't be the first time the visit of a painter or a music master had been twisted into scandal. Mary knew that it was always wiser to speak openly of the matter before people who mattered.

Although Anne chided her for spoiling her secret, she turned easily enough to her other guests with an explanation. "I've taken advantage of Edward's visit to have Master Holbein paint the child as a surprise for his father. I'm hoping it's going to be one of the best things he's done. Would you care to come and see it, Charles?"

Charles accepted the offer with alacrity. He had been thinking of asking Holbein to paint the two small boys Catalina had given him, but hadn't quite liked to since the man was under royal displeasure. But perhaps now this imperturbable woman had given him a lead. . . . Holbein, it appeared, was working in the great hall because of the light, but in that winter afternoon hour before the torches were lit the gallery leading to it was already full of shadows. And for Charles Brandon, it was full of memories. Like parts of many houses that are seldom lived in, it had become something of a museum, and there were things there which he hadn't seen since he was a boy. The long, iron-bound crusading coffer into which he and the first Mary Tudor used so daringly to drop adolescent love notes to each other, and the Saracen chessmen with which they used to play.

"Take them—as far as I am concerned," offered Anne, seeing how lovingly he dallied over each piece. "And I only wish Henry would take away that colossal suit of armour or have the gallery widened!" The finely wrought suit, shaped to Henry's size, stood near a small window almost blinding her in the rays of a low, red sun.

Charles looked up, quite horrified. "But it's solid gold. The Emperor sent it to him for a wedding present," he protested.

Emperor or no emperor, Anne hated the thing because she had to pass it every time she went to matins or evensong and it always made her feel as if Henry himself were in the house. "Which wedding?" she asked flippantly.

"Yours, of course," said Charles, carefully closing the box of chessmen and tucking it under his arm. "It wouldn't have fitted him before."

"Well, all that gold would have been far more useful to my new orphanage and almshouse for all he's ever likely to use it. Just think how funny he'd look in armour!" jibed Anne, with a little spurt of ribald laughter. She wanted to hurry down to the hall where Holbein was working—and where she would find baby Edward and possibly Elizabeth. They were the high lights of life for her. But Charles and the imposing suit of armour were blocking her way. "Why must you hate him so, Anne?" he was asking earnestly.

Anne simply stared at him in speechless amazement. That any man could ask such a question. Dear God, weren't there a thousand reasons why she should hate him? Hadn't he humiliated her in the eyes of all Europe? Hadn't he cheated her of children? But the only words that came to her sounded trifling. "Don't you suppose it hurts to be called a Flemish mare?" she almost shouted at him. It was queer how that seemed to have rankled most of all.

"Of course it did, my dear child," agreed Charles. "It was—inexcusable. But at least you must have known you were quite a personable young woman."

"Well?" demanded Anne, feeling that that made it all the worse. She knew that when she had been Queen he would never have dared—or bothered—to talk to her like this; but people said all sorts of things to her nowadays.

"What I am going to say is treason—but I think it will be between friends?" Charles had dropped that air of aloof superiority and was smiling down at her almost appealingly. "Hasn't it occurred to you that nobody cares to call Henry a fat old man—but he knows only too well that he is one?"

"I see," said Anne slowly.

They walked down the length of the gallery together and as they went he tried to make sure that she did. "We used to do everything together when we were young. And now when I am with him I feel apologetic because I have 'kept my figure'—as you women say. It is a very hard thing for a fastidious, intellectual man to grow fat."

Anne wanted to ask if fastidiousness oughtn't to extend the workings of a man's conscience; but at the top of the main staircase, Charles stopped to point out a less showy suit of armour. It was so plainly fashioned and so tucked away in a dark corner that, although she passed that way every day, Anne had scarcely noticed it. "Henry used to wear that in the lists," he said. In the growing shadows he ran his fingers from gorget to gyve until they found the particular dent he sought. "He only just warded off Northumberland's lance in time, I remember."

229

Anne looked from his almost reverent fingers to the work-manlike steel. It would have fitted a man slender as Culpepper, but considerably taller. A young man with muscles whipcord-strong, who would stride splendidly about the earth and spring lithely to the saddle. A young man with reddish hair, with Edward's fair Plantagenet skin and Elizabeth's fearless eyes. . . . One could fill in the details from that youthful smiling portrait by Van Cleef hanging in the music room.

"He must have changed a lot," she stammered awkwardly. "I remember someone telling me at the Bachelors' Pageant what a marvellous athlete he had been. But I supposed it was the sort of thing people always say about royalty."

Charles left the gallery of memories with a sigh. "Well, you can take it from me that we youngsters at any rate didn't fawn upon him with flattery. We went all out to beat him at tennis or wrestling or whatever we happened to be doing. He would have hated it if we hadn't. We loved him for his ardent spirit, his zest for fun and his good sportsmanship. He would have filled the centre of our stage anyhow, I think, even if he'd been a commoner's son. Some people have that kind of flame in them." Anne was about to descend the half flight of wide, stone stairs but he coaxed her back to the seat beneath the big mullioned window at the top. He was in the mood to talk—and here was Anne to listen. He had hoped to find her alone this rainy day, but there had been all those people in her private apartments and there would be others down in the hall. "I will tell you something," he said, settling the carved chess-box comfortably on his silk-hosed knees. "When Henry first came to the throne he had to marry his favourite sister to the King of France. He hated doing it because Louis was a much married old death's-head and Mary only fifteen and full of fun. She wept and entreated, and Henry was so moved that he promised she should choose her own husband next time. It's terribly hard on a girl, you know."

"I believe I do," said Anne, viciously plumping up a tasselled velvet cushion for her back.

Her erstwhile brother-in-law had the grace to look uncomfortable and hurried on with his tale. "Well, as it happened. Louis was extraordinarily kind to her and the kindest thing of all that he did was to die. Poor Mary was terrified at the time that she would be rushed into a second marriage with some dull Flemish prince——"

"Thank you," murmured Anne, from her corner of the window seat. Certainly, the courtly Suffolk wasn't at his best to-day. But he didn't seem to hear her and she herself was beginning to feel they *were* rather dull compared with some of the amazing people she had met in England.

"So she begged to come home and Henry sent me to fetch her," went on Charles. "God alone knows why, since he must have known we'd always cared for each other !"

Much to her surprise Anne found herself suggesting that perhaps Henry had really *wanted* them to be happy. It was Charles himself—the gorgeous parvenu—who pooh-poohed the suggestion. "Probably it never occurred to him that I would dare lift my eyes so high," he said, quite humbly. "You see, my father was only *his* father's standard-bearer. He saved Henry the Seventh's life at Bosworth when he was plain Henry of Richmond, and they gave us the Suffolk estates. I'm not related to all our Kings like Norfolk."

Anne leaned from her corner to lay an affectionate hand on his arm. "But I like you much better," she told him, touched that he of all men should speak to her so frankly.

He patted her hand absently. She was so soothing. It was nice to have her there, listening to him reliving the exciting past which had begun in this very place. "She clung to me and whispered her love—and I was as wax in her pretty hands. We were married in Paris. . . . She was sweet and fragrant as the dawn. . . ."

Something in Anne ached to touch the magic conjured by his low spoken words. She herself had been married near London—with much ceremony but precious little magic— and with all her frustrated heart she envied them the dangerous rapture they had shared. "And Henry?" she prompted, speaking scarcely above a whisper lest she should break the romantic spell.

"Mary took all the blame," he told her. "She appeased him with all her 'winnings in France'—as she so naïvely called Louis' fabulous gifts. And the new French King and Wolsey very sportingly interceded for us. So I brought her home to England—in the Spring."

"And Henry forgave you?"

"And Henry forgave us. He might quite well have killed me; but he stood godfather to our son instead."

"I didn't know Mary had a son," said Anne.

Charles turned from her to set her gift of chessmen on the seat beside him. "He died a year or two before you came," he said. "Until Edward was born we thought he might one day be King. Her other two were daughters."

Sensing a grief in which no words of hers could help, Anne said, "I think I have met your elder daughter, Lady Frances Grey? The one with the solemn little girl."

"Yes—Jane Grey. She is a solemn little thing, isn't she? All brains and no beauty. I've a suspicion they're too strict with her." He dragged himself from his abstraction to ponder doubtfully upon the up-bringing of this sedate little grandchild. He wanted to do the best for her for Mary's sake, and perhaps after all even if she *were* only a girl—the distant sound of Elizabeth's clear, ringing laughter gave him an idea. "Anne," he begged, "I believe it would be awfully good for Jane if you would ask her here sometimes to play with the other children."

"Of course," promised Anne placidly. "She'll be just the age for her cousin Edward."

Charles glanced round at her, uncertain just how far she had read his thoughts. But a servant was coming to light the wall sconces and they sat in silence until he had passed, Anne leaning back against her cushion and the Duke leaning forward with his hands loosely clasped between his knees. As soon as they were alone he began to grin. "You've almost the same devastating candour as Mary," he remarked. "I often wonder if Henry has noticed it."

"You started all that need-of-a-sister stuff before—out of kindness—when I fainted," laughed Anne. "But judging by her portrait she was another of these 'little women,' so it's no good your pretending I'm the least bit like her."

But Charles was regarding her quite earnestly. "I'm not pretending this time. You've changed somehow. You laugh more often. There really *is* something. . . ."

"You know very well this idea of keeping me in the family is just a convenient way out," Anne told him flatly. "Can you imagine Henry ever talking things over with me or telling me things about himself?"

Charles realized that that was exactly what he himself had been doing—dragging her through poignant scenes of his youth which obviously he couldn't dwell on with his wife—boring her no doubt. He rose and offered her his arm. "Don't we all—sooner or later?" he countered rather sheepishly.

"You love him very much, don't you?" she asked.

"The King can do no wrong," he quoted, as they went down the wide staircase together. "But as a man——" He shrugged with a kind of tired dignity. "Don't think I'm blind to his faults, Anne, and often these latter years I've had to do things for him which I hate. It is then that it comforts me to think that when he is acting most like an ogre, he too is looking for the lost splendour of his youth."

Anne squeezed the pearled white satin of his sleeve. "Perhaps he will recapture some of it—with Katherine," she said, lowering her voice as a couple of conspiratorial choristers came scuttling out from her private chapel. Whatever their unlawful occasions, they flattened themselves against the wall at sight of her, leaving the chapel door ajar. Anne smiled indulgently at their guilty faces, set like shiny pink pomegranates on the stiff white plates of their ruffs. The divers scrapes they got into were a constant source of joy to her. From the lighted chapel behind them their companions' voices floated out to her, sweet and pure and holy as only such graceless youngsters' voices can be. They were practising intoning the Lord's Prayer for Christmas. *Dimitte nobis debita nostra.* The sonorous Latin cadences were familiar to everyone. *Forgive us our trespasses.* . . . Perhaps this urgent honeymoon of Henry's which she had taken for sheer lust in him was in part a desperate effort to solve his sensitiveness about growing obese and old—so many people suffered pitiful embarrassment about some physical defect or other which they found too intimate to be spoken of even to their friends. *As we forgive them that trespass against us.* . . . Perhaps in time she might even be able to forgive *him*— her nature being what it was, Anne found happiness in the thought.

She stood listening for a moment or two more, her eyes soft with unshed tears. The two boys had disappeared down the turn of the stairs into the courtyard, and Charles was waiting for her by a great arched door which led into the hall. Anne went to him while his hand was still on the great iron bolt and, reaching up on tip-toe, kissed his cheek. "Give that to your Catalina from me," she said, "for keeping you so kind in spite of—everything."

CHAPTER XXI

It was good to walk into the banqueting hall of her own home and see Holbein working there. A dear familiar figure, always at ease in any company. His broad shoulders and finely moulded head were turned from her, his hands busy on a sheet of vellum. He was too much absorbed to notice her although the place seemed disturbingly full of people. Kate Ashley lifting Edward down from a high-backed chair near the fire, a servant waiting to carry him back to his nursery, the Lilgrave woman and her satellites repairing the dais tapestries and—at the far end by the buttery—Thomas Seymour and Elizabeth, with a pack of hilarious pages, chasing the elusive little monkey in and out of the serving screens.

"How *can* you work in such a pandemonium?" asked Anne, crossing to the open stone hearth in the middle of the hall. She couldn't very well reprove the late Queen's brother in front of the servants, but she hoped he would observe her displeasure.

Holbein turned and bowed formally, but his dark eyes welcomed her more warmly. "I'm afraid the sitting has come to an untimely end," he explained, with his deep easy laugh. "His Grace, it seems, is already over-tired and Mrs. Ashley finds it difficult to induce him and the infernal animal you gave him to sit still at the same time."

Remembering how annoyed he used to get with Amelia, Anne was grateful for his patience. "I'm so sorry," she apologized, as triumphant shrieks from the hunting party proclaimed the capture of their simian prey and Elizabeth came towards her, straightening her little lace cap as she ran. "It's so frightfully *public* here!"

She was thinking of his work; but he was thinking of her attractive maturity. She was no longer the unawakened girl he had found such delight in painting and teasing in Düren.

He laid his wet brush carefully on a metal tray. "Perhaps it is just as well," he muttered, for her ears alone.

Fearing further indiscretions, Anne hastened to make him aware of the Duke's presence behind them. "Don't you think the King will be pleased, Charles?" she called over her shoulder. Secretly she was rather disappointed with the portrait but mistrusted her own judgement. Thomas Seymour came and joined them to comment upon the solemn features of his young nephew and she left the two men to talk art and—she hoped—business, while she enquired anxiously about Edward's over-tiredness and received the onslaught of Elizabeth's tumultuous embrace. The children seemed to be glad she was no longer Queen. They still called her 'Madam' decorously enough in public, but they loved to get her away from the other grown-ups where she could be just 'Aunt Anne' and they could draw her into all their doings; and before Kate Ashley finally coaxed them away to their supper, their hostess found she had let herself in for a Twelfth Night party and promised to invite their cousin Jane for Christmas. "Even if Henry *is* home by then he won't want to invite them this year," she thought. "And Katherine is too young herself to be hankering after other people's children!"

Before rejoining the group by the fire she remembered to see how the mending was getting on and to say a few gracious words to Frances Lilgrave. But although they chatted for a few minutes with the mutual interest of experts, Anne fancied she detected a hint of hostility behind the woman's subservience and wondered if she had inadvertently given offence by starting on the precious tapestries herself. But probably it was just a reflection of the Howards' antagonism. For Lilgrave's widow was a striking-looking woman, graceful as a wand, to whom long association with important families had lent a gentility above her station. So Anne, observing that her fingers were cold from working so far from the fire, asked if she had made any friends about the palace and gave her permission to sit and rest sometimes with her own ladies. She felt oddly relieved, however, when the embroideress explained that she went home each evening to friends in London. "Well, I hope you have company for your journey now it gets dark so early," said Anne, dismissing her pleasantly. And something in the pointed way the woman assured her that she had very good company made her feel that Dorothea, at any rate, might not have approved of her.

After Mary and Charles and the Archbishop had hurried away to catch the afternoon tide, Anne wandered back to the hall fire and sat down in the chair in which Edward had proved such a fractious model. Holbein smiled at her but went on with his work. He was trying to finish a troublesome bit of background before the last of the light went, and Anne was content to watch. She often wondered rather wistfully what it must feel like to be married to a middle-class man and sit nursing his child or mending his clothes while he earned their daily bread. She had learned enough of this particular man's art to understand his technique and the exact effect he was striving after. She could appreciate the value of the pigments he used and the extent to which his clear ultramarine backgrounds enhanced the delicacy of a miniature. She knew too, instinctively, that this portrait she had commissioned was bothering him. She must try to keep the place less like a bear garden. Artistic people were so dependent upon environment—they needed someone to act as a buffer against the petty vexations of life. She glanced round the shadowed length of the hall from which the servants and tapestry workers were gone at last—all except Frances Lilgrave herself who had come down from the dais and was mending a beautiful firescreen banneret by the light of a wall cresset not far away. How conscientious such workers were, coming all that way and working from dawn to dusk with their poor fingers blue with cold! It would seem churlish to turn her away. "And Heaven knows," mused domesticated Anne, "those hangings need mending!" Yet what a pity Henry had sent his people just now.

"Does that woman annoy you?" she asked.

Holbein glanced round to see of whom she spoke and shrugged indifferently. "I've got used to her by now—and we're both artists of a sort," he said, with his habitual tolerance.

Anne picked up a pile of loose crayon sketches; and the monkey, exhausted from play and safe from children's teasing hands, curled itself up on her lap. Although monkeys were the fashionable pets of the moment, Anne didn't really care for them. She preferred dogs. But she had a feeling that the sad-eyed little creature was a foreigner in a strange land and began smoothing its straight, lank hair. It was pleasant sitting there idly with the fire warming her toes. Better, really, than being a Queen. And somehow, here in this quiet English household, one didn't feel like a foreigner any more.

She began turning over the sketches. Mere jottings, some of them were, as if Holbein had been putting stray thoughts on paper before deciding how to use them. Looking through them, one learned so much about the workings of the mind behind each masterpiece. There was a small drawing of the monkey, each hair so soft and vibrant that Anne laughed aloud with delight—and studies of various hands, each full of character. Little Edward's podgy one, grasping a ball— and an exquisitely poised hand with long, tapering fingers stabbing a needle into the heart of a Tudor rose. Frances Lilgrave's, of course. She remembered the cold, clever fingers. He must have enjoyed doing that. Anne looked across at her, seeing her for the first time with an artist's eye. What a perfect model she made with the candlelight on her white cheek and raven hair, the seductive folds of her black and gold dress and the slenderness of her wrist above the crimson banneret! Anne fell to wondering where Mistress Lilgrave had bought the black and gold material, and how much of the effect was due to extravagance and how much to a wand-like figure. "Henry and the Howards must pay her pretty well!" she thought, a bit sceptically; for she knew that the only place where such stuff was obtainable was the warehouse of one of the more exclusive merchants in the Steelyard. She was still trying to decide whether she herself would look well in such a daringly cut gown when she became aware that Holbein was putting away his brushes.

"Finished?" she enquired sleepily.

For answer he tore the half-finished portrait across and across.

Anne sprang to her feet, tumbling Edward's pet impatiently to the floor. "But all those hours of work——" she protested.

He shrugged with the almost exasperating patience of a genius to whom time counts as nothing against perfection. "After all I've taught you, you should know that it's about the worst thing I've ever done," he told her curtly. His voice was frayed with virtue gone forth. He mopped his brow with a lurid handkerchief and tossed off a glass of wine that had long been standing untouched beside him. "I'll rough out something better to-morrow," he promised.

He relaxed wearily onto a stool and Anne brought him a plate of chicken from a laden table the servants had left for him. She remembered how he would ignore his meals for hours when he was working, and how ravenous he always was when he had finished. "You're not looking too well, Hans," she said. The thought had come to her like a stab the moment he had turned to greet her. There were deeper lines about his eyes, and he had the look of a man whose creative urge is so prolific that he is burning himself up against time.

"Tush, Anne, you know I'm as strong as a horse! What you mean is you're afraid I'm drinking too much and leading a loose life," he teased, grinning at her comfortably over the plate balanced on his knees. "And, anyhow, looks aren't everything." He stirred the strips of painted vellum with the end of his shoe so as to turn one of them face upwards. "That boy, for instance, often looks the picture of health," he added ruminatively. "And yet there's a transparency about his skin . . . his mother had it too, I used the same tints for both of them. For all this cosseting, he won't last. A painter comes to know 'em as well as a doctor, Anne."

Anne looked down compassionately at the captivating curve of Edward's cheek. "I'm glad you've caught that illusive look of health," she said. "That ought to please the King."

"That's why you commissioned me to do it, isn't it? So that he should lift up the light of his countenance upon me and be gracious unto me and bless me," he demanded shrewdly, misappropriating Cranmer's lovely words with his mouth full.

Anne stood regarding him gravely, reproachful of his levity. "He's got to," she said earnestly. "You see, I feel responsible. And the royal retaining fee must be a big slice of your income."

"Three hundred and sixty pounds," he admitted cheerfully. "But he hasn't docked me of it yet. And, thanks to you, your erstwhile brother-in-law has just asked me to make miniatures of his two brats. Fifty pounds a piece I've asked for 'em."

There was a healthy coarseness about the man strangely at variance with the delicacy of his imagination. If Anne had expected him to resign voluntarily from the pay roll of a master who had treated her so abominably, she was mistaken. Body and soul, Hans Holbein represented both the realistic vigour and the spiritual tenderness of his work. Perhaps only such balance between the beauty of two worlds could enable him to illustrate with understanding the whole book of life—from cradle to grave, from obscene sot to compassionate Madonna. "What do you do with all the money you earn?" she asked, with a sigh for his generous shiftlessness.

He sat staring down into his refilled glass, twirling the liquor round and round with a careless tavern gesture. "Spend it on my mistresses—or lend it to my friends," he said lightly. Anne never flinched now when he talked like that. She knew that the love of truth in him would allow her no illusions about the kind of life he led. "You need a good woman to husband it for you," she advised him quietly.

"I tried one—and she turned out a shrew," he said slowly, without looking up. "And the only other one I really wanted was out of my reach."

For her protection every word he said deliberately underlined the difference of their lives in all but affection—yet Anne felt that he was sounding her. As far as the sanction of

Henry or William was concerned, she was still out of his reach. And in spite of her desires she had the sense to know that although fields of forbidden passion flowers might blow for other women, for her, only the lilies of righteousness must be allowed to bloom. All her up-bringing warred against illicit love, spoiling all joy in it. Even in summoning Holbein to Richmond she hadn't really wanted it—only the warmth of friendship, tender and intimate enough to disregard her rank, and the healing assurance that as a woman she was desirable. By striving hard to accept adversity she had—as Mary's wise confessor had foretold—twisted it into a kind of moral victory. She had won her immunity. And now, it seemed, she must be prepared to accept life in half-tones.

She knew that he was watching her—that she had only to beckon to all that was lawless and unconventional in him to unleash the passion that might have been between them. Because she was a great lady he must perforce wait for her to give him his cue. She could have taken up the challenge of his words; but instead she deliberately spoke of something else. And perhaps at no moment in her life had she ever been more intrinsically Anna, daughter of Cleves. "How are the children?" she asked, as prosaically as any middle-aged shopkeeper's wife.

He seemed too surprised to answer her. "Which children?" he stammered vaguely.

"Your children in Basle," smiled Anne. "Surely you aren't absent-minded enough to have forgotten them?"

"Of course not. But they're scarcely children now," he excused himself confusedly, and began to tell her how he had settled all his continental earnings on his wife and the younger ones and how he had just apprenticed Philip to a goldsmith in Paris.

"I was hoping he would come to England," murmured Anne. More than anything now that she might never have any children of her own, would she have liked to mother one of his. But he seemed long ago to have decided to keep his two worlds completely separate.

He went on telling her about them eagerly, as if it were a

241

rare treat to talk to someone who understood what it meant to a celebrated painter not to have the training of his sons. The time slipped by and presently he stood up and reached for his cloak. One of his servants had spread it across a stool to dry but the rain was still lashing the river, and driving in great gusts against the windows. Anne looked up with concern. "Why must you go, Hans?" she said wistfully. "There are a hundred and fifty bedrooms in this palace—and most of them unoccupied."

But Frances Lilgrave, who was packing up her things, broke the spell of their companionship by dropping her scissors with a clatter to the tiled floor. Suddenly reminded of her presence, Holbein frowned with annoyance. Usually her movements were so quiet that on her departure people found themselves wondering whether she had been there all the time and what they had been talking about. "I thank you, Madam, but I am well lodged at the house of my Antwerp friend in Goldsmith Row," he replied formally; and stood fumbling with the fastening of his cloak, waiting for the woman to go.

Anne's eyes darkened with angry pride. "I am not asking you because I am lonely," she said coldly, "but because it is pouring with rain."

Swinging round as if he had been stung, he saw how hurt she was. He came instantly and took both her hands, shielding her from the direction of the door with the wide folds of his cloak. "Dear Anne!" he said contritely, and turning her palms upwards bent to kiss them with passionate lips. "If I dared to stay it would be because I am very lonely indeed. You do believe me, don't you?"

"Dared," she repeated a little unsteadily, warming all her hurts of the past year at the blaze of affection shining in his eyes.

"Oh, not for myself," he explained hurriedly. "For you —you guileless woman! Didn't you know the new Queen's party still spy on you?"

Anne withdrew her hands reluctantly. "But—why ever should they?" she gasped.

He kicked savagely at a log that had rolled across the

hearth. "Because they're afraid. Afraid of your own incorruptible uprightness, of the place you hold in your friends' hearts and the way the people want you. Afraid— for all I know—that Henry himself may want you again one day—when he's tired of his latest toy." Anne made a furious gesture of dissent, but he hurried on. "They even open your women's letters," he warned. "Just because one from that new Lady Basset of yours happened to be addressed to Calais. . . ."

"But of course it was," broke in Anne indignantly. "Isn't her father Governor of the place?"

"I know it was just a family letter. But they hoped you might have been trying to curry sympathy on the Continent. And some of them would give anything to damn you in the King's eyes." He glanced over his shoulder and Anne noticed that although they were alone the door of the hall was not quite shut. "Specially that Rochfort woman," he added. "She has a pretty place as Queen's confidante and cousin by marriage, and if you ask me she would stoop to any depths to keep it."

Anne began to understand why the Howard's sewing creature had reminded her of a beautiful snake, and in a detached sort of way she was grateful to Holbein for his worldly wisdom. "How do you know all this?" she asked.

But he didn't answer her. Instead he picked up his brown, wide brimmed cap. "The world glittered with promise for you once," he said, "but as its exciting lustre changed to bitterness in your hands you never changed, except to grow stronger and still more kind. Out of the dregs of cruelty and ridicule you built up for yourself, out of your own courage and endurance, a lovely reputation. And in common with all decent men I want to keep it flawless—above the smears of scandal—for all time." He stopped talking like a man repeating some splendid creed and began turning the cap in his hands like a schoolboy. "It isn't only that," he confessed awkwardly. "Besides being lonely I am also earthy and inconstant—as I told you long ago. And there were all those cursed months—when Henry Tudor had you. I had to live somehow. . . ."

Anne smiled at him with all her heart in her eyes. "And man cannot live alone," she said compassionately. "You don't have to tell me."

So they stood there, facing each other in the firelight. Though they might meet again a score of times, both knew it was their leave-taking as lovers. "Oh, Anna—my incomparable Anna—how was I to know you would be divorced," he cried, reverting to their common tongue.

"Or I," she said sadly. "But it could have made no difference. We were born such poles apart!"

He went then, his cap crushed in his hands, and banged the heavy oak door behind him. The baleful sound of it echoed through the empty hall. The fat candle in the cresset guttered with a malevolent hissing sound and burned itself out. Anne stood for a long time by the dying embers on the hearth. She had never been so lonely in all her life.

CHAPTER XXII

It was a nine days' wonder when Anne went to Hampton Court to stay with her former husband and his new young wife. People in both parties were scandalized. Marillac found it the most piquant situation he had encountered in the whole course of his diplomatic career, and Henry himself couldn't help thinking what years of trouble and opprobrium it would have saved if his first Queen had behaved with half as much sense. But his daughter Mary was frankly disgusted.

"How *can* you go and sit at meat with that strumpet?" she asked, the evening before Anne left Richmond. It was characteristic of her that, although she disapproved so strongly of the visit, she gave herself the trouble of helping to decide which dresses were to be taken.

As Dorothea laid each one aside to be packed, Anne herself was choosing the particular ornaments which should be worn with it. Her hands were busy above the jewel case which Basset had placed on a table beside her, and the sight of it always reminded her of the wistfulness with which her youngest maid-of-honour had hung over it that dreadful day at Rochester—and of how shy and kind the girl had been after her spiteful step-mother had gone. How she had run back—with neither the slyness nor the brazenness of a strumpet—to warn an inexperienced foreigner about a world of intrigue hidden beneath the suave surface of nuptial welcome. "Why do you call her that?" she asked, holding two rival necklaces up to the light. "After all, they are married."

But Mary, standing stiff-necked and stubborn by the window, only sniffed contemptuously.

"If she were really bad he could just have had her for his mistress," persisted Anne, with dispassionate logic. "And he needn't have gone to all the trouble of divorcing me."

"Mother of God, give me patience!" prayed Mary, who found it difficult to suffer fools gladly. Would this dear, defenceless woman never look for motives less straightforward than her own? "Maidenly reluctance can be the handmaid to ambition," she explained. "And her people are powerful enough to see that he pays top price for their goods. The same as he had to with the Bullen. Only *she* was clever enough to see to it for herself!" Anne heard the rosary she had been fingering fall slackly from her belt with a faint clicking sound as she turned to stare out of the window, and noticed how her clever little hands clenched involuntarily as they always did at mention of Elizabeth's mother. Through the leaded panes was an enchanting picture of early Spring. Across the river people waited in homely little bunches for the ferry, a herd of goats grazed between clumps of golden kingcups edging the lush meadows and the rooks came cawing home across a pale April sky to their fat blobs of nests in the bare elm trees. But it was doubtful if Mary Tudor noticed any of these things. The inward gaze of her heart was fixed upon her mother, sick and lonely and discarded, beseeching a bemused husband to let her see their only child before she died. Her clenched hands came up to her breast, beating soundlessly one on the other. " 'Whom God hath joined together, let no man put asunder' ", she quoted, with the intention of one to whom the words had become a banner for which one bore much suffering.

The chosen necklace dripping from Anne's fingers slithered back with the rest to lie like a carelessly coiled snake in the sparkling cavern of the carved chest. She waved Basset and Dorothea and the lesser problem of fashion away. "Of course as a Catholic——" she began thoughtfully.

Mary turned and came to her immediately, affection shining through her habitual buttoned-up look of reserve. Life had left so few people on whom to release the pent-up burden of her love that her yearning to give often became pain rather than pleasure. Knowing how grievous a humiliation it had been for a proud daughter of Aragon to retire into obscurity, she failed to comprehend how relatively small a tragedy this was to Anne. And—looking upon it specially in the light of Heavenly consolation for the loss of an earthly crown—she did so want her friend to receive the full blessings of her own faith. "After all your talks with Father Feckenham you must realize that marriage is one of the Holy Sacraments," she reproved her gently.

Anne turned dutifully in her chair, her empty hands folded in her lap. As usual in such pose, she looked like a brooding Madonna; but actually it was only that a new idea was taking shape in her mind. And with her this was almost a physical process which needed cessation from all other effort. She knew it was stupid to assimilate any new train of thought so slowly. But it just hadn't occurred to her that while the Lutheran party were wanting Henry to take her back, plenty of people—and particularly the very Catholics who didn't—must still be thinking of her as his wife. She looked up questioningly at her friend's composed face. Her own attitude was that of an attentive child's. "Then although your own mother was divorced——" she prompted.

Her diffidence about all theological matters was so disarming that Mary bent to kiss her. "In spite of my father's second honeymoon and even a coronation service, she knew herself to be his wife until the day she died," she said. She spoke with a decisiveness which was meant to be reassuring; but somehow Anne found it oddly disturbing. To be tied all one's days to Henry in one's conscience like that. . . . Surely it would be very uncomfortable? "But then she loved him —she *wanted* it that way," she remonstrated.

Mary was calmly signalling to her ladies that she was about to depart. For her there was no need to grope and stumble and sort out one's mind. "It doesn't make any difference what you *want*," she said, with kind formality. "It just *is* so."

But even when Anne was at Hampton Court with Mary's words fresh in her mind she couldn't think of Katherine as a strumpet. The young Queen was too good-natured and too obviously discomforted by the presence of a former mistress whom she had wronged to try to triumph over her. Indeed, she had no need to, for all the world could see she was the apple of Henry's eye. She moved about the lovely rooms with the easy radiance of youth, her plain, almost childishly-cut gowns accentuating her adorable curves, sunlight or candlelight for ever enmeshed in the rich auburn of her hair. All the pleasures and adulation poured into her lap were so pathetically new to her that one had the feeling that she was still holding her breath lest they should vanish. She was always very sweet to Henry, though never quite losing a rather touching air of being on her best behaviour. And he, on his side, came nearer to being unselfish with her than with anyone who had ever entered his life. Like an indulgent father, he even resigned himself to watch her enjoying pleasures in which he himself could no longer participate. "It's a good thing she has Culpepper to dance and play the fool with," he remarked affably to his guests. "He's just the ideal companion for her."

The supper trestles had been removed and they were grouped about a brazier on the dais while some of the wilder spirits improvised a masque in the body of the hall. Anne glanced sideways at Henry. "Is he blind—or just sure enough of himself to think he can keep her?" she wondered, nettled at being included with some of his middle-aged cronies in a dissertation about Katherine's need of youthful companionship. The musicians were in fine fettle playing a pleasant little composition of his own and, well pleased, he softly hummed the air of it. His eyes smiled as they followed the graceful progress of his wife and Culpepper about the hall. Archbishop Cranmer was sitting near him, and without looking round, Henry stretched out a hand and pressed his knee. "She's like a rose, Thomas," he said, with a happy intake of breath. "A rose without a single thorn!"

Cranmer did not answer. But Marillac, who was leaning elegantly over the back of the King's chair, felt that some sort of compliment was expected. Swinging his agile mind from all sorts of interesting conjectures aroused by the sight of Anne sitting in sisterly amity beside her former spouse, he brought it to bear on the good-looking but apparently un-complicated couple in whom he was but mildly interested. "How perfectly they dance together! Youth and grace and gaiety—they have everything," he exclaimed, with facile Latin hyperbole. "How the Gods must love them!"

"Don't!" implored Anne involuntarily, turning sharply in her chair. Were they so blind, these middle-aged on-lookers? Couldn't they see the consuming flame in which those two young bodies moved? Nor understand the significance of the effulgence that illuminated them, bringing their transient beauty to too quick perfection so that they stood out from the earth-bound drabness of their fellows? The drama and the danger of Katherine, the King's rose, held heart high in her handsome cousin's arms?

Marillac looked down at her in surprise, supposing only that she hated him to praise her rival. But Cranmer, warming his white hands so that they showed a blood-red outline against the brazier, turned to smile at her with friendly understanding. "Madam of Cleves refers to the ancient Greeks' postulate that those whom the Gods love die young," he explained, profoundly touched by her disinterested uneasiness.

Anne was not altogether sorry when her visit drew to an end. People had been as kind and hospitable as possible but there had been one or two difficult moments chiefly engineered by Lady Rochfort, who seemed bent on spoiling the new Queen; and it didn't make it any easier that Katherine herself was an embarrassed and inexperienced hostess. So deciding that after all there was much to be said for the laws of conventionality, Anne left bride and bridegroom alone as much as possible and inevitably spent much of her time with Tom Culpepper. He was such pleasant company and so unfeignedly glad to see her again that he might have been an attractive younger brother. Besides, being the new Queen's cousin and recently knighted, his position at court was now very different. Henry, in his present mood of complaisance, seemed glad to leave much of the entertainment of his guests to a young man whose tastes and accomplishments had been so closely moulded on his own; and Culpepper, quick to remember in what settings the Flemish Queen had looked her best, contrived to arrange only the kind of pastimes in which she could easily take part. On the last afternoon of her visit when the Dudleys and Katherine's uncle of Norfolk were present, he adroitly lured them all into an archery contest in which he was sure that Anne, with her straight eye and unflurried aim, would more than hold her own against the other ladies.

"What a lot of trouble you've taken to make my visit a success, Tom!" she said, as they were strolling back together from the butts. She had scored more bulls than the detestable Rochfort woman, Henry had applauded her and altogether she had spent a thoroughly enjoyable afternoon. "And why, for instance," she teased, seeing that they both knew she couldn't sing a note in tune, "did you talk them all out of the King's idea of singing madrigals?"

"Because I wish to Heaven he'd take you back!" Culpepper answered unexpectedly. His nerves were on edge and he was off his guard.

Anne stopped short in the middle of a box-edged lawn. "Well—really!" she exclaimed.

He must have known that he was behaving outrageously but, having made the admission, he stuck to it. "Everybody does—except poisonous politicians and families rotten with ambition," he declared, digging a destructive heel into the velvety turf. "You're so suitable. And Kate's—well—just an adorable child."

This promised to be interesting, so Anne sank down on a stone bench beneath a budding hawthorn tree and looked him over apprisingly from fair head to long, silk-hosed legs. "Meaning," she murmured, after a precautionary glance round the twisted little tree trunk, "that you want her for yourself?"

It was a startling sort of conversation to be holding within sight of the royal party who were only a few yards ahead, trailing like a muster of brightly coloured peacocks in the direction of the terrace. But if there was one thing he had learned in Anne's household it was that she herself never gave anyone away. "If the King hadn't taken her there was no reason why I shouldn't have married her," he stated truculently.

The familiar sound of Henry's whole-hearted laughter echoed against the tilt-yard wall and was born back to them on the soft April breeze. "But if the King is happy?" said Anne.

In common with most members of the royal household, Tom Culpepper was more concerned with the King's temper. "Happy?" he repeated vaguely.

"Well, look at him. He's a different man."

Culpepper looked up sullenly from the havoc he had been wrecking on the diligently clipped lawn. Katherine was hanging on her husband's arm, looking up into his face; and as if to round off some jest they had been laughing at, Henry bent down to pinch her rosy cheek. "Oh, that!" he shrugged, discounting the half-pleasures of forty-eight with all the egoism of twenty-two.

Together he and Anne watched the little group straggle out of sight into the shadow of the garden doorway. Then he turned to her vibrant with all the urgency of his frustrated passion. They were alone among the little may trees and it seemed as though he must speak of it to someone or die. He tugged impatiently at a low hanging branch that came between them and it snapped off in his hand. "You don't know what it means to me!" he said thickly. "I love her. I've always loved her—since we were children. I was to have had her. My mother—all of us—took it for granted. And then that old Norfolk bitch must needs bring her to Rochester. . . ." He stood breaking the branch into little pieces. His strong hands shook. He tried to control himself and spoke presently with less violence. "She'd just come to care for me —the way I wanted. To trust me, and tell me things about her life. . . . He let the pile of sharp thorned twigs fall to the ground and stood staring down at his empty, bleeding hands. "I tell you I love her with a passion as pure as any man can have for a girl," he reiterated. "And almost every night I have to wash and perfume that lusty mountain of flesh to go to her—or send one of the backstairs pages to fetch her to his bed. I—whose body is on fire for her. Whose breath comes unevenly if she but touches me lightly in passing. I—who may only hold her publicly in the dance when but for him I might have lain with her crushed against my heart in the sweet stillness of the night. . . ."

Anne sat very still, overwhelmed by his plight. She had long suspected it but his vehemence had shaken her. He looked so white, so hopeless. How cruel it seemed that men and women must be consumed by blazing passions that were not of their own kindling! "Must you go on doing—all this?" she asked, with a gesture which included the gay company in the palace, a be-ribboned lute which some forgetful maid-of-honour had left on the seat, and the deserted butts where he had devised their afternoon's entertainment.

"I'd rather fight or go exploring the Indies, if that's what you mean," he answered. "But the King won't let me go. That's almost the worst part of it." He looked straight at Anne with the decency of his kind. "He's fond of me—and he relies on me so. I could cheat him a dozen times a day."

Anne yearned to comfort the misery in his eyes. She reached up and pulled him to the seat beside her. Somehow, sitting there, he seemed less alone. Less unguarded in this terrible daily fight of the flesh. "Tell me about when you were children," she said, in an effort to soothe him.

"She had no parents," he began more normally. "Her father, Edmund Howard, was a grand soldier but only a younger son. And when he died the Duke's second wife took her in."

Anne couldn't think of anything much grimmer. "Had she a terribly unhappy childhood?" she asked.

"I don't know that she was particularly unhappy—just neglected. The old woman didn't want to be bothered with her so she left her to the servants. My mother used to invite her sometimes to stay with us." A smile for the happiness of the memory warmed his face as Anne had hoped it would and—more or less irrelevantly—she made a mental note to give little Jane Grey a particularly good time at Christmas. Aloud she said positively, "I like your mother."

"But you haven't met her, Madam!" he ejaculated in surprise.

Anne drew the forgotten lute onto her lap and began thoughtfully smoothing out the crumpled ribbons. "No," she admitted, with one of her loveliest smiles. "But she probably looks like you and she made you what you are."

"She's a wonderful person," he agreed, his ingenuous face kindling. "And, in spite of everything, she is very fond of Katherine."

"In spite of what?" asked Anne, looking up sharply.

He fidgeted for a moment as a person does who wishes something unsaid. "Oh, nothing much. There was a bit of trouble over her scented fop of a music master—when she ought still to have been in the schoolroom. Kate, sweet child, came and told my mother all about it and she was furious. She said that no woman who looked after her household properly would ever have let it happen."

"I see," said Anne slowly. "Does the King know about that?"

"Good Heavens, no!" he assured her.

Anne felt she really ought to go indoors; but clearly the young man wanted to ask her something and she took her position as Lady Culpepper's deputy seriously.

"What do you suppose Katherine herself gets out of this marriage?" he blurted out presently.

She considered the question carefully, for she of all women should know. "Quite a lot, I should think," she told him. "She may love you, Tom—but she is normal enough to enjoy all the things he can give her. Not arrogantly, as some girls would—but with a healthy kind of greediness."

"I could give her things too," he raged. "Not all the adulation, of course. But I'm not completely penniless—nor half impotent."

Anne winced and laid a restraining hand on his knee. "But don't you see, my dear boy, marriage isn't only what one gets out of it. It's what one puts into it as well. And your little Katherine is far too honest for all her sweetness to him to be just pretence. . . ." She sat for a moment or two, sizing him up, weighing his chivalry against his virility—wondering to what measure of self-denial he could attain. "Couldn't you—let her alone—to make the best of it?" she suggested diffidently, thinking of how the mother who loved him would wish him well out of this dangerous affair.

But her words only produced the storm she had anticipated. "Couldn't I——" he began angrily. Then shrugged

253

and got up with an air of one resigned to disappointment. "But how *could* you understand?"

"I do understand!" she flamed back at him; and got up too, forcing him to face her. "Listen, Tom. You must trust me a great deal to tell me what you have just said. Would it help you if I trusted *you* enough to tell you something I've never told anyone else?" Having captured his surprised attention she began to speak more quietly. "When I first landed in your country there was a man who loved me. A man esteemed throughout Europe." It was so difficult to speak of that she hesitated between each sentence. She looked down as if surprised to find the gaily decked instrument still in her hands and began plucking a string here and there at random. "He wasn't royal. Nor even of a fine old family like yours. But he loved me so much that he tried not to spoil my marriage." She stopped on a jangling discord and handed him the lute with a wry grimace. "Well, as you know, it was doomed from the start——"

Culpepper took the thing blindly. His astonished gaze never left her face. "None of us ever guessed, Madam!" he stammered almost deferentially. "And you——?"

It was presumptuous to ask, of course. But she nodded without offence. "Yes, Tom, I could have loved him."

He was all generous indignation immediately. "And all the time people were making cheap jokes and being patronizing——" He stopped, knowing how his words must hurt her, and understanding for the first time a source of her proud indifference to such hurt. Never before had he seen her look so much like the miniature Holbein had painted of her, with that serene forehead and the calm candour of her clear brown eyes. He hadn't realized that she could look really beautiful. "I should think he must have been some sort of saint!" he exclaimed boyishly.

Anne had to laugh. "Oh, no," she assured him. "He was a very thorough-going sinner. But, you see, he had the inestimable help of being older and wiser than you."

Etiquette decreed that she really must follow her host and hostess and Culpepper walked in obedient silence beside her, swinging the foolish lute. But as they passed from the thin sunlight into the shadow of the palace walls she shivered and said earnestly, "For God's sake be prudent, Tom!"

But when the blood is hot, danger is but a spice to love. "What chance do I ever get to be *im*prudent?" he countered, lowering his voice because of the pages hanging about the door. "When is she ever out of his sight? Not a single night since his marriage has he lain away from home."

"Perhaps it's just as well," thought Anne, turning to give an order for her barge to be ready after supper. She heard him mutter, "I wish to God he would!" and was to blame herself bitterly that she scarcely heeded him.

Henry and Katherine both came down to the landing stairs to see her off. Anne parted from them with expressions of mutual regret; but she was glad to be going home. In the primrose light of a late April evening the Thames lay placid as a ribbon between fringes of gold and grey catkins and the gardens of great houses. As her watermen pulled out towards mid-stream she relaxed gratefully beneath the gaily woven canopy. Her senses took keen delight in their rhythmic motion and the swift, easy progress of her barge with the fluttering lion of Hainault parting the water at the prow. She loved the fussy little red-beaked moorfowl darting in and out of greening sedges under muddy banks, and the proud, conjugal swans leading their fleet of fluffy grey cygnets up-stream. As they passed Kingston church a heron, startled by the creak of rowlocks, rose croaking hoarsely across the tops of the dipping willows. And round the bend, full in the evening sunlight, rose the stately walls of Ham House, its sad poplars offset by a string of colourful barges moored in the boathouse creek. Anne wished that Holbein could perpetuate the whole lovely essence of Surrey in an English Spring.

And then, as they pulled into the Sheen reach, past its long island and sloping green hill, came the first glimpse of her own palace bowereed in garden trees. No wonder so many people stopped there! Mary and the children were at Havering and Holbein had long since finished his painting. But still it was good to come home. Home to her own life without the difficult dominance of man, the constant juggling with danger or the turmoil of passion. There were other things she had come to value. Her mind raced forward to the welcome of her people, the quiet of her own rooms and the pleasant, busy days ahead. She seemed to have lost all her nostalgia for the dykes and windmills and flat fields of the Maas. This was her home now, mellow and satisfying. A refuge, when she chose to make it so, for her friends. And yet—and yet——She was still young and it was Springtime. And Springtime in England made one's heart hunger for one knew not what.

CHAPTER XXIII

It was almost Summer and the tall Dutch tulips which Anne had imported from Guelderland were flaming along the edges of her garden borders when Henry came again to Richmond. This time he came alone, without courtiers and baying hounds. Early in the forenoon and so unostentatiously that only the gaping gatehouse porter knew he was there.

As he rode into the pleasant courtyard of his old home he heard a woman singing. Singing so tunelessly that the sombreness of his countenance broke into a broad grin. For, although the sound came from the kitchen wing, surely no one but his adopted sister could sing quite as tunelessly as that!

He swung himself down from the saddle with a grunt and told his groom to stable the horses; then walked across the wardrobe court to investigate. The kitchen windows were set low against the ground and there he found her, framed like a painting in a narrow arch of grey stonework. Apparently she was in a sort of private pantry. Someone had pinned a large russet apron over her gown, her sleeves were rolled back to her comely elbows while her hands kneaded diligently in an earthen-ware crock full of flour.

"By all the Saints!" ejaculated Henry. For a divorced woman she looked remarkably content and he didn't find the inference very flattering.

She looked up then, annoyed because his bulk was shutting out the light. And when she saw who it was she stopped short in horror, with her mouth open preparatory to taking a top note; and while thinking of something suitable to say, hastily tucked an escaping strand of hair back under her cap, leaving a streak of flour across her forehead. "My ladies and I were just having a trial of cookery," she explained rather unnecessarily.

Henry was aware of a stir of feminine fluttering in the

pantry beyond his range of vision and stepped close against the iron bars to peer down into the bowl. A delicious whiff of freshly spiced pastry assailed his questing nostrils. "What are you making?" he asked.

"Eel pie," confessed Anne, rather acidly. Couldn't the man ever let one know when he was coming? And if he must come unannounced, why in the world must he choose an hour when any woman reckoned on a little domestic privacy? Now probably he would think her more uncultured than ever and be as shocked as some of his haughty duchesses at the idea of a princess making pastry. But, on second thoughts, hadn't Cranmer once told her that Henry was almost as interested in domestic matters as she was? And now she came to think of it he adored eel pie.

He was still sniffing approvingly. "Finish it," he said. "And by your leave, Madam, I'll stay to eat it."

Anne dared not disobey although her housewifely mind had sped on to the more formal aspects of receiving distinguished guests. Would Guligh think to have dinner laid in the great hall? Had that Lilgrave woman finished the tapestries at last? And would Perce and Hawe, her cofferer and comptroller, be at the foot of the King's staircase to welcome them? While she was decorating the top of her pie and washing her hands, she gave hurried instructions; but by the time her women had released her from the hideous apron it appeared that no formal reception was necessary. To the consternation of the cooks Henry had wandered into the kitchens and was standing before one of the huge fireplaces examining a new type of spit she had had installed. "Where is her Grace the Queen?" she asked, surprised at finding him alone.

Henry was watching the way an iron handle beside the fireplace spun a couple of joints above their gravy pans instead of the unfortunate turnspit having to roast himself as well. "At Hampton," he told her shortly. "I see you've converted one of the bread ovens into a serving hatch and had a new door made by the buttery passage."

Anne had hoped he wouldn't notice. "I don't like my food cold," she murmured. And to her surprise he was quite

258

affable about it. "That's the trouble at Hampton Court," he agreed. "The meat's half cold before it comes to table."

Anne came and joined him before the fire. "Well, of course, when it has to be carried across the passage and up all those stairs——"

"You'd think Wolsey would have had the sense to put the kitchens nearer to the hall when he built the place," grumbled the man who had appropriated it. "I don't see that anything can be done about it now."

But Anne had given a good deal of thought to the matter during her honeymoon. "When I was living there," she began tactfully, "it occurred to me that perhaps a small kitchen could be erected in that little court behind the watching chamber."

"Not big enough," said Henry, beginning to move from table to table to sample the preparations for their midday meal much as he and Arthur and Charles used to do when they were boys.

"Oh, only just for your own family and friends," submitted Anne doggedly, if with still more diffidence. "If *you* had another door made the food could be brought straight through the watching chamber to the dais."

Henry lifted his nose from a jar of her special mint jelly with which the head cook was garnishing a boar's head. "I believe it could be done," he said, staring at her thoughtfully. "What made you think of it?"

"As your Grace knows, I am interested in houses."

If she were as interested as all that, he thought, there might be a few more useful hints to be picked up. "Then show me all the other improvements you've had made," he said. "And let's begin with the cellar." It wasn't in the least the sort of morning Anne had expected to spend but she found herself thoroughly enjoying it as she moved beside him between her well stocked benchings, where every barrel of ale on the stillages was as methodically accounted for in her cellarer's inventory as the choicest wines. At last she was meeting Henry on her own ground, showing him things of which she knew as much as he. "And to think that you yourself drink nothing stronger than Hippocras!" he marvelled, as they emerged into the sunlit back court.

She showed him her walled fruit garden, her dovecote and her vinery. He noted the size of her grapes with a jealous eye, and when he insisted mendaciously that his own peaches were sweeter or his pigeons plumper she never once contradicted him. But she hoped he remembered telling her that no one since his mother's time had ever been able to run the place; for she was confident that never could he have seen the courtyards tidier or the endless passages cleaner. "Even your scullions look wholesome," he admitted handsomely, as they returned to the hall. "How do you manage it?"

"Oh, I make my clerk of the kitchens an allowance to buy them each one garment a year—something that can be washed," she laughed, seating herself at table beside him.

"I should have thought you had enough expenses already," he remarked; for in view of all she had spent on the place his three thousand pound annuity began to look less lavish.

"But I enjoy my food better," said Anne, who had been secretly appalled at the dirt and waste in English kitchens. "Perhaps if her Grace the Queen has the same di-culty——"

But for once he didn't want to talk about Katherine. "Oh, I doubt if she has ever been in the kitchens," he said, and settled down to enjoy his hostess's eel pie. The trial of cookery must have been highly successful for he ate largely of it and, in spite of his weight and his gout, drank as much of her excellent Malmsey as he wanted. After dinner Anne signed to her ladies to go out softly and left him to sleep in his chair. He must have been abroad early and she knew that it did him good to rest in the afternoons, although when she was visiting at Hampton she had noticed that he had broken himself of the habit. Out of vanity, perhaps, or to keep pace with the young people. That seemed rather pathetic to Anne, who had been used to looking after her menfolk's health. Turning back to look at him as he lay with closed eyes she realized that, although he was certainly slim-mer and fitter, he looked tired. Living up to a restless young wife was beginning to tell upon him and Anne had a shrewd suspicion that that was why he had come to her, just as Cranmer and Charles and several of his ministers came when life was getting too much for them. As she sat embroidering in her own sunny room over-looking the river, she found herself thinking a lot about Henry and wondered if it were possible that she had really forgiven him.

In the evening she played cards with him in her private apartments and instead of letting him win as she always had when she was married to him she won three times running at 'Sent' and 'Pope Julian' and found that Charles had been right about his being able to take a beating. "You've improved tremendously," he said condescendingly, glad to find an opponent who could give him such a good game.

"I used to play for hours with my brother—when he was sick," she told him.

"But surely they don't play 'Pope Julian' over there?" he asked.

"No," said Anne. "But I learned some of your English games in Calais."

"To please me?"

"Well—yes—I suppose so," she admitted, with heightened colour. And then, to change the subject, she told him how surprised she had been to find all the people living there were English and he explained how, when Edward the Third and the Black Prince took it, they evacuated all the French inhabitants and sent over shiploads of their own people to colonize it. "They were the first subjects of yours I met—and they seemed to like me," she told him reminiscently.

He smiled at her ingenuous pleasure and swept up the cards with his smooth, plump hands. "And *you* seem to understand *them* much better than my other foreign wife ever did."

"Well, you see, I learned to know them as they really are right from the start. Not just as we see them when they travel——"

"When an Englishman travels he's at his worst," declared

Henry. "He's used to the sea and his own language all round him. And when a man doesn't feel sure of himself he tries to cover it up by behaving like a braggart."

"And, of course, it's mostly the rich who travel," agreed Anne thoughtfully. "We see their arrogance and their splendid retinues and we think of you all as being pampered, pleasure-loving—almost decadent. We're apt to under-rate you. But I saw these same elegant gentlemen in danger. And the seamen who man your great ships—stripped for action, do you call it? One of them fell from the—the——"

"Yard-arm," suggested Henry, following the gestures of her expressive hands.

She flashed him a grateful smile, pleased to find herself really talking to him at last about things she had experienced and felt. "And half a dozen of them would have gone overboard after him into the murderous sea if Sir Thomas Seymour hadn't forbidden the useless sacrifice."

Henry was always pleased when anyone praised his sailors. It was queer, he thought, that although this strangely acquired sister of his had no book learning she could be so interesting about practical affairs and talk so observantly about people. "And what were you doing all the time?" he asked, from the depths of his comfortable chair.

Anne picked up the cards and began shuffling them. "Oh, we were all terrified. Most of my women were prostrate and——"

"I said *you*," he bullied.

She arched her fine brows consideringly and let the cards she was holding in either hand snick down alternately into one complete pack. "Oh, I was just sick—and badgering people to teach me English."

Henry burst out laughing. "What divers occupations and admirable persistency!" He heaved himself out of the chair reluctantly. "I'm afraid you suffered a vile crossing. A pity I was so impatient."

Anne could scarcely believe her ears. It was the first time she had ever heard him apologize for anything. "Especially as you found there was nothing to be impatient about!" she added, with a wicked smirk at his broad back.

But when he turned he found her looking becomingly grave. That was the worst of these meek women, you never knew when they were laughing at you. "After all," he observed in self-defence, "you *have* changed, you know."

Anne raised those provoking long lashes of hers, unveiling lovely unresentful eyes. Henry's own eyes began to crinkle humorously at the corners. Their glances met and they smiled at each other broadly. "Shall I have your Grace's horse brought round?" she enquired, seeing that he had risen at last.

It was a long time since anyone had suggested to Henry Tudor that he should go. But certainly the situation was a little unusual. "What hour is it?" he asked.

Basset rose from her embroidery frame at the other end of the room and consulted Anne's egg-shaped Nuremberg watch. "It wants but a quarter to midnight, your Majesty," she said.

Henry was amazed to find he had stayed so late. He opened a casement to see if the moon had risen, but the weather had changed and the wooden shutter banged sharply in a squall of wind and rain. "It's pitch black," he reported, sucking his smarting thumb and glancing uneasily at Anne. "Perhaps I'd better stay the night. Unless, of course——"

Both her women were watching him. One could almost read their hopeful thoughts. But Anne ignored his deference to the delicacy of her feelings. "It is as your Grace pleases," she answered, completely unmoved. "The beds are all aired."

It was just the sort of thing Anne *would* say. Of course, she would have given anything for Wriothesley and the Dowager Duchess and all of them to hear him. But not by so much as the flicker of an eyelid did she betray the warm triumph that was racing through her. It was sheer balm that this man who had spurned her and was now nine months married to his precious thornless rose should be begging to stay beneath her roof. "I am afraid I've no gentlemen-of-the-bedchamber to wait upon your Grace," she said politely,

263

and picking up a candlestick from the table prepared to light him to his room herself. It was a gracious gesture, full of homely hospitality, and as she went before him up the King's staircase to the disused state apartments Henry thought he had never seen anything lovelier than the way she turned a little, holding the candle low to lighten his feet. Because his facile emotions were quickly touched he followed her in silence. And the little group of women and servants standing respectfully at the bottom noted how his gigantic shadow and Anne's comely one ran into each other on the stone wall. In their fondness they took it as an omen and began to hope that one day their mistress might be queen again.

The candles were lit in the great state bedroom and the door stood wide. Yet Henry stopped short on the threshold like a man stabbed by memory. Anne heard the sharp intake of his breath and knew that he was afraid—that he recoiled from the thought of sleeping there alone. Save that most of the valuable rugs had been removed the room must have looked much the same when his father lay there dead—and Henry hated anything to do with sickness and death. So she went in first suggesting in the most matter-of-fact way that perhaps he would prefer to have his own old room. He mumbled a few words of gratitude, and presently she saw him go to the far side of the great four-poster and draw back the crimson tapestry. He picked up the old-fashioned bedside hour-glass, cupping it in his hands as if it were a familiar friend. "My mother used to sleep this side," he whispered, as if he stood in some sacred place. He remembered it as if it were only yesterday, although he had been only twelve when she died, and he stood for a long time staring down at the empty pillow. There was an embroidered stool just within the bed hangings and Anne wondered if he used to stand on it as a boy to bid her 'Good-morning.' With what joyful pride must Elizabeth of York have looked up at him, seeing in his ruddy Plantagenet fairness a reincarnation of her beloved small brothers so cruelly murdered in the accursed Tower! Rejoicing in his strength and tallness, watching him play with her hour-glass. Smiling with all her love in her eyes, as mothers do.

When Henry followed Anne out of the room his cheeks were wet. "You've had fresh rushes put," he said, without looking at her. And Anne noticed that he walked carefully so as not to disarrange them.

"I have them changed every week," she told him.

"But you didn't know her."

"No," said Anne, softly closing the door behind them. "But I've seen her in that family group Master Holbein painted, and for six months she was in a sense my mother-in-law."

"I think she would have liked you," said Henry, unaware that he paid her the highest compliment a man has to offer.

They walked the length of a gallery in silence and waited for Guligh, who was in attendance, to open a smaller door. This time Anne left Henry to go in first and stood aside to watch his pleasure. There was nothing sacred about this room—no saddening memories of the beloved nor spectres of the dead. She had had it left just as he had last used it when he was a lad. The hangings gay with hunting scenes, the presses holding his first sartorial successes, chests still strewn with youthful sports gear. He went round lifting a model galleon here, a forgotten hunting trophy there, or bending a light-weight bow until Anne felt positively maternal over him. "You do prefer to sleep here, don't you?" she asked anxiously, wondering if it were grand enough.

His relief and pleasure were patent. He came and took the candle from her and held it so that the soft light fell full on her face. He was scrutinizing her in a baffled sort of way and Anne knew that he was trying to reconcile the liking he now felt for her with the angry exasperation he had exhibited that first night they had spent alone together in a bedroom. "You're an amazing woman, aren't you?" was all he said. And sighed, and put the candle down.

Anne bade him a formal 'Good-night' and went back to her own wing of the palace wondering what he would have been like if his kind, wise mother had lived, and whether after all he mightn't come to derive some of the comfort out of their own queer relationship that he had enjoyed with his sister Mary. She had spent an exacting day full of effort on his behalf and, as usual, she fell asleep almost as soon as Dorothea left her.

But in the early hours of the morning she waked suddenly, remembering for no particular reason that the King had never lain away from home since his marriage. She had been dreaming of Tom Culpepper. Of his handsome face white with passion, and his pleasant, laughing voice grown harsh as he muttered, "I wish to God he would!" Anne sat up gripping the bedclothes in consternation. Had Culpepper *really* said that? If so surely she oughtn't to have let Henry stay. For herself it mattered nothing—there was nothing between them. But for Katherine? This child of the first family in England, who had been so queerly brought up and who had had some ugly sort of bother with her music master. Evidently Henry wasn't in the best of humours with her at the moment, else why should he have ridden off without her and not wanted to be talking about her perfection all the time? Perhaps they had even quarrelled. And in this country it wasn't safe to quarrel with one's King. A dull sense of foreboding seized Anne. It was rather like waking to that old nightmare fear about the Tower. She felt as if some disaster were hurrying towards her; only this time it was fainter and further off and instead of mounting to a frenzy of horror it resolved itself into a nagging affair of conscience. Yet why should she of all people feel responsible for those two? She hadn't asked Henry to come, nor even wanted him. *She* had no lust to slake—but only pride to heal. And yet, nagged Conscience, need she have tried so hard to make him like her? And had she been merely fooling him all the time? Hadn't she been moved to sympathy—been aware of nascent affection? Could there be something about the massive man—some spark left over from his golden youth which in spite of all his gross selfishness and cruelties could charm the heart out of people still?

Anne shrugged her bare shoulders at the absurdity of the

idea. Out in the wet garden the owls were hooting derisively and a watery moon was silvering the misty tree tops. She crossed herself and snuggled down again, turning towards the window to watch it ride the scurrying, troubled clouds.

CHAPTER XXIV

The next day Henry said nothing about going home and Anne's people were seething with excitement. As no ministers or messengers had come to him it looked as if he hadn't told even the Queen that he was going to Richmond.

In the forenoon Anne rode with him through the home park and after he had had his dinner and his sleep she heard him playing the organ in the music room. He had left the door ajar so that the unwonted sound swelled gloriously through that part of the palace, showing her what had been lacking in her conception of a home. Lured by the sweet richness of the instrument, she went in and stood listening.

A feeling of well-being wrapped her about, and a new appreciation of the beauty of this long, oak panelled room. Nowhere had she seen such gracious houses as these wealthy English possessed. Golden bars of sunlight lay across the floor, flecked here and there with gems of colour reflected from armorial bearings on the casements of three long oriel windows. On the wall facing them a tapestry in russet and green held all the living loveliness of an autumn wood through which a lordly stag pricked his way with timid grace. From a gilded frame above the wide, stone canopied hearth Owen Tudor, the aspiring Welshman who had started the family fortunes by marrying a widowed queen, looked down complacently. There were beautiful pieces of furniture designed for comfort and a great painted globe of the world. On a long refectory table which looked as though it might have been filched from some splendid monastery were gathered in casual contiguity a pewter ink well holding a flamboyant quill, white sheets of music scored with square black blobs of notes, and a priceless collection of queerly shaped musical instruments of which Anne didn't even know the names. Everywhere were books and maps and signs of lively culture. Her father had had plenty of books but most of them were chained to gloomy desks, not scattered about family rooms so that the sunlight could wink cheerfully on their metal clasps. Only these Tudors, it seemed, understood the art of living.

Henry became aware of her standing there, but went on playing, passing in idle enjoyment from one well loved melody to another. "Do you know this?" he asked casually, as he might have asked of Charles or Culpepper or any of his family with their wide Continental education.

"No," said Anne, starting at finding herself observed.

"But you should," remonstrated Henry. "It's by one of your own Netherland composers, Adrian Willaert." Out of the tail of his eye he saw her touching the crimson binding of More's *Utopia* appreciatively. " I never see you reading anything either," he added.

"Most of your books are in Latin or French," she said evasively.

"But I thought Cranmer sent you some English ones?" questioned Henry, through the opening bars of his own song 'Pastime with Good Company'.

"Yes. But I hated them," she admitted, wondering how he knew. "Mary said it was my own fault for not understanding theology."

"It was probably Cranmer's fault—for not understanding women!" chuckled Henry. As a man of the world his own taste was more catholic. Although he prided himself on his own ability to write a theological treatise, he rose from the organ stool and sauntered to a near-by shelf, running his up-stretched hand along brown leather backs of books until he came upon a well-worn volume frivolously bound in green and gold. "Try this," he said, handing it down to her. "Geoffrey Chaucer loved life and people and laughter—it should be just the thing for you. If you find the old-fashioned English difficult ask young Bess to help you. She often reads his *Canterbury Tales*. And, truth to tell, so do I —whenever I feel I'm losing touch with my people."

He stood for a while by the table turning over some old songs while Anne retired to a window seat and opened the book across her knees. It was nice of him to bother, she thought. And he was perfectly right—these pages showed her a new, undreamed of expression of the warm life and movement that she loved. There were richly coloured illustrations of a party of people going on a journey—much as she had set out from Düren. All sorts of people, from priests to millers—and women just like herself—and looking at their cheery faces one felt they were all enjoying themselves immensely and wanted to know more about them. Anne began reading the widely spaced verses so clearly printed by Master Caxton from his press at Westminster. She scarcely noticed that Henry had seated himself at the virginals where Mary and Elizabeth sometimes practised and was playing over the accompaniment of a song more suited to the plaintive lightness of that instrument than to the organ. Presently he began to sing.

> 'Mine own sweetheart
> So stricken I
> With Love's fond dart——'

The sweetness of his true, well-trained tenor seemed to fill the room with harmony as well as sunlight. Anne lifted her head from the book and listened. "What beautiful words!" she exclaimed, when he had finished.

Henry played the last cadence over again softly, as if loath to let it fade. "They were written for a very beautiful woman," he said.

"Who wrote them?" she persisted, thinking how deeply in love the poet must have been.

"I did—in a Kentish garden," he answered. "And then rode home and set them to music like any love-lorn squire!" He spoke almost as if he were jeering at himself and without a trace of his usual conceit. Yet to have made so moving a song seemed to Anne far more wonderful than wasting midnight oil writing all those dry religious treatises about a theme which didn't really need them, because it began in a manger and was as simple as love.

It was drawing towards supper time, but neither of them noticed it. Henry's spirit, young and untrammelled, was back among the lavender and hollyhocks in Nan Bullen's garden at Hever. And Anne, looking at him across the quiet room as he sat dreaming before the virginals, was suddenly aware that she had found that 'other facet' of which Cranmer had spoken. The side of him that Charles still loved.

"It cost me so much to get her," he was saying, almost as if he had forgotten Anne's presence. "Months of humiliating waiting, a Papal quarrel that set all Europe by the ears, the goodwill of my people. And then the putting away of a fond wife for conscience' sake."

Anne slipped a taper between the pages of Chaucer's delectable fiction and closed them hurriedly. Here was an episode from real life. The most discussed tragedy of the century told by one of the two principal characters. "For conscience' sake?" she repeated, the new-found 'fairer facet' retreating before such monstrous self-deception.

The very fact that no one else had dared to mention the subject for so long made it sheer relief to speak of it—given the right atmosphere and listener. And these two days at Richmond had been like a home-coming to Henry, reviving old memories and loosening his reserve. "My first wife had been married to my elder brother, Arthur," he said. "I was only eighteen and thoughtless when I took her, but I've often wondered since how my parents came to arrange a union forbidden by the Church on grounds of consanguinity." He said the words with such precision that Anne felt them to be but a repetition of what he had been saying all these years in his own mind. Saying self-righteously over and over again until he came to believe them. She leaned forward eagerly, both elbows resting upon the closed book on her knees. "But why need you have worried?" she began impulsively. "Arthur wasn't sixteen when he died and Mary says——"

Henry's arm jangled an angry discord of notes as he swung round on her. "What can that obstinate little Jesuit know of something which happened before she was born?" he shouted. "My brother should know if the marriage were consummated or not, shouldn't he? And when he parted their bed curtains next morning the first thing he called for was a draught of wine. I saw the pages scurrying and tittering, myself. 'Marriage is thirsty work', he said. 'And I've been in a hot place this night—in Spain.'"

Anne let his coarseness pass. She was accustomed to it. She was listening to him with keen interest, for only by hearing both sides of a story could one judge.

"As the years went by I began to lie awake at night remembering what my brother had said." Henry had turned his back on the virginals and sat staring at the floor, his hands clasped between his knees. "It seemed God *must* be punishing me. Child after child I begat on her. I was young and lusty then. But they all died, except Mary. Even our sweet little Prince of Wales, for whom we made such marvellous processions and rejoicings. The rest never lived at all. Can you picture our grief and disappointment, Anne?"

Anne was filled with triumphant astonishment, for here was the incredible thing happening at last—the possibility at which she had always scoffed. Here was Henry Tudor himself confiding in her—as if she were his sister indeed! She stretched out a hand towards him with a gesture more compassionate than speech, and at sight of it Henry bowed his head in his hands. He loved sympathy, and always played up to it. "It must have been wrong taking her—or God wouldn't have punished me like that for eighteen years," he groaned. "I was faithful to her. But I wasn't getting any younger, and a succession of miscarriages had ruined her health and looks." He looked up at his fourth wife with a kind of shamefaced, defiant misery. "And then Sir Thomas Wyatt began writing verse to her wittiest maid-of-honour. She'd come back from France with my sister and her Circe eyes played the devil with men, and I wanted her."

No need to discuss *how* he had wanted her. How he had written her some of the loveliest love letters any woman ever received. Nor how she had flaunted the good Queen, whose heart he had ridden over to get her. Anne had heard all that from Mary, with concentrated bitterness. "At least she gave you Elizabeth," she reminded him gently.

To her that seemed an inestimable gift; but throughout his matrimonial troubles, Henry had been obstinately determined to see himself an injured man. He got up and strode to the empty fireplace. "Why did my daughters have to live, and not my sons?" he demanded of the complacent portrait of his more fortunate great-grandfather. "Why did it have to happen to *me*—who *must* have sons? Strong, able sons for England!" It was an obsession with him. He couldn't conceive of women reigning. And, for all his self-love, he cared passionately for England. He'd even planned to put his illegitimate son, Harry of Richmond, on the throne, and when he lost him at eighteen, it had been one of the bitterest personal griefs he had ever had to bear. He went on speaking with his back to Anne and the pleasant room. "My second wife was unfaithful to me," he admitted, in a strangled sort of voice. Even now he couldn't bring himself to mention Nan's name, but his hostess knew how it hurt his vanity to speak of her at all.

"Not—not with the poet Wyatt?" she ventured, having heard many conflicting stories, which even included Jane Rochfort's wicked accusations against her own husband, who was Nan's brother.

"Oh, no, not with Wyatt," answered Henry wearily. "He wrote that exquisite poem 'Forget not yet' in which he gave her up to me. But with lesser men. And, fool that I was, I kept her—knowing her to be with child. Though God knows if it were mine or some music master's!" Evidently, in his side of the story there was an uncurbed bitterness to match Mary's. "Even there she tricked me, knowing that while she carried the hope of an heir she was safe . . ." Henry sighed gustily and seated himself on the settle like a broken man. "One day I fell from my horse out hunting. The poor brute trod on my swollen veins and it was the beginning of all the trouble I suffer now in my legs," he went on, shading his face with his hand. "And that fool Northumberland, though he knew her to be near her time, rushed in and told her I'd been killed." His words came harshly, in broken sentences as though he had been running.

"A few hours later the child was born dead. And, of course, it was a boy!"

Anne averted her eyes, for even after all this time his agony was painful to look upon. If he—the vain-glorious Tudor—had been forced to woo patiently, had believed himself tricked, and then allowed himself to risk being cuckolded for the sake of a son, then such final frustration must have clouded his mind with veritable fury. Anne knew all about frustration, and what it could do to people. She could understand now why he hated the Dudleys. So what possible pity could there have been for Nan?

"Well, at least you have a son," she comforted him. She couldn't help speaking grudgingly, for it was more than she had.

His face softened and he crossed himself. "Yes, Jane gave me Edward—may God preserve him and rest her sweet soul!"

Trying to keep the conversation on more cheerful, everyday subjects. Anne asked how Katherine liked the boy. But it seemed that the day Henry had taken her to Havering, Edward had been particularly fretful so that she feared to take him on her lap and didn't want to have him at Hampton. "What chance has she had to know anything about children?" laughed Anne generously. "Wait till she has a nursery of her own!"

Henry wasn't too optimistic. "It's nine months now and no sign," he complained. "You know, Anne, I'm not too happy about her these last few weeks. I believe she's frightened about something. If one comes into a room unexpectedly she jumps."

"But I thought——"

"Oh, everything was wonderful while we were alone. That's why I stayed away so long. I wanted to keep my domestic happiness like any other man. It was like a bright bubble safely out of reach of people's dirty, clawing, ambitious hands—the interfering hands that have managed to burst most of my brief bubbles of happiness," he added, with ruminative self-pity. "But now since we came back there are all these people clamouring to take service with her—people out of her old life . . . I don't want to thwart her, but is it wise?"

"Lady Rochfort——" began Anne tentatively.

"Oh, Jane Rochfort's her cousin, so I suppose that's natural enough," said Henry. "But now there's this Bulmer woman, who calls herself her secretary—and Heaven knows the ill-taught child needs one!" He broke off to laugh indulgently, and then went on sounding half amused, half vexed. "And this week we're plagued with another relative of sorts she's taken into her household. A ferocious fellow called Derham, just back from Ireland, who seems to think he has some claim on my little Kate and glares at poor Culpepper if he so much as writes a sonnet to her. And a greasy-looking musician called Manox, who used to teach her to sing or something." Having found so good a listener, Henry warmed to the subject of his grievances. They must have been weighing on his mind a good deal, or it might have occurred to him how incongruous it was to be telling them to Katherine's predecessor. "That Rochfort bitch is always closeted with her," he complained. "I wouldn't mind so much in the day time, when I'm out hunting, or busy with my ministers. But only the night before last I had to stand outside my own wife's bedroom door in my nightgown among a pack of sniggering pages before they undid the bolt."

Anne began to see where the first thorn had scratched, and the reason for his early morning visit to Richmond. "Perhaps if her Grace's step-mother could drop a hint about manners," she suggested, trying to suppress a smile.

"She's all over her now she's Queen," growled Henry. "But it's a pity she didn't look after her better when she was only a poor relation!"

Anne stole a glance at his scowling face. Did he wonder who was behind that bolted door? Had he by any chance heard any rumours about this second music master? Any of his other wives, placed as she was, would have hoped he had, and improved the shining hour of opportunity by making certain. Anne held her rival's reputation in her hands.

But instead of trailing it in the mud, she told the King cheerfully that she had a pleasant surprise for him. She hated anyone to be unhappy in her house, and felt that opportunity could be better employed on behalf of a friend who was out of favour.

CHAPTER XXV

Henry had an almost childlike love of surprises, and by the time Anne had led him to the great hall, he was in the best of humours. He spoke affably to Mistress Lilgrave and her departing women, pleased with his own magnanimity in sparing them. Anne envied the grace with which the slender widow sank into the billows of her skirt and sent her humble duty to the Queen and Lady Rochfort, and while Henry glanced round approvingly at their almost completed work, she drew aside the piece of cloth veiling Edward's portrait and called a servant to light a candle on either side of it.

Henry was simply delighted. He viewed it first from one angle and then from another, and each time he looked at it he felt prouder of his paternity and more sure of his son's health. Evidently the children had loyally kept her secret about the sittings, although Edward was always chattering about the monkey his Aunt Anne had given him. "There's nothing anyone could have done that would give me more pleasure!" their father kept saying. "Although the boy is like his mother, he's growing more like me. And Holbein has caught the likeness. I must congratulate him at once. Where is he? I haven't seen him since—since our wedding."

"We were afraid—that is——" stammered Anne, always more nervous on her friends' behalf than her own.

"You were afraid that I would punish him—like Cromwell?"

"God forbid!" she shuddered. "But it was rumoured that he might lose his appointment as court painter."

Apparently all her anxiety had been for nothing. Henry laughed boisterously and shook her arm in kindly pleasantry. "My good woman, what sort of a Philistine do you take me for? I could create a whole regiment of new Chancellors to-morrow, but not another Holbein!" he assured her. But all the same—with disquieting tales about music masters fresh in her mind—she was thankful to be able to say that he wasn't staying in the palace. "He lodges with a Flemish friend in Goldsmith's Row," she told Henry. "I'll send one of my men to fetch him to Hampton first thing in the morning."

She turned to recall the servant who had lighted the candles, but found only Frances Lilgrave at her elbow, ready cloaked for her homeward journey. "Perhaps if Madam will allow *me* to deliver the message——" she was offering, in her mincing French way. Anne looked at her coldly. It was true that the King was momentarily occupied with some of Holbein's rough sketches; but the Howards must have spoiled this invaluable craftswoman of theirs very badly that she should so presume to thrust herself into a royal conversation. "Why should you?" she asked witheringly.

Mistress Lilgrave drew back with exaggerated meekness. "Only to save your ladyship the pain," she murmured, "because I live there too."

Anne caught the malicious gleam in her dark eyes, and felt as though an adder had darted out its fangs at her. Instinctively she recoiled, pulling aside her skirts. "Very well, then," she agreed ungraciously, because it seemed ridiculous not to; and stood staring at the closed door, even after the woman had gone. Henry was making a running commentary on a dozen or so crayon studies which Holbein, with his usual prodigality had left behind, but she had no idea what he was saying. Frances Lilgrave . . . Of course, that would explain her own instinctive dislike. Hans had never made any secret of his way of life—but that it must be this Lilgrave woman! A spy in the pay of her enemies—always in her house—watching her. . . . Probably that was how he knew about poor Basset's letters being opened. And how much more dangerous a spy could be if personal spite entered into it—if the woman suspected that she, Anne of Cleves, meant more to Holbein than wife or mistress! Anne heard Henry say something about the sketch of Edward's clenched fist being marvellously modelled—"Yes, just like the Holy Child's hand in the Solothurn Madonna," she agreed—but all the time she was trying frantically to remember what she and Holbein had been talking about in front of this woman that afternoon he had drawn it. Though why should she mind? Hadn't she been the soul of circumspection for William's sake? Always assuring him that she was well treated, and even leaving her letters to him unsealed so that the King's ministers could read them. And never trying to make trouble, as she could so easily have done, by culling sympathy from the people. No, there could be nothing for even the most venomous spy to report. It was just one of those crazy things that happened in this country. One must keep one's sense of humour and thank God that there was never a dull moment in Henry Tudor's kingdom!

He was holding out something he particularly admired. "Yes, lovely!" said Anne vaguely, looking down at a half-finished nude. It certainly was lovely—a woman's sinuous white body lying across a bed by candlelight with night-black hair cascading to the floor and the flesh tints cleverly thrown up against an exotic black and gold gown she had just discarded. The easy smile died on Anne's lips as her mind registered recognition of the material. It was so like Holbein to leave the thing lying about without subterfuge in her house!

"It's that Lilgrave hussy," Henry was chuckling obscenely. "And isn't this one of your women? In a stuffy blue Dutch dress with her hair down?"

Anne glanced at the more formal painting he held aloft which she herself had ordered and paid for. "It's Dorothea —one of my women-of-the-bedchamber," she said woodenly, stretching out her hand for it.

"The plain one who was with Kate Basset last evening? These painters get all the opportunities. Who else would have supposed she had such red-gold treasure screwed up beneath her appalling cap? Why, it's almost Tudor colour!"

"I specially wanted him to paint it because it's her only beauty," explained Anne. "I'm having portraits made of

279

the few Flemish servants who were allowed to remain with me so that they may send them home to their relatives."

"But she looks a lady. And I said all your 'jauntlewomen', as you used to call them, must go back." His heart applauded her rare kindness; but to off-set a hint of preoccupied terseness in her manner he spoke sternly. For herself there were few things Anne considered worth fighting for; yet there was a streak of obstinacy in her that would stand for certain principles and promises to the death. So she tucked the small painting carefully into her pocket and looked at him challengingly. "Dorothea *is* a gentlewoman," she told him coldly. "But she married one of my servants sooner than leave me. Guligh, the red-headed giant who helped you undress last night, is her husband."

Henry's eyes fell before hers. He had the grace to realize the distress his arbitrary command must have caused, and the devotion shown her. "Don't they quarrel—your English and your Flemish servants?" he asked uncomfortably, for the sake of something to say.

"If they do I never hear of it," said Anne.

He stared at her incredulously. The background of all his domestic life seemed to have been perpetual bickering among the officers and servants of his various wives. "What a unique household!" he remarked. But presumably he found it to his liking, for although Guligh himself appeared at that moment to announce that supper was served in milady's private apartments, the King made no mention of departure.

All he seemed concerned about was that he should not be parted from her gift. He had it set up opposite to them while they ate and called for a flagon of Gascony to toast the artist. And after supper he settled down to cards again. But Anne played badly. Her mind was following Frances Lilgrave home—home to Goldsmith's Row. Picturing her at supper with Holbein. In his littered studio, embroidering his shirts, perhaps. While she herself sat here, neither wife nor widow, playing Pope Julian—a game based on the first divorce proceedings of the man she strove to entertain. Why, even then he had been ridiculously concerned with a Katherine and an Anne, and the very points of the game—King, Pope, Matrimony, Intrigue, Divorce—showed with what shameless publicity the affair had been discussed. Well, there was no wrangling and publicity this time—everybody concerned could keep their dignity—and only one person had to pay for it. Three times in succession Anne was stopped by 'intrigue' and lost twenty crowns.

"You are reckless to-night, Madam," grinned Henry, scooping up his winnings.

"I feel reckless," she said.

He had been intent on the game but, looking up quickly, he noticed that her cheeks were flushed and her lazy eyes wide and bright. Such restless animation suited her, and yet he thought she looked more unhappy than he had ever seen her. His vanity led him to mistake the meaning of her mood. He had come to Richmond on the spur of the moment, piqued and in search of change and rest; but the excited twittering of her household hadn't escaped him and by staying like this no doubt he had given them cause for optimism. Obviously they adored their mistress and hoped that he would take her back, and he was well aware that a large proportion of his subjects still looked upon her as their rightful queen. But Anne herself was an enigma. He pushed the cards aside and leaned across the table, covering one of her jewelled hands with his own. "Do you still want to go home, Anne?" he asked.

Anne shrugged her shoulders but made no effort to escape from his caressing gesture. "Home?" she repeated bitterly. "Where do I belong—or to whom? What family have I? Or—come to that—what nationality?"

He had never heard her speak like that before. And he was surprised to find that—quite apart from political considerations—he didn't *want* her to go back. "You can be naturalized," he suggested. "I should *like* you to be naturalized. I will send Taverner, the Clerk of the Signet, to take out your papers."

"I will think of it!" she promised listlessly. "But—English or Flemish—when I look round at other women I feel that I am nothing."

281

He was in his kindest mood and she had listened to his troubles and now it seemed only natural that she should voice some inkling of her own. But he till supposed himself to be the well-spring of her rare mood of bitterness. "You feel that the Queen has everything?" he questioned, glancing round to make sure that her women and the servants were out of earshot. He was beginning to enjoy himself immensely.

Anne withdrew her hands and began moodily twirling the black enamelled ring on her thumb. She hadn't been thinking of the Queen, but there too was a grievance. "She has Elizabeth," she said. It was stupid to mind so much, of course. But the joy of the child's companionship had been denied to her of late because, owing to their blood relationship, Katherine had made a point of having her at her own table.

Henry was still more pleased. For all he might call young Bess his bastard, he was rightly proud of her boyish carriage and quick brain, and loved to hear her praised. "She shall come and visit you often," he promised. "And if it's any comfort to you to know it, she's been plaguing me to let her live with you altogether. Though of course I can't allow that. It would seem so slighting to the Queen."

But Anne was so touched that her unhappy eyes filled with tears. *That*—from Elizabeth, who adored the pomp and circumstance of Courts. It wasn't as if it were dear Mary, with her unassailable loyalty and her preference for he dignified seclusion of a quiet home. For no particular reason than that she was over-wrought, Anne began to laugh with the tears still running down her cheeks. Henry rose and went to her. He was quite alarmed at seeing so restrained a woman so upset. "Did you want children as badly as that?" he soothed, patting her shoulder with endearing awkwardness.

In her hurt and emotional distress Anne caught at the comforting reassurance of his arm. "I would rather have been her m-mother than Q-queen of England," she confessed, between sobs. But it was only because so much had been taken from her that she clung so tenderly to what little had been left.

Almost immediately she hated herself for her hysterical outburst. It was just the kind of weakness she always wrestled against for fear of becoming like William. Subconsciously, it did something to you, having a brother like William. If people would only realize—the people who thought her dull—that that was why she always used to hold herself so still and calm! But now, perhaps, there was no longer any need. For—dear as William was—it was a release not to have to look upon his malady. Besides which she knew herself to have gained strength of character and to have overcome many fears. So that now she could live her own life without holding anything back; finding expression of personality and spirit, and giving free rein to the strength of normal desires and emotions.

She wiped her eyes and found herself in Henry's arms, sniffing ignominiously against his familiar shoulder. "I'm behaving like a very *young* sister!" she apologized, trying to disentangle a gauze wing of her cap from the gold chain about his neck. But to her surprise he wouldn't let her go. He was whispering something about this sister business being all a mistake and basely—though possibly truly—excusing himself on the grounds that of late his feeling for Katherine had become almost fatherly. And suddenly it occurred to Anne that he was making love to her. That he wanted her. Really wanted her, for the first time—now that she was out of his reach. It was the sort of thing that she had set herself to achieve, out of revenge; yet here she was so overcome by surprise that she just stood there wondering what on earth she should do.

It was top score to her in their matrimonial game, of course. But it was so difficult to think with his demanding hands drawing her closer and lifting her chin. He could *make* her do anything, she supposed; but what *ought* she to do? Of course, he was lustful and inconstant, and she wasn't in the least in love with him. But she was used to him and he was her husband. Yes, still her husband. For in that moment of close contact, however unwillingly, she felt through

283

and through the truth of Mary's words. It wasn't just that Holy Church said so. A good woman like Catherine of Aragon had counted herself his wife until the end of her days. So there could be no sin.

"Indecency," thought Anne, as he pressed his lascivious mouth to hers, "but no sin." The sin lay with her promoted maid-of-honour—and she owed Katherine Howard nothing. She owed nobody anything. It was Life which owed *her* so much. She had schooled herself to renounce a lover and the prayers of her people, and she never had wanted Henry; but perhaps if she let him have his way she might yet have a child of her own. She was no wanton and it seemed improbable in the extraordinary circumstances that any second marriage would be arranged for her. This might be her last chance. . . . What the outcome of such a tangle could be she didn't know. All she cared for was that the hateful picture of Frances Lilgrave lying naked on Holbein's bed was wiped out by reckless resolution, aided perhaps by the unwonted warmth of her own good Gascony.

She freed herself from the King's greedy embrace and moved to the nearest window, jerking the heavy curtains apart. Outside a full moon rode clear of clouds. It was not yet ten of the clock and the grassy ride through the park to Hampton lay clear as day. She looked over her shoulder, mockingly. But her royal guest called firmly for his candle.

Anne herself carried it for him as she had done the night before. Comptroller, cofferer, confessor—all made way for them, only the mighty Guligh going before. And this time Anne turned on the second stair to offer Henry her hand. It was a regal gesture of reconciliation—a remitment of all his cruelty and unfaithfulness. "From now on we are friends," she thought cynically, "for I'm no better than he." A tolerant humanity flowed pleasantly through her. She even managed to laugh, rather deliciously, picturing the procession of women who must at one time or another have gone hand-in-hand to bed with him.

At the foot of the King's staircase Basset and Dorothea waited sleepily to undress their mistress. They waited a long time. In the uncertain light from the wall torches their eyes questioned each other, half triumphant and half afraid. Guligh had long since gone silently down the backstairs. The gatehouse guard had changed as a clock struck midnight. But although the King's fifth wife lay alive and warm in her bed at Hampton, his fourth wife did not come down.

CHAPTER XXVI

Months slipped by and ripened into autumn. Anne knew now that there would be no children of her marriage. At first she rebelled fiercely; then gradually learned to accept the disappointment with resignation. But Mary's confessor had said that that was not enough—that the only way to triumph over frustration was to make a free gift of the thing denied. So as time went on she spent her aptitude for motherhood more and more in the service of other people's children—preferably those who were more in need of love than her own could ever have been. October found her preparing to give some of them a party.

"Not a grand party like the Queen is giving on Twelfth Night with Edward and Uncle Charles's boys and the Dudleys and our best clothes," Elizabeth was explaining to her small cousin Jane, who was staying at Richmond. "Just a party in the guard chamber for Aunt Anne's orphans."

"What are orphans?" asked Jane Grey, who even at five showed a precocious passion for knowledge.

"Children with no fathers or mothers," Elizabeth told her curtly. Uncomfortably aware of the stigma attaching to her own mother, she supposed she must be half an orphan herself.

They were watching the rain fall steadily in the inner courtyard. It raced in rivulets down the outside of the leaded window panes and Jane, who was short for her age, had clambered onto a stool to trace their course with a stumpy finger. "Then they wouldn't get pinches and slaps when they fidget over their writing tablets, would they?" she asked enviously.

She had dared only to whisper the question and her cousin was watching a fascinating waterspout gushing from the mouth of a stone dolphin sticking out from the guttering of the chapel roof. But Anne heard her and paused in the middle of the instructions she was giving Hawe to pull the child onto her lap. Although she knew Charles disliked the strict way his daughter and the Duke of Dorset brought Jane up, she couldn't very well say anything about it herself without making trouble. Jane didn't expect to be petted as Edward did; but Anne often held her very close so that if life should frighten her when she grew up she would have some caresses to remember and be able to draw comfort from the promise that underneath are the Everlasting Arms. Jane, for her part, wasn't accustomed to being taken onto people's knees—except occasionally her grandfather's and on one terrifying occasion the King's—but sitting with Anne's arm round her was rather pleasant because one could get down whenever one liked. 'Why do you have orphans, Madam?' she asked, playing with the bright bead trimming on her hostess's dress.

"Because she is kind, of course," interrupted Elizabeth, whose quick-silver mind found Jane's grave persistence rather boring. But Mary, who had brought some gifts for the party, explained patiently that it was usual for ladies in Madam of Cleves' position to keep an orphanage for the poorer children on their estates. She didn't say what trouble she herself had been to to arrange this for her friend's consolation, nor how much pleasure it gave her to see Anne sitting there in happy serenity just as if she had been born one of the family—with the other Mary Tudor's grandchild in her lap and tall Elizabeth coming to lean on the arm of her chair. "May we help make the cakes again this time, Aunt Anne?" she was pleading.

"The little spiced ones perhaps," promised Anne, glancing through the list her comptroller handed her. "But there's to be one very special big one which the cooks are busy making down in the kitchen now. A birthday cake with sugar icing for a new baby who is coming."

"When?" asked Elizabeth eagerly, for Edward was getting much too big for her to lift.

"In time for the party we hope!" smiled Mary, considering the inconvenience Anne was being put to by the event.

"Will he be an orphan too, then?" piped up Jane, and hid

her freckled face against the attractive bead trimming when they all laughed.

"No, poppet," explained Anne. "His parents will be Dorothea and Guligh. That's why Mistress Lilgrave has been making fresh hangings with all those pretty embroidered birds for Dorothea's room."

"Then he ought to have auburn hair like me," prophesied Elizabeth.

Jane peeped up enviously at her cousin's tight red-gold curls. "Guildford Dudley says mine is mouse coloured," she lisped sadly.

"But then Guildford is a horrid, spoiled little boy," snapped Mary. She shared her father's dislike of the Northumberland family and knew better than the others why they encouraged their handsome young son and the King's plain grand-niece to play together, and in what direction their ambition lay. Her old irritation rose against Elizabeth too. For when excitement painted colour on the girl's pale, high cheek bones she could make everybody else look drab and colourless—and feel it! Mary was glad when she darted back to her stance at the window to see a horseman galloping into the palace yard, and the younger child slid off Anne's lap to join her. "How sad to see a mere babe of five cherishing a conviction that orphans are a particularly privileged set of people!" she remarked. "The Dorsets must think that book-learning is the only weapon with which to equip their children against life."

Anne dismissed Hawe and drew her chair nearer for a chat. "I should say that a happy childhood is far more efficacious," she said thoughtfully. "I know that if I'm able to face most things with reasonable serenity now, it's mostly because when I was small I always felt my parents were there between me and harm, standing deputy for God."

Mary nodded. She too had had a wonderful childhood until she was ten. "I hope your mother is better?" she said. "Last time I was here you had had disquieting news of her health."

But their conversation was interrupted by Elizabeth's clear voice calling, "It's Tom Culpepper's servant, Aunt

Anne—with the wet simply pouring off his hat and his horse all in a muck sweat!"

Anne rose hurriedly. Her eyes sought Mary's. "You don't suppose—it's any ill tidings about the Queen?"

But Mary knew nothing of Anne's cause for anxiety. "I was with them only yesterday for the festival of the Blessed Saints; and my father thanked God aloud that after all the strange accidents that had befallen his marriages he had been given a wife so entirely confirmed to his inclinations as the one he has now."

Anne was guilty of a ribald grimace. "I suppose I'm one of the strange accidents," she said. She was really waiting for the sound of hurrying footsteps and when Culpepper's letter came she broke the seal and read it where she stood. "He begs me to come at once," she told Mary, turning the hastily written note about in search of some explanation and continuing to speak in undertones inaudible to the children.

"To Hampton?"

"Yes."

"Whatever for?"

"I've no idea," lied Anne, struggling with a rare sense of premonition.

Mary always felt that Anne put herself out far too much for everyone connected with her household; but she rose with that dignity which was so surprising in so small a person. "Well, as you know, I'm crossing to the opposite bank to spend All Souls' Day at the Convent of Sion. But I thought you had Sir Richard Taverner coming to settle about your nationalization papers?"

"I know. It's terribly inconvenient. And besides——" Anne stood for a moment or two in indecision. It was eight or nine months now since Henry had come to stay. Part of the time he had been on a progress up North. But on several occasions he had ridden over or stepped off his barge on the way to Westminster to sample fresh trials of cookery or bring her a present of grapes from his vinery and show her what a properly grown bunch should look like. Her lips curved into a smile at the recollection of their amicable encounters, for their relationship was now on the safe and true basis where affection thrives on mutual banter. But all the same she didn't like the idea of going to Hampton Court without being officially invited.

"And besides," Mary concluded for her impatiently, "why should you of all people put yourself out over the Queen's affairs?"

But Anne didn't measure out kindnesses like that. "I *did* promise her my gold tissue May Day dress to have cut up into angels' wings for the Christmas nativity play," she remembered. "But it's Tom Culpepper I'm thinking of." Hurriedly she sent for the lavish looking garment, made her excuses to Mary and left instructions for the luckless Clerk of the Signet to occupy himself as best he might until her return.

By the time her closed horse-drawn litter reached Hampton the rain had ceased. She went in by the garden entrance and found Culpepper waiting as he had promised. No one else appeared to be expecting her and as it was nearly time for Mass there were very few people about. On their way across the Stone Court he drew her into the quiet gloom of the chapel cloister. There was an urgency about his speech and manner that precluded ceremony. "In less than an hour the King will have found out," he said.

Even by the light of a horn lantern fixed above the chapel doors he looked years older. All the boyish gaiety was gone —all the ruffling swagger of his fashionable Court clothes was belied by the drawn gravity of his face. "About—you?" she whispered back aghast, thinking of his danger and realizing how much she cared for him.

He shrugged as though uncertain, but made no admission. "About Manox—and Derham," he said.

"Derham?" A whole pit of hideousness opened before Anne's imagination, blackening the lovable picture of Katherine—the picture of a child neglected, more sinned against than sinning. Could it be possible that this high-born girl whom she had felt sorry for in spite of all her own wrongs was just a lustful wanton? And that when Henry behaved like an ogre he sometimes had provocation? "The

King once mentioned to me a man of that name," she recalled. "But I'm sure he never dreamed——"

"But most of us *knew*," interrupted Culpepper, in that strained, low pitched voice that seemed to have lost all its laughter. "It was madness to have all those people here who had served in the Duchess of Norfolk's household. I went to Katherine's rooms one night and reasoned with her for hours while Jane Rochfort listened for the King's coming. The poor sweet believed it was the only way to keep them from betraying her. She couldn't see that it was only piling up suspicion and dangerous evidence against herself." Voices were audible from the courtyard—the enviable, carefree voices of men who weren't face to face with disaster—and Culpepper glanced uneasily over his shoulder, talking against time. "It was the Duchess herself who urged her to stop that swine Derham's mouth with a good appointment," he explained. "I suppose she was terrified of what the King would do to her if he found out that she had encouraged him to marry her granddaughter, knowing her to be no maid."

"Tom! Was it as bad as that? And you loved her in spite of it?" Anne put a pitiful hand on his arm, moving closer against him to let the approaching chapel officials pass. Coming in out of the light they might easily take her hooded gure for any maid-of-honour indulging in a mild flirtation.

"It wasn't her fault," he declared obstinately. "Even the King might have admitted that if only she had thrown herself on his mercy instead of fooling him. It all happened before he married her and the most he could have done would have been to divorce her."

"I see," said Anne, avoiding a lively crowd of choristers scuffling along the cloister kicking a muddy ball before them. "And then some day perhaps you could have married her?"

"I would have waited all my life," he said, quite simply.

"And as it is?"

"As it is some cursed busybody has laid all the facts before milord Archbishop, and he feels it his Christian duty to write them down and hand them to the King."

"Cranmer——" Anne found it difficult to reconcile the prelate's habitual friendliness towards Culpepper with the young man's bitterness.

"Oh, to save his own skin, no doubt—now the Howards are in power with their Popish bishop Gardiner. Fear will make a man do anything. Sir Thomas Seymour thinks he means to hand it to the King here in chapel this morning."

The doors stood wide now and people were beginning to come in twos and threes from both directions. "But why in chapel?" asked Anne.

Culpepper laughed mirthlessly. "To prevent the King from making a fool of himself with a special public thanksgiving he has ordered for his thornless rose, I suppose!" He stopped to listen to as the new astronomical clock over the courtyard gateway struck a quarter to the hour. "Soon he will come into his private oratory upstairs," he said unsteadily, "and then her whole world will crumble about her." He said nothing about the danger to his own world.

A warm stream of light flowed out from the chapel, bringing fantastic beauty to the grey, groined roof of the cloister; and Anne stepped forward so that she could see the interior. It looked warm and inviting compared with the draughty place where they stood, and brought back a vivid recollection of how much she had liked going there when she was so homesick and uncertain, even though in those days she hadn't understood a word of the service. She wondered if Katherine found the same sort of comfort. "Will she be there too?" she asked.

"Some of her women have already been questioned by Wriothesley and she's afraid to leave her apartments."

"Surely it would look better if she went to Mass as usual?"

The upper servants were going in now. In a few minutes the doors would be shut. Culpepper threw out an appealing hand. "It's her only possible chance. To be with him when they tell him. Can't you possibly persuade her, Madam?"

Anne shrugged with exasperation. "But why ask *me*,

Tom?" she asked, feeling that she had already had her share of this awful waiting on the King's displeasure.

"Because they are already watching her and you are the one person whom no one would ever suspect of trying to help her."

Anne saw now why he had begged her to come. She looked round and beckoned to Basset who was waiting at a little distance with a basket containing the May Day finery. "I still don't see what I can *do*," she was protesting helplessly, when she felt Culpepper's lips pressed against her hand. "You can show her friendship and forgiveness—and God knows it may be the last time she'll ever see you!" he whispered in passionate gratitude. "I beseech you, Madam, tell her that if only she will face divorce by admitting she lived as Derham's wife, I'll wait for her. And that though they may pluck my eyes out I will never endanger her life by admitting that I have been her lover."

The urgency of his manner moved her. His trust moved her still more. She paused only for assurance that Lady Rochfort wouldn't be there. And before going to escort the King, Culpepper saw her disappear round a bend at the far end of the cloister. He knew her to be sufficiently familiar with the domestic part of the palace to find her way up the backstairs to the Queen's apartments.

CHAPTER XXVII

Everything was unusually quiet on the principal floor of Hampton Palace that All Souls' Day. The King's procession had not yet been formed and only a couple of ushers waited by the door of his oratory overlooking the chapel. Anne walked briskly along the gallery to the Queen's ante-room. A few servants and pages stopped whispering together in corners to stare after her. "Her Grace is indisposed and milady Rochfort left instructions that she was not to be disturbed," she was told. But no one appeared to have any definite authority either to receive or to hinder her; and after she had had the gold tissue unwrapped as the ostensible reason for her visit and had talked with reassuring complacency about the latest fashions the few ladies remaining on duty allowed her to go in to their mistress. "Either they must think me a complete fool not to sense that something is wrong, or that I have come to jeer at her," she supposed.

The familiar room had been part of her own honeymoon suite and for a moment Anne believed it to be empty. Then the sound of hysterical sobbing directed her gaze to a window embrasure where the little Queen knelt all alone. The dark stuff of her gown was crumpled on the floor and her bright head bowed on arms outstretched across the velvet cushions. Her discarded cap had been cast from her by a broken chin-strap. "If only I hadn't so misdemeaned myself!" she kept crying over and over again in a frenzy of fear and remorse. Once she raised a ravaged face to see who had come in and at sight of so unexpected a visitor her sobs grew wilder. Anne decided then and there that she was in no fit state to be seen in chapel or anywhere else, and sat down to wait. She was accustomed to dealing with hysteria.

"I see you're wearing my rubies to-day," she remarked cheerfully, picking on some commonplace theme. "I expected you would have given them to one of your women now that you have so many trinkets."

Katherine made an effort to pull herself together. "I always liked you, Madam," she stammered. "But I was so ashamed."

Absently, Anne stooped to pick up the fallen cap and smoothed the torn linen against her knee. "I'm afraid you didn't get many pretty things after all," she said. "Henry had spent more than he could afford on me—or rather on impressing Cleves. But when a man really loves you I suppose he doesn't need to pretend with gee-gaws."

Katherine began to sob again at the recollection. "I had such a sweet and gentle prince. But that's all finished now. They've told him at last—about . . ." She ceased crying quite suddenly and, casting a crafty glance at Anne, stopped her mouth with two childish looking hands.

"Not yet, I think," said Anne. "Perhaps if you try to keep calm we can think of something to do about it."

"We!" The girl sank back on her heels, staring up at her with wide eyes. "But why should *you* care what happens to me?"

"Because I can probably sympathize with you better than anyone else in England," Anne told her grimly.

"But no one found out—if you had a lover. . . ."

Anne ignored the imputation. In this country, it appeared, people were always on the look out for such infidelities in a royal bride. She leaned forward, beating a vexed tattoo on the arms of her chair. "I suppose your grandmother and that Rochfort woman always speak of me as your rival —someone who's trying to get rid of you?" she asked contemptuously.

"I did think—just now—that you'd come to get back your crown," admitted Katherine.

Anne almost laughed at her cowed naïvety. "Well, it's true I liked being Queen," she allowed. "And I'd have made a far better one than you because—although I wasn't English—I cared tremendously about my people. But I had Henry for six months—here in these very rooms for the most part—and I found him anything but a sweet and gentle

295

prince. He made my life hell." She leaned down and caught hold of her former maid-of-honour's shoulder as if to shake some sense into her. "Now I've my own life and my own neck and a comfortable degree of his liking, d'you suppose I want him back as a husband?"

The better part of Katherine which hadn't been spoiled by ambition could appreciate this. She herself had come to realize the price of pomp. But subterfuge had grown so much a habit that it was difficult to accept so disinterested and simple a truth. "You haven't come to trap me into a confession?" she parried doubtfully.

Anne sighed and sat back in her chair. "You may as well trust me," she advised wearily, "seeing that Tom Culpepper begged me to come and I daren't stay much longer."

At mention of her cousin's name a brief muster of dignity upheld Katherine. She rose to her feet and held out a hand for her cap. "Did he send me any message?" she asked eagerly.

"He showed all the loving care for you of which a man is capable, bidding you take comfort because he will never betray you," Anne told her. "And—for the rest—he beseeches you to admit a previous marriage contract with this man Derham so that the King may divorce you."

"That I will never do!" Katherine's whole neatly rounded body quivered with repugnance and disdain. It was as if a belated pride in her Plantagenet blood swept over her, sustaining her obstinacy. Her small white teeth bit into her lower lip in an effort to be done with tears, and she sat down on the window seat with some degree of composure. Anne didn't press the point because she felt sure that Cranmer, in common humanity, would urge her to it.

Katherine gazed out unseeingly at a world that once had looked so fair; and presently the whole pitiful, sordid story came out. "I was only a child when my mother died. There were a lot of us and my father had to go away. He was made Governor of Calais," she began in low, monotonous sentences. "As you know, my grandfather's second wife took me in. She didn't want me. At first I cried myself sick for my sisters and my lovely Aunt Culpepper who sometimes had us to stay with our cousins in Kent. But the happy orchards where we played at Lambeth and Hollingbourne were only memories out of a lost world. Except at meals I seldom saw people of my own kind. I had to sleep in a common dormitory with the Norfolk waiting women. While they thought I was asleep, I listened to their lewd stories. And sometimes they stole the key after it was given into milady's keeping at night and let their men friends in. They brought us fruit and sweetmeats left over from the Duke's table. I didn't understand. I thought it was fun—just romping and fun—at first." She withdrew her gaze from the window and looked earnestly at Anne. "You do believe me; don't you, Madam?"

Anne nodded. Her heart ached for such a childhood. "But how could you—who could remember your own gracious home—care for such clods?" she asked gently.

"I was only thirteen and terribly lonely. Mary Lascelles, who was supposed to be in charge of me, egged me on. And one of the men who came was less rough than the rest." Katherine was so accustomed to seeing him about her present household that she sat for a moment or two twirling her rings while she conjured up a picture of how he had appeared to her then. "He was one of the Norfolk musicians and taught me to play on the virginals. He was dark and handsome in a foreign sort of way. I thought him romantic but he was only—beastly. He used to come and sit on my bed . . ." The King's fifth wife suddenly covered her face with her hands. "Oh, why is it so much harder to speak of such things—even though they be scarcely one's own fault—than to confess to theft or murder?"

"It was those devilish sluts of women who should have spoken of it, not a child like you!" cried Anne hotly. The last time she had dined at Hampton she had noticed the man Manox, black-eyed and fleshy, leering down from the minstrels' gallery while he scraped his accursed viola-da-gamba.

Katherine uncovered her face. "Some instinct must have warned me of the danger I ran," she said with a shudder. "I gave up my music lessons. I even made Lascelles take me to another house where he was employed so that I might upbraid him for his presumption. If I hadn't become Queen no one would ever have known. But then—my beloved father died—and Frances Derham came to live with us. . . ." Anne saw the Queen's little hands twisting in her lap. They showed white against the darkness of her skirts, like pale souls writhing in some torment of remorse. "He was a sort of relation—like me—but not so poor. One of my uncle the Duke's gentlemen retainers. He was bold and generous, and he gave me the pretty things I'd been used to as a child. I was growing up then and I knew men liked me—yet I'd less pin money than the servants! After a while I let him buy me clothes. Silks and velvets and things . . . I meant to repay him. But he didn't want the money. He wanted me."

"Were you publicly betrothed to him," asked Anne.

But again Katherine denied it with scorn. "It was only that he coaxed me to call him husband among his equals, and nobody seemed to care. He used to go away sometimes, and always left his money with me as if we were married. He tore my heart saying his mission was dangerous and I know now that it was smuggling—and each time he came back he was still more jealous and fond. Oh, I hate to think of him—and still more I hate myself!" She got up and paced the room, back and forth between window and fireplace, tearing her dainty cap to shreds. Her remorse was heart-rending, and yet Anne felt that it was less for the betrayal of her virtue than for the betrayal of her pride. "You see, it went on for months—and the baser part of me—wanted it," she explained, sitting down again with bowed head by the window. "The excitement and the secrecy and the flattery." Now that she had at last brought herself to speak of it, confession of each detail seemed to ease her. "I remember I was crazy for one of those pansy love-tokens the court ladies were wearing just then and he had one embroidered for me by a hunchback in London. He gave me a little cap pearled with fennel. . . . He gave me everything—and spoiled my whole life. . . ."

Anne rose and joined her at the window. "Didn't the Duchess ever find out?" she asked.

"Someone told her at last. And she beat me for it. And Tom or one of my other cousins would have killed him if he hadn't fled to Ireland."

Anne pondered on the ill fate that had bestowed on this wronged wanton such a blaze of greatness as would inevitably uncover her sinning to the world. There seemed nothing she could say to comfort her. She saw Wriothesley and Wotton emerge from a doorway across the courtyard and stand talking with some papers in their hands, and knew that she must be going soon. But Katherine had to finish her tale.

She told it earnestly, sitting there with her hands in her lap, as if trying to impress it clearly on her own mind. "After that I lived differently," she vowed. "It had been such a shock—being found out—and the disgrace. Although my granddam, who was responsible, tried to hide it from the Duke. It turned all my desire to loathing. I began to dress soberly like a gentlewoman instead of a backstairs jade. When men spoke to me I answered modestly. I *was* different. And then, when the Duchess brought me to Rochester, I met Tom again. For the first time—as a grown man. And he was different from all the rest. He was beautiful in mind and body, and I thanked God I had changed myself into the sort of girl my dear dead father would have had me be." She turned suddenly with a wild light in her eyes and plucked at Anne's trailing sleeve. "But you see it was no good!" she declared desperately. "The King wanted me too—and for a time my silly head was quite turned. It's terribly exciting being wanted by a King, isn't it, Madam?" As Anne didn't answer she went on in a little spurt of triumph, "There were supper parties at Durham House and all the fine clothes I wanted, and instead of being a neglected poor relation, I became the most important member of the family. Nothing was too good for me. Henry called me his *rosa sans spina* . . ." She began to rock herself backwards and forwards. "I used to sing to him. I even sang some of the ribald little French songs Manox had taught me —and my husband found them amusing. It was funny, wasn't it?"

"Don't!" implored Anne, dropping a hand on her shoulder. Katherine caught at it and tried to stifle her hysterical laughter. "He was good to me," she testified, as soon as she could speak calmly again. "And I grew fond of him—in place of my father. And we tried so hard, Tom and I, not to deceive him . . . but he *would* keep throwing us together. And then one night, Henry lay away from home. We'd no idea where he'd gone and Jane Rochfort kept watch." She stopped making excited movements with her restless hands and clasped them together against her breast. This time they looked like two birds, buffeted by the storm, come home to rest. "Together we two owned the world that night," she whispered, "and we knew that nothing else mattered."

So it had all been as Anne had feared. And then they had gone up north on this royal progress staying at dozens of different places, and no doubt there had been other opportunities. It had been wrong and dangerous and inevitable, and now Youth—fleeced of its loveliest rights—must pay the reckoning. She glanced down hastily and saw Wriothesley and Wotton picking their way across the wet paving of the courtyard and looking up stealthily at the Queen's windows. There was a horrid, suppressed excitement about their movements. They might have been poachers about to pounce upon their prey. "For your own safety, you must forget that stolen sweetness—absolutely," she told the brooding girl. But to her surprise some metamorphosis seemed to come over this wayward daughter of the Howards. She stood erect and smoothed the folds of her gown with a quiet, proud gesture. Her head was lifted courageously so that the light crowned her rippling auburn hair; her violet eyes were deep and sweet and sane. "I would rather die the wife of Culpepper than live as Queen of England," she confessed.

Anne had never liked her so well. But there was no time for sentiment. She must take advantage of this high, exalted mood before it waned. "I promise you there will be no need for you to die," she hazarded firmly, "if you go straight to the King and tell him just what you've told me now—about your pitiful girlhood and those two men."

"It's too late now. They're all at Mass——"

Katherine would have shrunk back but Anne almost pushed her to the door. "Then you must catch him as he comes out—before his ministers get at him," she insisted, imposing her own strong will upon the girl's vacillating one. "He really loves you, Katherine, and he's such a coward!"

"Henry—a coward?"

"Oh, not physically. Just about the plague and saying hurtful things to people's faces," explained Anne hurriedly. "He always makes someone else do it. But, of course, you wouldn't have had occasion to know."

"Did he do that to you, Madam?" asked Katherine, smoothing her hair and calling for a fresh cap. For the first time she was beginning to understand what this other wife of his must have suffered.

"Always," said Anne, opening the door. "And not being able to speak your language easily I used to sit quiet and watch him so that I often think I understand him better than any of his ministers do."

They found the ante-room a scene of concentration. Basset stood by a table with the May Day dress half folded in her hands, looking very excited; but most of the Queen's women wept aloud or crouched in corners while a pale and breathless page told them that a guard had just been set at the end of the gallery. Whether by Wriothesley's presumptuous orders or the King's, Katherine was already virtually under arrest.

"If only we could bribe them!" she moaned, in a fever to take Anne's advice now—that it no longer appeared possible.

"Or find means to distract their attention—if only for a moment," suggested Basset, her quick wits taking in the situation and her main concern being to get Anne home without being mixed up prematurely in a tragedy from which she might ultimately profit. As she spoke her glance fell speculatively upon the gorgeous stuff in her hands. Instead of finishing putting it away she shook out the folds, inserting her hands invitingly into the armholes as she always did when dressing her mistress. Anne followed her movements and her thoughts. Out in the courtyard the silvery chimes told the half hour. A few minutes more then Henry would be coming out. But there was still a chance. What was it that incorrigible French ambassador was said to have reported to Paris? "Every day milady Anne of Cleves wears a new dress, and each more wondrous than the last." Well, a May Day dress of gold tissue should be wondrous indeed on a drizzly day in October! She nodded to Basset and before the astonished onlookers could realize what was happening the shimmering garment was over her head.

Basset opened the door a few inches and peeped. Two tall halberdiers stood at the top of the Queen's staircase. Anne could see them over her woman's shoulder. Beyond them, at right angles, lay the long gallery leading to oratory and great hall. If only Katherine could reach it unperceived, run into the oratory and cling to Henry with those unhappy, childlike hands, perhaps she might fan to flame that new tenderness she had lit in his heart. Without taking her eyes off the guards, Anne allowed her own fingers to close for a steadying moment on the girl's trembling wrist. "Kick off your shoes," she directed. "Wait till they begin to watch me go down the stairs, and then seize your chance."

Another moment and she was saying loud 'good-byes,' fussing over the possibility of rain spoiling her finery and finally making her way from ante-room to stairs like a golden galleon in full sail. Nothing could have been more unexpected than her appearance nor more unsuitable than her garments. The confused halberdiers gaped. In their hastily received orders, plenty had been said about not letting Lady Rochfort *in* but nothing about letting Madame of Cleves *out*. Everybody had supposed her to be safely put away in a sort of hypothetical spinsterhood at Richmond, poor lady! Though, if all these dirty backstairs stories about smugglers and music masters were true, what more natural than that she should want to come and crow over a girl who had stolen her husband and her crown? Or maybe the King himself had sent for her, intending to reinstate her. And if that were so it wouldn't pay to offend her. Neither would anything please most people better for—queer as her taste in dress might be—she was notoriously kind. So, to be on the safe side, the men made way for her and sprang to attention. But the moment she began to descend the stairs curiosity got the better of them. Anne heard their clumsy footsteps and the creak of their cuirasses as they leaned over the stairhead. Above the pounding of her heart she could almost make out their muttered remarks. And with some listening sixth sense she was aware of the faint whisper of a flying skirt as a swift presence, light as the girl who had danced like thistledown in Culpepper's arms, passed along the gallery behind them.

Anne went down as slowly as she could, stopping half-way to upbraid the following Basset for some imaginary fault. Framed by the wide archway before her lay the wet courtyard, glistening in the first pale beams of a watery sun. She had only to cross the deserted gardens to her waiting litter. She would be glad to be home again, for nothing less than Culpepper's desperate pleading would have induced her to interfere and already she was wondering what the outcome of it all would be. But before she set foot on the bottom step a confused medley of sounds broke out above her, warning her that her plan had miscarried. An oath and clatter of halberds, heavy footsteps giving chase along the gallery, scuffling and men's agitated voices in the distance and then —from the direction of the oratory—a woman's piercing screams.

Some passing page must have warned them and they had caught the erring Queen before ever she could open the oratory door. Anne tried not to picture them wrenching her from it. Henry too must have heard those heartrending screams—and his tenderly loved child-wife calling desperately upon his name. But he made no sign. Cranmer's note was already in his hands. The complacent roll of the organ droned on and the screams died away. The public thanksgiving for 'her whom I have now' would never be said.

Before slipping away as quietly as she had come, Anne

leaned for a moment or two against the courtyard wall. She felt too shaken and sick to walk. Though muddy water might still swirl dangerously under Traitors' Gate, she closed her eyes and thanked God for the strange, safe backwater of her life.

CHAPTER XXVIII

While all England sorted the soiled linen of the Howard queen, Anne lay tossing feverishly on her bed at Richmond. Like most people who are seldom ill, she was an obstinate patient and gave her women a good deal of anxiety. For one think knowing her malady to be rather of the spirit than of the body, she steadfastly refused to bother any of the court physicians and seemed quite content to rely on the homely remedies of Alarde, the household surgeon who tonsured her confessor and physicked her maids. She was furious with herself for collapsing in such a ridiculous manner; but the fever ran so high that the whole week since her strange visit to Hampton seemed one confused nightmare.

She had hurried home crazy with anxiety about Culpepper and not at all happy about her own unconventional efforts on his behalf. And on her arrival she had found a courier from Cleves waiting for her with the shattering news that the Duchess was dead. She could remember sitting huddled in her cloak with the frivolous gold dress crumpled beneath it, shivering before a blazing fire. Slow, hard tears had rolled down her cheeks as she tried to realize that never again would she receive the very breath of home in a letter from her mother or know the comfort of that efficient, uncompromising personality. She wanted Dorothea, who knew all her family and would know what to do when one felt so wretchedly ill. But poor Dorothea had started her labour and had pains enough of her own. So Anne had allowed Basset and a feckless, young girl called Jane Ratsey to put her to bed. There had been two cases of plague in the village, and she knew by the scared look in their eyes that they thought she had caught it. But even Alarde knew better than that.

She had lain like a log for days; but with the uncanny perspicacity of a woman accustomed to running her own household, she had been irritatingly aware of what was going on and of all the arrangements they made. Dorothea would have made them quietly *outside* the patient's room, hiding any agitation she might feel as cleverly as she had concealed the recent change in her comfortable shape. But Basset and Ratsey managed to bring the backwash of domestic disturbances to the bedside. It seeped up through flurried whispers as they smoothed the sheets, or overflowed in scraps of self-important conversation with people just outside the door; so that although Anne lay between drawn curtains with her eyes shut she knew that little Jane Grey had been sent home and that, after much discussion as to the propriety of letting Elizabeth return to the home of her disgraced step-mother, a wealthy and recently widowed neighbour, Lady Katherine Parr, had eased the situation by inviting the girl to her manor at Wimbledon. The King, apparently, had gone off to Oatlands and—with his mind full of his own grief and his wife's inevitable trial—he had left no instructions about his daughters. As for Sir Richard Taverner, after being told that milady of Cleves had been called away on urgent business, he had been put off a second time with the excuse that his hostess had suddenly been taken ill, and Anne gathered that the poor man, unable to conclude the business of her nationalization papers, had displayed understandable scepticism and departed in dudgeon. And to crown the domestic upheaval, Dorothea's baby had been born.

It was all a jumble in Anne's aching head, mixed up with grief for her mother, genuine horror at the latest tragedy in her adopted family and disappointment at not being able to see the new baby. As she began to get better she was annoyed, too, by an air of smug elation about all who served her. Basset must have told Jane Ratsey and all the other women what had taken place at Hampton and they were ghoulishly glad of it. All that Henry and Katherine and Culpepper were suffering was, in their eyes, divine vengeance for the way in which their beloved mistress had been slighted. "It's God working in His own way to make milady Anne queen again!" she overheard the chatterbox Ratsey proclaiming to someone. Anne roused herself sufficiently to rebuke them feebly; but outside her room their tongues must have wagged on, for a day or so later she found herself being nursed by two inept women-of-the-bedchamber who told her some wild story about Lady Katherine Basset and Jane Ratsey having been put in prison.

Mercifully, Dorothea came into her room at that moment. Seeing how her mistress was placed she had made the effort to come and sit with her, and Guligh had brought their little son to cheer her. The great fellow seemed almost ludicrously over-awed at having sired anything so minutely perfect. Anne made him lay his precious bundle on her bed while all three of them hung over it. "Milady Elizabeth *said* he would have red hair!" she laughed weakly. "What are you going to call him?" And when they both promptly answered 'William' she realized that they were her very own people and that though they might spend a lifetime in England nothing would ever lessen their loyalty to her house. And, seeing that she was alone with them, she spoke of the thing that had been worrying her. "What *is* all this about Basset and Ratsey?"

"Only that they were sent for to Westminster and questioned by the Council, Madam," Guligh explained. "They were over-excited and said things, and someone must have reported them."

"What sort of things?" Anne wanted to know.

"Oh, only what we all *think*, Madam," said Dorothea, beginning to stitch at a microscopic shirt. "Ratsey remarked that it was impossible for so sweet a queen as yourself to be utterly put down, and Basset—you know how impulsive she is, Madam—exclaimed, 'What a man the King is! How many *more* wives will he have?' And apparently in this country that is treason."

Anne couldn't help smiling. She appreciated their passionate partisanship; but it had created just the vulgar sort of publicity she had striven so hard to avoid and had she not been taken ill it would never have happened.

"It's really nothing to worry about, Madam," Guligh tried to reassure her. "Master Hawe rode down to Westminster for news and he says the Council are letting them come home to-morrow, which all goes to show which way the political wind blows."

"But I do worry, Guligh," Anne reproved him gently. "Because I should hate people to think that I exhibit such odious eagerness myself." It amazed her that even those who loved her best could suppose that, because she had taken her losses in the matrimonial game quietly, she had no more pride than to allow herself to be picked up again like a discarded shuttlecock.

The following morning she felt very much better. The sun was shining, a cheerful fire crackled between the iron dogs on the hearth and she waked to a happy remembrance that Mary was coming to see her. To make matters better still Dorothea insisted upon attending her. Anne stretched luxuriously, put an experimental foot to the floor and drew a furred wrap round her. She was still dawdling on the edge of the bed drinking a bowl of hot broth when her two chastened ladies returned for duty; but although they were both contrite at having caused her displeasure they seemed too full of indignation against someone else to accept her well merited reproof in silence. "It was that spiteful embroidery woman of the Howards who started it all," declared young Ratsey, going tearfully upon her knees.

"Started what?" asked Anne wearily. She had always felt they disliked the woman, with her expensive clothes and superior ways.

"Scandalmongering about things we said in private—and about Dorothea's baby——" muttered Ratsey, between injured sniffs.

"And what scandal can there possibly be about *that*," scoffed Anne, "since I specially mentioned her marriage to the King himself?"

"But they say it's *not* her baby."

Anne was still only convalescent and might be excused a little irritability. "Do be more explicit, Ratsey!' she complained. "Who are 'they'?"

But the crowded events of the past week had been too much for such an excitable scatterbrain. 'That snake in the grass went straight home from here after embroidering all those lovely birds and told the goldsmith's wife where she lodges that there was a cradle in the room and that we were all sewing covers for it," she garbled.

"Well, so we were," agreed Anne more placidly. "And I'm sure the Antwerp goldsmiths' family are kindly, sensible people—friends of a friend of mine. . ." She was still completely at a loss to understand what all the pother was about, and looking round for some sort of enlightenment her questioning glance rested on Basset—Basset who was well bred and intelligent and still pale with shame at having displeased a beloved mistress by her ill-considered words. "Unfortunately," the girl vouchsafed, "she seems also to have spoken of it to Sir Richard Taverner that day we went to Hampton——"

Anne stopped her with a gesture. She couldn't bear to be reminded of that day. "I suppose the poor Signet Clerk had to fill in his time somehow!" she sighed, recalling how fatally easy it appeared to be for gifted men to fill in their time with attractive widows like Frances Lilgrave. She reached for her half-finished bowl of broth. "Poor little William!" she commented idly. "And whose baby did she tell them all he was?"

There was an awkward silence which for once the loquacious Ratsey didn't feel disposed to break. "Yours, Madam," answered Basset courageously.

Anne lifted her head sharply to stare at her, both hands still circling the bowl. *"Mine?"* she repeated incredulously. "And why should anyone say such a thing?"

"To discredit you, Madam—lest the King should take you back," explained the little thoroughbred, intent upon giving true service to atone for her recent lapse. "There are relatives of the Queen who fear to lose their heads over this business if the Protestant party should come into power again. They are hideously afraid because the people want you, and no one can help noticing how merry the King is with you these days. And when we were in Westminster we heard it said that the courier who came from Cleves has gone on to Lambeth to see Archbishop Cranmer."

"I see," said Anne slowly. She saw a whole new set of

possibilities opening up before her, and a net of treachery being woven for her destruction. She only hoped that her brother wouldn't complicate the hard-won peace of her present life by charging into the lists on her behalf. But probably the Flemish courier was only improving the occasion of his visit to find out how the land lay.

"One member of the Council asked us if it were true that you had taken to your bed, Madam," chimed in Ratsey, rising from her knees. "Suspecting nothing, we admitted it—and then they wanted to know what doctor attended your Grace. Oh, Madam, wouldn't it have been better if you had let us send for one of the King's physicians? Then no one could have said that the baby——"

To stop the girl's excited prattle Anne set down her bowl and bade her take it away. As the door closed behind her she looked at her two favourite women—at Basset, slim, dark and piquante, standing before her and at fair, plump Dorothea, sitting by the fire. She knew that she could trust them both. "If this Lilgrave person says a thing like that she will eventually have to prove it," she said thoughtfully. "Who— in this feminine household—does she suggest is the father?"

It was Basset's turn to remain mute; but Dorothea laid down her sewing. She alone, who had journeyed with Anne, had the key to her mistress's frustrated affection; but she was not sure how much Anne had found out about the Court painter's relations with Mistress Lilgrave. "If you ask me, there is personal spite in this as well as politics," she said, picking her words carefully. "Master Holbein was about the palace nine months or so ago."

Anne forced herself to discuss the matter, but withdrew a little into the shadow of her old rose bed-hanging. "But Lilgrave was his mistress," she said coldly. "Why should she wish to implicate him?"

Dorothea picked up her needle again, glad that the moment was past. "They may have quarrelled," she suggested quietly. "In any case, it was very clever of her because everybody knows he travelled back with your Grace from Düren."

"But not quite clever enough," said Anne, on a low note

of triumph, "because he wasn't the only man here at the time She probably supposes that the King rode back to Hampton that night I gave him the prince's picture."

She sat cogitating on the edge of her bed for so long that Basset brought her ermine-lined slippers. "The sun is shining and you look so much better, Madam. Wouldn't you like to sit by the fire for a while?" she suggested.

"No," said Anne, with the firmness of one who has just made a momentous decision. Having made it, she drew her long, shapely legs back into the inviting warmth of the bed, hugged the covers round her knees and smiled inscrutably over the top of them. "I think I'm going to be confined to bed for some time yet. Another week or two probably."

The two who had waited for her to come down the King's staircase that night had never spoken of it; but now they realized that had the Lilgrave's aspersions been true their shared knowledge would have constituted Anne's perfect protection. They too perceived the flaw in the net of treachery which made it likely to produce unexpected results and rendered it far more dangerous for the trapper than the trapped. Their mistress had only to hold her tongue and bide her time. But deliberately to lead her persecutors on to their undoing and fool the King. . . . The issues were too big, and they were afraid. After a minute or two Dorothea laid aside her work and came and stood beside the bed. She was still weak and steadied herself by a hand about one of the great carved posts that supported the tester. "You mean—you'll let his Grace think . . ."

"It'll do him a power of good," snapped Anne, in a forceful idiom she had picked up from the tenantry she visited. "*And* all the busybodies concerned." Looking up and seeing Dorothea's face bereft of its usual rosy hue she sought to reassure her. "There's no law against staying in bed, is there? And who can blame us for whatever uncharitable construction people choose to put upon it?" she reasoned cheerfully.

She called for bread and honey for breakfast and settled back against her pillows to enjoy it. It was pleasant lying idly in the warm while her enemies wasted their energies and became entangled in a net of their own making. Anne felt she wanted to make someone pay for Culpepper's danger and Katherine's haunting screams. So it was agreeable to think of Henry, in the middle of his self-righteous condemnation of his fifth wife, finding out that he hadn't quite finished with his fourth one. He wouldn't know what to do. If he heard that she was the mother of a healthy, red-headed son, it would never occur to him that it could be any man's but his. And he wanted a healthy, red-headed son so badly that—if Anne knew anything about him—he wouldn't repudiate it for all the money in Christendom. On the other hand, what a fool he'd feel acknowledging his own inconstancy while getting rid of Katherine because of her shocking behaviour! Anne even hoped that he might withdraw the charge against Culpepper in order to hush the matter up; because this time it looked as if his pompous Council would be in the ridiculous position of holding delicate investigations about two of his wives at once! She could of course get up and fight for her maligned virtue; but it was definitely more amusing to stay in bed and bluff Henry. And, whatever happened, Anne knew that every time she fooled him she felt better about life. It melted her resentment against him for past slights and made it possible to like him better.

The trouble was that, apart from eating and sleeping, there was nothing to do. And Anne wasn't very good at doing nothing. "I know! I'll make my Will," she said, startling her entourage considerably.

"But, Madam, you are getting better!" protested Basset, hurrying to her side in consternation.

"I know. But everybody ought to make a Will," she insisted. "They might die suddenly of the plague or something. So go on and fetch Dionysius Thomow and tell him to bring pen and parchment."

"Please God you won't need it for a long time!" demurred Basset, feeling that they were somehow tempting Providence. But Anne only pulled her sweet face down and kissed her so that the devoted girl felt that all her small sins had been forgiven her. "*Dear* Basset," she laughed, "think how useful it will be to have one already drafted out when I do!" And when her beloved, white-haired chaplain came in he was delighted to find her well enough to undertake even such a lugubrious occupation. But somehow with Anne it wasn't in the least lugubrious—she made a cheerful kind of game of it, remembering her good friends and providing for the needs of her dependants. The old man had his writing desk placed beside her bed and together they spent a pleasant and diligent morning. So diligent, indeed, that Mary Tudor was announced before they were through with it, and unfortunately neither of them had considered what a shock it might give her to find them so strangely occupied. While priest and gentlewoman rose hurriedly Mary, the King's daughter, stood at the foot of the bed, her face grave with anxiety. "Why, Anne, they told me you were better!" she exclaimed, peering short-sightedly at all the ominous-looking legal paraphernalia.

"So much better, Madam, that I had to be doing something," laughed Anne. "I think we have remembered everybody at last, haven't we, good Dr. Thomow?" She took the imposing document from his frail hand and laid it at the bottom of the bed where Mary could read it; but—seeing that it was all set out in high sounding Latin phrases—she herself had to rely upon memory. "I've left my best jewel to you, dear friend, and one to Elizabeth. There are keepsakes for William and Amelia and all my family. A small sum apiece for the education of my alms-children and for the poor of Richmond, Bletchingly and my other manors." She ticked each item off with naïve pride on her fingers. "Something for each of my people who came over with me—in case they should want to go home, and a small dowry for two of my poor maids who want to get married over here." An anxious furrow creased Anne's serene forehead. She hated asking favours and rarely did so for herself; but once or twice in a lifetime one incurred the debt of a devotion which one would walk barefoot to repay. "And about Dorothea and Guligh——" she entreated. "You will remember how his Grace, your father, so generously promised that he would count my servants as his own, and their good services done to me as if it were done for him? Well, I was wondering—in the event of my dying before you—if you would of your charity make room for them in your own household? If I were *really* dying it would make me so much easier to know that."

Mary wasn't really reading the Latin effusion, but she fingered it gently because she thought it the most beautiful homemade Will she had ever heard. She was touched to the heart by the warm humanity of Anne's bequests. No one from august relatives to the laundry woman had been forgotten. Her warm Spanish brown eyes were suddenly wet with tears. "Of course I will," she said brusquely. "But you haven't asked anything for yourself."

"What is there to ask for—save the tender mercy of Christ—when one is dead?" asked Anne simply.

"One might need a tomb," suggested the worthy Dionysius, with an affectionate twinkle in his faded blue eyes. "Her Grace does well to remind us of a clause we have omitted. Where would you like to be buried, Madam?"

Basset, zealous for her mistress's status in this world and the next, had an idea. "They say there is room for *three* coffins in the great vault at Windsor where poor Queen Jane lies," she suggested eagerly.

"Heaven forbid!" ejaculated Anne, feeling that it was enough to have shared Henry in his lifetime. From the height of the great four-poster her gaze wandered over their heads to the wide vista of the park where oaks and beeches were still warm with the last burnishing of their autumn reds and browns. Why, she wondered, must important people like herself always be buried in stuffy vaults, or at any rate indoors? "Oh, wherever it shall please God," she added indifferently, seeing that her scribe's pen was raised expectantly.

Mary handed him back the parchment. "If I were Queen I would have her laid to rest in Westminster Abbey—as near the High Altar as possible," she said positively.

Anne flushed with pleasure. It was one of the best compliments she had ever received. "Well, write 'where God pleases' but remember what her Grace said and have my Will kept until the time comes," she bade the equally gratified chaplain, dismissing him with a smile.

When he had gone Mary came and sat beside her, looking round the great bedroom with its cheerful tapestries and contented occupants. Already everything Anne owned was typically English. And everywhere Anne went, Mary supposed, she would turn palaces into homes and paid service into devoted friendship. And—if she played her cards carefully—she would go on living the enviable life of a private gentlewoman. Whereas she, Mary Tudor, might be called upon to become Queen. . . . That unheard of thing that some men deemed impossible—the first Queen Regnant of England. . . . She had just come from Havering. And as usually, whenever she heard her young brother coughing badly, apprehension racked her nerves. But because she was both Tudor and daughter of Aragon all the amazing courage in her small-boned body rose to quell it. Whatever she had to do, she would do with all her heart and mind and conscience. And, above everything, she would bring England back on its knees to the faith of her dead mother! The way would be hard and lonely for a woman. But how much harder and lonelier without a room and a friend like this to come to sometimes! "Don't die for a long time yet, Anne!" she beseeched, her beautifully controlled voice deep with feeling.

Anne looked up in surprise and Mary's cool fingers lingered tenderly for a few moments on her forehead. "If anything should happen to Edward—" she began; then broke off with an embarrassing laugh. "Don't you know, you stolid, patient woman, that you're the best friend we tempestuous Tudors ever had?"

CHAPTER XXIX

Neither Frances Lilgrave nor the titled people behind her could have expected their allegations to be taken so seriously. All they had hoped for was an ugly little scandal smirching a woman whose virtue had hitherto been irritatingly unassailable, linking her name illicitly with a commoner and, so leaving her unsuitable for further royal attentions. Something disturbing enough to reach the King's ears and to evoke an enquiry of sorts—before a carefully selected tribunal and with a bribed witness or two if need be. To which end Sir Richard Taverner had been primed on all points. But from the moment that unsuspecting gentleman had felt obliged to unburden his troubled mind to someone in the royal household the affair had been taken out of their hands. For some seemingly unaccountable reason highly placed ministers who were above either bribery or coercion pounced upon each flimsy piece of evidence and began sifting it as painstakingly as though they were working on the evidence against the Queen herself. Indeed, there were whole days when the Queen's trial was held up on account of the relatively unimportant question of Madame of Cleves' morals. But the King seemed unduly perturbed and had ordered them to prove or disprove this rumour that his fourth wife had given birth to a son. And proof was the last thing its promoters wanted.

Dorothea and other members of the Richmond household were hauled before the Council and questioned; while Frances and the goldsmith's wife, instead of being snubbed for slandering their betters, found themselves being severely reprimanded for not having reported their suspicions sooner. And what must have surprised them still more was that Holbein's name was never officially mentioned.

Relief at knowing this may have emboldened him to come to Richmond Palace. But Anne knew that he would have come anyway. He had small regard for the conventions and the fact that people were talking against her challenged his conception of friendship.

"They said you were ill—and in trouble," he blurted out, the moment he was admitted to her presence.

But Anne was up and dressed and sitting by the solar fire. Even after two years' freedom from her mother's influence she still felt there was something vaguely indecent about receiving visitors in her bedroom. And in any case the welcome sight of him would have made her feel much better—he was so careless about his own safety and in such a lovable dither of anxiety about hers. "It was all such a shock," she explained confusedly.

"My poor Anna!" He threw his wide brimmed hat onto a table, by the very freedom of his movements bringing a breath of a wider, more vigorous life into her ordered room.

She smiled up appreciatively at his robust good looks. "Actually, I have been recovered these many days," she admitted. "But there seemed no need to tell the world."

"Your mother was a great lady. Even a reprobate like me must bow the knee to her unflinching virtue," he said, not knowing of any other shock she had sustained on the same day.

Tears welled into Anne's eyes as she motioned him to sit comfortably on the other side of the hearth. Coming just then, his sympathy was too precious for mere words; for, like most mourners, she had discovered that the world was divided into those who had known the loved one and those who had not.

"And now all this damnable persecution. . . . Even in your grief they won't let you alone," he growled. As she said nothing he leaned forward earnestly. "Anna, I came partly to ask you—you don't think that I was a party to it—that I even knew. . . . ?"

Anne looked at him reproachfully and blew her nose. "My dear—why should *I* think such a thing of *you*?"

As he bent unnecessarily to readjust a shoe buckle his wiry brown hair and muscular neck were dyed in a warm glow of firelight. "The jade was living with me at the time——"

"I know."

He looked up questioningly.

"She took care that I *should* know," added Anne.

Holbein's glance strayed irritably to Basset who was industriously sorting skeins of embroidery silk, and Anne asked her to go and play something for them on the harpsichord in the gallery instead. "Have I added to your hurts—even as much as that?" he asked, when she was gone.

Anne didn't answer directly. "When we learned what that woman had been saying Dorothea suggested that you—might have quarrelled——" she said tentatively.

"We did—furiously," he assured her. "But not before the damage was done. I find my friend's wife—kind as she is—has been circulating this abominable lie in all good faith to all our neighbours. And, judging by the way the Council have been questioning them, Frances seems to have shot her poison into some more important ear."

"She met the Clerk of the Signet here while I was out," explained Anne wearily, "and improved the idle hour."

"The Clerk of the Signet!" exclaimed Holbein aghast. "Why, he's hand in glove with young Edward's sanctimonious tutor. The bitch may have endangered your life!"

But Anne laughed scornfully. "No, Hans. You—and they—underrate my intelligence and overrate my virtue." He sprang up as if he had been stung and she rose with her usual leisurely movement to confront him. His whole tense stance was a blazing question and she looked him straight in the eyes. "Make your mind easy. I stand in no danger," she told him quietly. "Had I been fortunate enough to have a child these last few weeks it would have been the King's."

She saw him go white beneath the warm colouring of his skin. "Then it's true—what they're saying in the taverns——"

Anne reached to the fireside settle for the fan he had given her, using the ostrich feather tips as a shield against his searching gaze. "And what are they saying in the taverns?" she asked, to gain time.

"That he means to take you back—that almost before Culpepper had been arrested your brother had sent a courier to Cranmer."

So it was true, what Basset had heard. That poor Culpepper had been charged with adultery and the Protestant party were trying to make her Queen again. "When Henry finds that there is no son he may not want me," she parried.

Holbein came closer, one knee upon a little gilded chair he had tilted out of his way, his strong, sensitive hands gripping the back of it. "And you, Anna—you?" he demanded. "Would you go through it all again? Would you go back to him?"

Anne's own hands began to tremble as she fiddled with the fan. "I don't know. I don't know, Hans. . . ."

"Then why did you do this?"

Anne turned her tortured face from him. "I wanted—so dreadfully I wanted—a child of my own," she confessed brokenly.

He let go of the chair and seized her by the shoulders, striking his frivolous gift to the floor. His hot brown eyes blazed down onto the defenceless whiteness of her face—a complete pallor which left her plain and pockmarked. "Then why couldn't it have been ours?" he cried. "To what use have I denied myself to keep you untarnished, or eased my body and starved my soul with a treacherous strumpet that I might think of you as one of my painted Madonnas?" There was the whole gamut of the painter's nature laid bare —mysticism at one end and materialism at the other—the power to portray with equal feeling the devotion of an angel's wing or the disarray of a drab's dress. And the desire to keep them apart. Anne whimpered with pain but made no answer, and after a moment or two he let her go and answered the question himself—brutally, out of his own hurt. "Because it wouldn't have been so *safe*, I suppose!" he laughed harshly.

Each of them knew that what he said wasn't true. "It's not comparable. In the eyes of God—and of all good churchmen—he is still my husband," Anne defended herself.

Holbein might have pointed out that she had changed her faith—that there was no particular reason why the Protestant party should want her. But he stood in contemptuous silence, trying to get a hold on himself—waiting for her real reason. Through the open door leading to the sunny gallery came the thin, staccato notes of the harpsichord weaving themselves into a sprightly air at complete variance with their conversation.

"I swear to you that I knew no passion for him." Anne spoke slowly, painfully. To talk of such things still outraged the false austerity that clung about the warm, expanding nature that always leapt part way to meet his own. "But he had trampled on all the burgeoning belief in my own beauty —torn up the roots of confidence you had planted in me with your painting. That precious, vulnerable sense of poise that can give even a plain woman charm—that reliance on her own personality that she needs to be anything at all. He'd humiliated me until I shrank before ridicule—the cruellest ridicule of all, aimed at women who stir no man's desire. So that I had to make him want me—physically— just once. It mended something in me that he had broken. . . ." She turned aside, resting an arm against the stone chimney breast. "But being a man you wouldn't understand——"

Before such candid abasement Holbein's anger could not endure, and as an artist he drew upon the depth of all humanity, not just of one sex or the other. He lifted her hand from the folds of her skirts and kissed it—he would have given much to paint the tears that hung more preciously upon her lashes than any pearls that ever decked her grandest gowns. "I do understand, Anna," he said humbly.

Because she knew no way of receiving generosity save by meeting it with her own, her palm turned to his. Her face was suddenly smiling, rosily flushed and without blemish. "It was that night I learned that you were living with Frances Lilgrave," she told him, admitting last of all the only reason she would have concealed.

He drew her to him and kissed her with the tender licence of renouncing passion. "My poor, beautiful Anna!" he murmured. "That I of all people should have presumed to upbraid you!"

They moved apart reluctantly as voices and laughter sounded from the gallery and the music stopped; then went with one accord to a window and lingered there, staring out unseeingly on the wintry scene, adjusting themselves to more superficial things as might divers being newly drawn from depth to surface. "Then it looks as if Frances's subtlety may land her in the Tower," remarked Holbein conversationally.

Anne looked profoundly shocked. "Oh, Hans, I'm sorry," she exclaimed, not quite sure how much he cared. "Perhaps if I hadn't stayed in bed and let them think——"

But he only laughed and reached for his hat. "You don't suppose they'll bother to chop off her sleek, worthless head, do you?" he said callously. "It's only the children I'm worried about."

"The—children?" repeated Anne.

"Oh, I knew her before I came out to Düren. We've two small girls."

"What will you do with them?" asked Anne, still regarding him with distress.

"I don't know. I shall have to put them out to nurse, I suppose. If only I can find the right sort of woman——" He rumpled his hair and looked about as helpless as most men of genius do when faced with the more urgent material problems of life.

"What about the goldsmith's wife?" suggested Anne.

He shook his head. "I had thought of it. But she grows too old."

Like her small adopted relative, Jane Grey, Anne began to trace patterns on the window panes. It helped her to think. Her heart was beginning to beat crazily, and she kept her head bent over her childish occupation so that her companion could not watch the birth pangs of a marvellous new idea. "Are they at all like—their mother?" she enquired cautiously.

"No. Fair as angels," laughed Holbein. "And so far," he added more grimly, "she hasn't taught them to lie. Actually they haven't been taught anything. They're just babes and she's neglected them. But Lavinia is going to be able to draw." Parental pride began to inform his voice. "You would love Lavinia, Anna. She's the elder. She gets hold of one of my pencils and licks it solemnly and produces a portrait of her pet dog—like this——" After much rummaging in crowded pockets, he produced a piece of parchment bearing the forceful image of a strange, square quadruped. A scrap of parchment so crumpled that Anne guessed it had been shown to many amused fellow artists, and a quadruped that drew Lavinia straight into an aching corner of her heart and assured her, as nothing else could have done, that the fair mite was wholly her father's child.

"Would you consider me a suitable sort of person?" she asked, with mock meekness. And when he only stared uncomprehendingly she said on a more practical note, "Listen, Hans. If Frances Lilgrave should be kept in the Tower—or you should part—sooner than let them go to anyone who wouldn't be kind, I will have them here."

"You, Anna!" he gasped, cramming the little drawing back into his pocket. "Why, that *would* confirm this imbecile rumour about us and confuse the King!"

But Anne hurried on. "Oh, not to live with me. But with my orphans. Who would be any the wiser?" There was a distinct echo of the late Duchess's managing efficiency in her manner as she pushed open a casement. "Listen! you can hear them singing. I've had them brought into that wing of the palace for their lessons because it's warmer against the great kitchen flue. Jane Ratsey is down there teaching them their carols for Christmas. That girl ought to have dozens of babies!"

For a moment or two they leaned their elbows side by side on the wide window ledge—the most famous painter in Europe and the Flemish woman who had been Queen of England. An inrush of still, frosty air chilled their faces, and from across the snow-covered courtyard childish voices quavered uncertainly after the clear sweetness of a young girl's voice. Down by the kitchen archway a couple of cook's apprentices pelted each other with snowballs, and a stout porter snatched a kiss from a passing dairymaid; while from the chapel came an ageing priest and an acolyte bearing the Host to some dying tenant in the village. It was the ordinary, everyday world of the people. The world from which

Holbein extracted food for his art and in which Anne was so adequately equipped to walk. But they both knew that because of her parentage she could tread only the edge of it. Remembering that she was still only convalescent he closed the casement again. "You see they aren't just foundlings," she was saying eagerly. "They are well cared for—and loved. And I would have your Lavinia taught to draw."

'You are an amazing woman, Anna," he said, unaware that Henry Tudor too had used those very words. He stood staring at her almost in perplexity, his hat rolled into shapelessness between his hands. "You really mean—you would care for the children of a woman who has treated you so vilely?"

The obstinate lift of her chin reminded him of the days when she used to wrestle with her English. It was, he knew, the outward sign of a process which she called 'being firm with herself.' "I shall remember only that they are yours," she assured him.

The love he bore his small daughters did not obliterate the fact that he had begotten them lightly. And now the one woman he would have chosen to mother his legitimate children was offering them her love. He found it impossible to express adequate gratitude for such a gift. "We must come to some business arrangement," he insisted, flushing awkwardly.

"Of course," agreed Anne, knowing that it eased his pride not to become her monetary debtor as well. He would have taken leave of her then but she and her singing heart went walking down the gallery beside him. "You will be able to come and see them sometimes," she reminded him, knowing that he must needs come and see her too.

But out of his own hard work he had built his fame, and independence was his fault. Like many great givers, he was a poor recipient. Anne understood. Noting the sulky line of his full red lips, she had the wit to turn her gift into a debt. She had learned of late that when people are parting it is best to speak straight from the heart lest one should withhold some ultimate tenderness until it be too late. There were things she had meant to say to her mother—small endearments and confidences broken free at last from the fetters of undemonstrative reserve. And she had never really said "Good-bye' to Tom Culpepper. . . . Looking at the fine, loved face of this older man who was in no especial danger, she was driven by some compelling urgency now. Before coming within earshot of the usher who held open the door, she stopped with her hands folded before her so that she looked as though she had just stepped from her portrait. She knew that it gave Holbein joy to remember her like that. "I have always *wanted* your children," she assured him without shame or subterfuge. "And because they are yours my life will never be quite empty and purposeless again."

CHAPTER XXX

Grey fog wrapped each riverside mansion in a muffled world of its own and obscured with a desolate shroud the chill surface of the Thames. Neither boat nor bird stirred between the slimy banks. Save where the Archbishop's bargemen had hung a warning lantern at the bottom of the landing steps it was difficult to tell where land and water merged, and across on the Middlesex side only the tops of the tallest poplars struck up like unfamiliar, melancholy wraiths against the February sky.

But inside Lambeth Palace the candles were lighted although it was as yet early afternoon, and fresh logs had been heaped on the fires; for Archbishop Cranmer was entertaining milady Anne of Cleves. He had intended to visit her at Richmond but because he was suffering from a severe chill she had spared him the trouble. "It's this new-fangled coal that hangs a pall of smoke over London," he wheezed, sipping gratefully at the hot rose-hip cordial she had brought him. "We never had fogs like this when I was a boy."

Apart from his cold, Annie fancied that all this distressing business about the disgraced Queen had aged him. She picked up the sables she had worn in her litter and tucked them, as a daughter might have done, across his knees. Only a very devoted servant of God or of Henry, she felt, would have left his bed to see her on such a day. And Anne was never quite sure in which category to place Thomas Cranmer. Inwardly, she was wondering what official urgency made him so desirous of talking with her; but for the moment she managed to turn their conversation to the subject that was uppermost in all men's minds—the fate of the Queen and Culpepper, of which she was so anxious to learn more. "I did my best to save her," he was repeating sadly. "But the pride of her house which she forgot in her youth seems to make her more stiff-necked than ever now. At times she was hysterical and at others I reasoned with her ineffectually for hours."

Anne could well believe it; but she hoped that no one had told him of her meddling and unsuccessful response to poor Culpepper's appeal.

Cranmer had ceased to shiver but he took another sip or two of the cordial for its own sake. "If only she would have admitted a pre-contract with Derham his Grace could have divorced her without——" The sentences trailed off into a convenient bout of coughing and he sat all hunched up in the furs, staring sombrely into the fire.

"Without—*what*?" Anne's voice had shrunk to a whisper and her throat gone suddenly dry. Involuntarily she put her hands to it. Feeling her urgent gaze upon him, Cranmer looked up and nodded slowly. "As you probably know, she was sent down the river from Hampton to the convent of Sion in charge of the Duchess of Northumberland. And now milord of Suffolk has orders to fetch her from there to the Tower." The words came laggingly. As primate of the Reformed Church he had wanted her put away; but as a man he had hoped that her life would be spared.

"Then all Culpepper's courage went for nothing?" cried Anne accusingly. She stood straight and tall by the hearth, her dove-grey mourning gown splashed with shifting points of crimson reflected from the leaping flames. She was recalling what Tom had said about fear making a man do anything—fear of losing the King's favour. And Cranmer was sensitive enough to read something of her thoughts. Very carefully he set down his empty bowl. Unconsciously imitating Pilate, he made a repudiating gesture with his fine white hands above it. "Nothing could have saved either of them once Lady Rochfort was called as a witness," he assured her —and himself—for the hundredth time.

Anne bent forward, and now the firelight was reflected like dangerous dagger points in her eyes. "What did they do to him—before they did him to death, I mean?" she demanded.

A spasm of revulsion twisted the archbishop's features. "They tortured him," he admitted.

"I know." Anne's clenched fist beat unconsciously against the linenfold panelling beside her. "But how?"

He lifted a shocked, protesting hand. "It were better that you should not know," he evaded, with the irritating, conventional protectiveness which mild middle-aged men dole out to women who are far more used to bearing things than they.

Anne sat down abruptly simply because her knees played false. "But don't you see that I *must*? Surely if he could bear it, only a coward among his friends would shrink from sharing the mere *realization* of it?" She leaned back against a cushion, her hands clasped tightly together in her lap, speaking with closed eyes as if to see more clearly the pictures of her mind. "For six months he was in my household —and the very light of it. He did me dozens of kindnesses. I was homesick and ignorant of your ways—bewildered by conjugal moods. It was he who taught me to dance and steered me through difficult situations and never once made fun of my awkwardness. . . . He was tall and fair and debonair—with gallantry in every movement and laughter on his lips. And all his future in his eyes. I can see him now, with his helmet gone and the wind in his hair, riding down men twice his weight at the Bachelors' Tournament. . . . His mind was quick and cultured—and his hard, lean young body more beautiful than anything those paunchy self-seeking statesmen who destroyed it can ever hope to make——"

Anne felt a hand covering hers, gentle yet authoritative, and opened her eyes to find the archbishop leaning forward, his eyes pained and reproachful. "Truly, my child, I do not know," he said. "When he and Derham were—examined— Wriothesley and some of the others went. But I could not." He withdrew his hand with its flashing episcopal ring and began meticulously folding up the furs she had lent him. "I remember telling you once that I find it difficult to face physical pain," he added, with a kind of humble dignity.

But Anne was scarcely listening. She was staring thoughtfully into the heart of the fire. "Tom swore that nothing would make him betray her; and he didn't," she was saying.

"I think—whatever they may do to Katherine—she is to be envied for having had his dauntless love."

"And for the pleasure he had with this woman he was prepared to pay with the lingering ignominy of being hanged, drawn and quartered," murmured Cranmer. "I often wonder, poor sinner that I am, if I could so suffer for my God!"

Seeing that he was an ageing man still shaking a little with the ague, Anne strove to control her own emotions for his sake. "But the sentence was commuted," she reminded him. That much Guligh had made sure of for her.

"In his case, yes. Because he was of noble birth he was beheaded. Not that he made any plea, like Derham. But the King in his mercy arranged it because—like you, Madam—he had once had much joy in him."

Anne turned aside to a tray of sweet herbs he had had dried for her from his famous knott garden. To hide her feelings she began making little separate bunches of her thyme and lavender, her rosemary and rue. "Mercy!" she muttered, as audibly as she dared.

"It ill becomes any of us to sentimentalize over the justly punished and to forget that the King is a much wronged man." Cranmer tried to speak as sternly as he should in spite of the stirred fragrance that filled the minds of both of them with memories of those tragic lovers moving with youthful grace about the summer lawns at Hampton. "He was happy in his marriage. Why should any adulterer who broke it up expect less than the death penalty?"

Anne bit her lip. "If he hadn't had such provocation—and if it were proven!" she wanted to say. For—as everyone knew—since Culpepper refused to speak, he had been found guilty only on presumptive evidence. Much had been made, no doubt, of that night he admitted to when he had so rashly gone to the Queen's apartments and reasoned with her as a kinsman about the danger of giving Derham an appointment in her household—the night when Jane Rochfort had kept watch. And the fact that later the King had slept away from home—although few people seemed to know where. Some said at Pomfret while they were on the royal progress. "And is it true—what my people tell me—about—about the heads on London bridge?" she asked.

The archbishop glanced at her troubled face over the tips of his arched fingers. "It is the custom with traitors, Madam," he told her suavely.

One of the innumerable customs of this tradition-ridden land, presumably. Traitors' heads stuck on pikes on some gateway on the Southwark end of a death-trap of a bridge crowded with houses. The first time she had seen them, after a rebellion about the suppression of the monasteries, she had cried aloud; and the company of fine, scented courtiers with her had laughed. And even now, when other women screamed every time their barge shot through the dangerously narrow maelstrom between the piers of London Bridge it was the knowledge of those poor blackened, eyeless heads above which made her shudder. It was all a part of this robust, cruel, laughter-loving island—of the crazy contrasts that made it so much more exhilarating to live in than the Lowlands. Mighty warships and gentle May Day revels, bull baiting and book learning, the despotic King signing away people's lives at Westminster and Henry Tudor—well groomed and immaculately fair—singing exquisite love songs in his own home. The memory of his sweet tenor drove Anne to argue hotly. "But even so how could Henry allow *her*—whom he professed to love——"

But Cranmer, in his wisdom, silenced her. "He *did* love her. Even when she was sent to Sion he made out with his own hand a list of garments to be sent for her lest she should feel the cold. Everyone thinks of *her* suffering—but what of his?"

Anne remembered Henry's voice that day in the music room when he had told her of his first sweetheart's falseness. "It will make an old man of him," she admitted.

"And I fear it will break his belief in everything," said Cranmer. "It wasn't the first time rumours had reached him about the Queen's unfortunate girlhood, and he'd ignored them. But when we came out from Mass on All Souls' day he called us together—and when he had heard everything past believing in her any more he cried bitterly."

Anne, who had often seen tears of self-pity in her husband's eyes, stared almost incredulously. "Henry cried—in Council?"

"He put his head down on the table and sobbed. Seeing him like a broken man the others crept out one by one. I stayed——" Cranmer got up abruptly as if to escape from the memory and stood by the table with his back to her. "I can hear that terrible sobbing yet!"

After a minute or two Anne went to him and laid a hand on his smooth lawn wristband, as much for her own comfort as for his. "How can a merciful God allow the world to be so full of suffering, dear milord?" she asked.

His free hand caressed the jewelled cross hanging on his breast. "Only when we learn to see time as a little piece of eternity does this terrestrial life of ours make sense," he told her, with a smile of rare sweetness. "Death may be but a door. And what looks like deliberate cruelty is often unavoidable. For instance, how could I have received such vile reports about the Queen, and for mercy's sake kept silent? It might have affected the succession. Suppose she bore a son by Culpepper—which, mark you, might happen yet—to save her lover's life and her own she might have allowed that child to become heir apparent—some day even King of England."

"Of course—you are right," admitted Anne, who had not thought of it in that light.

"But we have been diligent to safeguard both the succession and the King's honour in future," he told her, with the sigh of one whose duty has been satisfactorily accomplished. "From now on any woman who comes to the King unchaste—or any who wittingly allows it—will be accounted guilty of treason."

"*From now on?*" repeated Anne, in amazement. All unbidden the imprudent words of Basset slipped into her mind —"How many wives *will* the King have?"—and even in the middle of so serious a conversation she had difficulty in keeping a straight face. "Then you think he intends to marry yet again?" she enquired, with apparent guilelessness.

Here was the opportunity Cranmer had been waiting for.

"That is what I wanted to talk to you about, Madam," he said. "I have recently received a letter from your brother's Chancellor."

Anne's heart began to quicken apprehensively. "I was afraid—of that, milord," she said, wondering how William could have heard so soon.

"He begs me to mediate with the King's grace for a reconciliation between you two."

Anne drew herself up proudly. "I don't think we stand in need of any reconciliation. But, as you know, I have never been able to convince my brother that I am indeed treated as one of the family and not merely as a hostage for his neutrality."

"I take it that the letter implies reconciliation with a view to matrimony," said Cranmer.

Anne was standing at the end of the table and her long, capable hands were busying themselves again automatically with her herbs. "Are there no small, well-read women left who can sing?" she enquired caustically.

One could scarcely blame her, of course. But the archbishop was too experienced at Convention and Council table to be without a bland riposte. "There is Lord Latimer's widow, who was born Katherine Parr," he said, watching her covertly.

Anne betrayed the shrewdness of his thrust by spilling some precious meadow saffron seeds upon the floor. Kate Parr. But of course Kate Parr had everything—good looks, good breeding, book learning enough to vie with the Tudors and the inestimable advantage of having amassed the inheritance of her father and two husbands. She would be kind to the children and almost as experienced in matrimony as Henry himself. A suitable match in every way—indeed, one would scarcely have credited a set of stuffy old statesmen with sense enough to think of it! But somehow it simply hadn't occurred to Anne that there might be somebody else so soon. Not a meaningless child like Katherine; but a woman of like age and home-making ability as herself. An admirable woman for whom Anne had never had much liking.

She didn't want Henry for herself, and yet the matter touched her pride and a sharp stab of jealousy shot through her. Not so much jealousy of Kate as a possible wife, as jealousy of her possible position in the family. What did this strange woman know of their ways? Would she have the sense not to encourage Elizabeth's vanity, and be careful never to rebuff Mary's bruised capacity for loving? How long would she take to learn that however terrified one might be of Henry the only thing to do was to get at him through either his stomach or his sense of humour? Though Anne doubted if anyone so deeply imbued with theological learning would ever stoop to such unseemly subterfuge.

Finding it so difficult to relinquish her influence to another, it was suddenly borne in upon Anne how much she herself had come to care for these Tudors. How savagely she would fight for the well-being of each one of them, and how she would almost be willing to give up her personal liberty to retain them. "Mistress Parr is a very charitable woman. When I was ill she took charge of Elizabeth," she said, seeing that Cranmer was waiting for some comment. "But I thought—that is—hasn't there been of late some sort of attachment between her and Sir Thomas Seymour?"

That was putting it mildly; for everyone knew that the little widow, in common with every unmarried chit at Court, worshipped the ground he walked on and that either her refreshing virtue or her well-filled coffers appeared to be making unexpected headway with that gay philanderer. But Cranmer waved aside their emotions as if they were of no more account than Katherine's pretty neck. "It is, of course, only a suggestion which has occurred to the Council," he admitted. "Indeed, there was a time when I hoped it might never be put to his Grace, for if, as some supposed, your woman-of-the-bedchamber—erroneously supposing your honour to be in question—had *lied*—"

Anne pushed the herb tray from her and faced him, gripping the table edge behind her. "I thought Mistress Guligh had convinced you all that the child is hers?"

The archbishop was swift to placate her. "Of course, of course, Madam! And the true explanation of the matter

332

will be made known to all. But it was a decision which a few of us came to unwillingly—being more in the King's confidence and considering the colour of the infant's hair——"

Anne said nothing. She felt breathless with incredulity. Here was a primate of England going as far as he dared to express regret that she had not, in her anomalous position, borne the King a son! It would, presumably, have made things much simpler—and much safer—for him. It would have provided the last straw to the Norfolk party's burden of defeat, and made inevitable that 'reconciliation with a view to matrimony.' Perhaps some of them had even counted on it when they let all the foreign ambassadors know so soon about the Queen's disgrace.

Leaning there against the table, she began to think furiously—as probably Cranmer had intended she should, for he at least had never underrated her intelligence. He kept very still so that there should be no sound to distract her save an occasional hiss as a log fell smouldering to the hearth and the melancholy calls of some fog-bound watermen out on the river.

"Suppose even now I refuse to kill this wishful thinking in his mind?" thought Anne, seriously perceiving for the first time her own opportunity to juggle with the succession. It was almost being pressed into her hands. The Protestant party still looked upon her as their lawful Queen, the people wanted her back, and all the bells in Cleves and Guelderland, Juliers and Hainault would ring wildly with vindicated joy. And Henry? Anne smiled, remembering how much she had learned since the old days—how much better she could manage him and how much she would like to comfort and mend him in his present trouble, poor soul!

But did she herself want to be Queen again? She wasn't sure. But even in those hurried moments she *was* sure that she didn't want Kate Parr to be. It might be horribly mean, but she would do a great deal to prevent her from strolling possessively beneath the pleached elms at Hampton Court and having complete charge of Elizabeth, who was already half-way to loving her.

Anne glanced across at Cranmer's inscrutable face. He

333

was Henry's confessor. He probably knew about that night at Richmond. It should be easy to persuade him. She allowed herself to toy with the idea. . . . Dorothea and Guligh would have other children. She had only to persuade their devotion—to restore Henry's self-esteem and happiness with the warm reality of a sturdy red-head, the longed for heir apparent who would bring peace to his old age. But suppose, as people were always saying under their breath, something *really* were to happen to Edward? Anne recalled the red, wrinkled bundle of humanity Guligh had placed upon her bed. "Poor little William the Third!" she thought almost hysterically, her bare excursion into the realms of imagination checked as usual by a sense of its absurdity.

She opened her mouth to speak but at that moment the distant shouts from the river culminated in a commotion beneath the palace windows. Some distressed craft in midstream was evidently hailing the Lambeth watermen. A door banged somewhere below, followed by the scuffle of men's feet and an answering shout from the landing stage. No one but Cranmer's master bargeman, she knew, could bellow like that. "It sounds like an accident!" she exclaimed, and with a hurried apology she hurried to the window and pushed open a casement against what appeared to be a wall of clammy wetness. Through the fog she could see two water-men hurrying down the slippery stairs, their lanterns bobbing like yellow will-o'-wisps as they ran. The sombre shape of a barge loomed out of the enveloping greyness, carefully nosing her way inshore. From the muffled interchange of shouts it was evident that she had bumped into something and broken the horn lantern hanging at her prow and her barge master was wanting to borrow one in its place. Clearly the men knew each other, and as her eyes accustomed themselves to the murky afternoon light Anne observed that there were people of consequence aboard.

"Why, it's the Northumberland barge!" she reported, over her shoulder. "But surely even the Dudleys wouldn't be going to a party today!"

No answering comment came from within the room nor any sound of roystering from the barge. Something more than the elements seemed to hold the motionless company beneath the canopy in thrall. Even the cheery voices of the archbishop's men were suddenly hushed as they handed over a fresh lantern, and only a circling curlew broke the wintry silence with its sad, shrill cry. There was something sinister about a boatload of people who did not speak—something uncomfortably reminiscent of the Styx. "When did you say milord of Suffolk was to fetch—the Queen?" asked Anne sharply.

Cranmer hadn't mentioned any time. He wished she would shut the casement. "This afternoon," he answered irritably, forcing a fit of coughing.

But Anne, with a hand on the latchet, leaned out as far as she could, regardless of the stream of fog she let into the room—regardless of anything but the mysterious, hooded figures in the boat. There was a consequential-looking person who might be the Duke of Northumberland himself, a tall stately one who looked like Charles, a huddle of women, a priest, some soldiers—and a girl sitting apart on the cushioned seat of state. Anne had seen her sitting like that in a moored barge before; but then her knee had been touching Henry's and Tom Culpepper was a romantic figure ready to hand her ashore—a carefree party arriving at Hampton stairs with a load of Cheapside toys. And now her little drab and gilded hour of life had come full circle. As the barge slid slowly away again on her lugubrious journey from Sion to the Tower the Lambeth landing lamp shone for a moment on the girl's desperate face. In her misery she neither knew nor cared at which lighted mansion they had stopped; but she must have known that they were nearing London and her journey's end. "Poor pretty, pleasure-loving Katherine!" murmured Anne, trying to remember her only as the girl who had tried to do her a kindness when she first came. Better than most she could guess what it felt like to be travelling out there, wrapped about with the dankness of the day and the strained sympathy of onlookers who could not help—with wide eyes staring ahead through the fog and the short, terrible future in Eternity. And this thing might have happened to her—Anne—whose life was yet fragrant with a hundred small daily pleasures. . . .

She felt cold—cold to the very soul. She crossed herself slowly and closed the casement. As she drew her shoulders back into the warmth of the lighted room her eyes were dark and distended with disturbing visions. Cranmer was still standing where she had left him and she had a feeling that he had been listening intently to a scene he would not look upon. She knew that all that had happened down there was stamped by imagination as clearly upon his memory as it was held in hers. "If she should chance to look up when they reach London Bridge—the light would be too bad, wouldn't it—to see—anything . . . ?" she entreated falteringly.

But Cranmer only said something in Latin which she didn't understand. "Sic transit gloria mundi!" it sounded like. So she went to the fire and tried to compose herself. She knew she had been rude, opening the window and leaving him in the middle of a conversation like that. She looked round at him questioningly while she warmed her hands. "You were saying, milord—when I interrupted so unpardonably?"

He absolved her with his charming smile. "I, too, had forgotten for the moment," he confessed, joining her before the hearth. But, of course, the matter upon which he had wanted to sound her concerned the future and was far more important than an unfortunate tragedy that was almost past. "Was it not", he recalled hopefully, "that some of the Council thought your woman might have lied on your behalf?"

Ah, yes. The whole conversation came back to her, and with it amazement at the absurd temptation that had assailed her. Those few moments at the window watching the suffering of Katherine Howard had completely altered her reactions. Nothing was worth bidding for—neither place in the home nor popularity nor even the chance of motherhood—that might have to be paid for like that. What was it that cheeky young Christina of Milan had said? "If I had two necks——" Well, she was about right.

Anne turned to the Archbishop with a friendly smile. She was still grateful to him for asking her to come—for letting her feel always that she had had the chance. "No, milord, I'm afraid their flattering wishes sired their thought," she said firmly. "for you can assure them from my own lips that there was nothing for my good Dorothea to lie about."

CHAPTER XXXI

"The years have dealt kindly with milady Anne of Cleves," observed Marillac, watching the buoyant way she trod the grass with a child clinging to either hand.

"Yet how she has changed during the seven years or so since she came!" said Charles Brandon, trying to reconcile the derisive epithet of 'Flanders Mare' with this buxom woman in her early thirties coming towards them.

"She is one of those people who have found serenity because they have never tried to dodge suffering," summed up Cranmer, who understood her better than either of them.

They were standing together under a cedar tree at Hampton Court in rather bored attendance at a May day festival given by Queen Kate Parr, the sixth of Henry's wives, and their personal remarks were safely covered by the merry fiddling of musicians and the rhythmic clapping and bell shaking of Morris dancers. There had been ribbon plaiting round the Maypole, the traditional Jack-in-the-Green and a charming masque in which Elizabeth and Jane and a score of other children had each been dressed to represent a different flower. And perhaps the most novel and successful item of all had been the glee singing of Anne's tiny orphans.

Between the various items of amusement the lawns were gay with childish shouts and tinkling laughter, while the grown-ups—strolling in little groups of silk and velvet finery —looked like bunches of multi-coloured flowers sprouting from the grass. And yet, in spite of all Master Carden's efforts as Master of the Revels, the proceedings were falling a little flat. There was something lacking. Anne was aware of it as she trailed towards the three notables under the cedar tree, a fair little girl on either side and the incorrigible Seymour, undeterred by his new dignity as Lord High Admiral of England, flirting light-heartedly with Jane Ratsey behind her back. Was it, perhaps, because there was little probability that at any moment these men must spring to attention and all the women in their bright dresses sway gracefully in one direction as if mown down by the wind—nor any need for everyone to be keyed up to meet the incalculable Tudor mood? For no matter how kind was the Queen nor how capable Sir Thomas Carden, no Court function could be *really* a party without the all-pervading presence of the King. Even of late when the pain in his leg had been almost unbearable and he could hobble only with the aid of a stick and someone's shoulder or lower himself with angry grunts into a chair—whether in ill or genial humour—he was still the core and centre of it all.

But to-day an attack of gout had made it impossible for him to come into the gardens at all. While answering the children's excited chatter Anne looked up at the west wing of the palace, picking out the windows of Henry's room. She knew the interior so well. She could picture him sitting there with his leg up, fuming at having to stay indoors on such a pefect day—he who loved colour and merriment and the outside world as much as she did. It seemed so silly not to run in and see him now she was here. He would be glad of a visitor—someone with whom he could spar good-naturedly, or pass the time playing cards. But the Queen hadn't suggested it. So she must just pay her respects to these three good friends of hers, take a look round her beloved pleasances and orchards and go. Round at the other side of the Palace her barge would be waiting to take her little party home, gaily beflagged for the occasion and bobbing on the tide.

Charles, ever courteous, came to meet her. She noticed that he was beginning to stoop a little. "We must congratulate you, Anne. Your orphans' charming songs were the hit of the afternoon."

"Congratulate the babes themselves—or Jane Ratsey here!" she laughed. "It was a happy suggestion of yours, milord," she added, greeting Cranmer affectionately. "The children were so delighted at the Queen allowing them to come." She turned to the elder of the two children who had hung back shyly before such important-looking gentlemen.

"Curtsey to the French ambassador, Lavinia, lest he think we English have no manners!"

Both little girls, dressed in exact imitation of their elders, bobbed obediently; but the legs of the younger were still so short that she toppled over among the pink-tipped daisies and—finding them more interesting than ambassadors and such—remained there contentedly collecting bunches of them in her chubby hands. They all laughed and Thomas Seymour, basely diverting his attentions from Jane, sat down on the stone edge of a fountain and drew Lavinia between his knees. "And which did you like best, Mistress Gravity?" he teased, intrigued by the plain intelligence of her face. "The Maypole, seeing the Queen, or the iced cakes?"

Lavinia thought profoundly. Politeness should have made her plump for the second attraction, but—as behoved her father's daughter—she was an independent and discriminating little creature. "Best of all I liked the barge ride with milady," she decided, fingering the modish gold tassels of Seymour's shirt. "The water was so blue and the puffy clouds so white!"

"Quelle originale!" laughed Marillac. And Anne explained with almost maternal pride that the child was going to be an artist. "Show Sir Thomas how nicely you can draw a dog," she bade her, passing Jane the tablet and gold pencil from her own belt. Because Elizabeth, either from policy or love of dancing, was still standing beside her latest stepmother and hadn't slipped away as usual to spend the rest of the afternoon in her adopted aunt's company, Anne's glance lingered the more gratefully on the pleasant picture of her best loved orphan drawing diligently on the low stone coping with her pink tongue thrust out and her whispy flaxen hair tickling the new Lord High Admiral's ear. No one was likely to take Lavinia away from her. Except for the child's neglectful mother who was imprisoned in the Tower, there was no one left to do so . . .

"How different from last May when all crowded assemblies were forbidden because of the plague!" Cranmer was saying, almost as if he were following the sad trend of her thoughts.

They stood a while in silence, remembering it. All except the two children who had played through that summer at Richmond unconscious of its horror, although it had bereaved them beyond any present. London, from which they had been removed a few months earlier, had been a sad place then. Infected houses had been sealed up with a great cross and the words "Lord have mercy on us!" chalked on the door, Court and Council had gone away and grass had grown between the cobbles in the deserted streets. Only the creaking plague carts had gone round at night with the terrible cry, "Bring out your dead!" Standing safely at Hampton in the sunshine it was difficult to realize that so horrible a scourge had swept over their land and passed them by; but the memory and the fear of it would be ever in men's minds.

"A thousand people it took in one week," recalled Marillac, who considered it part of his duty to be exactly informed about everything. "St. Denis send it doesn't break out again in Paris!"

"The only thing to do is to move immediately to one's country house," said Charles complacently. He himself had been feeling oddly tired of late and had been almost thankful for the plague as an excuse to stay away from Court.

"But what about all the poor Londoners who haven't country houses?" asked Anne, who had seen some of them trying to remove their household goods on borrowed carts, and how the villagers of Richmond had been afraid to take them in.

"Well, anyone who has means is a fool to stay," he insisted. "Take a man like Holbein, for instance. What an incalculable loss to the world!"

Anne closed her eyes for a moment or two, going through those dreadful days when she had first heard. She had begged Hans to come to Richmond but he had just begun to work enthusiastically on a large wall painting of Henry granting a charter to the Guild of Barbers and Surgeons. First he excused himself because he had been in contact with plague-ridden friends and feared to bring infection into her home, and afterwards it appeared he had urgent business to attend to.

"The King was terribly grieved," Charles was saying. "At any other time so renowned a painter would have had a public lying-in-state. As it is, no one seems to know even where he was buried."

"He was in the parish of St. Andrew Undershaft," said Cranmer. "But who can tell?"—for when things were at their worst they were throwing the bodies into common pits."

Anne winced and turned to look anxiously at Lavinia. She knew where her friend was buried but had forbidden her women to speak of it before his children. But mercifully the small girl was completely unaware of her elders' conversation because the beautifully dressed gentleman beside her had asked if she could draw a man as well as a dog.

Anne had hoped that they would let the matter drop; but the Frenchman's thirst for gossip was insatiable. "They say he left two bastards, but no one knows who the mother is," he was saying tentatively.

"Probably she died too," yawned Charles, "because I hear he left everything he had to the children. They were out at nurse somewhere, and he rushed a Will through in a few days—got some of his artist friends to witness it and an armourer and a goldsmith to act as executors."

Anne had known all this for months. She could see him hurrying through the hushed streets to do it, his honesty reviling his procrastination because he hadn't seen about it before. Walking with those long strides of his down the middle of the narrow City lanes where only the midday sunlight poured vertically for a yard or two between overhanging eaves. Avoiding doorways lest the pestilential breath should strike him, wondering if his own turn would come next. Thankful that his children were in the healthy parklands at Richmond. Thinking of her—blessing her—and all the time exposing himself to the danger of fresh contacts, entering more tainted doorways, that he might not leave the full burden of their upbringing upon her kindness . . . He had been no valiant soldier like Charles, nor a dashing admiral like Seymour, but he had scorned to make his escape to any country house . . .

"And within a week he and one of the executors were dead!" sighed the kindly ambassador. His glance rested speculatively upon Anne, who had contributed nothing to the conversation; and it suddenly occurred to him that being Flemish by birth she probably did most of her shopping at the Steelyard. "Did *you*, Madam, ever chance to hear who their mother was?" he asked.

The others could not forbear to smile at his shameless curiosity. "Why not ask the remaining executor?" Anne suggested, with her usual sound sense. She knew that he would ride first thing to-morrow morning to the Steelyard and get nothing whatever out of that staunch craftsman, Hans of Antwerp. Holbein's affairs and her own were quite safe.

Or were they?

A splutter of ribald laughter came from the edge of the lily pond. Seymour was leaning precariously over the water holding a scrap of paper at arm's length while the small artist viewed his mirth approvingly. Evidently, she had produced something very arresting. "Whoever taught you to draw *that*, you little monkey?" he asked.

"My father," she answered loftily. "He could draw *anything*."

Jane Ratsey's uneasy glance sought her mistress's, and Anne crossed swiftly from one group to the other. Over Seymour's vastly padded sleeve she caught a glimpse of a few firm lines representing a square, fat man in a flat, feathered cap who was cruelly reminiscent of his royal brother-in-law. Naturally, Seymour loved it. In a moment he would be handing it round. She stretched out a hand and snatched it from him, while with the other she reclaimed her pencil from the astonished child lest worse befall. "Run along now, both of you babes, with Mistress Ratsey," she ordered, speaking more sharply than they had ever heard her. The surprised admiral she propitiated with a

343

smile. "I think I will go and look round the gardens," she decided suddenly. And when they all offered to accompany her she reminded them gently that it used to be her home, and they understood that she would rather be alone. She wanted terribly to go alone.

CHAPTER XXXII

Anne walked away quickly, without choosing any particular direction. She was blindly trying to fight down emotions aroused by her companions' casual talk about Holbein and the sight of that absurd caricature, and to regain some measure of her hard-won serenity. Her pace slackened only as she found herself approaching her favourite bench under the little hawthorn tree. The boughs were a mass of pink bloom again—the annual miracle promising perfection from decay. It seemed a lifetime since she had sat there with Culpepper on their way from the archery butts! She sat down a little wearily, for it had been a tiring day—and quite an experiment. Ladies didn't usually take their orphanage children out for treats, but she hoped that she had set a new and kindlier fashion. The Queen had certainly been delighted with them and everything would have been quite a success if only that little monkey Lavinia hadn't emulated her father's impudence! But even if Seymour had been astute enough to put two and two together she knew he wouldn't wittingly give her away. His faults were divers and glaring, bless him, but meanness and tale bearing were not among them.

It was good to sit there with Lavinia's puffy white clouds in the heavens and the delicious scent of may drifting all around one. To dwell on tender memories of the past and sort out one's thoughts about the future. She could see part of the red brick palace framed between a lilac bush and a mulberry tree. Windows through which she had looked as a lonely bride, a huddle of gilt weather-vanes and twisted chimneys and one of the squat, square towers over-looking the tilt yard from which spectators must have applauded Henry in his prime. She smiled as her glance rested on the giant elms shading a straight stretch of the 'vrou walk'', as he used to call it. It was easy now to realize how strange her women must have looked to English eyes, and to remember without rancour her own innumerable *faux pas* and subsequent embarrassments. She was on such good terms with all the family and so comfortably settled into a state of quasi-spinsterhood that it all seemed like another existence. Old Mother Lowe and her maids were gone, Hans and Culpepper were gone, and Henry himself was a failing old man at fifty-five. There was no more to fear, no more to thrill over, no more to decide . . . Her life would flow on in half-tones now with more leisure for the joys and sorrows and hopes of other people. All her fierce resentments were burned out so that kindliness and common sense could light her frustrated life in a pleasant after-glow. . . .

A step on the path, a shadow on the grass and she was brought back to the present by the approach of Thomas Seymour. All his swagger was momentarily lacking and he looked unusually cast down. Anne was not sure whether he had followed her or whether he, too, wished to be alone. But in either case he was one of those completely natural people with whom she always felt at ease. So she merely gathered her wide, brocaded overskirt a little closer and made room for him beside her.

"I'm sorry—about the drawing," he said, without preamble.

"I didn't mind *your* seeing it," she said. "But I was afraid you were going to pass it round. And one of them might have shown it to the King."

"People have lost their heads for less," he agreed.

But apparently it wasn't fear that had moved her to snatch the thing from him. "Clever, amusing things can be so hurtful to the person concerned," she added.

Strange, he thought, that *she* should have any compunction about hurting *him*. "I was only half listening to what you were all talking about, but it must have given me the clue," he said. "I saw you with Holbein at Calais, and rather shared his admiration myself, if you remember." He looked round at Anne with his raffish grin, crossed his immaculately hosed legs and slid an arm along the back of the bench behind her shoulders. "I've often wondered—were you in love with the fellow, Anne?"

346

She was completely taken aback. He was the first man to stumble on her secret, but there was a straightforward friendliness in his manner which made it impossible to take offence. "About as hopelessly as you were with Kate Parr before she married the King," she admitted cautiously, taking care to remind him that he was in as delicate a case as herself. . . . He made no attempt to deny it. "Then there are two of us," he sighed. "Poor Anne! You've been pretty brave, haven't you? I'm glad you've at least got his amusing little bastards."

Anne liked him all the more because he entertained no poky suspicion that they might have been hers. So much of his life had been spent campaigning or carrying through various diplomatic missions abroad that his mind was a careless storehouse of more interesting things. "It must be hard for you to come to Court again and see Kate playing the devoted wife and Queen," she said.

"She does it very well," he remarked glumly.

"Almost well enough to last. But that's no excuse for you to go on being a bachelor. There are plenty of other attractive women—and all of them waiting. It's time you married *someone*, Thomas!"

She laid a cool, friendly hand on his knee and to her surprise he held it there. "What about *you*?" he said, brightening. "We've both had our disappointments. Would you take me on?"

Anne burst out laughing. "Not on your life, Tom! I know you too well. And England's just crammed with silly, goggle-eyed wenches who love a handsome sailor!" For once he seemed out of repartee and she wondered if he could possibly be in earnest. "And anyhow," she hastened to add, "the King wouldn't let me."

"We could be married secretly—and bide our time," he said.

"Bide our time for *what*?" she thought. This was an entirely different Sir Thomas from the free-handed, jesting one who habitually showed himself to the world. For a moment she had a glimpse of the shrewd, calculating mind that hid behind laughing eyes and idiotic jests, helping him to win battles and persuade foreign powers. He withdrew his arm from behind her and sat up warily with a keen eye on the surrounding shrubbery. "When the King dies my elder brother Ned will be Regent for Edward," he said quietly. "But if you ask me our young nephew won't live long—he has the same kind of cough as poor Jane had——" Anne sat up too at such foolhardy words; but he went on imperturbably. "As you know, there's precious little love lost between Ned and me. But I happen to be a lot more popular. With a woman who has been Queen beside me——"

"But I'm not Queen now!" she gasped.

"Neither was Henry the Fifth's widow, Katherine of Valois. But Owen Tudor married her and got the throne on the strength of it—that and his self-assurance."

No one could call him lacking in self-assurance himself. "Do you mean you'd alter the succession?" she gasped. She still wasn't sure if he were serious or just spinning one of his fantastic yarns.

"What good would it do England to have a woman rule? She'd only marry some over-weening foreigner," he countered. "Besides, why should *you* worry what happens? You're not even English!"

"I am. I've had my nationalization papers for years!" cried Anne, genuinely horrified at finding herself even tentatively involved in a plot against the Tudors. "And it would be cheating Henry after he was dead!"

"That's a good one—coming from you!" laughed Seymour bluntly. "Hasn't he cheated you out of everything?"

It was perfectly true, of course; but—as Anne had discovered before—she was prepared to fight for any one of them. "Wouldn't it help your ambition better to ask Mary and save England from the possibility of a foreign consort?" she suggested sarcastically.

"God forbid!" he muttered.

"I would have you remember she is my friend."

"I'm sorry," he said, without looking in the least contrite. "But every time I try to entertain her with stories of my travels she looks down her prim little nose as if I were proposing to rape her."

Anne, who had heard some of the stories, was not unduly surprised. "What you mean is you respect her, whereas I'm anybody's second-hand pickings," she said, with a mixture of bitterness and amusement.

Seymour scrutinized her in his bold bad way. "You're lovable and human," he said.

"Thank you," she smiled, well pleased. "But I positively forbid you to say such treasonable things again." Being accustomed to the silly tittle-tattle of Court life, she knew she oughtn't to be sitting here alone with him for so long and looked anxiously towards the thin, early Summer greenery that served them as a screen. But he was too full of his own ideas to consider the impropriety of monopolizing the King's sister at a public function. "Then I shall have to marry Elizabeth," he decided, picking at the gold threads in her spread skirt like a sulky boy.

"Don't be ridiculous," she laughed. "Elizabeth's only a child."

"When she was five she asked me to marry her."

"And you still carry her about in your arms. She adores you, of course. And so do Edward and Jane."

"She adores me and she'll do what I want. When she's a bit older I've only to entangle her fancy——"

Anne turned on him like a fury. "If you harm that child——"

But he only sat there smoothing his attractive little gold beard and looking at her through teasing, half-closed eyes. "A pity she's a bastard!" he had the nerve to say.

Anne stood up and stamped her foot at him. "You're the most conceited, irritatingly complacent man I know, Thomas Seymour!" she declared. "And I'll tell you this. Young Bess may love you—but that doesn't necessarily mean she'll do what you want."

"Why ever not? She's got plenty of spirit."

Anne stuck out her chin and bent confidentially towards him. "Because there's someone she loves still better," she told him, with an air of weighty mystery.

He was all interest at once, catching at the rosary hanging from her belt so that she shouldn't escape. "Who, Anne?

349

Who?" he demanded, till she had to smile at the anxiety she had awakened in his sea-blue eyes.

"Elizabeth Tudor," she told him lightly. She didn't see why *he* should do all the teasing.

He sat with pursed lips, hugging his knee and looking up at her in quizzing amity. Like a good many of their mutual acquantainces, he had found that this fourth wife of Henry's was pretty astute. "You really mean—you think that chit wants the crown for herself?" he asked, with an admiring whistle for a grasp even more far-reaching than his own.

"As much as you do—but with more reason and patience." Anne sighed feelingly. "She has had to put up with so much humiliation. 'Time will pass,' she's always saying——"

She found herself speaking with sympathetic understanding, and her words appeared to consolidate the Admiral's airy jest into the realms of seriousness too. "Then she has only to marry me," he said, standing up also to the full splendour of his gallant height. But Anne laid a warning hand on his fine slashed sleeve. "I said the crown of England, Thomas," she pointed out caustically. "Not just a royal wedding ring and her initials temporarily effacing some other woman's on palace archways, and the gradual stamping out of her own personality with the weight of a man's every whim."

Seymour stared at her as if he had never really seen her before. Even in the midst of his own scheming he wondered why they had all been such uninspired idiots as not to realize that, in spite of her apparent meekness, she must have felt like this. It suited her, too, having a snap of malice in her eyes. "But whoever she marries she'll have to knuckle under, I suppose," he pointed out awkwardly.

Anne broke off a bough of pink may and stood for a moment or two with down-bent head, thoughtfully making the little cups of blossom into a sweet scented nosegay. She was recalling how often Elizabeth, newly come on a visit to Richmond from her much harried stepmother, had stalked through the homely rooms declaring to a rather scandalized Dorothea that when she was grown up she was going to live like her beloved Aunt Anne, with no man to boss her about.

"Has it never occurred to you that she might not marry at all?" she asked him, although actually she herself was really only envisaging the unusual possibility for the first time.

Seymour burst into a great guffaw of laughter which could scarcely fail to draw attention to their whereabouts. "Not marry!" he exclaimed, with healthy masculine conceit. "A girl with hair like that live like a nun?"

Anne coloured self-consciously. "It *has* been done," she reminded him.

Apologetically, he took her hands in his, may blossom and all. In spite of his bluff audacity he hated to hurt people whom he liked. And he always had liked people with pluck. "That's different," he muttered. Obviously, he had already forgotten his wild idea of remedying it.

Anne withdrew her hands with gentle finality. "Well, I must be taking my infants home—and here's the archbishop strolling our way. For God's sake don't breathe to him or anyone else what you asked me just now—it's too dangerous a jest to make in public. I used to be terrified of Traitor's Gate, you know!"

He was grateful to her for taking it that way. They stood for a moment smiling at each other in mutual liking. "What a fool the King was not to keep you!" he burst out impulsively, as if speaking his thoughts aloud. And for the first time that afternoon Anne was quite sure that he was completely serious. She tried to look suitably shocked; but her heart was singing with gratitude—for was he not watering some of those tender shoots of self-esteem which were beginning to put forth sturdy leaf?

"I'll apologize if you like," he offered. "But when I like people I can't pretend."

Anne glanced calculating in the direction of the approaching primate. He was still only half-way between the "vrou walk" and their little arbour of greenery, and strolling at contemplative leisure. With a brisk swing of those neat ankles of hers she turned and reached a hand to either of Seymour's shoulders, and before he could recover from his gratified astonishment she had kissed him soundly on the mouth. "I

351

like frankness, and to repay your kindly impertinence, milord Admiral, I'll tell you a secret," she said, her laughing, glowing face close to his. From standing a-tiptoe she let herself down onto her heels and whispered with exaggerated gravity, "I have long had reason to suspect that the King himself sometimes agrees with you!"

The younger Seymour's blue eyes nearly popped out of his head. His firm mouth shaped itself into a soundless whistle above the devastating little beard. "And why not? For Christ's sake, why not?" he asked himself, looking after the woman men had made such fun of as she went sedately to join Cranmer. But then Sir Thomas was a sailor and all bemused by the warm sweetness of Anne's mouth and the unexpected fragrance of her body. Other women who had kissed him smelt of expensive perfumes that staled in over-crowded rooms; but Anne was like her garden—cool, spacious of outlook and refreshing as sweet herbs.

CHAPTER XXXIII

Early in the New Year Anne went down the river to Westminster. A bleak January wind harried her skirts as she disembarked and the sky was so overcast that the palace ushers lighted her way along the unfamiliar galleries with torches. She didn't know the palace of Whitehall as she knew Hampton and Greenwich, and had seldom been near London since she and Elizabeth had shared the same carriage in Kate Parr's wedding procession. People had thought it peculiar of her to go; but the King had invited her and she had wanted to see the festivities. Besides, she knew that there was nothing she could do which would show more publicly or more clearly that she bore no animosity in the matter. And her going had certainly pleased Henry. Hadn't he stopped specially to talk with her and called her his dear sister? And now Cranmer had warned her, "If you want to see him as we all remember him go to Whitehall *soon*." He had said it for her ear alone at one of the Dudleys' parties, so that neither they nor the ambitious Seymour brothers should hear.

So she had come the very next day, without any preparation or fuss. She had brought a cap of her own embroidering for Kate, an infusion of meadow saffron for the King's gout and a large bunch of grapes in a basket. When the ushers reached the royal apartments she took the grapes from Basset and carried them in herself.

Henry was lying in a great state bed hung with crimson and gold and blazoned hugely with the arms of England. It was grander than any bed she had ever slept in with him. She had thought them splendid at the time and they had been meet for bedding a queen; but this, she felt with a shiver of premonition, was a bed fit for a great king to die in. Kate, reading aloud from a book spread across her knees, looked like a little doll seated beside the low dais on which so much gorgeousness was mounted. But neither blazoned heraldry nor majestic elevation could help Henry much now.

353

Even as Anne entered he grunted with a fresh stab of pain and hunched a shoulder in rude protest against the erudite sound of his sixth wife's voice; and Kate—who was used to humouring sick husbands—laid the book aside and came to greet their visitor, welcoming her with unaccustomed warmth.

Poor Kate wasn't quite so composed as usual. "He fell forward across the table in the middle of Christmas supper and has lain like this ever since," she was explaining in a sickroom whisper. "It's so difficult to make him take interest in anything, yet if one isn't there beside him every time he wakes——" The little Queen broke off with an expressive fluttering of her pretty hands. After all, this capable-looking woman who had once been married to him should know how exasperating he could be.

Anne *did* know—better than anyone else. And Kate found it comforting to have her. "You look tired and everyone says you've worn yourself out nursing him," Anne said, in that pleasant practical way of hers. "Can't you get a little sleep?"

"He won't let any of his friends in. I think he doesn't want them to see him like this. It isn't as if Charles Brandon were still alive——" The Queen looked round anxiously at the great bed. "But perhaps if you would care to sit with him for a while . . ." It seemed a queer thing to ask of this other woman who knew his ways—almost as if they were sharing him. But her head ached so for want of sleep.

"And perhaps if he wakes he won't notice the difference," agreed Anne, with just the suspicion of a twinkle in those lazy eyes of hers.

Kate's own eyes were focused longingly on a comfortable pallet well out of range of the patient's vision. Anne gave her a kindly push and without more ado she tiptoed across the vast room and lay down. At no time in their strange relationship had these two women found themselves in such close alliance.

Very quietly, Anne took the chair Kate had vacated. It was no good doing anything about the book because it appeared to be another Latin treatise. A dull thing to read to a sick man, she thought. Almost before she had closed the pages the poor, tired Queen had fallen into a light sleep, and the weary gentlemen-of-the-bedchamber were only too thankful, at a sympathetic nod, to withdraw to some shadowed corner where they could relax. There was no one else in the room. It seemed almost as if Henry had done with ceremony and wanted only the quiet homeliness for which a part of him had always craved.

From where Anne sat she could just see the tip of his beard and the regular rise and fall of gold embroidered leopards sprawling over the mountain of his body as he breathed. But presently he stirred and flung out a badly swollen arm. "Tom, you young devil, where are you?" he growled, fumbling impatiently at the heavy counterpane. "Can't you see I want to turn over?"

Anne sat rigid, realizing that he was calling on Culpepper whose sightless head had mouldered long ago on London Bridge. But after a moment or two she got up and went to him and even when she slid a helping arm beneath his shoulders he aimed a jocular cuff at her, still believing himself back in the colourful days when his favourite gentleman-of-the-bedchamber had attended him. "Though I suffer fools to lift me now, time was when I could have spit you on my lance like a trussed fowl!" he growled. "And if milord of Suffolk were still here he'd tell you so."

He was strong enough to raise himself a little against the piled-up pillows, but his mind often played tricks with him. Between dozing and waking memory seemed to straddle a lifetime, mixing up all the characters who had strutted their brief hour across his stage with those who filled it now. And because he himself had then been full of vigour and keen perception those figures of the past often seemed more real than the subdued people who moved about his sickroom. Anne stood betwee the half-drawn bed curtains and took stock of him. In spite of his barber's recent attentions his close cropped hair stuck up here and there in ruffled tufts, and the full red-gold beard which had set a fashion throughout the kingdom was a travesty in rusty grey. The button of a mouth that had been wont to bark despotic orders was loosely open as a child's, the blue eyes blurred. Just as he had caught her unawares at Rochester, so now she saw him at his worst, pitiful with age and blowzed with sleep. Yet she looked down at him compassionately and touched his forehead with a cool hand.

He began to realize that it was a woman's hand and that it felt good against his feverish skin. A good nurse, Kate, he thought—if she wasn't always arguing about theology. "Why d'you have to read me that stuff? D'you think I want to be taught by women in my old age?" he complained.

"Would you rather I read you that lovely bit about the Wife of Bath from Chaucer's *Canterbury Tales*?" asked Anne.

Some easy, laughing quality in her voice betrayed her. It reminded him of homely domestic discussions, sunny walled gardens and delicious mulberry tart, and the oaks and grassy rides in Richmond Park—a pleasant, well-run place where no one ever argued or bothered him about statecraft or taking vile physic. "Why, if it isn't my Flemish Anne," he said, rubbing the sleep from his eyes.

"I'm not Flemish any more," she reminded him.

"No, of course not. Taverner got your papers fixed up at last, didn't he?" He lay blinking at her approvingly. His mind was clearing—his excellent memory functioning normally again. In a few minutes he would be recalling other matters connected with Sir Richard and his anxiety concerning her morals. "As your sister I begged leave to come and see you, Henry," she told him.

His arched brows and considering eyes looked ridiculously like Edward's, that day the child had first looked up at her at Havering. "You weren't always my sister," he said, taking scurrilous pleasure in her discomfort.

"I'm sorry about the pain, Henry," she went on hurriedly. "I know how brave you've always been about that awful sore on your leg, and I've brought you an infusion which may ease the gout in your toes——"

But he wasn't listening. He had begun to chuckle, still staring at her with the disconcerting curiosity of approaching senility. "I might have known it couldn't be you reading all

356

that doctrinal stuff! I've often wondered—what *is* your philosophy of life, Anne?"

Anne, busy straightening the tumbled sheets, threw him a reproachful glance. "Your Grace knows I am not learned——"

"Just as well perhaps!" he muttered. For somehow his learned wives hadn't turned out too well after all. True, he rather muddled them up now; but he seemed to remember finding Jane's gentleness very restful and poor little Katherine's ignorance rather amusing. But learned or not, this divorced wife of his was no fool. She had an unusual attitude of mind and strange reserves of moral strength which might be helpful if only one could get at them—and, in spite of his imposing title 'Defender of the Faith,' he felt badly in need of help these days. "But you must have *some* sort of creed, Anne," he insisted.

With that sensitive sixth sense of hers Anne heard in that insistence the groping cry of one scared human soul to another. So she tried, very diffidently, to put some sort of workaday creed into words. Nothing Latin or grandiloquent. Just simple, English words that even a frightened sinner or a very tired old man could understand. "I suppose I just try to live a little better to-day than I did yesterday," she said.

It was so typical of Anne.

"At least such a creed would create no wrangling parties to torment men's lives," smiled Henry. "And perhaps," he added wistfully, "it is all we need to take us from this world to the next." Because he was quite serious much of his old dignity had come back to him, and with it a new humility.

Anne looked down at the great, gouty hand he stretched towards her. Muscular as it still was, she had the impression that it was clinging to her slighter one rather than imprisoning it; and very gently she began smoothing back the reddish hairs that used to rise like a beast's hackles along the back of it whenever he was in an ungovernable rage.

"Are you afraid to die, Anne?" he asked presently. It

357

was so still in the state bedchamber that he may well have imagined that they two were alone.

"No," answered Anne, after a moment of surprised mind searching. But she had become poignantly aware that *he* was, and because he made no answer she sought to help him by amplifying her own. "I used to be," she admitted thoughtfully, "because, like you, I was so in love with life. Oh, I know that to you brilliant tempestuous Tudors I must seem dull and placid; but I had it in me to grow like you—to expand with happiness and motherhood. I have known what it is to be drunk with joy in some riot of colourful beauty, or breathless in anticipation of some exquisite moment. Now——" she paused and shrugged as if half ashamed of such self-revelation—"well, I enjoy my pleasures to the full—but they no longer pin me down to earth. You see, I have grown so impatient to see what is on the other side of death."

"What has changed you?" he asked, watching her shrewdly.

It was a question she dared not answer—least of all to him. She withdrew her hand from his and began restlessly plaiting the bright fringes of the counterpane. "There is a verse in Cranmer's translation—'Where your treasure is there shall your heart be also'——" she began vaguely.

He did not press her. Being Henry Tudor, he was too concerned with his own crisis. Although it hurt him excruciatingly to do so, he raised himself on one elbow. "But—what of—the actual coming to die?" he asked. The light blue eyes were pinpoints of concentration, the words almost stuck in his throat with urgency. Anne supposed that only some maternal quality in herself made it possible for him to ask of her what he would not sink his pride sufficiently to ask of wiser people. Through the minds of both of them must have passed in pale procession the ghosts of all those whom he had sent out to untimely death—his bewitching sweetheart Nan, Cromwell, Derham, laughing Culpepper and little, wanton Katherine. Always, Anne had marvelled at their courage when, guilty or innocent, they came to die; and she was sure that when Henry's supreme moment came he would grace it like the great King he was. But at this moment he was desperately afraid. Afraid because he was beginning to realize for the first time that sickness, which he had dodged so long, and so loathed in others, had him at last in mortal grip. And afraid, above everything, of mortal reckoning.

To-morrow, next week, sometime soon, they would all be crowded in this room—peers and prelates and the poor tired Queen—to offer comfort and give ghostly consolation. But she would be back at Richmond then—forgotten and unwanted—merely a woman the King had once discarded. This was her moment. If there were any last tenderness she would leave with him, she must speak it now. She kneeled down on the dais close beside him so that, screened by the splendid tapestries, they seemed to be in a small, comfortable world apart. "Listen, Henry," she said, picking with unconscious hardihood at one of the imposing gold embroidered leopards. "I'm only a woman—and you know so much. But I've loved and feared and suffered, and if among my poor spiritual gropings there be one thing I have learned —one thing to which I can testify through personal experience, it is this. It's quite useless to try to avoid the things we fear. If we do, our fears will gradually master us. But if we go forward resolutely to meet those things of which we are most afraid, as we come to them they will either dissolve into nothingness so that we walk through them undismayed, or else they will change their shape so that we can recognize in them some purposeful, merciful lesson of God. And so it may well be, don't you think, with this final universal bogy of death?"

Henry lay silent with his thoughts and presently two remorseful tears forced themselves beneath his closed lids. "She screamed and screamed," he murmured incoherently. "God knows I didn't mean to send that child out all ill-prepared to die! It was their fault . . . for once they were too clever for me. . . . Even while I wept they sent instant words to all the foreign ambassadors . . . so that even if I would it was too late to condone her shame. . . ."

He was rambling through the past again. For men so near

359

to death time has so little meaning. Past, present and future ran together like the grains of golden sand in the fascinating hour glass beside his mother's bedside at Richmond—all running out together into Eternity. There were moments when his love for his mother mingled with the better elements in his liking for this woman who lived there now, and one seemed no further from him than the other.

For her sake he tried to pull himself together. For a little while longer it was the present and he must play the earthly prince. "You are still comfortable at Richmond?" he asked with an effort after graciousness.

"Quite, I thank your Grace," answered Anne formally, rising to her feet.

"And you have let your manor of Bletchingly?"

"To Sir Thomas Carden."

"Ah, you've a good tenant there. He's been our Master of the Revels almost since I was a boy. And I make no doubt you've already invited him to taste your eel pie and made a good friend of him!"

"He stocks my cellar and helps me with my accounts," smiled Anne demurely. The gentlemen-of-the-bedchamber had drawn nearer and she could hear Kate stirring. "That reminds me," she added with matter-of-fact cheerfulness. "I've brought you some grapes from my south wall."

"They're out of season. All ours were finished long ago!" he scoffed.

"But I've a special way or preserving them in jack apple and white wine." She fetched the basket and let him feast his eyes on the finest bunch of purple fruit he'd ever seen. "Not so bad," he admitted. "But they're bound to have no flavour." It was the old friendly feud between them.

Out of the corner of his eye he could see Kate measuring something out of a bottle. She was making up for having slept by looking more sedate and capable than ever. In a minute or two she would be bringing him another foul concoction those damned physicians had ordered, and he wanted to make sure of the grapes first. If there was one thing he loved, it was a juicy grape!

Anne sought in the folds of her skirt for the gold-handled

scissors hanging from her belt. Deftly she snipped off the fattest grape of all and popped it into his watering mouth. He savoured it greedily and, after a furtive glance across the room, squeezed her hand with the obscene slyness of an old man who has lived lustily. "The pick of the bunch!" he said. And the faded eyes that blinked up at her from beneath his sandy lashes were full of fun—and affection.

"How kind of you to bring him grapes!" exclaimed Kate, bustling forward with a glass of medicine. Naturally, she thought they were discussing the fruit.

But Anne knew he was teasing her. He might equally well have been discussing his wives. . . . She felt sure he had been speaking her epitaph; and a flood of long-delayed triumph shot through her, warm as wine. She wasn't ravishing like Nan Bullen, nor the mother of his son like Jane, nor yet his 'rose without a thorn'—but at least he had admitted his mistake and tried to make amends for calling her a Flanders mare.

CHAPTER XXXIV

Edward Seymour, Earl of Hertford, sat at the head of the long Council table. Because his young sister Jane had given the late King a boy he had become Lord Protector of England. And, according to his lights, he meant to fulfil the office worthily. He would be accessible to all and see that rich men no longer filched common lands from the poor, and make milady Mary's life a misery until she gave up hearing Mass. But all the first morning had been taken up by making arrangements for the royal obsequies at Windsor and haggling over the annuity and rent rolls to be paid to the Queen dowager. This would be Kate Parr's third matrimonial legacy and, because she was always such an exemplary wife, Henry had even allowed her to keep some of the royal jewels. Hertford had conscientiously read out that part of his Will, although he knew how fiercely his own wife coveted them. "And I think, milords, that is all," he concluded, thankful that his first Council meeting hadn't gone off too badly.

He had already risen in courteous dismissal when Cranmer leaned across the table to remind him of something, and the timely whisper was drowned by the movements of men eager to depart to dinner. But the Protector raised a hand to stay them.

"There is just one thing more," he apologized, raising his voice above the scraping back of chairs. "If no one has already advised the Lady Anne of Cleves of King Henry's death, it would be well to send someone to her for that purpose."

"With an intimation, of course, that she is now free to return to Cleves or to marry again should she so wish," the archbishop hastened to add.

Little King Edward's younger uncle raised his handsome head from a hasty reckoning he was making of Kate Parr's total assets. "A pity no one ever considered her wishes before," he remarked.

But his powerful elder brother ignored him. "Richmond is, perhaps, too large a jointure in the present circumstances," he was suggesting parsimoniously. "But we can go into that anon." And before the meeting broke up John Dudley, Earl of Warwick, was understood to say something about her having plenty of other houses to live in.

"Vultures!" snorted the Lord High Admiral of England.

"You feel strongly about the lady's misfortunes?" suggested Wriothesley at his elbow, under cover of the general hubbub. He was naturally curious to find out *which* royal widow the man intended to marry.

But Tom Seymour went on with his encouraging calculations, only pausing to add a memorandum to make sure that they handed over Jane's jewels. He could scarcely explain that Anne had once kissed him under a hawthorn tree and that he had found it an amazingly pleasant experience.

When their messenger reached Richmond he found Anne standing by one of the long windows over-looking the river. It was Sir Anthony Browne, Master of the King's Horse, who had offered himself for the part; and she seemed almost to be expecting him. Mary had told her of the King's passing and of how at the end he had pressed Cranmer's hand; and there was a sadness about her face and movements very different from poor Kate's tactfully concealed relief. One felt that, although Anne wore no mournful weeds nor knelt beside his bier, here in this quiet room she mourned Henry Tudor far more sincerely than his official widow.

In his own mind the kindly old courtier couldn't help comparing this encounter with the first time he had been sent to wait upon her. It seemed only fitting that he who had then brought her sables and an unwilling bridegroom should be the one to bring her freedom now. But had she looked half as posed and comely at Rochester, he reflected, how different things might have been. . . . And how many people might have kept their heads! "Milord Protector would have you consider how this sad matter affects your own life, Madam," he told her. "Naturally, you are now free to marry again should you so desire, or to return to Cleves. And he has asked me to bring him word whether you decide to go or stay."

Anne had not been unmindful of these possibilities before, but there had been so many immediate things to do. She had written to Mary, inviting her to stay over the funeral; and to Sir Thomas Carden, asking him to come and see her. She would hate to turn him out but it had already occurred to her that she might have to live at Bletchingly. And then there had been one of those dreadful letters of formal sympathy to compose to the new King—ridiculous as it seemed to have to be formal with a child one had smacked! But now she really must come to some decision about her own affairs.

She went and stood in the deep bay of the window. The Thames flowed before her eyes, pleasant and busy as the Roer or the Rhine. But it was only a background to the current of her thoughts. There was no one she liked well enough to marry. If her thoughts turned momentarily towards Thomas Seymour, it was only to realize that Kate Parr was now free too and that he was not the man to let love and ambition slide. To go back to Cleves would mean taking up a fresh life all over again. Her parents were dead and both her sisters married. William had gotten himself a bride and had no more real need of her. And all Flanders would pity her and know she had been a failure. Whereas here people were more inclined to envy her peaceful life and to accept her as she really was. Many of them loved her and confided in her. Even Henry himself, who had humiliated her in the eyes of her own countrymen. He had given her a fine English home and taught her English ways, and hadn't she voluntarily taken out her nationalization papers? She had lived in England for seven years and surely no country was so crammed with endearing, changing loveliness? To go back to sleepy Cleves would be to stagnate. No, she couldn't go back. She was Anne Tudor still.

These Tudors had adopted and absorbed her. It needed

no conceit to know that they would all be heartbroken if she went. And she wanted to stay and see what happened to each of them. Whom they would marry and which of them would reign. Would Edward grow up pompous? And would he marry his studious, stumpy little cousin Jane? Or—like his Uncle Arthur—would he not grow up at all? And if so which of his sisters would be hoisted by her religious party to the throne? Self-controlled, conscientious Mary who would fight courageously in a minority for a faith that was feared—Mary who was a good woman but who might not be so good for England as some unadulterated Tudor? Or Elizabeth who had her father's 'common touch'—that strange mixture of splendid egoism and wholesome vulgarity on which the people throve? Elizabeth who was so utterly English that everything she did was bound to bolster up their insular conceit. Elizabeth who would fleece and cheat and bully them to buy herself lovers and finery and all the pomp she had been starved of, and yet fight for them in times of stress and go among them with the heart and stomach of a king? For that was just how they behaved— these irritating, incalculable English. Covering the thing they cared for most with an assumption of frivolity so that their enemies believed them to be effete and did not perceive the parlous danger of mocking at them until it was too late. . . . Anne didn't need books to teach her that; she understood people. And interested onlookers invariably see most of the game. She wanted to see this through. This fascinating game played by people she cared for on the chequer board of England.

A discreet cough brought poor Sir Anthony to her mind. She turned at once, full of contrition for having kept an elderly man standing. "I am afraid I have tried your patience," she apologized.

"It is a big decision to make, dear lady; and you yourself have been very patient with *us* for seven years or more," he said gallantly. "But may I—quite unofficially—beg you to take into consideration that many of us would find England a drearier place without you?"

Anne smiled at him warmly. He was one of Henry's

oldest friends and when people said things like that it made her feel that she hadn't been such a failure after all. "Dear Sir Antony, you must stay to dinner and taste my eel pie," she said, ringing briskly for the servants. "And I would have you remember me to his young Grace the King and thank milord Protector for his thoughtfulness. But I pray you tell them I do very well as I am."

Brief
Gaudy
Hour

All Sphere Books are available at your bookshop or
newsagent, or can be ordered from the following address:

Sphere Books, Cash Sales Department,
P.O. Box 11, Falmouth, Cornwall.

Please send cheque or postal order (no currency), and allow
5p per book to cover the cost of postage and packing
in U.K., 7p per copy overseas.